Kiss Me Goodbye

Kisses and Combat Boots, Book 2

Jennifer Shaw Wolf

J.S. Wolf Publishing LLC

One

Waiting

November 2004

H is face on the screen. His voice, calm and clear, makes my heart soar and ache at the same time. I hate that he's here and not here. It feels like I could reach out and touch him, but he can't see me. I can't even talk to him directly.

Having his voice, his presence, even if it's only on a screen, makes this whole thing bearable. Makes reliving the worst night of my life a few feet away from the cause of that night possible.

"I've been thinking about you."

Brad's voice pulls my attention from the screen and sends cold prickles down my back. His lawyer hushes him before the judge notices. Brad's just trying to get to me. He's been staring daggers at the back of my head for the entire trial. I won't give him the satisfaction of turning around and acknowledging his words. The only time I faced him was when I gave my statement. I looked him square in the eye. I made sure he was the first to look away.

This isn't a full-fledged trial. As charismatic as Brad can be, I don't think his lawyer thought he could sway a jury. He waived the right to a jury trial, refused the plea bargain, and now we're together in this little room. The person I hate most is less than five yards away. The person I most want to be with most is almost 7,000 miles away.

"In the statement you made before, both you and Ms. Roberts indicated you hadn't ever been romantically involved. Is that still true?" Brad's lawyer asks Jacob.

Jacob's answer is firm. "At the time we made that statement, that was true, but in all honesty, the nature of our relationship has changed since then."

"And what would the nature of that relationship be now? Are you and Ms. Roberts dating, or..?"

Jacob laughs. "To be fair, sir, I can't be dating Ms. Roberts or really anyone now. I'm in the middle of a war zone."

"I guess that's a good point," the lawyer responds. "Let me rephrase that. Would you say you have a romantic relationship with Ms. Roberts now?"

My lawyer interrupts, even though I really want to hear Jacob answer that question. "Your honor, Sergeant Ricks and Ms. Roberts' relationship is not what's on trial here."

The other lawyer jumps in. "It goes toward whether we're talking about a domestic dispute here or an assault. These three have a long history–"

"Answer the question, Sergeant Ricks." The judge's voice is clipped and efficient. "I'll determine if it's relevant."

"Okay, yes. I would say it's a romantic relationship, and I hope Jess, Ms. Roberts, would view it the same way. Long distance as it is. But it began after Mr. Wilson attacked her in the barn."

"What would you say the impetus was for the change in your relationship?" Brad's lawyer asks.

I hold my breath, waiting for my lawyer to interrupt again. Maybe it isn't relevant to the case, but I want to hear Jacob's answer.

He doesn't hesitate, like he's already thought this through. "Well sir, I guess when you're put into an intense situation, like when I found Ms. Roberts after Mr. Wilson attacked her in the barn, and frankly, like the one I find myself in now, it makes you realize what's really important, and what you stand to lose by waiting too long."

"Three years?" The anger in Jacob's voice crackles across the bad connection.

"Actually, they counted the time he's already served, so it's less than that. He'll be out in about thirty-four months."

"That isn't nearly enough time for what he did to you and what he tried to do before."

"There wasn't enough proof of anything else. We had to stick to what happened in the barn. The judge sounded like he was throwing the book at him. I guess three years is a long time for a domestic assault."

"They still called it that? I don't get it. He came onto your property and came after you. Simple assault."

"The prosecuting attorney warned me he'd likely just get 'time served,' so this is better. Apparently, when he put his hands on my throat it crossed the line between domestic assault and felony domestic assault. That's why he got the longer sentence."

"Not long enough, but at least he won't be out before I get home."

"I hope I've forgotten his name by the time you get home." I close my eyes and try to control the shake in my voice. "Thanks for being there. It was so good to hear your voice."

"Well, you know, subpoena and all of that. Hard to refuse." His voice gets softer. "But you know I would have been there anyway. I wish I could have been there in person. I wish I could have been there to hold your hand, just hold you in general. I wish I could have at least seen your face. I'm sorry you had to face him alone."

"I wish you could have been there too." I take in a deep breath. "It's over. That's all that matters now. I miss you, Jacob."

"I miss you too. I wish we could talk longer. I'll send an email and call again as soon as I can."

"I'll be waiting."

"Love you." His face fades from the screen before I can say it back.

Two

Home

December 2004

I close my laptop, lie back on my bed and wrap my comforter around me, imagining Jacob wrapping his arms around me. Re-reading the emails between us has made him feel closer, but further away.

I miss him so much.

I've only heard his voice twice since he left—at Brad's trial and then the day when he called to find out the verdict. Email has been sporadic as he's moved around Iraq. I never know how long it will be before the next time I hear from him.

I sigh and watch the rain sliding down the window. It's good to be home. The spicy smell of Christmas permeates everything. I helped Mom with the Christmas baking earlier today. We wrapped the cookies up in little boxes and Mom is delivering them to the neighbors. I'm home alone. Dad is still at work, and Tyler is snowboarding with his friends.

Christmas is in five days. I'm looking forward to eight days of blissful laziness before I have to get back to my job in Pullman. No homework until I go back to school. The only thing that would make this better would be if Jacob were here.

I wonder if he got my package yet and if he'll get to call on Christmas. I'm dying to hear his voice, to ask him something and not have to wait days for him to answer back.

I'm trying to decide whether it's worth the effort to go all the way downstairs to get one of the leftover cookies when the front door opens.

"Hey, is anyone home?"

At the sound of his voice, I jump off the bed and run down the stairs. "Matt!" I almost knock my brother over when I fling my arms around him.

"Hi Jess," he untangles himself from my arms. "It's good to see you too."

I stand back and catch my breath. "You weren't supposed to be here until Christmas Eve."

"We caught an earlier flight into McChord." Matt sets his bag down.

"We?" I look beyond Matthew and notice another soldier standing just behind him.

He walks forward and smiles. "If I had known Matthew was going to get that kind of greeting from you, I would have come in first."

"Jess, I'd like you to meet my friend from Fort Bliss," Matthew starts.

I'm not listening. His friend looks familiar. "We've already met."

"You have?" Matthew says.

"Yeah." I look into his bright green eyes. "Michael, isn't it?"

He smiles. "I didn't think you'd remember."

"It's your eyes." I can't seem to break his gaze. "How could I forget those eyes?"

Three

The Guest

Matthew looks from me to Michael, like we spoiled his big surprise. "When did you guys meet?"

"Michael showed up at my spin class last year." I forgot how unusual the color of his hair was, red, not bright red, but more of a dark copper brown, kind of like the inside of a cedar tree when it's wet from the rain.

"Yeah," Michael steps inside and sets his bag down. "I tagged along with my friend from basic training, Sargeant Carson."

"Bryan?" I ask.

"Yeah." Michael turns to Matt. "Hardest workout I've done in years. Your sister about ran me into the ground."

"I must have. You never came back."

Michael pushes the door closed and steps toward me. "I was at Fort Lewis on a temporary assignment. I left right after that, or I would have been back."

"What brings you here now?"

"Actually, Matt showed your picture to the guys at Fort Bliss, and then held a lottery to see who got to go home with him." His eyes dance, and a sprinkling of freckles stands out across his nose.

Matt leans against the door. "It was the picture from your prom. I told him not to be too disappointed, that you clean up okay, but normally you aren't much to look at."

"Thanks a lot, Matt." I slug him in the shoulder.

"Actually, I was hoping to stay a couple of days before I go to Pullman to see my family," Michael says.

"Pullman, huh? I'm going to WSU now," I say.

"That's what Matt said. My dad's a dean there."

Matt looks around as if he just noticed the house is empty. Where is everybody?"

"Mom is out delivering cookies, Tyler is snowboarding and Dad is still at work."

"That's why it smells so good in here," Michael says. "Ginger-snaps?"

"Yep. You guys want some?"

"Definitely," Matt says. They leave their bags and follow me into the kitchen. I pour them a glass of milk and set out the plate of cookies.

Matt pauses between bites. "It's great to be home."

"I know." I sit down on the chair beside them. "I never imagined that I would miss this place so much." I chew for a minute. "I'm surprised you didn't go straight to Kendra's."

"Oh, I'll get there soon enough. I had to drop Mike off, and I wanted to show you something before I go." A smile plays around the corners of his mouth, and I know he has some kind of secret. Usually that means something I can't tell Mom and Dad.

"Something to show me?" I ask. Matt nods. I look at Michael. He raises his eyebrows, but he appears to be in on whatever Matt's secret is. It takes a second before I understand. "You bought a ring!"

Instead of answering, Matthew goes to his bag, digs through it for a second, and comes back with a little black box. He flips it open. Inside is a white-gold ring with a princess-cut diamond. The wedding band has two smaller side diamonds. It's elegant and delicate and absolutely perfect.

"Oh, Matt," I breathe, taking the box from him. "It's gorgeous."

Michael grins. "Mike helped me pick it out. He knows way more about diamonds than I do."

"Are you getting engaged too?" I ask Michael.

Michael shakes his head. "Oh no, I just...I've bought jewelry for my mom and sisters before."

I look at Matt. *Diamonds for a sister*? *Who is this guy?*

Matt looks unsure. "Do you think she'll like it?"

"She'll love it." I hand the ring back to him. "It's just pretty enough to cover your most obvious faults."

"Thanks a lot." Matthew studies the ring in his hand. He gets serious. "You really think she'll say yes?"

"I think it's a given. I've lived with Kendra for the last three months, and I'm totally sick of hearing how wonderful you are."

"Even if I have to leave her for a year?" Matthew doesn't meet my eyes.

"Why would she have to..." I cover my mouth. "You're being deployed."

Matt nods.

"When?"

"End of June. I haven't told anyone but Dad yet. Let me figure out a way to tell Mom, okay?"

"Don't worry, that one is totally you. There is no way I'd want to break that news to Mom," I remember Michael. "Are you going too?"

Matthew answers for him. "No, Stevens here is waiting on an educational deferment."

"Educational deferment?" I ask.

"Med school," Michael shrugs like it's no big deal.

"That's pretty impressive," I say.

"Isn't it though," Matt rolls his eyes, but he looks impressed too. "Michael wouldn't even be hanging out with a grunt like me if I hadn't saved his life."

"You saved his life?" I say skeptically.

"Yeah, actually," Michael says. "During jump training."

"Jump training? Isn't that where you go up in a perfectly good airplane and then jump out?" I try to look serious.

"That's the one. Your brother figured out my chute was screwed up. To be fair, I probably would have figured it out eventually, but maybe not. Either way, it cemented our friendship," Michael says, helping himself to another cookie. "Have you ever tried skydiving? It's the best feeling in the world."

"Jess is afraid of heights," Matthew breaks in.

I give him a dark look. "Not as much as I used to be. Actually, skydiving is something I've always wanted to try."

I refill Michael's glass of milk. He touches my hand as I hand it to him. "I'd love to take you sometime."

Matthew looks from me to Michael with a satisfied smirk. I pull my hand away and take another cookie. "So, Kendra doesn't know you're going to Iraq?"

Matt shakes his head. "I guess I'm hoping the ring would soften the blow. Do you think she'll wait for me to get back?"

"Absolutely. Kendra is definitely a one-guy girl." A weird guilt seeps into my chest. I wonder how Jacob would feel about the conversation I was having with Michael.

Matt looks at his watch. "Now that I've dropped off the package and gotten the sister's approval on the ring, I'm off to surprise the love of my life." He stands. "Can I borrow your car, Jess?"

I don't move. "Sure, but you might have to push it to Kendra's house."

"It's not working?"

"Not since September."

"What are you driving at school?" Matt asks.

"Jacob's car." I can't look at either of them when I say that.

Matt lets out a low whistle. "He's letting you drive his car while he's gone. Doesn't he know your driving record?"

"I have a perfect driving record," I say.

Michael looks at me curiously. "Jacob? You mean Jacob Ricks?"

Matt breaks in before I can answer. "Yeah, Jake is an old family friend. He used to live in our rental across the way. We were all kids together. He's like another brother, right Jess?"

I don't know how to answer. I'm still not comfortable using the word *boyfriend* when I describe Jacob. Does kissing in the barn, saying "I love you," and a bunch of emails make him my boyfriend?

"I'll take Jake's car then."

"You can take the rental if you want," Michael says.

"That's okay. I wouldn't want you to be stranded here with my sister." Matt gets my *Jess* keyring from its place on the hook. I don't stop him. Jacob told me not to let any other guy drive his car, but I'm pretty sure my brother is an exception to that rule.

Michael leans back against the counter and crosses his arms. "I can think of worse places to be stranded."

Matt shakes his head. "You only say that because you don't know her yet."

Four

Animals

"**D**o you need any help?"

I jump at the sound of Michael's voice and drop the fork I was holding. I'd slipped into the dining room to set the table for dinner when Matthew and Kendra came in. Seeing them together highlights the fact that Jacob isn't here. I needed to be alone for a minute.

He bends and picks it up. "Sorry, I didn't mean to scare you."

"It's okay." I take the fork without looking at him. "I guess my mind was somewhere else. It's nice to have everyone home." I put my hand on the spot where Jacob sat the last time he was here. Then I finish putting the silverware around the table.

"But not everyone's here, right? There's one more, isn't there?" Michael asked.

How does he know I was thinking about Jacob? "One more?"

"Don't you have a little brother?" Michael replies.

"Oh yeah, Tyler." I feel stupid. "He's fifteen, so he's never here anyway."

"Does that mean I won't get to meet him?" Michael follows me into the kitchen.

I pick up the salad bowl. "I imagine he'll sulk in at the end of dinner and demand to be fed before disappearing into his room again."

"I can understand that." Michael grabs the butter dish and follows me back into the dining room. "I was a teenage boy once."

"Strange animals, those teenage boys." I set the bowl on the table and face Michael.

"*Animals* would be the appropriate term." Michael says. "As I recall, there are only two things that can tame a teenage boy: food and, of course, a teenage girl."

"What about cars, sports, and violent video games?"

Michael waves his hand dismissively. "Distractions. Things to keep them occupied until the next meal or the next pretty girl comes along."

"Good thing you grow out of that stage," I say sarcastically.

Michael shrugs. "Actually, I think we just require more food, and older girls. But maybe we learn to control it better."

"Wow, thanks for that insightful look into the male psyche."

Michael shrugs. "I don't think any guy ever claimed to be hard to figure out, at least not any normal guy."

I sigh. "And yet we spend way too much time obsessing about what you guys are thinking, or at least I did when I was a teenage girl."

"I thought you were still a teenager. Don't you turn nineteen next month?"

"Yes, thanks for pointing that out." I'm not sure why he knows when my birthday is. How much did Matthew tell him about me? I turn around and struggle to get a basket from the top shelf.

Michael comes behind me, grabs the basket easily and hands it to me. "Does that mean you still obsess about what guys are thinking?"

I give him a strange look as the oven timer dings. "Actually, the only thing I obsess about now is whether I'm going to pass my next chemistry test."

"I get that. Chemistry is hard." He leans against the cabinet. "But guys are easy. Like right now. What am I thinking?"

I pull the biscuits out of the oven and pretend to think. "You're hungry and you're wondering if you could get away with stealing one of these biscuits?"

He smiles. "Close. I am hungry, and those biscuits smell fantastic, but like I said, I've learned to control that part better."

"So, no stealing?" I ask, piling biscuits into the basket. One falls out and rolls across the counter.

"Nope." He reaches over and picks it up. He takes a bite. "Unless it gets me the pretty girl."

When I walk into my room after everyone has gone to bed, Matt is sitting at my desk holding the picture I put on my nightstand of Jacob in his full dress uniform.

"Hey sis." He sets the picture down without comment.

"Shouldn't you be in bed by now?" I ask.

He sighs. "Yeah. But we have to be up early tomorrow, and Kendra's entire family is at her house, grandparents included. I doubt they'd be impressed if I followed her to her room." He laughs as my face flames. "Wow, Jess. You blush easily."

"That's not exactly a topic I want to discuss with my brother. Ever."

"Okay, sorry," he grins at me.

"So what do you want to talk about, Matt?" I glance at my computer. I was planning to email Jacob before I went to bed.

"Can't I just come in to talk without having an ulterior motive?" he says innocently.

"You never have before."

Matthew fidgets in the chair. "I was hoping I could convince you to come skiing with us tomorrow."

I sigh and sit on my bed. "I would love to go skiing with you, but as I said at dinner. I'm low on funds, and I promised Jasmine I'd go Christmas shopping with her tomorrow."

"Michael offered to pay for you," Matthew points out.

I sigh, remembering the discussion at dinner. Turns out Michael grew up in Colorado and was part of a junior racing team. He acted as if he were being modest about it, but I saw through his act. "And I said no."

"What if I paid for you?" Matthew asks.

It takes me a second to realize he's serious. "Why would you do that?"

"Call it an early Christmas gift. Call it wanting to spend more time with my little sis while I have the chance. Call it—"

Matthew is laying it on too thick for me to believe those are his only motives. "You need a favor, don't you?"

He breaks. "Yes. Actually, I'm kind of desperate. I have no idea how to propose to Kendra."

I don't think I've ever seen Matthew this stressed before. "You don't have a plan yet?"

"Not a clue."

I rack my brain, trying to remember if Kendra mentioned anything about a perfect proposal scenario. I can't think of anything. "It has to be something cool, something really romantic. Something she isn't expecting."

"I already know all of that. It's the details I need help with." Matt picks up a snow globe off my desk, shakes it, then looks at it as if might be a crystal ball that holds the answer.

"Hmmm." I watch the snow swirling around the globe. "Maybe something tomorrow, on the ski hill. That could be romantic."

"Tomorrow would be good." Matthew sets the globe down. "Waiting is killing me."

I consider my options. Matt seems desperate. I'd much rather ski than go shopping with Jasmine, and I'd really like to be there when Matt proposes. "Okay. I'll tell Jasmine I'll go shopping with her in a couple of days. Bring the ring with you tomorrow and give me some time to think. I'll let you know what the plan is in the morning."

"You're the best!" Matthew says. He stands and gives me a spontaneous hug. "You might want to let Mike in on it. He's good at romantic stuff."

"Yeah, sure." I glance at the computer again. I feel guilty for wanting Matt to leave, but I haven't checked my email since this morning. He doesn't. "So..."

"I don't have a plan yet. I said in the morning."

"Not that. What do you think of Michael?"

My thought process is shattered. "Michael?"

"Yeah, you know, the guy I brought with me." Matthew makes it sound like I actually don't know who he's talking about.

"Hot-shot, pre-med, diamond-shopping, ski boy? He's nice, I guess."

"Nice, good-looking, smart, funny..." Matthew starts.

"Wow. If you feel that way about Michael, maybe you should re think your engagement to Kendra."

Matthew makes a face at me. "You know what I mean. Mike is a great guy." He hesitates. "You should give him a chance."

"Give him a chance?" If I wasn't so shocked I might laugh. "Are you trying to set me up?"

"Maybe." He picks up the snow globe again. "How do you feel about that?"

"Honestly, Matt, there's a problem with that. Before Jacob left, things kind of changed between the two of us." My face flames. Here s another conversation I'm not comfortable having with Matthew.

"I know." Matt still won't look at me.

"You know?"

"Mom told me you've been writing to him. She said you drove all the way home to say goodbye to him when he left for Iraq." He gestures toward the picture. "Nice picture, by the way."

"Thanks." I pause. "If you know about Jacob, why did you bring Michael here?"

"He needed a place to stay while he went to visit some old friends." Matt keeps shaking the globe.

The motion is getting on my already fraying nerves. I take it away from him. "I know that. But you just admitted you were trying to set me up."

"Don't get me wrong, I love Jacob, almost like a brother. He's a great guy. But he's not..."

"Not what?" My irritation level rises.

His voice softens. "Michael is also a great guy. He comes from a family with money, and he's going to be a doctor."

"Please don't tell me this is all about money."

"Of course not." Matthew lowers his voice. "Jacob is a soldier, a good soldier, but right now that's all he is, and the road to advancement is a long one."

"How can you say that, Matthew? How can you say, 'Jacob's just a soldier.' When that's exactly what you are? How can you tell me that Jacob isn't right for me because he's a soldier, when you are asking Kendra to accept you on the same credentials?"

"It's a little different, Jess." He says it patiently—like he's explaining something to a child. "I'm just in it for the training and money for college. I'll do my time in the Army and then I can get my degree and a good job. It's a great place to get started. I've learned a lot. But for me, that's all it is, a jumping-off point. For Jacob, it's his whole life. Think about a life of long deployments and moving all over the country. He's already got you waiting around for him."

"Michael's in the Army too, right? Wouldn't I have the same life with him?"

"He'll owe the Army some time after medical school, but then he'll be done. For his family, the military is a rite of passage. Every great-grandfather for years has been a soldier. Michael has been in ROTC since high school. He's only a year older than me, and he out-ranks both me and Jake. He could walk away from the Army tomorrow and probably live on his trust fund for the rest of his life. He has everything in life, but he's still a good person. He wants to be a doctor so he can help people."

I glare at Matt. "How would you feel if while you were in Iraq I set Kendra up with some rich guy from college?"

"That's different. I've been dating Kendra for almost three years. By the time deploy, Kendra will be my fiancé, and if I can swing it, maybe my wife. You and Jacob had one make-out session in the barn. I'm not sure that's a relationship."

"It was a lot more than that. It was... I... he said..." I hate the way Matt put it, and I hate how flustered it makes me trying to defend my relationship with Jacob. "It had been building for a long time before that."

"I know you've had a thing for him forever, and yeah, he deserves all the credit for saving you from Brad in the barn. I can see how that cemented the feelings you already had for him, but are you sure it goes both ways? "

The thread of insecurity I feel every time I think about my relationship with Jacob forms into a rope that twists in my stomach. "What's that supposed to mean?"

"Look, I know Jake in a different way than you do. He's a good guy, but girls have always gone for him. He's always had one or two back-ups."

"So you're saying what? That I was his back-up?"

"I didn't mean it like that. It's just...if you really mean that much to him, why did he wait until just before he left to let you know how he felt? And why did it take him so long to get rid of that other woman?"

I'm ready to throw Matt out. Apparently, Kendra told him a lot about what went on between me and Jacob. More than I wanted her to.

Matt seems to get that he pushed things too far. He stands up. "I didn't mean to insult you. It's just...you're only eighteen, Jess. Keep your options open. If Jacob is the one, then you have my blessing. Not that you need it," he adds hastily. "But I know that Michael already likes you. It might be worth giving him a chance."

"If you think so much of Michael. You should go out with him."

"Not my type," Matthew says. Then he adds meekly, "You'll still help me tomorrow, won't you?"

I let out a frustrated breath. "I'll help you. Because I love Kendra, and I'm actually that desperate to have a sister. But honestly, Matt, butt out. I don't need your help when it comes to finding a guy."

"You'll still be nice to Michael though?" Matthew stands up to leave.

"Don't push it, Matt." I growl.

"I love you, Jessica," he says sweetly.

"Yeah, whatever. Go to bed. You're going to need your sleep. You have a big day coming up tomorrow, unless I decide to tell Kendra what you're really like."

As soon as Matthew leaves, I flop on my bed. I'm too irritated to think. Why does everyone have an opinion about who I should be with? Up until a couple of months ago, "everyone" included Jacob.

No way am I doing anything tomorrow that might give Michael any encouragement, or anything that will give Matthew the satisfaction of seeing us together. And I definitely won't be confiding in Kendra again for a long time.

I'm supposed to come up with Matt's perfect proposal plan. I look at the clock—11:30. Great. We're leaving early tomorrow, and I have to keep up with a guy who used to race on skis. Keep up with him and avoid him at the same time.

Five

Hot and Cold

S kiing. I'm going skiing.

It's the only thing that gets me out of bed when the alarm rings. It was probably two o'clock. before I fell asleep. I can't think of any brilliant ideas to help Matt propose to Kendra. I can't stop being annoyed at him for trying to set me up with Michael.

It's going to be a beautiful day on the slopes—sunny with new powder. My mood brightens. I should check my email, but I need to get going if I'm going to beat the bathroom rush.

I wrap up in my robe and hurry to the bathroom. Too late. Someone is already there. Matt, the king of long showers, somehow beat me to the bathroom. I pound on the door. "Save some hot water for the rest of us!"

I stop and listen. There's no answer, but someone is singing, actually singing in the shower. Singing well. It can't be Matt or Tyler. It has to be... I lean against the door and recognize the voice.

I forgot about Michael.

I don't want to stick around until Michael gets out of the shower. It's bad enough that I just yelled at him. I detour to the bathroom in my parent's room, but stop short when I hear the shower running there too. Matt must have had the same idea I did.

Back to my bedroom. At least now I have time to check my email. I'm dying to see if Jacob got my package or if he liked anything I sent. I'm thinking about that, so I don't notice Michael coming out of the bathroom, wearing nothing but a towel, until I run into him. I look up, and come face to chest. I look away quickly—not quickly enough not to be impressed. Not as much bulk as Jacob—but not bad.

"Sorry, Jess." He's blushing too, or maybe it's just his fair skin and the hot water. His entire chest and face are red. "I guess I've gotten used to living with guys."

"It's okay," I'm still averting my eyes. "I've only ever lived with guys. I mean my brothers. My roommates are all girls. I mean, I guess I'm used to it too." If I was blushing before now my face is on fire.

He steps aside and gestures to the door. "The shower is all yours. I even left you a little hot water."

"That's okay." I'm looking down, not at his face. It's not a very long towel. He has nice legs too. "Matt's probably finishing it off right now."

"What am I finishing off?" Matt comes up the stairs, chewing on a piece of bacon, already dressed.

"The hot water," Michael answers. I wonder how long he's going to stand there wearing nothing but a towel. I wonder if he or Matt would notice if I took another quick peek in his direction.

"Not me." Matt leans against the wall. "I showered an hour ago. I've been up since five. I couldn't sleep."

"Who's in Mom's shower then?"

"I think it's Tyler." A grin spreads across Matt's face.

"Tyler?" I shake my head. "Since when is he into being clean, especially before snowboarding?"

Matt's grin spreads to his cheeks. "It's possible our little brother is bringing a girl to the hill."

"A date? With a girl? Wow. I guess he really has turned into a teenage boy." I look at Michael again, forgetting he's not dressed.

"So Jess, did you come up with any brilliant ideas for today?" Apparently, it doesn't bother Matt that Michael is practically naked.

It bothers me. "Can we discuss this later? When we're all dressed?"

"Sure." He smiles at me wickedly. "I'd hate for Dad to come up and catch the two of you leaving the shower together."

"Matthew!" My face is blazing.

Michael takes this as his exit cue. I catch the look in his eye when he leaves. He thinks this is funny.

As I climb into the shower, I mentally move Matthew to the top of my hit list. Michael isn't far behind, even if none of this is his fault. Maybe I won't help Matt today. Maybe I'll ditch them all and ski by myself. The idea sounds nice. The water goes cold. Tyler hits number three on the list.

I hurry to get dressed. Since I didn't have time to wash my hair before the hot water ran out, I braid it back. I sit in front of my computer, but Matt calls me.

"Jess, are you ready? We need to make plans, and we're picking Kendra up in less than a half-hour."

The boys are devouring stacks of blueberry pancakes and bacon. Mom isn't a morning person. I'm surprised she got up early and put in that much effort. It must be for Michael's benefit.

Matthew and Michael are talking as fast as they're eating. "Hey Jess," Matt says when I sit down to eat. "You're fired."

"Fired from what?" I'm not in the mood for pancakes, so I get an orange and a piece of bacon.

"From being my romantic consultant," Matthew says between mouthfuls.

I pour myself a glass of milk. "Who's taking my place?"

"Michael," Matthew answers. "He has some great ideas for today."

Michael stands up, spreading his arms like a director selling a shot. "Picture this—the top of the ski hill, breathtaking views, a little grove of pine trees, lights in the lower branches, music in the background, a table, chairs, candlelight, champagne chilling in the snow, feathery snowflakes falling softly."

"Sounds complicated," I say thoughtfully. "But cool. Where exactly are we going to set this up?"

"I know every inch of that hill," Matthew says. "I know just the spot. It's out of bounds, but I think we can get away with it."

"How are we going to do the lights?" I ask.

"I have some battery-powered ones left over from the Christmas decorations," Mom is in on the plot now.

"The music?"

"Easy, iPod and speaker," Matthew replies.

"What about the table and chairs?"

"Leave that to me," Michael says. "I'm sure someone at the resort let us take some up."

"Michael can be very persuasive," Matthew says, looking at me. "He's used to giving orders and getting what he wants."

"Okay," I turn toward Michael, issuing a challenge. "Where are you going to get the 'feathery snowflakes falling softly?'"

Michael grins confidently. "That one is really up to the Big Guy Upstairs, but I've already put in my request."

"What do you think, Jess?" Matthew's face is beaming. It's hard to stay mad at him when he looks so eager.

"Unless you have a better idea," Michael says graciously.

"No, I think we should go with Michael's plan; it's brilliant," I admit. Michael does a poor job of looking modest. "You're still paying for my lift ticket."

"Of course. We need someone to ski with Kendra while we set things up." Matt is glowing. I've never seen him this excited about anything in his life. It makes it hard to stay irritated with him.

Six

Keeping Up

Somehow, I get stuck taking Michael down to the rental shop while everyone else heads to the lift. He walks up to the counter and asks if they have any demos available. When they bring them out, he spends a lot of time looking at a snowboard.

"Jess," he says. "Would you like to try snowboarding? I could teach you how."

"Not today." I'm already annoyed that he's using up my ski time.

"Why not?" Michael asks. "I'm sure you'd be great at it."

I sigh. "I have limited time and limited funds for skiing. I'm afraid I might actually like snowboarding, then I'd have to blow a bunch of money on new equipment. Besides, I don't want to waste today. The snow is great. You're welcome to get a board though. I'm used to skiing with knuckle-draggers."

"I'll pay for your rental," Michael says. Apparently, he likes to throw his money around.

"No, thanks."

He puts the snowboard back and picks out a pair of racing skis.

"What skill level?" the man behind the counter asks. He looks like he's trying to size up Michael.

"Expert." I answer for Michael. He doesn't contradict me. If he's trying to impress me, it's not working.

By the time we get to the hill, everyone is gone.

"Matt, where are you guys?" Michael says into the two-way radio we brought with us.

Matt's voice crackles through the radio. "Already on our third run."

"Should we wait for them to get down?" Michael asks me.

"I'm done waiting." I don't even try to keep the irritation out of my voice.

"We'll catch up," Michael says to the radio.

"Good luck with that," Matthew replies.

As we step onto the skis, I compare the skis I bought used four years ago to the demos that Michael is putting on. It's going to be hard to keep up with him.

"Beautiful day," Michael remarks on the lift. The sun is shining, and the sky is the deep blue that only shows up at this altitude.

"Perfect." The view lightens my irritation. "But where are the feathery snowflakes you promised?"

"Give it time." Michael lays his arm on the back of the chair, almost over my shoulders. "I just put in my request. Besides, we don't really need them for a few hours, anyway."

Saying Michael was a good skier would have been a colossal understatement. It takes less than half a run for me to realize that I could never keep up with him. As hard as I push myself, Michael is always waiting for me. My only advantage is that I know the mountain. I try taking him on the hardest run I know. Two turns in, I catch an edge that sends me headfirst down the mountain.

Before I'm even sure what happened, Michael is beside me, holding my skis. "Are you okay?"

"Fine." I'm covered in snow and bruises, but my pride is what's most damaged.

"You caught an edge," Matthew helps me up and sets my skis in the snow next to me.

"Really?" I'm trying to get into a position on the side of the hill so I can get my skis back on.

"Let me help you." Michael reaches to steady me.

"I've got it." I ignore him and slam my feet into the bindings.

"Do you mind if I give you a few pointers?" Michael asks.

"Not at all." He doesn't catch the dripping sarcasm in my voice. He launches into a demonstration of how I should bend my knee in, keep my upper body still and shift my weight. All the stuff I learned at age six from a ski instructor.

"When you're going down a steep hill like this, you really need to plant your pole and pop yourself up, like when you're doing moguls."

"Let me guess," I say flatly. "You were a ski instructor."

"Just for a couple of seasons." He pretends to sound modest about it. I don't buy it. "I mostly taught little kids and a few privates."

"Great. Thanks for the lesson." I start off without looking back.

"Anytime," he follows me cheerfully. "Should we see if we can find everyone else?"

Our next run ends at one of the beginner hills. Half-way down that hill we meet up with my brother Tyler and his date, Alex, sitting on the side of the hill. The classic scenario—good-looking girl doesn't tell gullible guy that she doesn't know how to board. Either that or Alex had been honest, and Tyler thought teaching her how to snowboard was a good way to get her to like him. It isn't working. She looks close to tears.

"You guys need help?" I ask.

"I'm trying to help Alex get the hang of this." Tyler is trying to sound patient, but I catch the frustration in his voice.

It hits me that I can help Tyler and get rid of Michael at the same time. "You guys are in luck. Michael used to be a ski instructor. I'm sure he would be happy to give Alex some pointers."

"Sure," Michael says easily. "I'd love to help." Michael and Tyler pull Alex to her feet.

I see my escape. "I'll go take a run or two by myself. It'll give me a chance to work on my technique."

"Are you sure it's a good idea to ski alone?" Michael asks.

"Alone?" I look around the crowded ski hill. "I'll be fine. After all, it's not like I'm heli-skiing in Alaska." I'm referencing the experience Michael had thrown out when we were all swapping ski stories on the way up.

"Okay. We're all meeting up for lunch in forty-five minutes, anyway. I'm sure we can have Alex riding down the mountain like a pro by then." He smiles encouragingly at her.

Forty-five minutes go by too quickly. I'd like to keep skiing by myself, but I promised Matt I'd ski with Kendra while they set up, so I head to the lodge. It's packed, but eventually I spot Matt and Kendra saving a table. Michael, Tyler, and Alex sit down beside them. I head to the table.

"Hey Mike," Matthew looks over the group. "Where's Jess?"

Michael picks up a sandwich. "She went off by herself while I was helping Alex. I think I did something that ticked her off."

"You weren't telling her how to ski, were you?" Matthew asks, grinning.

"Maybe," Michael says slowly.

Kendra laughs.

"Big mistake," Tyler says, taking a drink of his soda.

"Why? What did I do?" Michael looks confused.

"She hates being told what to do," Kendra says. "She likes doing things her own way."

"You couldn't have warned me about that?" Michael says.

I stop before they can see me. Am I really that bad? Bad enough that even Kendra noticed? I wait another minute before I join them. "Hi." I try to sound nonchalant. I sit next to Kendra. "How did the board lesson go, Alex?"

"She's doing great," Michael grins at Alex, and she beams back. It looks like my plan backfired for Tyler with his date. She appears to be infatuated with Michael.

"Dude, Jess," Tyler says. "You should see what Michael can do on skis."

"I've seen him." I take a bite of my sandwich.

"No, not on the hill," Tyler says impatiently. "On the terrain park, you know, with all the jumps."

"Freestyle too, huh?" I don't feel guilty about ditching Michael anymore. He doesn't need another admirers.

"Nah, it's just something I've messed around with." Michael's voice drips with false modesty. "But if you're interested, I could show you later."

I open my mouth to tell him I'm not interested, but Matt cuts me off. "I'll do the terrain park with you after lunch. Jess and Kendra can have some girl time."

He stands. "Help me take the cooler out, Michael." He tosses me one of the walkie-talkies. "We can meet up later with this."

Seven

Proposal

T he sun is just going down when I get the call on the radio. I listen to Michael's instructions and then turn to Kendra. "The guys want us to meet them at the top of the old lift."

"It's about time." Kendra says. "I bet they've been messing around at the terrain park this whole time."

"Probably." I'm trying hard to keep my voice casual.

"We'd better hurry," Kendra says. "It looks like we only have time for a couple more runs."

The anticipation is killing me. I have to keep ahead of Kendra so she won't see my face as we ski down to an old lift, just before the ski boundary.

Kendra stops beside me. "Where are the guys?"

Before I can answer, Michael walks out of the trees like a red-haired snow god.

"Mademoiselle." He takes Kendra by the hand. "Right this way; we have a table waiting for you."

Kendra unbuckles her snowboard, looking at me for answers. Michael leads her into the trees.

The grove couldn't be more perfect. It's almost round, completely sheltered from the outside world on one side. The opposite side has no trees. The ski hill falls away to reveal a breathtaking view of the mountain range, just beginning to be touched by the pink hue of the setting sun. Christmas lights hung in the lower branches of the trees cast an ethereal glow on two snow-sculpted chairs set in the middle of the grove. A giant snowball, flattened on both ends serves as a table. Two candles flicker next to a crock in the middle, also sculpted out of snow. It holds a bottle of champagne.

I'm blown away. I plant my skis in the ground and step behind the trees to watch as Michael leaves Kendra in the center of the grove and then joins me at the edge. "Perfect," he whispers, opening his palm to the sky. I was so caught up in the scene that I didn't notice the feathery snowflakes falling softly.

I look at Michael in amazement. He smiles and shrugs. Matthew appears in front of Kendra. He goes down on one knee. Michael touches my shoulder and motions for me to follow him. Reluctantly, I give them privacy.

I don't move away when Michael reaches to help me while I put my skis back on. The mood of the grove lingers, and I forget that I'm supposed to dislike him.

We wait until we're out of earshot to celebrate "We did it!" Michael gives me a double high five and then grips my hands. "Could that have been more perfect?"

"No way," I answer.

"Now all she has to do is say yes." His face glows with excitement.

"Trust me, she will."

Michael doesn't let go of my hands. I'm staring into his eyes. He really has beautiful eyes. "I'm sorry I was an arrogant jerk earlier."

I look away. "You weren't. I was being oversensitive."

"Friends then?"

"Friends."

He holds my gaze and my hands for a minute more. "Let's get in our last run and then we'll come clean up after those guys. Matt said he would call us when they were leaving."

We take an easy run and stay together the whole way down. I like Michael better when we're not trying to impress or outdo each other

On the way back up the lift, he keeps looking at me. Finally he says "Can I ask you a favor?"

"I guess so." I sway my feet and look down at the mountain.

"Matt told me you were going back to Pullman a couple of days after Christmas."

"Yeah. I have to get back to work."

"Will you be there for New Year's?"

"Yes," I answer slowly.

"Are you working that night?"

"I'm working until about four that afternoon, why?"

"Every year my family has a huge New Year's Eve party. For the last three years, my sisters or one of my aunts has set me up on a blind date. It would really help me out if I could tell them I already had a date."

"Would you like me to find you a date?" I don't meet his eyes.

"That would be pretty much the same thing as one of them setting me up," Michael replies.

"I guess you're right."

"I was wondering if you would go with me. Just as friends?" The pompous rich kid I thought Michael was melts. He seems almost unsure of himself. "That is if you don't already have plans."

I think about his offer while we get off the lift. He used the word *friends*. It'll make Matt happy, and maybe get him off my back. Besides, Michael is stationed in Texas. It's not like I'll ever see him again.

"Okay." I answer without looking at him.

"Is that a yes?" he asks.

"Yes, I would love to go to the party with you."

"Sweet," he says. Too late, I remember that I wasn't going to give him any encouragement.

"Now I have a favor to ask you," I say.

"Anything."

"Show me what you can do on the terrain park."

"Are you sure?"

"Absolutely."

I find a place at the bottom of the jumps to watch. It's easy to be an appreciative audience. Michael wasn't lying when he said he was an expert. After he finishes the first run, he comes over to me.

"Okay. I'm impressed."

"There's one I haven't done for a long time, a back flip." He hesitates. "Maybe I shouldn't try it."

"Go ahead," I urge.

"Okay." He takes his skis off to hike back to the top. "But if I break my neck, you have to be my private nurse for the rest of my life. Oh, and watch for ski patrol. I don't want to get banned from the mountain."

While he's hiking up, Tyler and Alex meet up with me. Alex is snowboarding pretty well for her first day. Maybe I should have let Michael teach me how to board.

"What are you doing sitting in the snow?" Tyler asks.

"I'm getting ready to watch Michael break his neck," I answer.

"Cool." Tyler and Alex sit down beside me.

Michael comes rocketing down the hill, building speed as he goes. He hits the biggest jump dead center. I have to force myself to watch and not close my eyes. He's going to die, and it'll be my fault.

He flips backwards almost too effortlessly. He hangs in the air for what seems like a long time, then lands perfectly.

I can't help it. I jump to my feet, clapping and screaming as he skids to a stop next to me.

"That was so awesome!" Tyler slaps Michael on the shoulder.

Alex is falling all over herself to tell Michael how cool she thinks he is.

Matt's voice comes over the radio. "Be quiet," I say. "What was that, Matt?"

"I said, ski patrol is ready to kick us out. Mom and Dad and Kendra's parents wanted to meet us for dinner at the lodge, so could you guys come take care of things up here, please?"

"That depends, Matt." I smile into the radio. "What did Kendra say?"

"I said yes!" Kendra screams from the other end. Tyler and Michael cheer. Alex hugs Michael, then turns bright red when she realizes everyone is watching her.

Michael takes the radio. "We'll be right up. C'mon, Jess, race you to the top."

"Even you can't do that." I'm still smiling. It's getting harder to dislike Michael.

Eight

Letting it Slip

December 21, 2004

M atthew walks into my room the next morning before seven without knocking. He sits down on my desk chair.

"I think you're picking up bad habits from the Army." I glare at the alarm clock sitting on my nightstand. "What happened to my brother who could sleep in until noon?"

"He got engaged." He appears to be floating, or maybe just bouncing on my chair. The motion, or his aura of bliss, is making me nauseous.

"What do you want now?" I pull the covers to my chin. "I'm not planning your wedding."

"Don't worry, Kendra has that part covered."

I know," I mumble. Kendra showed me a scrapbook she's kept for years—wedding ideas from the perfect dress to the place settings for dinner.

"So..." Matthew begins. I don't like the inflection in his voice.

"What?"

"Michael tells me you two have a date."

I groan and roll over so my back is to him. "I agreed to go to a party with him, as a friend."

"I told you, you'd like him."

"As a friend," I repeat. "I have a boyfriend."

Matthew raises his eyebrows, but doesn't comment. He stands up to go. "Like I said, it doesn't hurt to keep your options open."

"Wait, Matt." I climb out of bed. There's something that has been bothering me ever since I told Michael I'd go with him to the party. I lower my voice. "How rich is Michael's family, anyway?"

"Does that interest you?"

"No," I'm annoyed again. "I'm just not sure what I should wear to the party."

"Why don't you ask Michael?" Matthew stands with one hand on the doorknob. "I don't know anything about clothes."

There's no way I can get back to sleep now. I don't want to risk running into Michael on his way out of the shower again, so I wrap up in a blanket and open up my laptop. I haven't checked my email for almost two days.

I have two emails from Jacob. That's never happened before. Usually, I have to wait days before he answers one of my emails. He's never sent one when I didn't send an almost immediate response.

Jess,

Sorry it's taken so long to answer. I've been on patrol for a while, doing sweeps. Basically finding and deto-nating IED's (homemade explosives.) They're one of the biggest hazards around here. They can be hidden anywhere on the road and in anything and they do a lot of damage.

Most of the time things are slow. We spend a lot of time on equipment maintenance. The sand gets into everything so it's a constant battle to keep everything running.

I'm not sure what Christmas will be like here. I know we're getting some kind of a dinner, but I think that I'm on patrol that whole day, so it won't be much different from the other days I'm here. I wish we could be together. I miss you.

Love,

Jacob

I study the email looking for any evidence that Jacob thinks of me as his girlfriend. He always closes his emails, Love Jacob, never Love you, or I love you. I don't sign my emails that way either. This is the first time it's bothered me.

Even my friends close their e-mails with, Love ya. We've been big on saying that since we all moved away to college. If my friends Jasmine and Taryn can say it, why can't Jacob?

Dumb.

Despite what I said to Michael, I can still obsess over what guys are thinking, or more appropriately, what one guy is thinking.

Matthew is at my door again, but he doesn't come in. Now he respects my privacy. "I know you're up, Jess," he says through the doorway. "Mike's getting ready to leave. He wants to say goodbye."

Reluctantly, I pull myself away from the computer. The other email from Jacob will be a treat for later. I'll write him back a long one with all the details of skiing and Matt's engagement. Well, maybe not all the details.

I pull on a pair of jeans and a t-shirt and twist my hair up on top of my head. I don't care how I look around Michael, but he's seen me in my pajamas enough already.

Mom made crepes, my favorite breakfast. I grab a plate so I'll get some before my brothers come down. "Did Michael already leave?" I ask between bites.

"I think he's upstairs getting his stuff," Mom says. She adds two links of sausage to my plate. I'll have to go for a long run when it warms up to work all this off.

"Where's Matt?"

"Getting ready to go to Kendra's." Mom slides another crepe out of the pan. "So I guess no one gets to sleep this morning."

"Not unless you count Tyler. He's probably going to be out until noon."

"Lucky kid," Mom says. Tomorrow, when Michael is gone, I'm sure we'll all be sleeping in and eating cereal for breakfast.

Matt comes strolling in, whistling as he walks. I wonder when his euphoria will wear off. "Good morning, Jess. Sleep well?"

"Not long enough," I mutter, just loud enough for him to hear.

"Maybe the guys will stop bugging you if you get a little less beauty sleep." That's about as close to a compliment as I ever get from Matt. He sits down and digs into the crepes.

Mom slides another crepe onto the plate in front of us. "Save some for Michael and Tyler and Dad."

"Their fault if they miss out," Matt says, around a mouthful. "Maybe they should learn to get up earlier or move faster."

I look at Matt for a minute. "Did you ever get around to telling Kendra that you're going to Iraq?"

I realize my mistake instantly. The look that simultaneously cross-es Mom and Matt's faces leave no doubt. The question of whether Kendra knows anything about Matthew being deployed hangs in the air. The reality that Mom hasn't found out yet is answered immediately.

Nine

Emotional Minefield

Mom's face is ghostly pale. The crepe in the pan scorches. Matt is glaring at me. I mouth the word "Sorry," and go to take care of the neglected pan.

Finally, Mom speaks. "Matthew," she barely breathes his name. "When?"

I'm not sure if her question is "when is he leaving," "when did he find out," or "when he was planning on telling her?"

Matt walks over to Mom and puts his arms around her shoulders. "I'm sorry, Mom, I wasn't sure how to tell you."

Mom turns and pulls him against her chest. At that moment, Dad walks in, whistling like Matthew had been just a few minutes ago. As soon as Dad looks at Mom and Matt, he stops whistling and looks guilty.

"You." She points her finger at him. "How long have you known about this?"

"About Matthew and..." he hesitates. "Matthew and Iraq?"

"And Jess?" Mom is going from shocked to mad. "Does everyone know about this but me? Tyler, and Kendra too?"

No one says anything. I dump the scorched crepe and get ready to pour another one.

"Leave it," Mom orders. "I need to talk to your dad and Matthew. Jessica, go back upstairs.

I obey. I wish I could somehow erase the last few minutes. Mom looks hurt, angry and afraid all at the same time. Dad looks guilty. Matt just looks mad, mad at me.

Half-way up I run into Michael. He's whistling *Jingle Bells*, carrying his bag, and taking two steps at a time.

What is it with the whistling this morning? I catch him by the arm. "You don't want to go down there."

"I don't?" Michael stops mid-stride. "Did Matt already eat all the crepes?"

"No. Emotional minefield. Me and my big mouth." I sink down on the steps and put my face in my hands. Michael sits down beside me.

"What exactly did you do?" he asks.

"I let it slip that Matt is going to Iraq. Apparently, Mom didn't know about it yet."

"Oh," Michael says.

"Stupid, stupid." I shake my head. "I knew I should have stayed in bed this morning."

"It's not entirely your fault." Michael puts his arm over my shoulder. "When was Matt planning on telling her? When he was on the plane headed to Iraq?"

"It might have been safer for him," I answer. "I don't think I've ever seen Mom this mad."

"That would be a new one, a mother killing her son so he couldn't go to war."

I turn and give him a look that shows I don't appreciate his humor.

"It had to come out sooner or later," Michael tries again.

"Yeah, but I didn't have to be the one to tell her. Sometimes I just talk without thinking."

"We all do." Michael hasn't moved his arm. "It's probably better that it came out now. It will give her some time to process the idea. I can't blame Matt for taking this long, though. I would hate to tell my mom I was going to war. She would completely flip out."

"You mean like that?" The voices from downstairs get louder.

"Probably exactly like that," he sighs.

I stand up. "I'm sorry if this is keeping you from leaving. You want me to sneak you out the back door?"

"I can wait a little longer."

I'm out of things to say. I want to get back to my email, but I can't exactly leave Michael sitting here, waiting for the voices downstairs to calm down. Not talking is worse; now we can hear exactly what's going on downstairs.

Michael breaks the silence. "Um, maybe we should go somewhere else."

"Yeah." I follow him back into the rec room. It doesn't look like Michael slept here. He folded the bed back into the couch and stacked the bedding at the end. None of Matthew's other friends are this neat.

Michael sits down at one end of the couch, and I sit at the other. "I was thinking we should exchange cell numbers, so it will be easier to meet up on New Year's Eve."

"Oh yeah. Let me get my phone." I go into my room to get my phone, glance at my computer with the unopened email, and then head back to the rec room.

It feels weird to program Michael's number into my phone. Way too permanent for one party as just friends. Another question comes to mind. "Uh, Michael. What exactly is the dress code for this party?"

"The dress code?"

"You know, casual, formal, semi-formal, what?"

"Oh," he answers seriously. "A dress like what you wore to the prom would be just fine."

I try to keep my voice even. "Really? That formal?"

His face breaks into a grin. "No, not quite, but you did look incredible in that dress." I guess Matt really showed him my prom picture.

"Thanks. What then?"

"Hmmm." Michael looks thoughtful. "I guess you'd say a little more than semi-formal; a skirt or nice pants, maybe a dress, but not too dressy. My mom isn't into bling and nothing too short or too bare. Kind of like what you might wear for Christmas dinner."

"Oh." I don't tell him dressing up for Christmas dinner at our house means a sweater and jeans. I guess it's different at his house. I'm silent for a while, mentally considering the options that my closet presents. Not many.

Michael breaks into my thoughts. "I'm sure you'll look great no matter what you wear. Come in a grain sack if you'd like."

"That's great. I think there might still be a couple up in the barn loft. Should I wash them or just wear them with a natural coating of dust?"

"Oh, leave the dust on," Michael says. "It gives it an air of authenticity."

I'm trying to think of something clever to say to that when my phone rings. It's Jasmine. The clock reads 9:05. Impressive, Jaz is actually up.

"Sorry. I need to take this." I walk over to the corner of the room and answer the phone

"Jess!" Jasmine screams. "Where have you been? We need to get to the store as soon as possible! I have a ton of shopping to do."

"Come now, if you re ready. I'm looking forward to it." That's a lie. I am looking forward to seeing Jasmine, but the last thing I want to do today is fight crazed last-minute Christmas shoppers.

"Great," Jasmine says. "I'll pick you up in half an hour. It will be fun, I promise. I have loads to tell you about school."

"Last minute Christmas shopping?" Michael says when I hang up. He makes a face. "Have fun. Sorry, I couldn't help but hear."

"I know," I sigh. "Jasmine is my most enthusiastic friend."

"Cheerleader?" Michael guesses.

"Three years of high school."

"What about you?"

"No cheerleading—track and cross-country."

"I should have guessed," Michael says. "Those long legs."

I glance at the door. I need to get ready if Jasmine is coming that soon. "I wonder if it's safe to head down yet."

Matt answers my question by coming in. He gives me a look that makes me think I'll hear about my slip later. "You taking off soon, Mike?"

"As soon as I can," Michael answers.

"Not without breakfast. Mom will be offended if you don't eat." Matt says. "And she's already kind of riled up... I guess you probably heard."

"I'd better get ready to go." I stand. I don't want to give Matthew the chance to catch me alone.

"Where are you headed?" Matthew asks.

"Shopping, with Jasmine."

"Good," Matthew says. "I need you to find something that I can give Kendra for Christmas. Since I already gave her the ring, I'm kind of without a present."

Now I'm buying Kendra's Christmas present? I guess I owe him.

Jasmine arrives while I'm still doing my hair. I glance at my computer again and agonize.

Jacob's email will have to wait a little longer.

"Hi, Roberts family," Jasmine says when she comes to the door. "How is everyone?"

"Jasmine," Mom gives her a hug. "It's good to see you. Would you like breakfast?"

"No thanks. We need to get going," Jasmine says.

"Here are some ideas for something for Kendra." Matthew hands me a piece of paper.

I take it and look at the handwriting, too nice to be his. "Your ideas or Michael's?"

"A little of both," he says sheepishly.

"Hello." Jasmine notices Michael. She's eyeing him as if he's her next conquest.

I turn and introduce them. "Jasmine, this is Matt's friend Michael. Michael, this is Jasmine."

"Nice to meet you, Jasmine," Michael extends his hand.

"Nice to meet you too," Jasmine's voice has a familiar flirtatious ring to it. She doesn't let go of his hand immediately. "How long are you staying?"

"Actually," Michael shoulders his bag. "I'm leaving right now."

"Too bad," Jasmine replies.

"I'd stay longer, but my mom is ready to kill me for not being home already." He turns to me. "It was nice to see you again, Jess. Call me when you get back to school and we can make plans."

"Sure." I ignore the curious look Jasmine is giving me. "I guess I'll see you in a little over a week."

"I'll be waiting." Michael replies.

I'm afraid of that.

Ten

Out of Reach

Jasmine accosts me in the car. "Who's Michael?

"Matt's friend from Fort Bliss." I adjust the heater vent in Jasmine's car without looking at her.

"What did he mean by *plans*?" Jasmine won't let this go without details.

I take a deep breath. "Michael's family is in Pullman. He invited me to a New Year's Eve party there."

"He's cute. So you're going?"

I nod.

She gives me a long look. "Are you going to tell Jacob?"

I hesitate for a minute. "I haven't decided yet. It's a party, not really a date, but I still feel guilty about it."

Jasmine flips through the stations on the radio. "My advice, go and have fun. Don't tell Jacob anything. It'll be better that way."

I've learned to be selective about which of Jasmine's relationship advice I follow, but this time I think she might be right.

"I'll treat you to dinner," Jasmine says when we're driving home from shopping.

"Sounds good." It's taken all day to get through Jasmine's list and find something for Kendra. I'm exhausted and starving.

"What are you in the mood for? Italian? Chinese?"

"Actually, I'm kind of in the mood for a good burger. We could—" A report on the radio stops me.

"...Fort Lewis soldiers killed when a suicide bomber walked into a crowded mess hall in Mosul yesterday."

An electric chill races down my back.

Jasmine's forehead wrinkles in concern. "Where is Jacob?"

"Mosul." I turn up the radio, but the report is over.

"Don't worry," Jasmine starts. "I'm sure he's okay."

"Yeah." I'm trying to keep my voice steady. "Can you take me home? I'm actually not very hungry."

"Okay." Jasmine keeps glancing at me, but she doesn't say anything else.

As soon as Jasmine stops the car, I jump out and run up the stairs. Mom is at the door. "Mom, we just heard on the radio..."

"I know," Mom replies. "I just got off the phone with Trina."

"What did she say?" I hold my breath, afraid of her answer. I wrap my arms around myself. My whole has gone cold.

"She hasn't heard anything. She said they go into a communications blackout whenever someone...she said no news is probably good news." She hugs me. "I'm sure Jacob is fine."

Jasmine hands me the bag with Kendra's present.

"Would you like to stay for dinner?" Mom asks her.

"No, I need to get home." Jasmine hugs me. "Thanks again, Jess. Call me if..." she trails off. "Call me tomorrow, okay?"

I watch her drive away.

Mom puts her arm around me. "Matt is at Kendra's and Tyler is spending the night at a friend's house, but we have leftovers if you're hungry."

"No thanks, Mom, I'm just going to go up to my room."

She nods. "Try not to worry, Jess."

Dad is watching the news in the living room. "... the largest attack thus far. No names have been released pending notification of the families."

I walk into my room and sit down at my desk. I tap the keyboard and wait for the screensaver to disappear. My email is still up. The unopened message from Jacob stares me in the face.

I take a long breath and open it.

Hey Jess,

This is the second email from me and nothing from you (hint, hint). You didn't forget me already did you? I hope you made it home okay. I hope you're having a great Christmas vacation. Did I mention I miss you? I got your package. I already opened it. Sorry, I couldn't wait. I love the pictures of you. I wish there were more. It was so good to see your face. Did I mention I miss you?

I'll call you when I can. Maybe I'll try for New Years. It
won't be the same as a kiss at midnight, but I'm dying
to hear your voice.

I hope everything is good at home. I heard from Mom
and Gage. They'll all be together for Christmas. Mom
has banned all political discussions over Christmas to
keep the peace since Nathan's bringing Angel. Kind
of glad I won't be there for that.

Love,

Jacob

I read the email over three times. He was heading to the mess hall.
What time did he write the email? What time was the attack? I try
to find out on the internet. The story is everywhere, but they're all
different. Some say there were nine people killed, some say more. I
can't focus. I try to write a reply to Jacob, but I can't bring myself to
write something I'm not sure he'll ever read.

I shut my computer and lay down on my bed. I have two pictures of
Jacob on my nightstand, one of us sitting by each other on the couch
from last Thanksgiving and the one of him in his dress uniform. I pick
that one up and look at it. It looks too much like something that would
be displayed next to a flag-draped coffin. I set it down and pick up the
one of us together and hold it to my chest.

What will I do if he's gone?

I need everything that reminds me of Jacob close to me. The locket
he gave me is around my neck, where it always is. I search the floor of
my closet until I find the plastic bag that contains the shirt Jacob was
wearing the day he saved me from Brad. It somehow ended up in the
bag of my things from the hospital.

I hold the shirt to my face and breathe it in. It still smells like Jacob—sweat mixed with his cologne. It also smells like the barn—dust and musty hay. There's a long rip down the back and dark brown stains on the front. Blood. Jacob's blood. It makes me think about Jacob being hurt, Jacob bleeding. It makes me sick to look at it. I wad it back into the bag and put it back in the closet.

I try to focus on other things. I study the picture of us together. Jacob saved my life. Jacob held me, Jacob kissed me. Jacob loves me. I know he loves me.

I love him too. Why didn't I write it in every single email I sent him?

"Please, God, let him be safe." I pray out loud as I lie back down on the bed and trace my lips with the locket.

I get ready for bed and turn out the light, but I can't sleep. I keep listening for the phone ringing. If Trina got any news from Jacob, she would call immediately, wouldn't she? My heart feels hollow. I run through every moment of our time together. Somehow, he has to be okay.

I have to see him again.

When I finally sleep, I dream about Jacob. I'm running down a long, dark road. He's calling my name, but I can't see him. He's right in front of me, but always just out of reach.

"Jacob!"

His name is on my lips when I wake up. As I shake myself out of the dream I realize two things; the house phone is ringing, and my locket is gone. I must have been twisting it in my sleep. The chain is on the floor by my bed, broken.

I search my bedding frantically, as if finding the locket will make Jacob safe. I tear the bed apart before I find it, underneath my pillow. I press it against my lips.

"Jess."

Mom stands in the doorway with the phone in her hand. Her face gives nothing away.

It has to be Trina. She must have found something out in the middle of the night and decided not to wake me.

I take the phone with trembling fingers. "Hello."

Eleven

Bittersweet

"Hi Jess."

"Jacob." I gasp. "Thank God." I grip the phone tighter and the tears I held in all night flow down my cheeks. I can't say anything else.

"Are you okay?" Jacob's voice is tender and full of concern.

I laugh, relief almost giving way to hysteria. "Am *I* okay? Are you okay?"

"I'm fine. Sorry if you were..."

Terrified, heart-sick, grief-stricken. "I'm okay. Now. Oh, Jacob, thank God you're okay."

"Say that again," he says.

I take a deep breath. "Thank God you're okay."

"Not that, just the first part. My name," Jacob replies. "It sounds so good to hear you say my name."

"Jacob, Jacob, Jacob," I say it over slowly, savoring his name on my tongue. "Jacob, thank you for calling. I was so afraid."

"I'm sorry, Jess. I wish I could have called sooner. They lock down all communications when," he draws in a breath. "Things are pretty tight here right now."

"Jacob," I ask quietly. "Is Bryan okay?"

"He's fine. No one you knew was there."

Relief and guilt flood through me. No one I knew, but people had died in the explosion. Someone else received a very different call, a much different visit. Families were hurting—wives, kids, moms and dads. Was it fair to feel so happy when someone else was devastated?

I pick up the tone of Jacob's voice. "But men you knew."

"Yes, men I knew. We lost a lot of good men." His pain comes through in his voice.

"I'm so sorry, Jacob." Silent tears slip down my cheeks.

"So am I, Jess."

The line stays quiet. I can hear him breathing, like he's close enough for me to touch, but still so far away. His voice is soft when he finally speaks. "I got your package. Thank you."

"I got your emails. I'm sorry I didn't get back to you. Things have been kind of crazy. We went skiing, and Matt got engaged. I went shopping with Jaz." I'm blabbering like an idiot. It all seems so trivial.

"Wow, tell him I said congratulations."

"I will."

"Thank you for the pictures. I love them all, especially the one in the leaves."

"Kendra took that one for her photography class. She took a bunch that day, kind of like a photo shoot."

"Are there more?"

"A lot more. It was kind of embarrassing."

"Send them to me, please."

"All of them?"

"Every one. I don't care if you have your eyes closed or if they're out of focus. I want them all. I miss you so much." Jacob sounds different—vulnerable. It's sweet and sad at the same time. I can only imagine what he's been through in the past few hours. I can barely imagine what he's seen since he got to Iraq.

I wish I could hold him. I wish I could take away the pain in his voice. An idea comes to me. "Close your eyes."

"What?"

"Trust me. Just close your eyes. My arms are around your neck. My breath is on your face. My lips are on your lips." His breath comes through the line—close, like our lips could really touch. "Anytime you need a kiss from me, just close your eyes. I'll always be there. I promise."

"Thank you," his answer is breathless, like we actually kissed. His tone changes, more like himself, mischievous. "Can I count them?"

"Can you count what?"

"The kisses, so I can redeem them when I get home."

I laugh. "Absolutely."

"Jess, I... I got you something for Christmas. Mom said she'd make sure it got there in time." He sounds unsure.

"I told you I didn't need anything," I say, but I'm dying to know what it is.

"I know, but I thought you needed something a little nicer than a cheap locket. I hope you like it."

"I would love anything you gave me," I say.

"Thanks, I—" He's interrupted by someone in the background. He swears under his breath. "Sorry. I have to go. I wish I could talk to you forever."

"I do too."

"Do me a favor. Could you check on Becky, Bryan's wife? He said that she's really shook up. She knows the wives of the men who were killed."

"I'll call her today."

"Thank you; you're amazing."

There are voices in the background again. I'm afraid we'll get cut off before I can say what I really want to say.

"I have to go," he says again. "I'll call you again as soon as I can."

"Please, anytime, day or night. Call my cell phone. I'll keep it with me all the time."

"I will. I miss you so much. Good-bye, Jess. I love you."

"I love you too, Jacob. Good-bye."

The call disconnects, but I don't want to hang up. I'm clinging to the phone. I wish I could bring him back.

Bittersweet, always bittersweet with Jacob. He's mine, really mine. But so far away. Safe for now, but... I try not to think about the months that he has left in Iraq.

Twelve

Diamonds and Emeralds

K endra and Matt are cuddled on the couch, more into each other than the stack of gifts around them. Tyler is tearing into presents like a three-year-old. I'm trying to be patient as Mom digs through the gifts under the tree. Finally, she hands me a little blue box with a white bow on it. The card reads, "To Jess, Love Jacob," in handwriting I recognize as Jacob's mom's.

I slide the bow off carefully and lift the lid. Inside is a little velvet box that looks a lot like the one Kendra's ring came in. I hold my breath as I open it. Diamond stud earrings sit on a bed of red velvet. Small, but I know immediately they're real. The gift takes my breath away.

"Let me see," Mom says.

Kendra comes over to see. "Wow. Those are the real deal. Put them on."

I slide them into my ears. I stand up and go to the mirror, turning back and forth and watching how the diamonds catch the light.

Kendra stands behind me. "You're glowing." She holds her hand up so the diamond on her fingers sparkles. "There's just something about a diamond, isn't there?"

I touch my ears. "I'm never taking them off."

Kendra laughs, "I'm never taking mine off, either."

Matt doesn't say anything. I can't help but feel smug. Maybe now he understands how me and Jacob feel about each other.

I'm ready to go up to the computer and thank Jacob for the earrings now, but Matt picks up another present, wrapped in gold with a wide green bow.

"This one's for you," he says, handing me the box.

"Thanks," I reply.

"It's not from me." The way he says it makes me dread reading the card. In square, bold letters it says.

"Looking forward to New Year's, Michael."

I'm afraid to open the box. I slide the bow off and unwrap it slowly. Inside is a beautiful red sweater, a lacy white camisole to go underneath, and a white lace skirt to match. There's a smaller box inside the big box. Inside that is a silver choker of snowflakes inset with little emeralds. I hope they aren't real. The snowflakes and the green make an odd combination, but I get the message—a gift from the guy with emerald green eyes who can make it snow on demand.

I wonder how Michael pulled off this miracle. When did he buy the clothes? Where did he find the necklace and how did he get his gift to my house in time for Christmas?

I'm in my bedroom working on a long email to Jacob when voices come through the wall between Matt's room and mine. It's something I've never heard before—Matt and Kendra arguing. They're talking loud enough for me to hear without trying.

"...five months may be plenty of time for a guy, but not for me." Kendra is saying, "I have plans for our wedding, plans that will take longer. I need a dress, flowers, and a reception hall. All the things you would never think of."

"I'm just saying, things would be better for you if we got married before I leave." Matt is trying to keep his voice calm. "There are benefits that you would have as my wife that you wouldn't have as my fiancé."

"You're talking about if something happens to you," Kendra's voice is pinched. "I don't want to talk about that. Don't ever talk that way."

There's a long pause before Matt's voice comes back, deep and soothing. "You're right. You're always right." I can picture him putting his arms around her. "Whatever you want is fine. Take all the time you want with the wedding. Make it perfect. I'll be right beside you whenever you're ready. I'm getting the better end of the deal. I know that."

Kendra says something I can't hear. They laugh. I wonder if Matt knows how thin the walls are between our rooms.

I can't concentrate on the email anymore. I close my laptop and look at the picture of Jacob and the broken locket on my nightstand.

The last few days have made the war all too real. I don't want to think about Jacob and Matt being there.

Thirteen

The Hard Part

A blond-haired, blue-eyed little boy opens the door when I knock. A hugely pregnant, dark-haired woman is close behind him, putting on an earring. I'm struck by how young Becky is. When I met her at the self-defense class Jacob taught, she seemed a lot older than me. Now she seems almost the same age.

"Connor," Becky scolds. "You aren't supposed to open the door without Mommy there."

"It's just her," Connor points at me.

Becky stops in the doorway. "Jess. It's good to see you."

"Good to see you again too. You look great," I say. Becky's blue eyes are rimmed in dark circles, but her face is radiant.

She gives me a sideways hug to accommodate her belly. "Huge is more like it, but thank you."

Connor is staring at me, his eyes wide. "I know who you are. You're Jacob's girlfriend."

I love hearing that. I kneel to meet his eye. "My name is Jess."

He squirms away. "Jacob is with my daddy, in Iraq."

"I know," I answer softly.

"Jess is going to play with you while Mommy is gone," Becky says. I offered to babysit for her while she went to the memorial service for the men killed in the attack in Mosul.

"What did you bring me?" Connor asks. He reaches for the bag I brought with me.

"Connor, that's rude," Becky says.

I hold it behind my back. "A present." His eyes grow round. "And some cookie dough. If it's okay with your mom, I thought we'd make sugar cookies."

Becky smiles. "That's so sweet of you. Just watch him. He'll eat all the dough if you let him."

"I'm with you, Connor. I love cookie dough."

Becky picks up her purse and stuffs a wad of tissues inside. "You might be able to get him to nap in a couple of hours. But don't stress if you can't get him to settle down. He's at that age where naps are optional—at least for him. I can always use one. You have my cell number." She looks around the room. "What am I forgetting?"

She looks nervous about leaving Connor, or maybe just nervous about where she's going. "We'll be fine. Don't worry about anything."

"I know. You're wonderful for doing this. I can't imagine trying to go to this thing today and wrestling Connor the whole time."

I can't imagine going at all, especially in her position.

Connor is asleep on the couch, and the cookies are cooling on the table when Becky gets home. Her eyes are red, and she looks exhausted.

"Why don't you go lie down? I can stay while you take a nap," I say.

"No, that's okay." She takes off her shoes and settles onto the couch beside me. "I know you need to get on the road, and we really haven't had the chance to talk yet."

"How was the service?" I ask delicately.

"Very nice, very formal, very military." Becky sighs. "Absolutely heart-wrenching. I've never been to anything like that before. I didn't realize how hard it would be. I can't imagine what those families are going through."

I swallow hard. "Me either."

"I was so happy and so relieved when Bryan called me, but I felt so guilty. I knew there were other wives who were getting a very different call, or a different visit. When they show up in person, it's never good news."

"That's how I felt too—relieved and guilty." I can't look Becky in the eye. I study the patterns on the couch.

"It's not easy, is it?" Becky leans over and touches my hand. "These reminders that what they're doing is dangerous."

"No." I shake my head to clear the tears gathered in the corners of my eyes. I feel stupid crying in front of her.

Becky sighs. "They're gone for months at a time, the pay isn't great, and they're putting their lives at risk. And yet we choose this because we love them." She shakes her head. "Well, I should say I chose this. I guess you haven't quite reached that point yet."

I haven't really thought about what my life would be like if I chose Jacob, or if he chose me. Right now, whatever sacrifice I have to make seems worth it to have him. The last few days made me realize it might be harder than I thought.

She sits back. "I'm sorry, Jess, I didn't mean to make you sad. How's college going?"

Everything in my life seems so trivial after where she's been, but she seems ready to change the subject. "Good, kind of hard, but I'm doing okay."

"I remember that part of it—the hard part." She leans closer. "What about fun? Are you having fun?" I shrug. "That's the part I missed after I left." She ruffles her fingers through Connor's hair. "Of course, that's the part that got me in trouble." Becky told me she'd dropped out of college when she found out she was pregnant with Connor. Connor isn't Bryan's son—his bio dad isn't in the picture. "But it can't be all work and no fun. Do you go out, go to parties?"

My stomach tightens. What would Becky think about my not-a-date with Michael? "I don't know. Not a lot. I have a couple of roommates who are really into that, but I'm not... I mean, with Jacob gone..."

She laughs. "Don't sound so guilty when you say that. It's okay to enjoy yourself at college. You're only eighteen. Jacob might kill me for saying this, but a year is a long time. You don't have to put yourself in cold storage. You're young, you're beautiful. Enjoy it before you end up like me." She puts her hand on her stomach and smiles. "Don't get me wrong. I'm happy with how things turned out. I wouldn't trade my boys for anything. But if I could have a few of my teenage years back..."

I'm about to burst. I need to tell someone about the date with Michael. Someone who knows Jacob. Someone who won't tell me that Michael is better for me.

"I have a confession to make." I run my fingers through the fake fur on the blanket slung over the back of the couch. "I'm going to a New Year's Eve party."

"That's not really a confession."

"Even if I'm going with a guy, a guy my brother really wants me to be with?"

"Is this a guy from college?" Becky's face scrunches in concern. I immediately wish I hadn't mentioned it.

"No, he's in the Army. He's stationed at Fort Bliss with Matt. His family lives in Pullman, though. He came to our house for a couple of days and went skiing with us. He asked me to go to the party with him, as a friend." I emphasize the last word.

"Do you like him?"

I shake my head. "He's a nice guy, kind of arrogant, and he's not..."

"He's not Jacob," she finishes and smiles.

"Nothing like Jacob, and honestly, I can't imagine being with anyone but Jacob."

"Then go have fun. Fort Bliss is far away, and if you aren't really interested in him, where's the harm?" She raises her eyebrows. "Jacob is one of the sweetest guys I've ever met, and you're an absolute angel. You two are perfect for each other."

I blush. "Thanks, I think so too."

"Then a few parties while he's gone won't make that much difference. Just be happy. Enjoy yourself."

"Thanks for everything, Becky." I stand up. She looks tired, and it's late. "I'd better get going."

"Thanks for what?" Becky asks. "You're the one who babysat for me and made cookies."

"It was fun, and I appreciate all the advice you've given me."

"Anytime." It takes effort for her to stand. She gives me a hug. "Don't be a stranger, please. I'm stuck with a toddler all day, so any adult conversation I get now is a plus."

"I'll stay in touch. I promise."

"And keep praying for our guys. They still have a long time ahead of them."

I swallow hard and nod. "I will."

Fourteen

Kiss at Midnight

I study my reflection in the mirror. The outfit Michael gave me looks like something that Laini, Jacob's snobby ex-girlfriend would have worn. Except it's not all white. I'm not sure I can forgive Michael for that. He guessed my size pretty closely, or maybe Mom helped him. It couldn't have been Matthew, he's clueless about women's clothes.

My hair is up so I can see Jacob's earrings sparkle when I turn my head. I can't get rid of the stab of guilt in my chest. I picked up the phone to call Michael and tell him I'd changed my mind, or I was sick, or I had to work late, but I couldn't do it.

I hear a knock, then Michael's voice comes from the living room.

"Jess, your date is here," my roommate, Nichole, says. To Michael, she says. "It's about time someone got her to leave the apartment."

The word 'date' makes me cringe. It's not a date; it's a favor.

"You look stunning," Michael says when I walk in the room.

"Thanks." I'm suddenly self-conscious. "And thank you for the outfit. You have great taste."

Michael makes a face. "I know. It's a curse."

I laugh. "What's wrong with that?"

"I have three older sisters. They taught me more about clothes and fashion than any guy needs to know."

I laugh again. "Maybe I should get you to go shopping with me. Nichole is convinced I don't know how to dress myself."

"I hope I didn't offend you with the gift. Matt told me that you weren't sure what to wear. I know that's a big deal for women. I didn't want you to worry about being underdressed." Michael sounds sincere, but as he helps me with my coat, my thoughts go back to my ex-boyfriend, Brad. He always had an opinion about what I should wear.

Michael's parent's house is just off campus. It looks like the college buildings around it—red brick exterior, wide front porch, and white balcony over the front door, but it stands out, a notch above everything around it, bigger, somehow more elegant. The lights around the pillars and in the trees, and the decorations and wreath adorning the door all look like they were done by a professional decorator. They probably were.

"You've never lived in this house?" I ask as Michael helps me out of the car.

"No, I grew up in Colorado. Dad took this job after I left for the Army. It's kind of a compromise. Mom is from Washington, the

Bellevue area. She wanted Dad to retire here, but he's not quite ready to stop working. She was hoping for UW, but that didn't pan out. She didn't want him to take the job at WSU. She thinks it's cow college, no offense."

"None taken. Actually, that's what I like about it. It still kind of has that small college town feel."

Michael holds my arm as we go up the long sidewalk, past the fountain, and toward the ornate front door. "Did you order this?" I indicate the snow. There's a couple of inches of snow on the ground, and a few feathery snowflakes are falling against the lights.

"Oh no, that order came from a much higher power than me."

"And who would that be?"

"My mother, I'm sure God himself would have to answer to her if something wasn't perfect at this party." He rolls his eyes. "Silvia has got entertaining down to a science."

"Silvia is your mom then." I realize how little I know about Michael and his family.

"Yes, and Ronald is my dad."

"And you have three sisters, but no brothers, right?"

"Yep. Karen, Kelsey and Kandice are my sisters."

"Shouldn't you be named Kory or Kevin or something like that then?"

"You would think so, but Michael is my grandpa's name he was a lawyer for the Army for a lot of years. I guess I'm supposed to live up to it somehow."

"Tell me about your family." I slow my steps, feeling like I need to be prepared.

"Karen and Kelsey are married to Will and Thomas, respectively. Karen is a neurologist and has twin girls, Andrea and Gracey. Kelsey graduated from Stanford with a degree in communications. She has her own PR firm and two little girls, Emma and Katie. And she's pregnant; this one is actually supposed to be a boy."

My head is spinning with the credentials he spouted off for his family. I focus instead on what I feel qualified to talk about. "That sounds like a lot of estrogen for one family."

"It is. Y chromosomes run when they see our family. My mom has all sisters and my dad has all sisters. I'm an anomaly. My mom didn't know what to do with me when I was a kid."

"So what about your third sister?"

"Kandice just graduated from UW. She's engaged to Jeff. They're getting married in June. That will be Silvia's crowning achievement. The third daughter's wedding is her chance at absolute social perfection."

"Is there anyone else I need to know about?"

"I could get started on my aunts and cousins. Most of them are girls too, but I think we've crammed enough for now."

"Is there going to be a test?"

"Usually our last party game involves a quiz about the Stephen's family. Anyone who fails it has to clean up after the party." I must look panicked because he squeezes my arm. "Don't worry about it, Jess. They're all so giddy that I'm showing up with a date that I found on my own that they would love you even if you only had one eye and an extra arm."

"That's encouraging."

He stops at the base of the stairs and looks into my eyes. "Sorry, I didn't mean it that way. They will love you because you're beautiful and you're wonderful."

I pull away, embarrassed. "Thanks. You obviously don't know me very well. Besides, I don't buy that you couldn't have come up with a date on your own."

"Oh really? Why would you say that?" Michael doesn't move. He's still looking at me.

"I assume you own a mirror. And I'm pretty sure you've noticed the effect you had on my brother's date when I went skiing."

He laughs, tucks my arm closer into his side, and starts up the stairs.

"Thanks, but I'm not into girls who are still in high school."

"What about girls who are barely out of high school?" I ask. Then I realize it sounds like I'm flirting, or at least expressing interest.

"You seem a lot older than eighteen. I forgot you just got out of high school."

"Well, I am very mature for my age."

"I've noticed," he says. "But to answer your question, when you were a social pariah in high school, it's hard to remember that you're not that person anymore. I guess I can't imagine anyone would be interested now."

"Ski racing team? The red hair and those eyes?" *Money too*, I add to myself. "There's no way you were as big of an outcast as I was."

"That sounds like a challenge. Maybe later we can compare yearbook photos and see who was the bigger geek, but I'm sure I'll win."

"Don't count on it," I laugh, but there's no way I'm showing Michael pictures from my long awkward stage.

The door swings open before we reach it. Standing in the doorway is an attractive dark-haired girl who looks a little older than me. I assume she's one of Michael's sisters.

She turns and yells over her shoulder. "Mike's here, and he actually has a girl with him. A pretty girl."

Michael glares at her jokingly. "Jess, this is Kandice, Kandice this is Jess."

"Hi, Jess, nice to meet you." Kandice has the same green eyes as Michael. They dance with mischief. "How much is my brother paying you to go out with him?"

"Kandice." An older redheaded woman walks towards us. She has a slim figure and is wearing a fitted blue silk blouse, dark skirt, and a gold coiled necklace. I'm suddenly grateful that Michael picked out my outfit. "Don't be so rude to your brother's guest." She turns to me. "It's nice to meet you, Jessica. I'm Michael's mother, Silvia Stephens. Thank you for coming." She leans over and kisses me on the cheek—literally something I've only seen done in movies.

"You have a beautiful home, Mrs. Stephens." I try not to sound overwhelmed. It's an understatement.

The inside of the house is ornate on its own, but it's covered with elaborate garlands, lights, and flowers for the party. Music floats through the large room from a white grand piano. Tables loaded with elegant food are sit at either end of a huge great room. Adorable blonde twins in frilly white dresses are chasing each other between the legs of the guests. They look like part of the décor. The whole scene feels like something from *The Nutcracker*.

Michael introduces me to a dizzying array of relatives, friends, and faculty from the college. I meet his dad, Dean Stephens. He's quiet and polite, but he spends most of his time talking with other members of the faculty.

I like all of Michael's sisters. Karen, Dr. Nelson, is professional and formal–like her mother. Kelsey is sweet and very pregnant. Kandice is closest to my age. She's fun and mischievous. I think if we had the chance, we'd be good friends.

Beautiful, professional family photos fill a smaller room off of the main room. A picture of a baby with curly red hair catches my eye.

"Which sister is this?" I point to the picture.

Michael grimaces. "That one is actually me."

"Wow, you were a beautiful baby."

"I guess so. My sisters used to love playing dress-up with me, make-up, nail polish, everything."

"Hats, frilly dresses," Kandice is standing to the side of Michael. "He was adorable. We have pictures. I'll show you later."

"No, absolutely not." Michael steers me out of the room. "Now do you see why I never bring girls home?"

An hour into the party, Kelsey approaches Michael with a guitar. "Mom wants you to play."

"You're much better than I am." Michael pushes the guitar back to her.

"I can barely get my arms around my belly, much less actually reach the strings to play," she hands it back to him.

"This is embarrassing," he mutters. "You have to sing, Kels."

"We'll sing together, okay."

The two of them take chairs in the middle of the large living room. Kandice stands behind me and whispers, "Mom insisted on music lessons for all of us, piano, violin, voice, you name it. Kelsey and Mike were always the best at it. Have you ever heard him sing?"

"Only in the shower." I say, then blush. Kandice raises her eyebrows and grins.

Michael and Kelsey's voices blend beautifully. They sing Christmas songs first, and then a couple of folksy, John Denver-type songs. They end with *Springtime in the Rockies*. I think I can see tears in both of their eyes when they sing that one.

"That was beautiful." I say as he puts the guitar in its case.

"Thanks, I'm a bit rusty."

"That was rusty?"

He nods. "I don't have a lot of time to play."

"You must miss Colorado."

"Kind of." He shrugs.

"But that song..." Maybe I was wrong about the tears.

"That song reminds us of our little sister, Kaylee," Michael isn't looking at me.

"I didn't know you had a little sister."

"She was a couple of years younger than me." His voice cracks. "She died in a car accident when she was fourteen." He swallows hard. "We were close."

"I'm sorry."

A cloud passes over his face. "It was a long time ago."

Mrs. Stephens is watching Kelsey's husband help her get out of the chair. She shakes her head and looks at me. "I hope she knows what she's getting herself into. Nothing in raising girls taught me how to cope with one little boy. Michael was always getting into trouble, always jumping off of higher and higher things. That led to the whole skiing thing. I used to get so scared when I watched him. I finally had to ban myself from watching his sports altogether." She smiles at me. "It's good to see him finally settling down."

I don't know how to answer that.

At twenty to nine, Michael takes me upstairs to a playroom. "Mom always lets the little kids have their own countdown and celebration at nine before we put them to bed. They just started letting me stay up the whole night a couple of years ago."

I laugh.

"You think I'm kidding. I don't think my sisters will ever realize I've grown up."

"I guess we kind of feel that way about Tyler."

Michael hands out party hats, poppers, and noisemakers to his nieces and younger cousins. One twin comes up to me and pulls on my skirt. "Are you Michael's girlfriend?" She asks. She has the same beautiful green eyes as her uncle.

I blush. Michael kneels down in front of his niece. "I like Jess a lot, Gracey, but she's not my girlfriend. Maybe if we're really nice to her, we can get her to come back."

Gracey wraps her arms around my neck and kisses me on the cheek. "I like you a lot, too, Jess."

"Those girls are adorable," I say after we come down from the kids' party.

"Yeah, they are." Michael replies. "I'm kind of looking forward to having a nephew, though. It will be nice to have another boy around. I've always been outnumbered."

"Me too. I always wanted a sister. I guess I'll finally get my wish when Matt and Kendra get married."

"Maybe you'll get lucky and marry someone with a lot of sisters," Michael says.

I don't answer. I'm thinking about midnight. Going out with Michael is one thing. I can't kiss him. That would be too much like betraying Jacob.

At 11:45, everyone crowds into the living room for the countdown. Michael and Kandice are handing out funny hats and glasses of champagne. Even Michael's stoic father and proper mother put on a party hat.

Michael chooses a feathery red tiara and places it on my head. "More fashion advice?" I ask.

"This goes perfectly with your outfit." Michael jokes. He handed me a glass. "Sorry, this isn't real champagne. Dad has issues with providing one of his underage students with alcohol at his home. He's trying to change WSU's image."

"Good luck with that." I answer, taking the glass.

"I'll just have a small glass," Michael says. "I have to drive you home unless you'd like to stay."

His question makes me uncomfortable, but I brush it off. "No, that's okay. I didn't bring anything to sleep in, and I'm sure the house is packed with everyone here."

"I have three sisters, remember. I'm sure they have something you could wear. And my bed is always open." He catches the look on my face. "I mean, I'd take the couch for the night if you want to stay."

I shake my head.

I get more nervous as it gets to midnight. I spot the older Michael, Michael's grandpa, sitting on the edge of the room. I slip away from the crowd and stand by him.

When the clock strikes midnight, I lean over and kiss Michael Senior on the forehead. Michael kisses the young, female professor standing by him.

"Happy New Year, Mr. Stephens," I say.

He laughs and kisses me on the cheek. "I like your girl, very much, Michael."

Michael comes over and slides his arm around me. "I like her too." He kisses me on the other cheek. "Happy New Year, Jess."

"Happy New Year, Michael." I feel like I dodged a bullet.

I close my eyes and think. "Happy New Year, Jacob."

Fifteen

Checking Up

January 2005

I can't concentrate on what my professor is saying. My mind is on the two reminders of my birthday that showed up at my apartment this morning. The first was a dozen white roses. I immediately assumed they were from Jacob. They're from Michael. As beautiful as they are, they make me feel guilty just looking at them.

The second was the birthday card my roommate got from the mail and left on my dresser. The return address was missing, but the handwriting looked familiar. I didn't realize why until I opened the card. It was a generic card—a birthday cake on the outside, blank on the inside except for three words.

Thinking of you.

I tried to convince myself that it was a coincidence or someone's idea of a sick joke, but I know Brad's handwriting. He's not supposed to contact me. I thought about calling my lawyer, but there's probably no way to prove it was from him. I threw it away.

My cell phone vibrates. I jump and clap my hand over my leg to silence it. I keep my head down as I head to the back of the lecture hall, walking as fast as possible.

I manage to answer it before it goes to voicemail.

"Happy Birthday, Jess."

"Jacob!" I scream, not caring that I'm still in earshot of the class.

"You didn't think I would let today go by without at least a call, did you?" I can picture his lazy half-grin when he says that.

"Jacob, it's so good to hear your voice. I cried for an hour when I realized I'd missed your call on New Year's Eve. I should have told you about the stupid party."

"No, I'm sorry. I should have known you'd be out. There's no reason for you to be alone on New Year's Eve, sitting around waiting for a phone call." His voice sounds far away and lonely. My chest aches.

"The chance to hear your voice is a huge reason for me to sit around by myself. I don't care what day it is."

"How was the party?"

I suck in my breath. This is the last thing I want to talk to Jacob about. "It was okay."

"It wasn't a wild frat party, was it?" He's teasing, but I sense something beyond curiosity in that question.

"No way, I told you I got my fill of those the second week of school. This one was at one of the deans' houses. It was much more formal."

"Did you get a kiss at midnight?" There's a jealous edge to his voice, something I've never heard before.

"Jacob, how can you even ask that?" I'm glad I can answer him honestly. "Yes, I kissed a little old man on the forehead. Is that okay?"

"It sounds perfect to me. Speaking of which, do you want to know how many you owe me now?"

"How many what do I owe you?"

"Kisses."

I grin. "Sure, how many?"

"Let's just say you'd better stock up on lip stuff now."

"Good, I hope we get to spend the first three days after you get home just kissing." Cheesy, mushy, I don't care how it sounds. I love talking to him this way.

"You have no idea how good that sounds to me right now. Holding you. Kissing you. Whatever that leads to..."

My checks burn. I'm not ready for this conversation yet. "So how are things there?"

"Wet, muddy, basically a mess. What about there?"

"Cold, a little snow. I didn't think I'd ever miss the rain, but some days, I'd be willing to trade the rain for the cold. At least we get to see the sun."

"I'd love to come keep you warm."

"I'd love to have you here keeping me warm."

"How's school?"

"Okay, you just got me out of the king of all boring lectures."

"I called in the middle of class? I'm sorry."

"Don't be. I'd much rather be listening to you right now."

"Are you going to get into trouble with your professor?"

"Not if I bring a signed note from my mother." I laugh. "It's college; you don't really get into trouble like that. He might not be happy with me for ducking out, but I can deal with that. I would deal with a lot more than that to hear your voice."

"Hey, I was going to send you flowers or at least a card, but it didn't work out. I'm sorry."

Images of the dozen white roses sitting on my dresser and the card smashed into the bottom of the trash can flash through my mind. I can't tell Jacob about either. "Don't be. A call is the best thing you could ever give me. Besides, you've already given me more than enough. Did I mention I love the earrings? I'm never taking them off."

"I'm glad to hear that. Thank you for the long letter and all the pictures. I definitely have the best-looking girlfriend of any guy here."

I don't miss the word *girlfriend*. I'm sure it's the first time he's said it, but I try to keep it casual. "Yeah, right."

"Seriously, we lined everyone's pictures up and took a vote. You won."

For a second I wonder if he's telling the truth, but I catch the teasing in his voice. "You're such a dork."

"Yes, but I'm your dork."

My heart swells. "I love to hear you say that."

"That I'm a dork?"

"No, that you're mine."

"I am. Slave for life if you'll take me."

I try to sound coy. "You might regret saying that. I might just take you up on that."

"You can absolutely take me up on that."

I press the phone closer to my ear, savoring the implied commitment behind his words, even if we're joking around. It's everything I've ever wanted. He's everything I've ever wanted. If only he weren't so far away.

His voice gets more serious. "Hey, Bryan wanted me to thank you for watching Connor for Becky. She really appreciated it. She loves you."

"I really like her too. We email back and forth a lot. She's kind of becoming a big sister to me."

"I'm glad. Becky needs all the support she can get. I guess the baby will be here soon."

"Three weeks, and she's so ready for it to happen. Two boys, though, that will be a handful, especially if this one is anything like Connor."

"Bryan is dying that he can't be there."

"I can't imagine having a baby without a husband there. Actually, I guess I can't imagine having a baby at all right now." I stop myself. This is a really awkward conversation to be having with Jacob.

We're both quiet for a minute. Finally, Jacob says. "I miss you all the time. I can't believe it's only been four months."

"Please don't mention that. Time is going by so slowly."

"I know, but it will pass. I guess we're guaranteed at least that." He pauses for a minute. "Time. Damn. I hate this. I have to go. I'm sorry. I wish we could talk all day."

"I do too." I'm suddenly desperate to keep him on the phone. There's so much I want to say.

He's leaving. "I'm sorry. Have a great birthday, Jess. Don't forget, I love you."

I'll never get tired of hearing him say that. "I love you too." And Jacob..."

"What Jess?"

"Close your eyes."

"Mmmm, thanks for that. You'd better block out that whole first week after I get home."

"Already done. Hurry home. Take care of yourself. I'll be waiting."

I wait until class is over to sneak back into the lecture hall. I wouldn't have gone back at all, but I left my backpack in my rush to leave. I'm hoping my professor is already gone.

No such luck.

"Miss Roberts," he says. "I think I made it clear at the beginning of the term that I don't appreciate cell phones in my class."

"I'm sorry. I had to take that call. It's my birthday, and that was my boyfriend calling from Iraq."

His face softens. "I guess I can let it go. But I would appreciate it if you left the phone on silent for the duration of my class from now on. I find the vibrate feature just as annoying as a ring."

"I won't let it happen again." I shoulder my backpack and turn to leave.

He stops me. "I thought Dean Stephen's son wasn't going to Iraq."

The question shocks me. It takes me a minute to understand what he's implying. "You mean Michael? He's still in Texas. That's not who I was..."

He seems embarrassed. "Oh. I saw you together at the New Years Eve party. I just assumed..."

"We're just friends." I feel like I'm being checked up on. I wonder who else on campus knows anything about me and Michael, or what his dad or anyone else might have said about me.

Maybe I should have been more honest with Jacob about the party. I have this sudden fear that rumors about my friendship with Michael might get back to Jacob all the way in Iraq.

Sixteen

Conflict and Interest

March 2005

A s soon as I walk into the living room, I drop my suitcase. "Jacob."

I'm in shock. Sitting on the couch, playing video games with Tyler, where he's been a hundred times before, is Jacob.

He turns around. "Sorry, Jess. It's just me."

"Gage!" I'm almost as happy to see him as I would be to see Jacob.

He throws his arms around me, picks me up and kisses me—hard and on the lips. I'm too stunned to pull away.

"You totally owed me that one." He steps back. "You aren't going to slap me, are you?"

I'm trying to recover. "No. I should. I would if I weren't so happy to see you."

"Good. As I remember, you slap hard."

Tyler is grinning at us. "What are you looking at?" I ask him.

"Just taking it all in," he replies.

"Don't." I try to look stern. "I don't want you to pick anything up from this guy." I turn back to Gage, he's grinning too. "What are you doing here?"

"A stop on the way," he answers. "We're heading for combat simulation training in California, but we have a couple of days here."

"We?" I ask.

"You don't think Matt would pass up a couple of days with Kendra do you?"

I shake my head. "Not a chance."

Gage looks at me appraisingly. "Some snobby lieutenant wanted to tag along. But you already know him, right?"

My heart drops as I realize who else is here. I work to stay casual. "Michael. Yeah, he was here for a while over Christmas."

Gage is studying my face. Finally he says, "Are there any girls around?"

I put my hand on my hip and fake annoyed. "I'm a girl."

"Sorry, Jess. No offense, but when I told Jake I was coming here, he made it pretty clear you were off limits."

"You just kissed me."

Gage's face breaks into a grin. "We don't have to tell Jake about that. I'd hate for him to come all the way back from Iraq just to kick my ass."

I roll my eyes. "Jasmine is spending Spring Break in Mexico, but she said something about being home for a day or two. She'd probably like to hear from you."

"Cool." Gage already has his phone out. He heads into the next room to make the call.

I pick up my suitcase, suddenly realizing what Gage just said. How am I to get through two days with Gage and Michael in the same house?

"Hey. You want to play with us?"

I stare at Matt in disbelief. "You want me to play football with you?"

He shrugs. "Why not?"

"Is Kendra playing?" I ask.

"No way. She'd get crushed." Matt wraps his arms protectively around his fiancée.

"What about you, Jaz?" I ask. Jasmine is cuddled up on Gage's lap.

"I'm not into guy's sports," she answers. "Except as a spectator."

"I don't want her to get crushed either," Gage replies, nuzzling her cheek. "Unless it's by me. I can be very gentle when I tackle."

I think I'm going to be sick. Jasmine and Gage have a talent for picking up exactly where they left off, no matter how long it's been or who else they've been involved with since they last saw each other. I'm not sure who's worse, Matt and Kendra or Jaz and Gage.

"I guess nobody cares if I get hurt," I answer pitifully.

"Naw, we just know you're tough." Michael punches me in the arm. "We need you to even out the teams. Besides, we're playing touch, not tackle."

Gage narrows his eyes in Michael's direction. Gage has assumed the role of my watchdog every time Michael is around. I get the idea that they don't like each other. The air crackles with a kind of electric tension every time they're together.

I shake my head. "Okay, I'll play."

"Cool," Michael says. "You're on my team."

Matt takes the ball from him. "Sorry. We're playing Roberts against non-Roberts. You, Gage, and Tyler's friend Seth against me, Jess, and Ty."

I get why Matt divided the teams that way. He wants Gage and Michael on the same team so they don't have an excuse to go after each other.

Playing football, even touch, is a good way to work out the pressure I've felt ever since the guys got here. We run the plays like this—Ty blocks for Matt and I run. Matt throws me the ball. I'm fast enough to get a few yards each play before anyone catches me. On defense, I block Michael. He's too much of a gentleman to mow me over. Matt manhandles Gage, and Ty makes a run for it.

Michael catches on to our plans and sticks to me like he's my shadow. We're a few yards from the goal. I go out long and catch the ball. I'm almost in the end zone with Michael getting closer. Something slams into me from the side. I go down hard, but land softly, cradled in Gage's arms.

He does know how to tackle gently.

He's on top of me. Not crushing me. "What are you doing?" I ask.

"Looking out for my brother's interests, and saving the game." He doesn't let me go.

"Knock it off," I struggle under his grip. "I can take care of myself."

"I'm not sure..." He's cut off by Michael barreling into him.

I'm thrown sideways. Gage ends up on his back.

"What the hell were you thinking?" Michael is yelling at Gage. "Jess, are you okay?"

"I'm fine." I sit up, more stunned and hurt by Michael's heroics than by Gage's tackle. I shake myself.

Michael offers me his hand, but Gage is on his feet, toe to toe with him.

I stand up. "I'm okay, really."

They aren't paying attention to me anymore.

"This game is touch, not tackle." Michael says through tight lips.

"Maybe I didn't want you *touching* Jess." Gage's hands are clenching and unclenching into a fist.

"She's better off with me touching her than she is with you tackling her." Michael's whole body is red and his green eyes are on fire. I've never seen him mad before, but he looks like a volcano about to blow.

"I doubt that," Gage says.

"Don't you think that's up to her?"

"We aren't on base now, rich boy," Gage says. "You can't order me around and you sure as hell can't order Jess around."

I'm tired of being talked about as if I'm not standing here, as if I can't take care of myself. "Knock it off! I'm sick of this whole thing." I turn and start walking away.

"Jess—" Michael starts. I ignore him.

"Alright, boys." Matt is between them now. "Jess is right. You two need to cool it."

I keep walking into the house and up to my room. This is stupid. I'm furious with both of them for ruining my Spring Break.

Seventeen

Intruder

I don't talk to Gage or Michael for the rest of the night. Dinner is pretty silent. Afterwards, Matt takes off with Kendra. Gage and Jasmine stay at my house to watch a movie, probably so Gage can keep tabs on me and Michael. Michael leaves, saying something about meeting some friends from Fort Lewis. I head upstairs to take a long bath.

The house is quiet when I get out. Jasmine and Gage must have left too.

I walk into my bedroom and pull the towel off my head, rubbing my hair to dry it. I pull my pajamas out of my drawer and start to take off my robe.

"It goes against all of my principles..."

I scream and wrap the robe back around me.

"...but you'd better stop there. I think my brother would kill me if I saw you naked before he did." Gage is sitting on my bed.

"What are you doing here?" My face is flaming with rage and embarrassment.

"I wanted to apologize for what happened today."

"You couldn't wait until I got dressed?" I hold the robe close to my chest.

"It's more fun this way." He has the *I'm too cute for you to be mad at me* look on his face. This time it only makes me mad.

I point to the door. "Out!"

He isn't moving. He picks up the picture of Jacob from my nightstand. "I'm glad to see Jacob is still hanging out in your bedroom. You show this picture to Stephens?"

"What's that supposed to mean?" I ask, even though I know exactly what he means. "I barely know Michael."

"Right, but have you shown this picture to him?" Gage asks.

"No. He's never been in my bedroom." I hold my hand out for the picture. "And you shouldn't be either."

He hands me the picture. His voice gets serious. "You need to watch out for him. There's something off about him, and he wants to be more than friends with you, Jess. I can tell."

I set the picture back on my nightstand without meeting his eye, because I know he's right. As much as I've tried to keep Michael at arm's length, I can tell he wants more. "I thought this was supposed to be an apology."

He leans back and gets comfortable. On my bed. "A warning and an apology."

"You need to leave, Gage."

"One thing. I've heard some things about him. You should probably–"

A knock on my door stops him. "Jess. Are you in there?" It's Michael.

Gage stands up. "I'll get it."

I point at him. "You stay quiet. I don't want him getting the wrong idea about us."

"Maybe that would discourage him."

I draw my finger across my throat. He grins and mimes locking his lips.

"Jess, are you there?"

I open the door and stand just inside, blocking Michael's way to come in or to see who's in my room.

"I wanted to apologize." He steps closer, and I hold my ground. "I didn't mean to lose my temper. I thought Gage had hurt you. He's kind of a hot-head."

I flip my hair and say loud enough for Gage to hear, "You don't have to tell me about Gage. I've known him since we were kids. He always acts before he thinks."

"Yeah, I don't know what his deal is. He's like that on base too. He doesn't have much respect for authority. I have a hard time keeping him in line."

I hear Gage moving toward the door. I take a step forward and shut the door with my foot.

"Is there a problem?" Michael asks.

"I'm not allowed to have guys in my room."

"Oh, sorry." Michael leans against the door frame. "I'm sorry I messed up the last couple of days for you. I'd like to make it up to you. We could go for a walk, or go out for ice cream or something."

I'm positive Gage has his ear pressed against my door. "It's late. I was just getting ready for bed."

Michael steps back. "We can stay here. Watch a movie in our pajamas."

"I'm tired. I'd probably just fall asleep."

"Oh." He acts like he wants to say more, but doesn't. "Good night then. I guess I'll see you before we leave in the morning."

"Good night, Michael." I wait until he's down the hall before I push my door open, with more force than necessary.

"Ow." Gage rubs his forehead.

"You were listening."

He makes his voice high and squeaky. "We could just watch a movie in our pajamas." He looks disgusted. "Who does that guy think he is? I know why he wants to get you in your pajamas. That's just one step away from—"

"This from the guy who was hiding in my room when I got out of the tub."

"I didn't see anything." His voice drips fake innocence.

"Thank you Gage for being so gallant. Now could you leave? I was serious when I said I was tired."

He isn't listening. "*I* have a problem with authority."

"You do. Remember when our soccer coach told you to take a lap? We were like seven. I'd never heard that word before."

"Yeah, Mom heard me too. I can still taste the soap." He sits on the edge of my bed, getting comfortable again. "I do have a problem with Michael's authority. He's a huge pain in the ass. He thinks he's all that and the rest of us should just fall in line."

"Isn't that how the Army works? Doesn't he outrank you?"

Gage ignores my jab. "That's not all. Have you asked him why he isn't going to Iraq with us?"

"He said he's waiting on an educational deferment, medical school, I think."

"And yet he hasn't started yet, has he? I guess it pays to have rich parents."

I'm not sure I believe what Gage is implying about Michael. He doesn't seem the type to dodge an assignment, still... Something strikes me from the conversation I had with my professor *I thought Dean Stephen's son wasn't going to Iraq.*

I can't think about any of it. This entire conversation is getting to me. "Okay, Gage, you really have to go." I reach to open the door.

He stands up. "I'll take the express route." He heads for my window. "I told Jaz I'd meet her back at her place." He holds out his hand. "I need to borrow Jake's car."

I get the keys from my dresser, but keep them against my chest. "He told me not to let any other guys drive it."

"I'm not a guy. I'm his brother."

I let him take the keys. His hand lingers on mine for a minute. He's more serious than I've ever seen him. "You mean a lot to Jake. I don't want to see him get hurt."

I look him in the eye. "Jacob means everything to me. More than you'll ever know. I won't hurt him."

Eighteen

Trust

I glance at the clock, wondering if I have time to go to the Wi-Fi area and send a quick email to Jacob before my plane boards. Mom and Dad surprised me with a plane ticket to Texas. Matt and Gage are deploying in a couple of days, and the base is having a deployment ceremony.

"Jess?" A somewhat familiar voice calls me from the crowded terminal. "Jess Roberts?"

As soon as I see her, I'm frozen in shock. It's Laini, Jacob's old girlfriend.

She sits down beside me. "Wow, you look so grown up I almost didn't recognize you. What are you, a senior this year?"

"A sophomore, actually." Not officially until I start summer classes next week, but close enough. "At WSU."

"College. You have grown up." I wonder if it's possible for her not to sound condescending. "Where are you heading?"

"Texas." I shift uncomfortably in my seat. Now it feels like I have too much time before my flight. "My brother Matt is being deployed." Her voice goes soft. "I didn't realize he was in the service."

"He is. Army."

"Tell him I said good luck." She glances at her expensive watch. "I need to get going. I have a long business trip ahead of me. I'm always on the run these days." She straightens her skirt and stands up. "I'll have to tell Jake I ran into you the next time he calls. He'll get a kick out of that."

I freeze. She either doesn't notice or pretends not to notice the look on my face. "He's doing okay. They had a bit of a scare just before Christmas. Maybe you heard about the attack in Mosul? You can imagine how relieved I was when he called me to tell me he was okay. He didn't give me very many details. He doesn't like to worry me." She looks at her watch again. "I'll tell him you said hi."

I mumble some kind of goodbye. At least I think I do. I can barely breathe. She strides away, her high heels clicking toward whatever important destination she's heading to. I should follow her, ask her exactly when she last heard from Jacob.

I can't move.

My thoughts are churning. Is it possible he's been playing both of us this whole time? Has he been lying to me?

I make a quick decision and cross the terminal to the Wi-Fi area. I connect and type in Jacob's email address. The message is quick.

Jacob,
We need to talk. Call me when you can.
Jess

I look at it for a few agonized heartbeats before I hit send. Am I jumping to conclusions? Am I that gullible? Laini brought him up so casually. It didn't seem like she was lying. My stomach twists.

How can I be sure?

The flight is excruciating—my heart aches, and I'm searching my memory for details I could have missed. Everything I thought was real is in doubt. I need to talk to Jacob. Hearing his voice will fix everything.

I hope.

I'm pacing the empty hotel room I'm supposed to be sharing with Kendra when my cell phone rings.

It's Jacob.

"Jess," he sounds worried. "Are you okay? I got your email."

"I'm not sure." My answer is painfully honest. "I ran into Laini at the airport."

I gauge the tone of his voice when he answers. "Wow, small world. What did she have to say?"

"She told me she'd tell you hi from me the next time you called her."

"What?" he sounds genuinely confused. "What's that supposed to mean?"

"I was hoping you could tell me."

"Hold on, Jess. I'm not sure what you're asking. Maybe we have a bad connection."

"I'm asking you if you're still seeing Laini."

He laughs. A nervous laugh? A guilty laugh? "I'm in Iraq. How could I possibly be seeing her?"

"You know what I mean." I'm getting impatient. Is he trying to avoid the question? "Are you still talking to her?"

"Talking to... Laini? How can you think that? You know me better than that."

But do I really know him? How can I be sure his confusion is genuine?

"The last I heard anything about Laini, she was coming to our house for dinner just before you left. You told me you broke up with her. Now I see her, and she acts like she hears from you all the time, like you've been calling her. What am I supposed to think?"

"You're supposed to trust me. Besides, you know that was a lie. How often do I get to use the phone here? How often do I call you?"

"You got to it pretty fast after I sent that email."

"I thought something was wrong, with you or at home." He sounds irritated. "I didn't know it was something so..."

"So stupid?" I finish for him.

"I didn't say that."

"But that's what you're thinking. Why don't you just give me a straight answer, Jacob? Are you still talking to Laini?"

"No." He says it firmly, but the irritation is still there. "I haven't heard from her since I left. I might have gotten a Christmas card from her parents. I don't remember."

"She knew about Mosul."

"Everyone knows about Mosul. It was all over the news. Damn it, Jess. Don't you trust me?" The edge in his voice is getting sharper.

"I thought I did. Now I'm not sure." I'm suddenly that awkward little girl again, begging him for attention, unsure of what he thinks of me.

"Laini." Her name comes out in an angry breath. "I don't know what her game is. I don't have time to deal with this. I'm trying to fight a war."

"You mean you don't have time to deal with me."

He hesitates for a minute. "I didn't say that."

"You didn't have to." I close my eyes. I wish I hadn't emailed him. More than that, I wish I hadn't seen Laini. I wish I could push away the doubts swirling in my mind and just trust him.

"What about you?" I pick up on the edge of suspicion in his voice.

"Me?" Guilt prickles in my stomach.

"Yeah. You and New Years Eve. What exactly were you doing that you couldn't answer my call?"

Suddenly, I'm the one playing defense. I suck in a breath. "I told you where I was."

"But not the whole story, right? You gave me the where, but left out the who."

My thoughts flee in panic. I don't know how to answer that, so I don't say anything.

"The Army isn't as big as you think it is," Jacob says. "What am I supposed to say when some guy here sees my picture of you and says he saw you at a party with one of his friends on New Years?"

My heart pounds with guilt and fear, but my first reaction is to strike back. "You're supposed to trust me." I throw his words back at him. "It was a party with a friend. Am I supposed to put myself in cold storage until you come home?"

"I never asked you to do that," his voice is calm. The kind of calm that I know means he's mad. "I guess we never talked about it, whether or not this is an exclusive thing."

This? Thing? Is he trying to justify himself? I think about what Matt said about Jacob always having an extra girl on the side. Am I the extra girl?

"And I guess I never asked you *not* to keep in touch with your old girlfriend. So I have no reason to be mad either."

"Jess, listen to me, I'm not..."

But I'm too worked up to stop. "She had you for four months. I got you for what? Four hours? Why shouldn't you still be talking to her?"

"Jess, stop." He swears under his breath. "This isn't working."

Fear slices into my chest. The line is quiet for a long time. Finally, I ask, "What's not working?' I choke back a shivering breath, "Us?"

"We need to—" Static comes through and then the line goes silent.

I grip the phone, willing his voice to come back, willing him to finish that sentence, wishing there was a way I could call him back—almost. I'm afraid of what he was trying to say.

Is he done with me? Is it over between us before things even got started, because I let Laini get to me, because I was jealous and immature?

Seeing her brought back a tidal wave of insecurities. Why would he want me when he could have her? Beautiful, polished, sophisticated—Laini can make me feel like a little kid without even trying—and she did.

My conversation with Matt keeps playing in my head. *"If you mean that much to him, why did it take him so long to get rid of that other woman?"* What if he hadn't really gotten rid of her?

And what about my "not" date with Michael? How did he find out about that? And so what if he did? It was all perfectly innocent. I lie on the bed, still holding the phone, still arguing in my head with myself, with Jacob, with Matthew, even with Laini. I can't believe I got in a fight with Jacob, over the phone, in Iraq. I bury my head in the pillow and cry.

By the time the knock comes at the door, I'm cried out. I get up and peer through the peephole. For a second, I'm not sure if I should answer.

I try to sound normal as I open the door. "Michael. I didn't think you were going to be here."

"This is my unit leaving. I wanted to be here for the ceremony tomorrow." He hugs me. If he realizes I've been crying, he doesn't mention it. "It's good to see you, Jess."

I step back. "It's good to see you too." And it is good to see him, better than I thought it would be. Maybe better than it should be.

"I asked your parents if they wanted to come to dinner, but they'd rather stay here and eat in. Tyler is talking with a girl down by the pool, and Matt and Kendra are 'unavailable'. Would you like to get something to eat with me?"

I hesitate for a minute, glancing at my phone on the nightstand. I need to get out and clear my head. "Sure," I manage a weak smile. "Give me a minute to put on makeup and get changed."

Nineteen

No Angel

June 2005

"**M**om's cousins personify the word 'redneck.'" Gage is sitting beside me in his parent's car on the way back from the deployment ceremony. "Some of them actually have all their teeth."

"Gage, be nice," Trina says from the front seat. "Uncle Jack is really proud of you. He's throwing this barbecue in your honor. He's a nice guy. A little back-woods, but nice."

"I can't help but feel like we're imposing on a family thing," Mom says for the hundredth time.

"No imposition." Trina shakes her head. "You guys are basically family. You took care of Jacob while he was at Fort Lewis. I'm glad to give something back."

My heart hurts at the mention of Jacob. He didn't call back, and I haven't gotten an email from him in the last two days. Maybe he's not in a spot that he can call or email, or maybe he doesn't want to talk to me.

Rednecks maybe, but Trina's Texas cousins know how to throw a party. I half expect to see an entire cow roasting over a spit. There's music and incredible food and a lot of hugging and slapping Gage and Matthew on the back.

Gage sits by me, polishing off a rib that would put even my dad's to shame. "I can't believe there are no girls here. How's a guy supposed to go to war without someone to send him off?"

"There are lots of girls here." I look around. There are more tank tops and cut-off jeans than I thought existed.

"Yeah, they're all my cousins or aunts or some twice-removed relation."

I poke him. "I thought you Southern boys were cool with the whole cousin thing."

He rolls his eyes. "Ha ha, Jess. At least you could have brought Jasmine here for me. As a going-away present."

"Jaz is probably spending the break between semesters in Europe or Hawaii or someplace exotic."

"Mexico," Gage answers. "She's at her grandma's house again. Abuela isn't doing great."

I look at him strangely. "How did you know that?"

"She had a layover here on her way to visit her." He looks embarrassed. Nothing embarrasses Gage, but he won't look at me.

"How long was the layover?"

He shrugs. "A couple of days."

"That's a long layover."

"Not long enough." He sits back. "You don't think she'd mind if I wrote to her once in a while, do you?"

I get the idea that their on again/off again casual relationship has morphed into something more. "I think she'd like that. She might even write you back."

"I'd like that," Gage says. "Actually, I'd—Who invited him?" I turn around to see what he's looking at. Michael is walking toward us.

I shrug. "Don't look at me. This is your Mom's party."

Michael holds his hand out to Gage. "Good to see you, Ricks." Gage shakes his hand begrudgingly. "Your family sure knows how to throw a barbecue."

"Thanks," Gage mutters.

Michael asks Gage about the guys in their unit and what they'll all be doing once they get to Iraq. I tune them out. Across the yard, another arrival is causing a big fuss.

Gage follows my gaze. He lets out a low whistle. "I can't believe it. He actually showed."

Above the crowd, I catch a blond head. "Who's that?"

"Nate."

"Nate? You're brother Nate?" I ask in disbelief.

"Yep, and never far from his side, you guessed it. No Angel."

I stare at the couple. If Gage hadn't told me it was Nathan, I wouldn't have recognized him. His hair shaved short in the back, spiked on the top. He has more than one earring and a couple of tattoos. The one on his shoulder says "Angel". He's wearing a black tank top and black jeans, almost off his butt, held up by what looks like a chain. Angel is bone-thin and pale. Her hairstyle mimics Nathan's except she has dark hair with a brush of green to the tips. She has two eyebrow piercings and one in her nose. She has her hand in Nathan's back pocket. His hand is in hers.

"Nice touch." Gage nods at Angel's tank top. It says, *Stand Up for Peace*. "Do you think she'd be offended if I added, *Through Superior Fire Power?*"

I look for something positive to say. "She's pretty."

"Yeah," Gage snorts. "Pretty awful. She's got him so tightly by the ba—"

"Gage!"

"Yeah, sorry, Jess. It's the truth. He smokes now too. What kind of an idiot starts smoking when he's twenty-one? Isn't that supposed to be a stupid teenager thing?" Gage looks across the yard in disgust. His mom motions for us to come over. "I always knew the first girl who paid any attention to Nate would have him good. No offense, Jess. I think you were the first girl he ever kissed."

Michael is studying me with curiosity. "You kissed him?" He nods toward Nate.

I blush. "It was a long time ago."

Gage is grinning at both me and Michael. "Not that long ago." He turns to Michael. "She looks innocent enough, but don't let her fool you. New Year's Eve a couple of years ago, Jess kissed Nate, and me, and about a dozen other guys. All in one night."

I'm not sure whether Michael looks shocked or impressed.

Gage's eyes are sparkling with mischief. "And I have it on good authority that she's kissed Jacob too. That's three for three in the Ricks family."

I can't stop blushing. "I think your mom wants you, Gage."

"Come with me, Jess. You can meet the devil herself."

"You're Jess?" Angel's painted red lips turn up in a smirk after Nate stumbles through the introductions. She looks me up and down. "I guess I expected more."

I ignore her 'not even thinly veiled' insult and focus on Nate. For as much as he's changed outside, he acts just as awkward and shy as before. I still feel terrible about everything I did to him, but I don't think this is a good time to apologize. "How's school?"

"Taking a break." Nate tightens his grip on Angel's waist.

"Exploring other options," Angel adds. "What about you?"

"I just finished my first semester at WSU, but I'm starting summer classes next week," I say, but Angel turns her back on me before I finish.

"Hey babe." She puts her arms around Nate's neck and leans in. "Remember how you said we'd only stay a couple of minutes?" She kisses his neck. "Time's up."

"You haven't eaten, or said hi to Steve, or really anyone," Trina says.

Angel ignores Trina and pulls herself closer to Nate, resting her forehead against his. "Remember that place we were going to go to, babe?" She kisses him in a way that makes my face burn. "We don't want to be late."

Nate looks uncomfortable as he pulls away from her. "Sorry, we have a thing. I promised Angel."

"Seriously?" Gage's face is red too, but for a different reason. "What about hanging out with your brother? The one you aren't going to see for an entire year."

Angel turns back to Gage, her arms still around Nate's neck. "Not our fault. You're the one who sold your soul to Uncle Sam."

"At least I didn't sell it to one of Hell's angels," Gage says.

Nate steps away from Angel. "What's that supposed to mean?"

"You're the smart one," Gage says. "I'm pretty sure you can figure it out."

Gage stands his ground as Nate moves closer, his fists clenched. "You don't know—"

Trina steps between them. "Please, Nate, just stay a little while longer. We've hardly seen you."

Nate looks from his mom to Angel. A tortured look crosses his face. "Sorry Mom. Angel's right. This is Gage's choice. We can't stay." He raises his hand. "See you on the other side, bro."

For once, Gage is speechless.

"Bye," Angel waggles her fingers in our direction. A satisfied smile crosses her lips as Nathan tucks her under his arm and they walk away.

The barbecue ends with a big bonfire and everyone sitting around talking. I'm alone, staring into the flames. Michael left early after saying he had "arrangements" to make. I guess that means he has a date. That thought does little to ease the weight of guilt I've carried this whole weekend. I'm sure the whole "Nathan screwing up his life" thing is my fault, and I completely screwed up everything with Jacob.

Matthew is cradling Kendra in his arms a few feet away from me. She's crying. "I changed my mind, Matt. Let's just do it now, tonight. I don't care about a big wedding. I just want to be your wife."

He kisses her forehead. "I would do it in a heartbeat, babe, but we don't have a marriage license, and your parents would kill us if we got married without them." She lays her head against his shoulder. "Just keep planning the wedding. Time will fly by. Don't worry, I'll be standing right by you when you take your vows. I promise."

My eyes fill with tears, and I feel like I'm eavesdropping, so I walk away. I find Gage sitting by himself on the fringe of the group.

I walk over and take his hand. He grins at me. "You'd better not do that. Mom told everyone here that you're Jacob's girlfriend. I don't want them getting the wrong idea about us."

I keep his hand and close my eyes. "I'm sorry about everything with Nathan, I—"

"Not your fault, Jess. Nate has the freedom to screw up his life on his own. We've fought our whole lives. He's being an idiot now, but we're brothers and we love each other. We'll work things out." He nudges me, noticing the tears. "You okay?"

I want to ask him about Jacob, about what he might know about Laini. If he knows anything, I don't think he would tell me the truth. I'm sure there's some unbreakable brother code about that. "Just thinking. About you and Matt leaving. I'm worried about you guys."

Gage puts his arm around me and pulls me close to his chest. "Don't worry about me. I'll be fine."

I look up at him earnestly. "I'll be praying for you, Gage."

He laughs and kisses my forehead. "Save your prayers for Jake and Matt. I'll be fine. Only the good die young, right?"

I pull away. "Take care of yourself. I mean it."

He laughs. "I've always been pretty good at that."

"When you get to Iraq, if you see Jake..."

"I won't. We'll be on opposite sides of the country."

"But if you do." Tears are clouding my vision. "If you do, tell him that I..."

He pulls me close again. "I know, Jess. He loves you too." He holds me for a minute. "If you see Jaz, tell her..."

"Tell her you'd like to hear from her?"

He shakes his head. "Yeah, something like that."

Twenty

This Moment

I t doesn't feel like we're headed towards the airport. I read the freeway signs, and I'm almost sure we're heading in the wrong direction. Michael is driving. Mom, Dad, and Tyler left for their flight early this morning.

"Michael, are you sure we're going the right way?"

He smiles and keeps his eyes on the road. "We're going exactly the right way."

I catch his tone. "But not the right way for the airport."

"Not *your* airport."

"I'm going to miss my flight." A flutter of panic settles in my stomach.

"You won't miss *your* flight." It bothers me that he won't give me a straight answer.

"What is that supposed to mean?"

He still hasn't faced me. "I changed your ticket."

"You did what?"

"Believe me, it wasn't easy, but I changed your flight. You aren't flying out until late tonight. That should give us plenty of time."

I narrow my eyes. "Plenty of time for what?"

"Do you trust me?" His green eyes are glittering with a secret.

I lean back. "I'm not sure."

He tries to sound serious. "No, Jess, this is important. You have to trust me. If you don't trust me, this isn't going to work."

"What isn't going to work?"

"I guess you'll never know if you don't trust me." Whatever it is, he won't stop grinning.

His mood is infectious. "Okay, okay, I trust you."

"Good." He turns his attention back to the road. He's still trying to be serious, but there's a smile playing around the corners of his mouth.

"So...where are we going?"

"I thought you said you trusted me."

"I did, I do. Now you can tell me where we're going." I put my hand on his leg, trying to flirt.

He looks straight ahead and doesn't answer.

I shake my head and look out the window. At least I can make Michael think that I'm not that interested in what he has planned. I'm racking my brain about where he could take me, but nothing comes to mind.

Michael is still grinning when I look back at him. He looks cute like that—inviting. A stab of guilt hits me in the chest.

Jacob.

I'm not sure how to feel about everything. It's been three days since our argument, and I still haven't heard from him. I'm too afraid to write to him. What if he hates me?

I try to shake off the guilt. Whatever the story is with Jacob, I'm not consciously betraying him, even now. It's not like I knew Michael was going to kidnap me on the way to the airport. I don't know what he has planned.

I steal another glance in his direction. He's whistling nonchalantly and still grinning—bursting with his surprise. He looks good—one hand on the steering wheel; the sun turning his auburn hair the color of the sunset. Too good. I turn away and watch the road for any clues about where we're going. He turns off a little sidestreet, and then I see an airport. This one is much smaller than the one listed on my plane ticket—a little hanger, an office, and a few small planes.

We pull into a parking lot. Michael gets out and comes around to open my door. "Now, are you going to tell me what we're doing here?"

"Why don't you guess?" Michael is holding the door open and grinning. His face must hurt by now.

"You're sending me to Iraq, to be with..." I almost say Jacob. Should have said Jacob. Instead, I finish "... with Matt and Gage."

"Yeah, like I'd send you anywhere with Gage. Sorry, our flight isn't going that far."

I stand up. "Our flight?"

"And there's a possibility that we might not make it to our final destination. We may have to bail out early."

A wave of excitement and fear hits me so hard that I have to lean against the car for support. "You want me to jump out of a plane?" I whisper.

Michael puts his hand on my shoulder. "You said you've always wanted to try skydiving."

My panic comes out in my voice. "I said someday. Like when I'm terminally ill or something. I didn't mean now."

"No time like the present."

I lean into him. "I'm not ready for this. I'm not sure if I can do it. I'm not, like, mentally prepared."

He wraps his arm around me and squeezes. "The best time to do this is when you aren't mentally prepared. You think about things too much and you'll never do it. You'll never jump."

I close my eyes and shake my head.

"You don't have to do this if you don't want to." His voice is thick with disappointment.

I open my eyes. "Now or never... okay now."

His grin is back. He gives me another squeeze before stepping back. "You won't regret this."

"I hope that doesn't mean I won't live long enough to regret it."

He takes my hand and pulls me toward the building. "It's the best feeling in the world. I promise."

There's a mountain of paperwork and scary waivers to fill out. Michael is hovering the whole time, dancing with impatience.

"It won't be a real jump," he apologizes. "You don't have time to do the training, so it's going to be a tandem jump. The part that sucks is I don't get to be your tandem. Something about a lack of experience on my part. Like I haven't logged as many jumps as any of these guys." The guy at the counter is shaking his head at Michael's bravado.

Our trainer and the man who will be my tandem is retired military. He's probably as old as my dad. Michael calls him Sergeant Owens. Everything with him is straight down the line. I don't think he cracks a smile once. He treats Michael like he's a little kid, except that he calls him "Sir."

I'm so freaked out that I grasp at every bit of information from our training session. After I put the gear on, I realize I can't remember any of it.

I look up at him, panicked. "I can't do this, Michael. I forgot everything."

"Turn around," he says.

"What?"

"Just turn around." He wraps his arms around my waist. "Now bend your legs. Pull them up to your stomach."

I obey him. I think he's doing some kind of trick to calm me down.

"When you jump, keep your legs up, your knees bent. Spread-eagle in the air. That's all you have to remember."

"What if something goes wrong? What if one of those worst-case scenarios happens, like he said?"

"Don't worry. It will only hurt for a second when you hit the ground." He's terrible.

"That doesn't help," I snarl.

He wraps his arms around me. "You'll do fine. You're one of the bravest girls I know. If something goes wrong, Sergeant Owens will talk you through it. Remember, I saved Matt's life during a jump. I wouldn't let anything hurt you."

"I thought he said he saved your life?" I ask.

"Yeah, well, it didn't go exactly like Matt said. But either way, I've done this a lot and I've got you."

His reassurances just reinforces the idea that something bad could happen. I want to do this almost as badly as I don't want to do this. I make it onto the plane. My legs are shaking, but I'm still standing. Michael holds my hand while we climb to altitude.

"I don't think I can do this." My voice sounds small and terrified.

"Think about it this way—there is no future, there is no past. All there is now, this moment. That's what I always think before I jump."

"You're trying to tell me I don't have a future? Sorry, Michael, but that doesn't really help."

He puts his hand on my cheek and turns my face toward his. "I didn't say you don't have a future. I just said don't think about it. The past either. Just this moment. Then jump."

The door opens. For a second, I expect to be sucked out of the cabin like in one of those bad plane crash disaster movies. Sergeant Owens is shouting last-minute instructions. I'm trying to listen, but the roar of the wind and the pounding of my heart in my ears are too loud. My harness is strapped to his chest. I fumble with the buckles, so Michael reaches over and helps. When we're all set, he gives me a thumbs up. This is all routine for both of them. Michael looks calm. Sergeant Owens stands up, and we walk to the door. I'm wondering if I threw up if we would still go on with the jump. Would it get sucked out of the door or blown into Sergeant Owens' face?

We stand at the doorway for a terrifying second. I clench my hands together to keep from grabbing the edge of the door.

Just this moment.

I'm both happy and terrified that I'm not the one deciding to step out of the plane.

I squeeze my eyes shut, pull my knees to my chest, and feel the safety of the solid mass of metal and engines fall away. My stomach lurches. I think I'm about to test my theory about throwing up. I clamp my jaw tight.

"Relax. Open your eyes, Jess." I know Sergeant Owens is yelling so I can hear him, but his voice sounds calm and strangely soothing.

I open my eyes and see the world, a huge unending expanse, opening up before me. The rush of the wind hits me in my face. I spread my arms and legs. I'm flying. "It's beautiful!" I yell.

Michael is next to us. Trying to get my attention. I look at him and give him a grin that probably looks more like a terrified grimace. He gives me a relaxed smile, reaches out, and grasps my outstretched hand.

Sergeant Owens is screaming something like, "Too close."

Michael lets go, pulls his chute, and disappears far above me. I have a moment of panic as I realize we're still falling. There's a sudden jerk. My helmet knocks into Sergeant Owens'. The wind slows, and we're drifting. I look up and see the canopy overhead. Our chute. We're safe. I scream in triumph, finally breathe, and enjoy the view. An almost spiritual calm comes over me. I look across what feels like the entire world below.

No future. No past. Just this moment.

The ground comes up faster than I'm ready. I remember to stay tucked while we land. Sergeant Owens runs forward, holding me up.

"You can put your feet down now. It's solid." Now that jump is over, he actually sounds friendly.

I put my feet down. Euphoria and adrenaline spark through my veins. I want to hug Sergeant Owens, but I'm still strapped to his chest.

Michael comes over, his face flushed and grinning. "You were awesome." He gives me five and grasps my hand. Then he hugs me, Sergeant Owens still attached.

Sergeant Owens bawls Michael out for getting too close, still calling him 'sir.' Michael works to unbuckle my harness.

As soon as I'm standing on my own, my knees give out. Michael catches me. "What did I say? The best feeling in the world?"

"That was..." I struggle for the right thing to say, "beyond words!" I hold him tight. "Thank you." I release Michael and turn around and give Sergeant Owens a big hug.

He turns from drill sergeant to affectionate parent. He pats my back. "You did really well, Jess."

I pull away and blush. "Thanks."

We gather up the chutes and gear and start heading back to the hangar. Michael stops me. "Wait, we need a picture."

He pulls a camera out of his jumpsuit and hands it to Sergeant Owens. He drapes his arm over my shoulder, and I grin like an idiot while he snaps the picture.

Once the gear is put away, Michael walks with me back to the tarmac, holding my hand. The surreal euphoria from the jump hasn't faded. The sun is going down, a beautiful expansive sunset. Michael stops and wraps his arms around me. I look up. He's gazing down at me. "I was thinking."

I should move out of his arms, but I can't make myself do it. "What are you thinking?"

"I was thinking about what Gage said."

"I try not to think about anything Gage says. It gives me a headache."

He puts his hand under my chin, stroking my cheek with his thumb. "About the other guys you've kissed."

My heart pounds against his chest. I can't move.

"I was wondering what I have to do to earn one of those kisses."

I don't know what to say to him.

He holds me in his gaze. "Can I kiss you, Jess?"

I've never had a guy ask me if he could kiss me before. Usually, they just do it. I look at him for a long moment.

No future. No past. Just this moment.

"No."

Twenty-One

Unforgetable

"**N**o?"

Michael steps back, staring at me in disbelief. It strikes me he isn't used to being told no.

I look into his beautiful eyes, searching for anger or hatred. I see only shock and confusion. "I'm sorry. It must have taken you a long time to arrange all of this, and I'm sure you spent a lot of money. It was amazing, the best date I've ever been on, something I've always wanted to do." I look away, my heart still pounding. As much as I'm not sure of what's going on with Jacob right now, I can't betray him. "But I can't kiss you, Michael. I'm with someone else. I'm with—"

"Jacob. I know." He sighs. "I know about Jacob."

I look up at him, wondering how long he's known. "Did Matt tell you?"

He shakes his head. "Not Matt, Gage. Gage told me all about you and Jacob. "I think he put it something like, 'what kind of a jerk would go after another guy's girlfriend when that guy is off fighting a war? What kind of soldier would do that?' Only with more colorful language."

"Michael, I'm so sorry. I should have told you about Jacob from the beginning. I shouldn't have let you go to this much trouble. I should have—"

He steps back, shaking his head. "I guess it's my fault too. I should have listened to Gage when he told me you'd never leave Jacob, but I have a hard time giving up something I want." The intensity of his gaze when he says that makes me look away.

"I'll pay you back." I'm not sure how much he spent on all of this, but I know it's more than I can afford.

He shakes his head. "No. You never gave me any sign you felt anything but friendship for me. Besides, I didn't actually give you a choice about coming here. I basically kidnapped you. The money isn't important, anyway. I'm sorry I assumed you were interested, when clearly a girl like you wouldn't be interested in me."

"Why would you say that? You're a great guy. A great—"

"Friend? Brother?" He laughs. "Yeah, I get that a lot."

"You'll be so much more than that to the right person. If it weren't for Jacob, I'd..."

He waits for a long moment, like he wants to hear the end of that statement, but I can't finish it. Finally he smiles. "I'm glad you had a good time. I hope we can stay friends."

"Of course."

"Great. A guy can never have too many friends." He glances at his watch. "We'd better get going. I wouldn't want you to miss your actual flight."

I step forward and pull him into a hug. "Thanks Michael. Today was absolutely unforgettable."

He leans back and brushes a stray hair off my cheek. "It was, wasn't it?"

I sit up in bed and reach for my phone. Michael told me to call him when I got home last night.

I didn't.

There are four voice messages. Still nothing from Jacob.

The last one is from Michael—late last night. "I guess you made it home. Thanks for jumping out of a plane with me. I've never done that with any other girl."

I remember the moment on the tarmac, what it felt like to be that close to Michael. How hard it was to say no to him. I squeeze my eyes shut, wondering if I made a mistake. I probably ruined everything with Jacob. Maybe he won't ever talk to me again. A little voice in the back of my head says, *He's probably happier with Laini anyway.*

I go to my computer, checking email. My heart stops. I have three emails from Jacob from three different days. They were probably delayed by a tech glitch on the other side of the world. They all have the subject line "I'm sorry."

I open the first one.

> Jess,
>
> I'm so sorry I lost my temper. You hit me at a bad time, on a bad day. I don't know what Laini is trying to do. I haven't talked to her, written to her, emailed her, or heard from her since I left. I honestly never thought

I'd see her again. Please believe me. I love you. I would never betray you like that. I would never hurt you. And the thing with the New Year's Eve party, forget I brought it up. You told me what happened. I'm sorry I let it bother me. I trust you.

I love you,

Jacob

I'm already crying when I open the second one.

Jess,

Again. I'm sorry. Please write me back and say something. Even if it's that you hate me and you don't want to talk to me ever again. I wasn't lying to you. I should never have been with Laini. She's a controlling little snake and apparently vindictive too. I never loved her. I only love you.

Please write me back.

I love you,

Jacob

One more, really short.

Jess,

I'm sorry. A thousand times. I miss you. I love you.

Jacob

I stare at the blank screen, a sick pit in my stomach. I can't believe I ever thought Jacob would hurt me. Why did I let Laini get to me? Why did I let Jacob see my stupid insecurities?

I waited so long for him to notice me and made so many stupid mistakes along the way. Even with all of that, he stood by me, first as a friend and then as more. I never dreamed I'd ever be able to hurt him. I don't deserve him.

I take a deep breath and write him back.

> Jacob,
> I'm the one who needs to be sorry. I believe you. I trust you. I love you. I'm sorry for jumping to conclusions. It was all so stupid.
> I'm sorry I didn't answer sooner. Your emails just came, and I wasn't sure if you wanted to hear from me.

I work to keep it light.

> I was in Texas at Matt and Gage's deployment ceremony. We went to a barbecue at your mom's uncle's house afterwards. I think we ate a whole cow. I got to meet Nate's girlfriend. Yikes! Maybe we can chalk it up to temporary insanity. I hope it's temporary.
> It was so hard to send Gage and Matt off. Kendra couldn't stop crying. I know how she feels.
> I'm sorry we got in a fight. I'm sorry for everything.

I look at that "everything" for a long time. I wonder if I should tell him everything that I'm sorry for; if I should confess to jumping out of a plane with Michael, in case he hears about that somehow too. It would be too much to explain in an email.

I close the email with a bunch of "I love yous" and "I'm sorrys".

Jacob doesn't have to know about anything that happened with Michael. What happens on the tarmac after you jump out of an airplane stays on the tarmac.

Twenty-Two
Blurring the Line

I'm actually relieved when Michael calls. He's not mad at me. He barely mentions the jump. Mostly, he talks about getting ready for med school. He's hoping the Army will let him go to the University of Washington via a military scholarship, but likely he'll be across the country at the Uniformed Services University in Maryland. In the meantime, he's still at Fort Bliss as part of something called rear D or rear Detachment, because the rest of his unit is deployed.

It's nice to have someone to talk to. Communication with Jacob, even via email, is always sporadic. My roommates have busy social lives, and Kendra is in full wedding planning mode. I relax and let my friendship with Michael grow. It's not like I'm going to see him again anytime.

The invitation comes on embossed stationery with gold writing, no picture. I'm invited to the whole thing—rehearsal dinner, wedding, reception. I barely know Michael's sister Kandice. To be honest, I barely know Michael.

I don't mention the invitation to Michael, but he brings it up casually a couple of weeks before the date. "Don't worry about the RSVP for my sister's wedding," he says. "I already told Mom you'd be there."

It annoys me that he just assumes I'll be there. I'm not sure how to tell him that. I'm quiet long enough for him to notice.

"You are going to be there, aren't you?"

I take a breath, trying to figure out how to let him down easy. "I don't want to intrude. I barely know your sister."

Michael laughs, "You don't have to know Kandice. You're coming as a favor to me. My family already knows you, and they like you. It will take a ton of pressure off me. I don't have time to come up with a date on my own."

The word date has me tongue-tied. "But the rehearsal dinner...isn't that usually a family thing? Or an attendant thing."

"I actually tried to get them to let you be a bridesmaid. Mom wasn't going for it. I'd much rather walk down the aisle with you than with my cousin."

I can feel things moving in a direction I'm not comfortable with. I struggle to put on the brakes. "I have to work on the day of the rehearsal. And it's in Seattle. That's a long drive. I don't know if I'll make it."

"Can't you get it off?"

"I don't think so."

"It's okay if you just come to the wedding and reception. It's at the most exclusive country club in Seattle, one my grandparents have belonged to for years. The gardens are beautiful, and the food will be fantastic. I promise it will be fun."

"I don't know Michael."

"Please, Jess. I'll owe you. Whatever you need. Anything, anytime."

But it's what I owe him that gets to me. He paid for me to go skydiving and he's still talking to me even though I told him I didn't like him that way. "Okay, I'll be there. I'm excited to see this place."

"Just the place?" he asks.

"It will be fun to see your family again too," I add.

"Not exactly what I was fishing for, but I'll take it. See you soon, Jess, and thank you."

When I hang up the phone, I sit for a long time, trying to analyze my feelings for Michael—realizing I *have* feelings for Michael. I'm working to convince myself that I'm only going to the wedding as a favor for a friend. I can still keep him at arm's length.

I can't tell him I'm excited to see him too.

Twenty-Three

Tow Trucks and Lace

W e're in the middle of the dance floor after the wedding. Michael leans back and looks in my eyes. "Did I mention you look incredible?"

"Thanks, I thought you'd be impressed that I picked out a dress by myself." *By myself* is a bit of a stretch. I borrowed the dress from my roommate Nichole. It's a great dress, light blue, form-fitting, but also flowy. As Nichole put it—elegant, but not too formal, sophisticated yet flirty, sexy yet conservative.

Michael ducks his head. "Sorry about that."

"You look pretty good yourself." I answer as he spins me in an easy arch. He's a great dancer, and he looks incredible in his dress uniform.

The next song is slower. He pulls me against his chest and sings in my ear. I've had guys do that before. It always bothered me. This time I find it incredibly romantic and sexy. Too romantic, too sexy. I pull away, establishing a more *friendly* distance and focus on the crowd around us.

The bride, Michael's sister Kandice, is in one corner, dancing with her new husband. They aren't cuddled up like most newlyweds would be. Her eyes are alive with mischief, and they're talking in conspiratorial whispers.

Michael notices them too. He shakes his head. "Here it comes. She's been too good this whole time. Kandice loves to make my mom crazy. This is her wedding, and she's got something in mind to prove that."

I watch the couple with more interest. When the song ends, they leave the dance floor and go to a corner by themselves.

Michael watches them go. "That reminds me, I have some groomsman, brother of the bride duties to attend to. Are you okay if I leave for a little while?"

"I'll manage."

Michael steers me to a table populated by one of his aunts and a couple of his cousins. As soon as he's gone, they start in on a sales pitch of Michael, almost like they've been coached. I listen politely and keep one eye on Kandice. So far, nothing interesting has happened.

The cake cutting and the bouquet toss go off without incident. Michael comes back in, rubbing his hands with a paper towel. He stands between me and his dad.

Dean Stephens glances at the streaks of grease on Michael's hand. "What did you do?"

Michael shrugs and tries to look innocent. "Nothing permanent." To me he says. "Did I miss anything good?"

I shake my head. "They barely smeared the cake all over each other's faces."

The last thing on the list is the garter toss. Michael lines up with the other bachelors and waits.

Kandice daintily puts her foot up on a stool, and Jeff reaches under her skirts to retrieve the garter. He gets a perplexed look on his face and continues up her leg. Silvia looks mortified. Karen and Kelsey shepherd the little girls to the other side of the room. Jeff comes out from under Kandice's skirt holding a piece of lacy blue fabric. He turns backwards and shoots it across the room. It hits Michael squarely in the face. As he holds it up, his look changes from triumph to shock and horror.

Instead of a garter, it's a stringy piece of lingerie.

Kandice walks over to Michael. "I don't think it's quite your size." She puts her arm around him. "You know what this means, don't you?"

Michael holds the lingerie with disgust between two fingers. "It means I'm going to need years of therapy to get over touching my sister's sexy underwear."

She laughs and takes it from him. "No, it means you're the next one who gets to use this. I mean, the next one who gets married."

She heads towards me. Everyone is watching her. My face flames as she hands it to me. "I don't need this now. Maybe you can get some use out of it."

Jeff walks over and takes his bride's hand in solidarity and triumph. "Thank you all for coming. We have a plane to catch, so we'd better get going."

They head for the door. Sylvia's expression is a mixture of dumb-founded shock and embarrassment. I'm stuck holding a stringy bit of lace that's too small to be called underwear. Everyone is staring. I'm not sure what to do next.

Michael's older sister Kelsey saves me. She takes the lingerie from me. "I'll take care of this."

The crowd dissipates. Someone announces that Mr. and Mrs. Jeffery Collins will say their final goodbyes on the front porch of the country club.

Michael walks over and puts his arm around me. "Sorry about that. Don't worry. Revenge is already in the works."

We wait on the front porch of the country club with little bottles of bubbles for Kandice and Jeff to make their big exit. The valet is supposed to bring Jeff's car around. Michael's mom looks flustered. I can't tell if she's eager for this to end or if she's worried about how it will end.

Michael tightens his grip on my waist, and I sense his anticipation through his fingertips.

The car arrives towed by a dirty gray tow truck. Its engine sputters, and black smoke pours out of the tailpipe. The driver gets out—huge, long-haired, tattooed, greasy. Michael is trying to keep a straight face. His mom sends him a dark look from across the room.

Kandice and Jeff come through the door. The little girls are blowing bubbles like crazy. Jeff stands and stares in disbelief at his car—a shiny black Lexus. Besides the fact that it's being towed, the front tires are missing, and it's covered in whipped cream, balloons and streams of toilet paper.

Kandice squeals and turns on Michael. "What did you do?"

Michael is doing his best to look innocent. "Me?"

Jeff looks as if he wants to hit someone. Kandice puts her hand on her husband's arm. "It looks like we need to borrow a car so we don't miss our flight. Does anyone have one we can use?"

The tow truck driver steps forward. "Don't worry, Miss or I guess, Missus, I can get you to the airport."

"In that thing?" Jeff points at the grimy truck. The tow-truck driver doesn't look like he appreciates Jeff's assessment of his vehicle.

"It'll get you there. Of course, I can take only one passenger up front. I assume you want that to be the bride. You'll have to sit in back." He jerks his thumb towards the disabled Lexus.

Kandice waves to the crowd and kisses her parents. Then, she allows the tow truck driver to hoist her into the cab. Jeff climbs into the front seat of the Lexus, tossing out balloons and tissue paper as he struggles to close the door.

There are cans tied to the back of the Lexus, but the roar of the tow truck's engine drowns them out. The couple drives away in a cloud of smelly diesel exhaust.

"Michael," Sylvia warns. "They had better not miss their flight."

Michael moves away from me and wraps his arms around his mom. "There's a limo waiting for them a mile down the road. Clyde will take care of the car."

"Clyde?" Her eyebrows shoot up. "I don't even want to know how you know him."

"Old Army buddy," Michael says. "He's a decent guy."

Sylvia puts her hand to her temples. "You kids... I need a drink."

Kelsey puts her arm around her mother and leads her back inside. "Don't worry, Mom, three down, one to go." She looks at Michael meaningfully.

"I'd better get going," I say after Michael's family has gone inside.

He reaches for my hand. "You didn't get the chance to see the gardens."

"I don't want to take you away from my family."

He laughs. "Actually, I think that's what they're hoping for."

I raise my eyebrows. "It's dark."

"They're even prettier in the dark. Trust me."

I'm in less of a hurry to leave than I should be. "Actually, a walk sounds nice. Once I get out of these shoes." I slip off one high heel and rub my toes.

Michael directs me back into the country club. Most of the guests are gone or saying their goodbyes to Michael's parents. I slip into a bathroom to change.

I change slowly, my thoughts swirling. I like Michael. I like his family. If things were different, maybe I could... I close my eyes and touch the diamonds on my ears. Things aren't different.

I'm in love with Jacob.

An unbidden thought crosses my mind. What if I hadn't gone back to say goodbye to Jacob? What if the second kiss in the barn had never happened? Would I be free to be with Michael, guilt not included?

I shake my head.

How can I wish away the sweetest memory of my life?

Twenty-Four

Deciding

Michael is right about the gardens and even about the dark. There are winding cobblestone paths branching in every direction, lit topiaries, and beds of gorgeous flowers glowing in moonlit beds. He shows me the place where he got in trouble when he was six for playing in the fountain and at eight for trying to swing on the long limbs of the willow tree.

"I honestly thought I was Tarzan," he says. "My mother was mortified. It was in the middle of my grandmother's seventieth birthday party and about a hundred guests."

"You had a very different childhood than I did." I'm thinking of the casual dining, cake and ice cream party we had to celebrate my grandmother's eightieth birthday the year before.

"Not that different, really," he says, taking my hand and pulling me to a rock structure he called *The Tower*. He puts his hand on the side of it and a shadow passes over his face. "This was Kaylee's favorite place.

No one told us you weren't supposed to climb it." He looks so sad that I reach for his hand and squeeze it. He doesn't let go for the rest of our walk.

We walk for a long time. Long enough that it feels like we're the only ones left in the gardens. Long enough that it feels like we might be the only ones left in the world.

Finally he stops. We've reached the edge of the gardens, a few feet away from the parking lot. I'm driving back to my parents' house, and Michael is flying out tomorrow.

"Thanks for inviting me, Michael. You were right; this was fun. And this," I spread my arms out to indicate the garden, "is absolutely gorgeous."

He steps closer, his eyes locked with mine. "This is absolutely gorgeous."

He's so close I'm having a hard time breathing. I look down so I don't have to face the question I see in his eyes. "I should go," I say, but I can't make myself move.

He brushes a lock of hair that's come loose from my up-do back from my face and then rests his hands on my shoulders. "It's been a long day. You're tired. Stay tonight. Stay here with me."

My body stiffens, and I close my eyes against the familiar guilty ache in my chest. "I can't."

"Why not?" he asks.

I meet his gaze. "You know why not."

He moves closer, close enough that I can feel his breath on my face. "But are you sure you know?"

I hesitate long enough for him to jump into the space. "I asked Matt about it, about you and Jacob. He told me Jacob ignored you the whole time he was at Fort Lewis. That he made you crazy. That he didn't pay any attention to you until the day he left, and then he kissed you and told you to wait around for him."

"It wasn't like that. It was... We were... I..." If I don't fully understand the depths of my relationship with Jacob, there's no way I can explain it to Michael.

He grips my arms. "I would never have treated you that way. I won't treat you that way now."

I shake my head. "I can't—"

He leans closer, his eyes pleading. "There's something I need you to understand, Jess." I'm having a hard time focusing, a hard time breathing with him so close. "I'm not what he thinks I am—what Gage thinks I am. I'm not the kind of guy who goes after another guy's girlfriend, especially not another soldier who is at war, but I wouldn't have stayed away even if I'd known about Jacob sooner. I recognized you the minute Matt showed me your picture, even though I'd only seen you that one day at your spin class. There was a connection between us, and I knew I wanted to see you again. The more I get to know you, the more I feel that connection. I know you feel it too."

"Michael," I start, but I'm not sure what to say because he's right. As much as I've tried to fight it, I know it's there.

He bends down. His hands slide along the back of my neck. His breath brushes my lips. "Please. I can give you so much more than he could. You know that's true. Just give me a chance."

I push him away. "I can't do this. I don't... I love... Jacob."

He tightens his grip on my shoulders. "You don't have to—"

I break away from him, my heart pounding. "Don't tell me I don't have to decide now. Don't tell me I can have it one way now and another way later. That isn't fair to any of us. I have to go. I don't..." I can't finish that sentence. I can't bring myself to say the words that will release him. Words that might release me too. I can't tell him I don't feel anything for him.

He reaches for me again, but I turn away and start for the parking lot. I won't look back. I can't see the pain in his eyes. I can't let him see the pain in mine.

He catches up to me and puts himself between me and the car door. "Jess, wait—"

I look down at the ground. "I'm sorry, I'm sorry I didn't tell you the truth from the beginning. I'm sorry if I hurt you. I'm just sorry, okay Michael."

He stands for a long moment, his hands clenched, his jaw set, before he finally moves out of the way. I fumble with the keys in my hand. Too long, it's taking too long. I force my fingers to work. The tears are ready to break through. I have to get away as soon as possible. I can't let him see me fall apart.

I manage to get into my—into Jacob's car. Somehow, I hope it will make me feel safe, like it always does, but it just makes the ache of guilt that much worse.

I make the mistake of looking at Michael before I drive away. He looks so hurt. I hate that I'm the cause of it.

I can't go back.

Twenty-Five

Time

August 2005

I 'm pulling into the driveway of my parents' house when my phone rings. I'm positive it's Michael. I'm positive I should let it ring.

I answer it anyway.

"Jess?"

His voice breaks me I hold my breath, trying to keep the sob from escaping my throat.

"Jess, are you there?"

"Jacob," I barely whisper his name.

"I'm sorry; did I wake you up? I wasn't paying attention to the time. We had a rough night last night. I needed to hear your voice."

"Jacob," his name comes out stronger the second time. "I'm so glad you called."

"Were you sleeping?"

"No, I..." I hesitate, not sure how many details I can share, how many questions I have the strength to answer. "I was at a wedding in Seattle. I just got back to my house. I..."

Another sob rises. I force it down, but he hears it. "Are you okay?"

"I'm fine." I work to keep my breathing steady. "What about you? Are you okay? Why did you have a rough night?" It strikes me that a bad night for him could be so much worse than a bad night for me.

"I don't want to get into it. I just... I miss you so much."

I close my eyes and lean into the phone. "I miss you too. Your call couldn't have come at a better time. I really needed to hear your voice tonight, too." Tears slide down my cheeks and my heart aches, but in all of this, it's a good ache. It's an ache that tells me how much I love Jacob, how much I miss him, and that I made the right choice tonight. "It seems like you're so far away. Like you've been gone forever. Like none of it was real."

He's quiet for a long time. "I feel that sometimes too, like you're this incredible dream I made up, and when I get back, you'll be gone. But it was all real, kissing you, holding you, finally figuring out what it took to get together. The most real thing I've ever had. I just wish it hadn't taken so long for me to figure out we should be together. I wish we'd had more time."

I brush the tears out of my eyes and work to sound positive. "It doesn't matter now, not really, because we'll be together again soon. We're down to eleven weeks. Less than three months."

"Eleven weeks," he repeats. "And then I'll get to hold you in my arms and kiss you and... I don't know. Right now I'd give anything just to hold your hand."

The reality of our situation, even after he's home, hits me. "But we won't be together, not exactly. I'll be at school, five hours away. You'll be on base all week and... we won't get to see each other very often."

His voice is low and soothing. "We'll figure it out. I'll come see you when I can. You'll come home when you can. Five hours isn't ideal, but it's a hell of a lot better than what we have now."

"I could take a semester off. I'm taking summer classes, so it wouldn't put me too far behind." My mind races. After everything that's happened, I don't want to lose him, but I don't know if skipping a semester would work. "But the nursing program is pretty competitive. I don't want to lose my spot." Fear and something like desperation come out in my voice.

"Slow down. It'll be okay. I wouldn't ask you to do that. Like I said, we'll figure it out. The most important thing is that I love you and I never want to lose you."

"I love you. And I don't want to lose you either, so I should..."

"Close your eyes." He breathes into the phone. "My arms are around you, pulling you close. My lips are on your lips. Anytime you need me, I'll be there."

The words I used for him months ago work for me too. My heart is full. My lips tingle as if we'd really kissed. "Thank you. And thank you for calling tonight. You always know exactly when I need you the most. You're my hero. My best friend. Everything. I love you."

"I love you too, Jess. Eleven more weeks. We can do this."

"We can do this," I echo. "See you soon."

Twenty-Six

Everything After

September 2005

I 'm not one-hundred percent. I can feel it in the first few strides of my run. It's not just the usual mental anguish I've felt since the whole thing with Michael. I can drown that out by pushing myself to where all I can hear is my heartbeat, all I can feel are my legs moving me forward.

I think I'm sick.

I've been a model girlfriend waiting for her boyfriend to come home for almost two months now. I spend the weekends doing homework or hanging out with Kendra and helping with wedding stuff. I live for Jacob's emails. We talk about when he gets home, all the things we want to do together.

I haven't answered any of Michael's phone calls, emails, or texts. Not even when he sent flowers. Not even when he said he wouldn't push anymore, that he was okay with being just friends.

Eight more weeks, eight more weeks. That's my running mantra now. In eight weeks, Jacob will be home and everything will be perfect again.

I never get sick, but this time I'm pretty sure there's something physically wrong. The flu is going around. I feel dizzy, nauseous, and my energy is gone. My legs are like bricks. I cut my route short and quit before I've even gone two miles. I always feel guilty when I do that—like I'm wimping out.

By the time I get to my apartment, I know I'm sick.

"Are you okay?" Nichole asks when I walk in. She touches my forehead. "You feel hot."

"I just finished a run. But I don't feel good. I'm going to take a shower and go to bed."

"You must really feel awful," she looks at the clock. It's only 6:30.

I shower, leaning against the wall for support. Getting into my pajamas leaves me exhausted. My whole body aches. I glance at my computer. I've been emailing Jacob every night before bed. Usually, it's just a quick goodnight. I don't even have the energy for that.

About one o'clock I wake up flushed and barely make it to the bathroom before I throw up. As I crawl back into bed, I pray this is a short bug. I can't get behind in school. I lie back down, exhausted.

"Jess," Nichole is calling for me.

I look at the clock, seven-thirty a.m. If I'm going to make it to class, I have to get up now. I sit up, and my head pounds.

"Jess," she calls again.

I get up and walk towards the door. It takes all my strength. I'm not going anywhere today. I lean against the door frame. "I'm not going to class today. I feel terrible."

"It's not that." She walks into my room. She's holding my cell. I must have left it in the living room last night. "You have a phone call."

Something about her face makes me dread taking the phone from her. I wonder if it's Michael. I told my roommates that I can't talk to him.

"Hello."

It's a man's voice. Not Michael, but one I immediately recognize.

"Dad?"

Dad never calls me. Usually when Mom calls, she puts him on the phone and we talk for a minute, but he's never initiated a phone call.

"Jessica, baby." The tone of his voice is scary—quiet, tender, deadly serious. He hasn't called me baby since I was little. "We had a visit from the Army this morning."

I clutch the phone tighter. I already know what he's going to tell me.

It's never good news if they show up in person.

"Matthew is gone. He was killed yesterday when a rocket-propelled grenade hit his Humvee." Dad's voice wavers.

I breathe in once. Matthew, not...my mind can't finish that sentence.

I clutch the phone, and lean against the wall for support. I can't speak, I can't cry. Nichole catches the look on my face and puts her hand on my shoulder.

"Jess, are you there?" Dad asks.

"I'm still here," I whisper.

"There's more."

"More," I squeak. I can't wrap my head around what he just told me. How can there be more?

"Gage was with him. He was killed too."

Twenty-Seven

Just a Dream

I'm back in my bed. My body is on fire. Everything hurts. I struggle to push the covers off. It all must have been a dream, some horrible fever-induced dream.

I'm afraid to open my eyes. What if it wasn't a dream? My heart feels hollow. I force myself to look around. My room is gray. It must be daylight, but the blinds are closed. Someone's hand is covering mine. I struggle to focus on his face.

"Michael?"

He takes my hand. His voice cracks. "Jess, are you okay?"

I struggle to make sense of anything. "Michael," I croak again. "Why are you here?"

"I was in town for my mom's birthday. I would have called, but I didn't think you'd want to see me. I came as soon as I heard." He turns away, still gripping my hand.

As soon as I heard you were sick. I want him to finish that way. I don't want to believe there's another reason for him to be here. It's just a nightmare.

He leans close to my face and strokes my hair. His eyes are wet. "Please, what can I do for you? I only want to help."

I pull my hand from his and press my fists into my eyes. I want to shut him out, shut all of this out. I want the world to go dark again. I feel like I'm going to throw up again. This time I don't think it's physical.

"Kendra," I say suddenly. "Find Kendra. I need to know if she's okay."

Michael covers my hand with his. "I'll find her. I'll be back as soon as I can."

He leaves. I close my eyes again, no tears. Why can't I cry? Someone is coming in and out of my room—rummaging through my closet, through my drawers. I don't know who it is. I don't care. I can only focus on the pain and horrible emptiness in my chest. I drift away again.

I wake up to voices in my room. This time I'm not naïve enough to think everything is a dream. "Has she taken anything?" It's a woman's voice I don't recognize.

Nichole answers, "I don't think so. She threw up last night. She's only been up once since then, when she got the phone call."

A hand on my forehead. "She's burning up. Get my thermometer. In my work bag."

I open my eyes. My head pounds. Michael is kneeling beside my bed. "Did you find Kendra?"

"She's already on her way home. I brought my sister, Karen, back with me. She's a doctor."

Karen takes my temperature. When she looks at the display, she shakes her head. "103.1," She hands the thermometer to Nichole. They're all hovering around my bed. "Have you taken anything for the fever, Jess?"

I shake my head.

"How do you feel?" She hesitates. "I mean physically."

"Achy, hot, pretty horrible."

"You have the flu. It's been bad this year. The vaccine wasn't a good match. You need to stay in bed, rest, get lots of fluids. You look dehydrated."

I start to sit up. "I need to go home."

Karen shakes her head. "Your family doesn't need this right now. Get a few days of rest. Then, have someone drive you. I wouldn't recommend your going now."

I lie back down and press my hand into my face. How can I possibly stay here?

Michael takes my hand. "I'll do whatever you want."

I open my eyes and look into his, pleading. "I want to go home Now."

Karen shakes her head. "There's nothing you can do now, Jess, nothing but make them sick. A couple of days."

"No." I moan and turn my face to the wall. Swallow. My throat aches; it's sore too. When they're all gone, I'll drive myself. I have to be home.

Michael touches my face. "I'll take you home."

"Mike, you can't," Karen starts.

"I have to do something." His voice is choked with tears. The sound makes my throat hurt more.

Karen sighs. "Okay. But I want her to take something to bring the fever down. Keep an eye on her temperature. If it goes any higher, you'd better take her to the ER." She lowers her voice. "I don't recommend this for either of you, but I know I can't change your mind." She leans over me. "I'm sorry, Jess, for you, for your family." She leaves. Michael gets up. Nichole is standing over me with medicine and a glass of water. I take the pills and then lie back down. They're talking in the hall outside my door.

Nichole comes back in and sits on the side of my bed. "I packed for you. Extra everything. A couple of dresses for...the service. I'll be coming...when you know the details." She squeezes my hand and turns away so I don't see her tears.

Michael comes back in. "Are you ready?"

Ready? I'm in my pajamas. My hair is crazy, wild and wet with sweat. I should get up and get dressed. I should at least comb my hair—stupid things to think about now.

He doesn't wait for me to answer. He picks me up, blanket and all, and carries me out of my apartment, down the stairs, to Jacob's car. I remember Jacob telling me not to let any other guys drive his car. There isn't anything I can do about that now.

Michael slides me into the back seat. There are pillows and blankets piled in the back. "Are you comfortable?"

My whole body is hot and achy. My heart is hollow. The seat is too short for me to stretch out on. Comfortable isn't possible. I nod anyway.

He climbs behind the wheel. I close my eyes. The effort of being carried to the car has left me exhausted. I drift in and out of consciousness, in and out of reality.

My cell phone rings. I open my eyes. It's on the seat next to Michael. He reaches over and picks it up. "Hello...yes...Michael Stephens." He's talking quietly. "Oh... hi. Yeah. I'm sorry, very sorry to hear about your brother."

I strain my ears to hear. Tyler?

"I'm taking her home. She's sick...the flu...she's asleep in the backseat. No, don't worry, I'll take care of her...Sure, I'll tell her you called. Again, I'm sorry about your brother. He was a good man... I'll tell her you said that...You're welcome, Ricks."

Jacob! An involuntary moan escapes my lips as Michael snaps the phone shut. He doesn't hear me. "Jacob." I whisper his name. All I can think about now is how he must be hurting. How much I need to talk to him.

Michael keeps driving. His eyes on the road. He must not hear me.

Twenty-Eight

Anything and Nothing

I'm lying on my bed. My own bed in my own house. Vague memories come crowding in—a car ride, Michael carrying me in the house. Two soldiers standing on our porch. My parents talking in low voices. Mom's face, pale, her eyes rimmed in red.

Tyler. Where was Tyler?

I focus on the form lying on my floor. Mom? Her arms are wrapped around a pillow and a blanket is lying in a heap next to her. Her breathing is even, but her face looks haggard. What is she doing here? Why is she asleep on my bedroom floor?

I adjust my position. The noise wakes her. She sits up and rubs her eyes, kneels beside my bed, and touches my forehead. "Jessica, baby, you're still so hot. How do you feel?"

How do I feel? The irony of what she said is laughable, or it would be, if everything wasn't so horrible. "Mom." I try to sit up, and my pulse hammers in my ears. "Why are you here? Did you sleep on the floor? You need to rest."

She stands up slowly and sits on the chair beside my desk. "I need to be a mom right now. I can't do anything for... for Matt." Her face twists, and she turns away.

"What about Dad and Tyler?"

"Dad slept in Tyler's room last night. He hasn't come out since we told him. You looked so sick when Michael brought you in. I needed to be with you to make sure you're okay." Her voice is halting, as if every word takes an effort. She needs to sleep. She needs to get away from me. I can't make her sick. Maybe Karen was right. My being here is making everything worse.

There's a soft knock at the door. Michael comes in. He has two glasses in his hands, with some kind of brown liquid. "I brought you guys some protein drinks, something to keep your strength up."

Mom takes hers. "Thank you, Michael. And thank you for bringing Jess home."

He walks over and sits on the edge of my bed. "How are you doing?" Dumb question. He touches my cheek. "You still have a fever. Have you taken anything?"

I shake my head. I wish everyone would stop fussing over me. It makes me feel guilty for insisting that I come home. Mom looks like she's aged a hundred years. Somebody should take care of her.

"Drink this," Michael coaxes. "You need liquids." He's holding the glass like he's going to press it to my lips and hold it for me while I drink. I take it out of his hands before he can.

I stare at the brown liquid. I can't imagine anything less appealing. Mom is swirling hers around in the glass. Michael is watching me. Mom is watching me. I take a tentative drink. It's chalky, completely tasteless, and it hurts my throat on the way down. I take another swallow and then set it down on my nightstand. Mom gives up on hers too and sets it on my desk.

Michael stands up. "I made some phone calls," he says delicately. "I'm working on travel arrangements for the memorial service, things like that. They put me in charge of your family, in charge of taking care of you. Whatever you need, let me know."

Mom takes his hand. "Thank you so much, Michael." She stands. "We should let you rest, Jess. Drink your breakfast. I'll bring you something for the fever." She carries her glass with her.

Having the flu is my salvation. The phone rings and rings, the doorbell too. I get to shut it all out, stay locked up in my bedroom. "Michael is fielding the calls and the visits." Mom says when she brings me lunch. "Keeping the newspeople away. I don't want to talk to them." She sighs and sets the tray down on the nightstand. Nothing looks good to me. "Becky called, and Taryn. Jasmine has called about a hundred times."

I want to know whether Jacob called back. I'm not sure where my cellphone is. Michael comes in before I get the chance to ask Mom.

He sits on my bed again. "I talked to Karen. She said to give you this." He hands me a glass of pale pink liquid. "To keep you from getting dehydrated."

"Thanks." I take the glass and take a sip.

Dad walks in. "How are you doing?"

"I'm still alive," I grimace at my poor choice of words. "I feel better." I'm mostly lying. "Where's Tyler?"

Dad shakes his head. "He won't come out of his room. He's not eating."

"He wants to shut down," Michael says softly. His face goes dark. "He doesn't know how to handle this. He feels like he should be tough, be a man about this, but he's not sure how." We're all watching

Michael. He looks up at my dad. "My sister died when I was about Tyler's age. I reacted the same way."

Mom looks at Michael. "Maybe you could talk to him."

Michael nods. "I will later. Right now he needs his space."

Mom stands up. She takes Dad's hand. "You need to rest."

"So do you," he answers.

"Sleep, all of you." Michael takes the untouched drink from my nightstand. "I'll take care of the calls and the door."

"Thank you," I whisper.

He touches my face. "Anything, anytime."

Twenty-Nine

Pieces

M y whole body is shaking. I wrap my arms around my shoulders to try to stop, but I can't. I'm freezing. The bed is shaking too. My hair is damp with sweat, and my pajamas are clinging to my back. Even my bed is wet. I need dry clothes. Dry sheets. I don't have the strength to get up and help myself.

I hear a tap on the door. I don't know how he heard me, or knew I needed help, but Michael is standing there. "Jess, are you okay?"

I shake my head between shivers. "I can't get warm."

He crosses the room in two strides and puts his hand on my head. My bangs are plastered against my forehead. "Your fever is gone. Now you feel cold. We have to get you out of those wet clothes."

He rummages through my drawers. He sets a pair of sweatpants and a T-shirt on my bed. "I'll be right back."

I pick up the shirt and pants and shiver out of my wet things. I'm curling back under the covers when Michael comes in with an armload of blankets. He strips the sheets off my bed and throws them in the corner. "Lie down."

I lie on the bed, and he covers me with the blankets. Even with dry clothes and extra blankets, I'm shaking like crazy. He climbs in next to me, wraps his arms around me and presses his body against mine—holding me against the shaking. His body heat mingles with mine.

"Better?" he asks.

I nod and relax against his chest, soaking in his warmth. He leans his chin on my head and brushes the damp hair out of my face. "Try to sleep."

I close my eyes and hope for sleep, but without the haze of the fever, the horribleness of everything hits me full force. My heart aches, a gaping bleeding hole. I'm shaking again. Michael pulls me tighter against him.

My mind spins in circles as I try to grasp the reality of my brother's death. He's never coming home. There won't be a wedding. He'll never tease me or give me advice, or drive me crazy again. I try to remember the last thing I said to him. The last email I sent. Did I tell him I loved him? I suddenly want to talk to him, to call him, to hear his voice. The hole is there, sucking the life out of me. I'm powerless to fill it.

And Gage. Wonderful, obnoxious, full of himself Gage. So alive, so larger than life. Gone. How is it even possible?

Jacob. He must be hurting as much as I am. I want to talk to him. I want to make sure he's okay. But I can't even help myself.

I lie there for a long time, watching the clock advance in slow motion, listening to my breath and feeling Michael's arms around me. He stirs, moves to get up. He brushes his hand against my cheek. "You seem okay now. The chills are gone. I'll let you rest."

I reach for him, suddenly terrified at the idea of being alone in the dark horribleness of this reality. "Please. Don't go."

He slides his arms back around me, and I lean my head against his chest. He kisses my forehead. "I'll stay. Go to sleep. I'll be here as long as you need me."

Michael is gone when I wake up. I can't believe I slept so long. The clock says almost noon. I move around testing my body. I'm not burning up or freezing anymore. The aches, at least the physical ones, are gone. I'm weak. My stomach—disconnected and emotionless—rumbles, reminding me I've barely eaten for two days. The rest of my body has no appetite for anything.

I slide off the edge of my bed, stand and make my way slowly down the hall.

The mirror in the bathroom shows a face I don't recognize. I'm pale, with dark circles under my eyes. My hair is half-wild, clinging to the side of my face.

On the way back to my room, I stop at Tyler's door. It's shut tight, but I need to see him. There's no answer to my soft knock, so I push it open. My brother is lying on his bed, his arms wrapped around his knees, his back to the door.

I take a step inside. "Ty?" He doesn't answer. I walk into his bedroom and sit down beside him on the bed. I touch his back. "Tyler, it's Jess."

For a minute he stays still, then slowly he rolls over to face me. He looks just as haggard as the rest of us. "They said you were really sick.

That I needed to stay away so I wouldn't get sick too. I was worried that..." His eyes slide away from my face, losing focus.

"I'm okay." I leave my hand on his shoulder. "What about you?" He shakes his head. "You haven't left this room since Tuesday night?" He doesn't answer. He won't even look at me. On his dresser is a plate of breakfast, untouched. I stroke his hair. "Have you eaten anything? You need to eat. You need to..."

"Don't tell me what I need to do." The anger in his voice surprises me. "Don't tell me I need to keep my strength up. Don't tell me what Matt would want me to do. Don't tell me that everything will be okay because it won't. Not ever again. Matt is gone, blown to pieces. He's never coming home." His shoulders shake with sobs.

I wrap my arms around my baby brother, taller than me now. I hold him while he cries. I don't cry. As big as the hole is in my chest, as sharp as the anguish of watching my almost-grown brother reduced to body-wrenching sobs, I can't cry. I can only hold him as tight as I can, hoping I can hold the pieces together.

Thirty

Connections

I'm absentmindedly sorting through a pile of sympathy cards. Not reading the sentiments or the names, just transferring the pile from one place to another, anything to keep my hands busy. One stops me—a plain, steel-gray envelope. The handwriting looks familiar, and there's no return address. My hands shake as I slide my finger under the flap and open it.

It's a flowered card, blank inside except for four words.

You're in my thoughts.

I stare at it for a long moment. It could be a harmless sympathy card. We've gotten them from all over the country. It could be from a stranger who saw what happened on the news and decided to reach out. I know it isn't.

I rip the card in half and push it to the bottom of the garbage can. No one notices but Michael. There's a question in his eyes I can't answer.

"Jess." Mom's voice pulls me out of my trance. She's holding the phone, her hand over the mouthpiece. "It's Jasmine. She keeps calling. She sounds desperate."

Jasmine always sounds desperate. Right now, her desperation feels like it's intruding on my family's grief. The drama queen in her can't stand not being part of this. I don't want to talk to her, but I can't make Mom deal with her either, so I take the phone.

"Jess," she sounds breathless. "I'm so sorry. I can't believe this."

"Thanks." I don't even try to keep my voice from sounding cold. I'm tired of talking, tired of everyone reminding me how horrible this is. I was better off when I was too sick to talk to anyone.

"When is the memorial service?" Jasmine asks.

"We're leaving tomorrow for the one on base in Texas. The funeral will be here next Thursday." Details I've heard repeated a hundred times.

"Have you talked to Gage's family?" Her voice breaks when she says his name.

"Mom talked to Trina twice." This is where she makes this her pain too. She and Gage barely had anything. It's heartless, I know, but I don't have the energy to include Jasmine in the scope of my grief. Seeing Kendra last night—not talking, not crying, just twisting her ring—completely shattered. I can't deal with Jasmine feeling like she has a share in this too.

"How are they doing?"

"Destroyed. Like the rest of us." I close my eyes and shake my head. "Listen, Jaz, I can't talk. I have to..."

"Jess, I need to tell you something." She's talking fast, like she's worried I'll hang up on her. "I wouldn't bring it up if it weren't important. I don't know who else can help me."

She has my attention now. I've never heard Jasmine sound so scared. "What?"

"I'm pregnant."

I lean against the wall. Michael comes behind me and puts his hand on my shoulder. "Gage." I breathe his name. She doesn't answer. She doesn't need to. I already know. "Does he... did he know?"

"Yeah. I was in denial for a long time. I didn't tell anyone. My mom came to visit, and she figured it out. She was furious, but she convinced me to tell him." She laughs. "He totally freaked out at first. Asked me if I was sure it was his. We had a huge, stupid fight about it." Her voice gets shaky. "He called back a couple of days later and said he was sorry. He said whatever I decided was okay with him. He said if I wanted to keep the baby, we could get married when he came home. He said he'd take care of everything. He said he loved me." She starts sobbing. "What should I do? I don't think he told his parents. I don't know how to tell them. I was going to keep the baby. I even thought about marrying him, but now he's gone."

One o'clock in the morning.

I miss the haze of the fever. I can't sleep. My mind won't shut off. The hole in my chest is consuming me. I should have taken a sleeping pill, like Mom finally did, so I could abandon myself to a black, dreamless sleep. I keep thinking about Kendra, about Tyler, and now Jasmine. Gage is going to have a son he'll never know. Matt will never have kids.

If I face the window, I see Gage's face, grinning at me the night he snuck into my bedroom. If I face the wall, I see Matt sitting in my desk chair, asking me to help him propose to Kendra. When I lie on my back, the glowing stars on my ceiling remind me of the day Matt helped me put them up when I was eight. I pull the pillow over my head and try to shut it all out.

The door opens. "Jess."

I turn. "Michael, what are you doing here?"

He stands in the doorway. "I'm sorry. Did I wake you? I just wanted to see if you were okay. A lot of bombshells got dropped on you today, on top of everything that's already happened."

"I wasn't sleeping, but yeah. Today was insane. Jasmine..." I shake my head.

He comes into my room and closes the door behind him. "That wasn't all. You got something in the mail that upset you. I was wondering what it was."

I can't meet his eyes. "A card from someone who I thought was out of my life for good."

He sits on the bed beside me. "Something you want to talk about?"

"No." The last thing anyone needs right now is for me to share my suspicion that the card came from Brad. My parents have enough to worry about. Besides, he's still in jail. He can't touch me. It was just another stupid attempt to get to me. "Why are you still up?" I ask to deflect questions I don't want to answer.

"I couldn't sleep either. I just keep thinking about them—Chandler and Monroe, Ricks, and especially Matthew. My friends. Just gone. They were good men. All of them."

"You knew all four? Not just Matt and Gage."

He nods. "Chandler had a wife and two kids. Monroe was an only child of a single mother. I met his mom at the deployment ceremony. She was so proud of him." He closes his eyes.

I remember Matt telling me the guys in his unit were like his brothers. For a minute I forget my grief and hurt for Michael and what he's lost.

He leans forward and puts his hands on his face. "I should have been there, Jess. They were my guys, my unit. I should have been with them. If I weren't such a coward, I would have been."

I touch his back. "You're not a coward, Michael. You choose to go to medical school. That's not exactly the easy way out."

"Isn't it?" He shakes his head. "I'm sorry. You're the last person I should dump this on right now."

"It's okay."

"Can I stay?"

"Yeah." I can see he needs to talk. I'm not sure how much more I can handle, but I feel like I owe him. He's done so much for us. I move over to make room for him on my bed. He lies next to me and puts his arm around me. I lean against his chest. He runs his fingers through my hair, absently untangling the knots.

After a few silent moments, he looks at me like there's something he needs me to understand. "Do you want to know why I couldn't go with them, why I applied to medical school?"

Another conversation comes back to me, almost a year ago, when Jacob admitted he was afraid to go to Iraq. "I would guess you were afraid of being killed. There's nothing wrong with that."

He shakes his head. "No. I wasn't afraid of dying. I was afraid I'd have to kill someone. I don't think I could do it, no matter what the situation. No matter how honorable they make it out to be." He closes his eyes. "I took an oath, and I didn't want to go back on it, but I didn't want to be put into a situation where I had to shoot someone. That kind of hesitation in a battle could be deadly, not just for me, but for everyone I'm with. I didn't want that on my conscience. I had the grades, so I figured if I could be a doctor, then I could help people instead of hurting them."

"That's not a bad thing, Michael. Some people might even say that's noble." I close my eyes, thinking about Brad and the card and all that I've been through because of him. "I was in a situation where I could have, maybe even should have, killed someone, but I couldn't do it. I shot him in the leg and now he's..." I almost say, *still tormenting me,* but that's not something I'm ready to share with anyone, "now he's in jail."

"The guy who attacked you in the barn? Matt told me about that." He pulls me closer. "I'm so sorry that happened to you, but I guess that means you understand what I'm saying better than anyone could."

We lie there for a few moments, breathing together, both of us lost in our own pain and fear.

Then he talks slowly, like he's afraid of my reaction. "I understand that there are situations where lethal force is justified, and I wouldn't ever blame someone for defending themselves, but that's the thing with this war. It's not a defense. There's no justification for being there. There's no reason good men like Matt and Gage had to kill or be killed. They shouldn't have been there at all."

I lay in stunned silence. Michael almost sounds like Nathan. I've never heard a soldier talk about the war this way. It's so different from what I've heard Jacob say about being in the Army.

"My dad and my grandpa pushed me into ROTC when I was in high school. *The honorable thing to do, a rite of passage.* But the longer I was in, the less honorable it felt. Then the whole thing in Iraq started. The more I've studied what's going on, the more I've felt like we shouldn't be there. There's no way it's going to end quickly or cleanly. It's already cost too much. I don't have to tell you that." His mouth sets and anger resonates in his voice. "Matthew shouldn't have had to die to pay for a college education."

I don't know what to say. Part of me wants to yell at him, to tell him he's wrong about all of this. My brother was a hero. He died for what he believed in. He died defending people who couldn't defend themselves. But there's another part, a part that thinks he might be right, a part that's screaming about how unfair and senseless this whole thing is.

He reaches up and puts his hand on my cheek. I flinch at his touch. He rolls away from me, onto his back, staring at the ceiling. "I'm sorry. I shouldn't have said anything. I made it worse, didn't I?"

I can't answer him. The hollow place in my chest fills with an anger I didn't know I had. My hands ball into fists until my fingernails dig into my palms.

He takes my hand, rubbing his thumb over it, as if he'll soothe the hurt by loosening my grip. "I'm sorry, Jess. I didn't mean to hurt you. Matthew was a good man. He was doing good things there. I know he was. I just..."

"It's okay," I whisper, even though none of it's okay.

He props himself up on his elbow, searching my face. "I've never told anyone what I just told you—about being afraid, about how I feel about the war. There's just something about you, something that makes me want to tell you everything. Something that makes me want to be with you. I've never had this kind of connection with anyone, and honestly, it's a little scary, but Matthew asked me to take care of you. I know what it is to lose a sibling, a best friend, someone you've fought with and loved and known your whole life. I understand Jess, so if there is anything you need, anything, anytime, just ask."

I stare up at him. There's something in his expression, a connection, like he keeps saying, something that feels safe and honest and solid. Something that could take away the fear and the gaping emptiness inside of me.

"Will you kiss me, Michael?"

Thirty-One

Snapshots

Excruciating. That's the only word I can use to describe the memorial service. It's very military, very filled with ceremony. For me, it's only excruciating. The line of four sets of boots with helmets perched on top of rifles, with dog-tags draped over them are beyond painful. Four pictures—Matt and Gage and two others. The lines of men and women in uniform. Michael is with them. They tell stories about the guys who died. Stories that are meant to make people laugh and cry. Somehow, this is all supposed to make us feel better, but it doesn't.

Someday when I look back on this day, I know I'll remember it in snapshots—twisted snapshots that shred my heart. Gage's dad, Steve, saluting the gun and boots set up to represent his son. The roll call that the men who died don't answer. The echo of gunfire outside the auditorium in some kind of salute. Kendra's narrow shoulders shaking uncontrollably as I wrap my arms around her. Jasmine, too afraid to face everyone, taking a seat in the back, away from the families.

Michael called in some favors and got us all a private plane into Texas. He knows how to work the system. We have a nice place to stay for a couple of nights. Food, transportation, everything. He's taken care of our every need. My parents think he's wonderful, that he can do no wrong.

We stay in our places after the service is over. Strangers come to tell us they're sorry and tell us what a great man Matthew was. That he was a hero. They circle around us so there's no room to move or to escape. I want to crawl out of my skin. The world is closing in on me, and I can't breathe. I want to stand up and run, but I can't move.

I look up to see Gage's parents, Steve and Trina. They're by themselves. "Where's Nathan?" I ask without thinking.

Darkness clouds Steve's face. "He said he wouldn't participate in any military service. Not even for his own brother."

A pang of disloyalty hits me because I understand how Nathan feels.

Trina puts her hand on his shoulder. She looks around me, searching. "Your friend, Jasmine. Is she here?"

I scan the seats behind me. Jasmine is slowly making her way towards. Her arms are wrapped around her shoulders and her head is down, but I can just make out the bulge under her black dress. Steve reaches out a hand to steady her as she steps down next to us.

Her red eyes dart from face to face as if she were a scared animal. She sways on unsteady feet. I put my arm around her waist. She looks up at Trina. "I don't know if you remember me."

Trina wraps her arms around Jasmine and pulls her into a hug. "Jasmine, of course I remember you. Gage talked about you all the time." She steps back and touches Jasmine's stomach. "Is it true?"

Jasmine blinks back tears and digs through her purse. She pulls out an ultrasound picture and hands it to Trina. "Your grandson." She says softly. "Gage wanted to name him after his dad."

Trina studies the picture and then hands it to Steve. She pulls Jasmine against her chest and sobs.

I'm struck by a strange stab of jealousy. Like I don't belong here anymore. Like I'm an invader on this scene. The room is getting too close again. I take a step back and bump into someone.

Michael steadies me with a hand on my shoulder. "Gage's parents?" I nod. He steps forward to talk to Steve.

I back away and push through an opening in the crowd. Slowly at first and then almost running. I don't stop until I'm outside. I slide down a cement pillar and sit on the stairs. I can't breathe. I haven't had a panic attack for a long time, not since Brad went to jail. I don't think I can stop the one that overwhelms me now.

My vision clouds. I'm falling into a dark tunnel. A voice comes from the other end. "Breathe. Breathe. Blow out. It's okay. I've got you."

I grasp his voice first and then his hand. Slowly I emerge from the tunnel.

"Jess, are you okay?" Michael is holding me. I don't remember where he came from, how long he's been beside me, or even how long I've been here. "You scared me. No one knew where you went."

I pull back from his embrace. It feels too tight.

"Are you okay?"

I want to scream at him. I want to tell him that nothing is okay and it will never be okay again. I shake my head and suck in enough breath to answer him. "I had..." breathe in, "...I had to get out of there."

He nods. "It will take time. A long time to heal. You need to be patient with yourself. I wish I could stay with you, help you through

it, but I've used up my leave time. The Army has been pretty understanding about the situation, but I have to leave from here. I can't go
back to Washington with you. I can't even come to the funeral. I'm
sorry." He puts his hand under my chin. His touch suddenly makes
my skin crawl. "Call me whenever you need me. Anything, anytime.
Okay?"

He leans forward and kisses me. I don't have the strength to push
him away, but I can't make myself kiss him back.

He keeps his hands on my shoulders. "Do you want me to walk you
back inside?"

"No. I don't want to go back in there. I need—" But I have no idea
what I need or who could give it to me.

"I can find your mom..."

"No." I practically yell at him. I want him to go. I want him to leave
me alone and to stop touching me. Somehow I let things go too far
between us. Somehow we crossed a line, and I don't know how to pull
things back. "I just need to be alone."

"If you're sure." He stands. "Oh, I almost forgot." He pulls my cell
phone out of his pocket. "I've been keeping this for you. Sorry. I think
the battery is dead."

I take it from him and stare at it like I don't remember what I'm
supposed to do with it.

"Remember, anything, anytime." Michael kisses me one more time,
then he walks away. After he disappears into the crowd, I lean forward
and put my head in my hands.

I still can't cry.

I sit there for a long time before I feel another hand on my shoulder.
I look up as Steve sits down beside me. I barely know Steve—Gage's
real dad and Jacob's step-dad. He was in special forces, so he was gone

all the time when we were growing up. "How are you holding up, Jessica?"

I sit up. He always makes me feel like I need to sit up straight, pay attention, say "yes sir," and "no sir." Jacob said that all the time, even before the Army. "I'm okay."

He leaves his hand on my shoulder. "This is so hard on you kids. It's been really hard on Jacob. I'd appreciate it if you wrote to him. Gave him some support. I have a feeling it will mean more coming from you than coming from me."

I nod. I wonder if he saw Michael kissing me. I wonder what he thinks.

He stands up and helps me to my feet. "Your family means a lot to us. Your parents took care of Trina and the boys when I was away so much. I'm so sorry about Matthew. He was a good man, a good soldier."

I should say something about Gage. That he was a good friend. That he could always make me laugh. The words catch in my throat. I can only say, "Thank you."

Thirty-Two

Existing

I stare at my computer screen. There are twelve emails from Jacob. Four voice messages on my cell phone that I didn't get because Michael was keeping it for me. I haven't answered any of them.

Matthew has been gone for seven weeks. I've been back at school for five. At first I wasn't going to go back, but after a week of existing in a house over-crowded with memories, I fled to the emptiness of an apartment where Matthew had never been. Kendra hasn't come back.

I'm way behind, so I've put my focus on school. Cold, logical facts in my calculus and chemistry classes are easy. Anatomy is harder. I keep imagining what happened to Matthew and Gage when their Humvee exploded.

I run every night. I push myself to the absolute limit so I can sleep. It doesn't help. Food has no appeal for me now. All of my clothes are too big, but the idea of shopping for something new is beyond my ability to deal with.

As I sit, another email comes up, Jacob again. Only two lines this
time.

> Jess,
> I just need to know if you're okay. I love you.
> Jacob

I should write him back. I've started a hundred times, but what do
I tell him? That the service was excruciating? That it was impossible
to say good-bye to a box—a flag draped coffin? That my entire world,
everything that made me feel safe and happy and normal has shattered.
That Mom quit work to homeschool Tyler because he couldn't handle
going back? That I'm jealous of Jasmine and her connection to his
family?

Or how about the other connection, the one I made with Michael?
I kissed him. I slept in his arms when the pain of being alone was too
much to handle. He calls me every night now. He tells me he loves me.

Or maybe I could tell him that the more I read about the war, the
more I hate it. And I can't stay away from it. It's like an obsession now.
I could tell him I blame him for all of this. He talked Matt into joining
the Army. Matt should be home right now, finishing college, planning
his wedding with Kendra.

My phone rings.

It's Michael.

"Hey Hon. How are you doing today?"

"Okay."

"So you survived your Chemistry test?"

Survived. What a stupid word to use for a stupid test. "I think I did
okay."

"That's good." He hesitates, like he's waiting for me to say something. When I don't, he starts talking about what's going on in his life—about the delays in his approval for medical school and how he's getting transferred to another unit at the same base. I barely comment. This happens a lot. I don't know if he's that self-centered or if he's just used to my silence and he feels like someone has to make these phone calls meaningful.

I realize he's waiting for a response from me. "What?" I ask.

"I said, 'What kind of car did you decide on?'"

"Actually, I'm not sure. Dad picked it out. It has a lot of miles on it, but he said it runs pretty well." I'm tracing my finger over the trackpad on my laptop, watching the cursor circle Jacob's words.

"I wish you would've let me help you with the car. I'd like to see you in something nicer. Something really reliable. You've spent enough time on the side of the road."

"It's fine."

He's quiet for a few minutes. "I wish you'd talk to me, Jess."

I close my eyes and inhale through my nose. "What do you want to talk about?"

"Talk, Jess, just talk. I've been through this before. I know you need to talk about things. I meant what I said. Anything, anytime."

Bring my brother back.

"I need to go, Michael. I have to be up early."

"That's right, you're going home tomorrow. How long are you going to be there?"

"Just there and back. Long enough to pick up the car. I have to work on Sunday." I can't tell him that I volunteered for an extra shift so I'd have to leave early. The idea of being home even overnight terrifies me—too many reminders that Matthew isn't there and that he isn't coming back.

"When is Jacob coming home?"

The question catches me off guard. I look at the email again, feeling guilty. "Next week."

He doesn't ask if I'm going to see him. I don't volunteer that information. He breathes into the phone like there's something he wants to say, but he doesn't. Finally he says, "I'll let you sleep. Drive carefully, okay? Call me when you get there. I want to see a picture of your new car."

He knows that I'll do none of those things, but maybe he feels like he has to say them anyway.

"Goodnight, Jess. I love you."

"Goodnight Michael."

I snap my phone shut, close my laptop, and open my calculus book, immersing myself in a sea of logic and numbers to drown out the emptiness that threatens to send me over an invisible edge.

Thirty-Three

Jacob: Home

October 2005

S he has to be here.

I scan the crowd, too large to make out faces. The guy talking drones on and on. Doesn't he know? Doesn't he understand that we just want to be out of here, to leave this place and find the ones we love? Away from them for a year, isn't that long enough?

She has to be here.

We didn't talk about it, at least not for a long time. Me coming home. Actually, we haven't talked about anything. No response to any of my emails. She won't answer my phone calls. She's hurting. I know that. I'm hurting too.

She'll be here.

I'm trying to convince myself. She'll be here. I'll hold her in my arms, and we can make everything better together.

When the speeches are over, I make my way through the crowd, looking for a familiar face. Mom finds me first. She flings her arms around me and holds on like she'll never let go. She's crying. When she finally lets go, Steve grips my hand and then hugs me too. I don't think he's ever done that.

"It's good to have you back, son." I don't think he's ever called me that either.

Behind them are Mr. and Mrs. Roberts. Jess' parents. Nice of them to come.

Jess isn't with them.

Mrs. Roberts sees me searching. She gives me a hug. "Jess couldn't make it. She's really behind in her schoolwork. She was home for a long time when..." She trails off and grips my hand. "She's having a hard time right now."

We go back to the Roberts' house for dinner. My car sitting in the driveway makes my heart pound. She is here. She couldn't handle going to the ceremony, but she's here waiting for me. The car is empty. For one insane second, I consider going up to the barn. Like she'll be there waiting for me like she was before.

I stop before I go inside the house and run my hand down the side of my car. "It looks okay." I almost wish it didn't. A little ding in the side of the door, a scratch, something to show that she's been driving it for the past year.

Everything inside the house is exactly the way it was when I left, except for the picture of Matt in his uniform on the fireplace mantel and a triangle flag in a box beside him.

And she isn't here.

It's really nice of Jess' parents to have me over. It must kill them to see me, knowing that their son isn't coming back.

Tyler comes out. I don't ask what he's doing at home in the middle of the day on a school day. He looks taller, taller and thinner, and lost. His hair has gotten long, so it hangs in his face. He doesn't talk at dinner.

I hang around making conversation for a couple of hours. Mom and Steve are staying with the Roberts. I need to leave. Go back to the barracks. Back to the guys who understand what it's like to be in Iraq. What it's like to be home. I make some excuses about being tired, about needing to get settled. They all nod like they understand, but not one of them does.

When I get in my car, I'm searching—a little scrap of paper, a hair, anything to prove that this has been her car while I've been gone. She would have had to spend a long time detailing my car to get it this clean, this devoid of any trace of her.

I open the glove compartment and a white envelope falls out. I take a deep breath and open it up. It's full of money. There's probably a thousand dollars here. I'm more interested in the note written in her smooth handwriting.

Jacob,
Thank you for letting me borrow your car. I'm glad
you're home safe.
Jess

That's it. Just Jess. Not even love, Jess. Definitely not, I love you; I miss you; I'll come see you as soon as I can. It's like the kiss in the barn never happened. Like there hasn't been a thousand emails back and forth. No phone calls. Like she never promised me a million kisses. It's all been erased.

I'm suddenly angry. I slam my hand against the steering wheel. Damn her. Does she think she's the only one hurting? Does she think she can just toss everything we had aside? Just toss me aside?

I scan the note again, count out the bills—one thousand dollars even. Rental for my car, I guess. I search the envelope. She didn't return the earrings. Stupid how that makes me feel better. Stupid how it makes me feel like she's holding onto some piece of us, some reason to talk to me again.

Thirty-Four

Asking

I'm getting out of my gear when the phone rings. I hate how my heart leaps every time I see the Roberts' name come up on my caller ID. It always takes a second to remember she doesn't live there anymore.

They've been more than decent. They've had me over for dinner a couple of times. It was weird at first, but I'm getting used to being at their house again. I've almost stopped looking for Jess when I'm there.

This time it's Tyler. "Jake, do you hunt?"

I used to hunt deer with my step-dad and I guess I spent the last year hunting insurgents in Iraq. "That depends. What are we hunting?"

"Chicks," he answers. I can picture him rolling his eyes. He's starting to act like a teenager again. "Deer. We're hunting deer. Next Saturday. Dad wanted me to invite you. We start early, but Dad says you can stay here."

"I don't have a gun. At least not one I can hunt with."

I know he's rolling his eyes again. "I don't think we're short on guns around here. I'm sure you could borrow one."

"Sounds like fun." Something to divert my attention away from thinking about Jess or remembering Iraq.

Mrs. Roberts is shaking her head. I finally brought myself to ask the question that's been eating me up. WSU, where Jess is going to school, is only five hours away. I keep wondering if I should get in my car and head over there, talk to her face to face, maybe get some answers.

"I don't think that's a good idea," Mrs. Roberts says. "She needs time right now. This has affected her more than any of us."

This. She can't even bring herself to say it. I don't push for more.

Maybe I can get more from Tyler. I approach him casually when he's distracted, playing video games. "Hey Ty, how's it going?"

He shrugs and doesn't look away from the screen.

I try again. "How have you been? How has your family been since e..." I'm a coward. I can't say it either.

"Since Matt died?" He says it. His voice is flat, emotionless.

I sit by him. Consider putting my arm around him. Pull back. He's still playing the game. "Yeah." I say quietly.

"How's your family?" he throws back.

"Surviving." The only answer I can give him.

"Us too." Still no emotion. He could probably play this game in his sleep for the effort he's putting into it.

"What about your mom?"

He shrugs again. "She's doing okay."

"What about..." I can't say her name either. So many things I can't bring myself to say anymore.

He pauses the game. Turns to face me. "Look, Jake, I'm not a little kid anymore." She used to say that to me all the time. "If you want to know something about Jess, just ask."

"Okay." I take a deep breath. "How is Jess doing?" There. I said her name.

He looks down. Studies the couch. "Not good."

"Not good?" I'm hoping for more.

He still doesn't look at me. "She didn't cry. Not even at the funeral. You'd think that would mean she's okay, but she's not. Mom cries all the time. I hear her at night sometimes. But she still smiles. Jess doesn't do that either. I've even seen Dad cry, but not Jess. Not that she ever comes home. She's avoiding all of us, like somehow that will make it less real."

I lean back on the couch to take it in. He has a lot of insight for a kid. At least I know I'm not the only one she's avoiding. But knowing how much she's hurting rips through me. Protective instincts, always strong when it comes to Jess, are killing me. I want to help. I want to wrap my arms around her and take away the hurt. She won't let me near her. Won't let anyone near her.

Except... I remember Gage's warning. "Watch out for Stephens. He's getting closer to Jess than he should. I don't know if she realizes it. She thinks he's a friend. He wants it to be more."

He answered her phone. He was there with her, driving her home, after Matt died. *I'll take care of her.*

How far does taking care of her go?

I feel like a jerk for asking this, but I have to know. "Is she dating anyone?"

Tyler shakes his head. I'm not sure if it's a yes or a no. "There's this guy—Michael. He came from Fort Bliss with Matt. He stayed at our house for a couple of days over Christmas last year. Went skiing with us. He brought her home after Matt died, then came with us to the memorial service. He likes her a lot."

"How does she feel about him?"

"You'll have to ask her." He un-pauses the game so I get that he's done talking. I stand up and leave him alone. He looks so tired. So much older than fifteen right now. He's carrying around a huge weight. I can't push anymore. I can't make it worse.

Thirty-Five

Treasure

I'm lying in her bed.

Alone.

It's been a long time since she slept here. The sheets smell like they were just washed. I wish they'd left them from the last time she was in this bed. Mr. Robert's friend is sleeping in the rec room. No one suggested I sleep in Matt's room. I'm not sure if anyone has been in there since he left. It hasn't even been three months.

I lie in her bed, staring at the glowing stars on the ceiling. They've been here since Jess was a little kid. I used to tease her about making a wish when they fell. They're all stuck tight. No wishes for me tonight. I can't sleep, so I get up and wander around the room—slide my hand over the curve of the headboard, pick up a pen she left on her desk, look out the window where I saw her watching me the first time I worked on her car. I'm trying not to snoop. Wanting so bad to snoop. I want to know what Jess left in this room.

There's a picture stuck in the side of the mirror—Jess and her high school friends Jasmine, and Taryn. They have their arms around each other on some beach, shorts, sweatshirts, and bare feet. They must be about 16.

I lean in to study the picture closer and accidentally knock into a blue box sitting on the edge of the dresser. I try to catch it, but it falls on the floor. The lid comes off and the contents scatter.

I look around, feeling guilty, like someone heard the noise and is coming to see what I'm doing in here. I try to scoop everything up without looking. A little label on the lid of the box stops me. "Jessica's treasure box," written in a childish scrawl.

I change my mind. I'm full-fledged snooping now—going through the papers and the things that fell. I need to know what Jess's treasures are. What they were.

She started this a long time ago. The first thing I see is a picture of her and Gage on a soccer team. They were about six, maybe seven. There's a running medal–Capitol Lake Marathon. A picture to go with it, Jess and her mom, arms around each other, holding their medals. Everything is mixed together, a 100% spelling test from grade school next to a picture of her college roommates.

Something silver slides out of a pile of papers. I pick it up, already knowing what it is. The locket I gave her, no chain at all now. There are patches where the silver has gotten dull from her rubbing it.

I think back to the day we moved away from here. The day I gave Jess the locket. I've spent a lot of time trying to sort out what happened that day. She used to follow me around like a puppy. "Hero worship," my mom called it. But I didn't mind.

There was always something about Jess. Even when she was a little girl. She was tough. She never seemed to care what the other kids said to her, or how many times she got left out. She kept coming back, kept trying to be part of everything we did. It got to the point where I cared more about the teasing than she did. I went after anyone who hurt her. When I found out we were moving, I bought the locket, but I wasn't sure I was brave enough to give it to her until I found her crying in the barn.

And the kiss?

That one I'm still not sure about. I only knew that it would make her happy. When I saw her again, all grown up and beautiful—seventeen, I was worried that she would think of me as some creepy fifteen-year-old who stalked a kid four years younger than him.

She didn't.

She told me the kiss was perfect. I wish I knew the perfect thing to do now.

Another picture catches my eye. We're kids. It's a picture her mom took after we spent the day digging a hole in the ground to make a fort. My idea. Me, Matt, Nate, Gage, and Jess are gray, covered in dirt. Jess wasn't afraid to get dirty. She'd do anything to keep up with the boys. She never cried, even when she got really hurt. Gage would cry before she would.

Never cried. Never cries. Maybe she's still trying to be tough.

I'm done snooping. I pick up a pile of papers and pictures and shove them into the box. The next handful stops me. This time it's a picture of us. Grown up. My arm is around her, her head is on my shoulder. She sent me an identical picture right after I left. It's the only picture I have where we look like a couple. I looked at it every single day in Iraq.

It was taken before we got together, the time I came over for Thanksgiving dinner and we played cards and bet on chores. I won breakfast in bed from her, something I'd hoped to collect as soon as I got back. Now I'll probably never get the chance.

The program from the memorial service is next. Weird to see Matt and Gage's name with the other two men killed. Mom sent me a copy of this. I shoved it into my footlocker without looking at it. Now I study it. Read every detail until the pain is replaced with numbness. Then, I put it back in the box. I'm suddenly tired. I scoop up the last of the papers. I doubt there's anything else in here that I want to see.

I'm wrong.

Another picture—Jess and Lieutenant Stephens. His arm is around her. They both look flushed. They're wearing parachute gear.

On the back it says,

> *Looking forward to our next adventure. I'll be thinking of you. Love Michael.*

I figure it out pretty easily. He took her skydiving.

When?

Where?

How do you compete with that?

I study her face in the picture. She looks excited, happy. Beautiful.

Lieutenant Stephens is a big thrill-seeker. Skydiver, extreme skier, all of that. I study the picture. What happened after they jumped out of the plane? What was his next adventure? Her?

Looking at the picture makes me sick. Jess said she loved me, that she would wait for me, but I know too well how the heat of the moment can change everything. Especially after something as adrenaline-filled as jumping out of an airplane. Where did they go after this picture was taken? That will haunt me.

I put everything back in the box, establishing my own hierarchy. The picture of us and the locket on top. Stephens at the bottom. I resist the urge to rip him out of the picture completely.

I lie down on the bed and try burying my head in the pillow. Nothing but dryer sheet smell. No Jess.

I close my eyes and try to see her face. Now I see two faces. Her face and Michael's, smiling, arms around each other. I can't separate them in my mind.

Thirty-Six

Game

I 'm back in Iraq.

We're doing a building-to-building search. Tense, not knowing what's behind the next corner.

Jess is with me. She's wearing a T-shirt and jeans, no Kevlar. No gun. No helmet. I keep telling her to get back, to take cover. She won't talk to me, won't even look at me.

Sniper fire.

I put my body between her and the gunshots. I raise my gun and fire. The sniper fires back. I'm trying to keep track of Jess while I shoot. I hit the sniper. He falls from the top of the building.

Jess screams and runs into the street. I'm trying to stop her, but she fights me off. She kneels beside the fallen man. I see his face.

Stephens.

She's screaming at me. "You killed him." She's holding his body. Blood and sand are everywhere.

She looks like she did in the picture, covered in gray dust. Now she's a little kid again. I'm trying to carry her out of the street. She's fighting me. She gets free and runs.

"Jess!"

A sharp knock on the door brings me out of the dream. "Jacob, are you up?" It's her dad.

I sit up in a daze. My legs are tangled in her sheets. I wonder if I yelled her name out loud. I can guess how that would sound to Mr. Roberts, standing outside the door. Me, yelling his daughter's name in my sleep.

Tyler is way into this. He stops and examines every footprint, every broken branch, every dropping, like he's some expert hunter. I'm trying to shake the feeling that I'm back in Iraq. I keep checking for my Kevlar, feeling naked without it.

Mr. Roberts and his buddy went one way. I'm with Tyler. I hope we don't end up shooting each other in the crossfire.

Tyler taps my shoulder. I look up and see a little herd—three or four deer, just down the slope in a little meadow. They're too far for a good shot.

"Let's split up," he whispers. "I'll head down the hill on the right. You can go straight. If they see you, you'll spook them in my direction."

"Sounds like a good way to get shot." I touch my chest again, no body armor.

"I won't be opposite you, just to the side." He heads downhill and right.

I head straight down the hill—slow, cautious, trying not to kick up any rocks. The deer don't see or smell me. I'm almost close enough for a good shot when something spooks them. They take off.

I raise my rifle. One deer goes down. I didn't hear any shots. It stands, but it's caught in an old barbed-wire fence. It's a young buck with little knobs for horns. He's big enough to be considered game, but not quite an adult.

I raise my rifle level with his head. He turns—rich brown eyes staring back at me. It's an expression I recognize—the look of a sentient creature who knows his number is up. I peer through my sights at him. The shot would be clean, easy.

I can't make myself pull the trigger.

Rocks kicked down the ravine spook him. With one desperate tug, the buck frees himself and bounds into the trees.

"What are you doing?" Tyler looks confused and disgusted. "You had a clean shot. Why didn't you take it?"

I lower the rifle and breathe in. I'm not sure how long I've been holding my breath.

I lean against a tree and face him, a little sheepish, a little nauseous. I can't answer. I breathe again. My heart is pounding. "I don't feel good, Ty. Let's go find your dad. You can hunt with him for the rest of the day."

Thirty-Seven

Rifts

December 2005

I hear the argument before I get out of bed—my brother Nate, and our step-dad Steve, going at it. I'm surprised they lasted this long. Last night, Christmas Eve, was tolerable, not pleasant. More like strained with an aching hole. I keep reminding myself that Gage wouldn't have been here anyway, even if he weren't dead.

Angel showed up late last night. Her arms were full of presents. She had a kiss for Mom and a hug for Steve and me. Mom and Steve are trying to be tolerant. We all know Angel and Nate are living together. Mom has never approved of "shacking up," as she calls it, but for the sake of peace she's keeping her mouth shut.

Ironically, it sounds like "peace" is what they're arguing about. From what I can gather from the conversation, now more than loud enough to overhear, Angel and Nate want to skip out on Christmas and go to some peace rally.

"Anti-military is more like it." Steve's voice is even, but I recognize the calm before the storm.

"This is how we're choosing to celebrate Christmas. I thought you were Christians—that peace is what Christmas is all about." Angel's argument might be more believable if she hadn't already expressed her opinions on the general stupidity of any kind of religion.

Steve loses it, shouting at Nathan, "How can you do this to your mom? You're going to leave her alone on Christmas and go off to some anti-military rally. How can you go against everything your brothers have fought for? You wouldn't even attend Gage's memorial service, but you're willing to skip out on your family to go against what he died for?"

Nate's voice is almost as loud. "Don't tell me what I'm doing to my mom. Not after all that you've done to her. After all you've done to us. You were never part of this family. You were always out chasing glory, looking for a fight, while Mom took care of everything. And then when you got too old to go yourself, you filled my brothers' heads with your war stories. You started living through them. You sent them off to die for your ego, and now you have the audacity to tell me I'm not being fair to my mom or loyal to my brothers."

He pauses, and I hear the hurt and the shock in the silence. He starts up again. "You were never a dad to me, and you were barely one to your own son. Now he's gone, and you're still spouting off the same red, white, and blue rhetoric that you filled our heads with when we were too young to know any better. I've grown up now, Steve. I've learned to think for myself. You can't keep giving orders and expect me to follow them blindly."

"Nate, stop." Mom's voice cracks. "You aren't being fair. You're entitled to your opinion, but I can't let you treat my husband and the only father you've ever had that way. We did the best we could. We're all hurting over Gage's death. We can't let it destroy our family."

"Steve is not part of my family," Nate spits out the words. "I'm sorry, Mom, but as long as he lives here, don't expect me to come back."

"Nathan, please don't—."

I can't stand the desperation in Mom's voice. I get out of bed. Maybe I can talk some sense into my brother.

The door slams before I make it to the front room. I follow him into the street. "Don't do this."

Nathan doesn't even turn around. "I can do whatever I want, Jake. I'm not under his thumb anymore. I don't have to follow orders."

"For Mom's sake."

"I'm sorry about Mom. I guess she's a casualty of all of this. You're a soldier, right? You know all about casualties. Do yourself a favor and get out of the Army before you become one too."

His attitude disgusts me. "Grow up, Nate. Go back in there and face Mom. Tell her you're sorry."

"Ha," Angel sniffs, "you grow up, soldier boy. Playing with guns, trying to play hero in a place where we don't belong."

I turn on her. "You stay out of this. This isn't your business anyway."

"Don't talk to her that way," Nathan snaps. "I should have known you'd take his side. You're just like him, Jake. You've always been Daddy's little soldier. I'm done with this. Go ahead and get yourself blown up too. Don't expect me to cry over it."

Angel wraps her arm around him, and I watch them walk away and get into his car. I'm too hurt and too furious to do anything to stop him.

Thirty-Eight
Walking Out

Mom is leaning over the sink, peeling potatoes, silently continuing the business of making Christmas dinner even though Steve and I are the only ones who are going to eat it. She tried so hard to make this work. She made all of our favorites, homemade stuffing for me, candied yams for Steve, orange rolls for Nate, some vegetarian tofu thing for Angel. Even lemon meringue pie for Gage.

I put my hand on her shoulder. "Can I help, Mom?"

She shakes her head, but I pick up a potato and start slicing it into the kettle.

She sighs. "You didn't feel that way, did you, Jacob? Like you didn't have a dad. Mark was a bad choice. I knew that almost from the beginning. I shouldn't have married him, but Steve. Steve has been a good dad, hasn't he?"

I think about the difference between my bio dad, Mark, and Steve. Mark was fun to visit, fun to hang out with. He had every game system available. He always drove a nice car, even though I knew he didn't pay what he was supposed to in child support. He was like a favorite uncle who never took any responsibility, the kind of guy you outgrow pretty fast.

Steve was tough on us, but he loved us. I knew that. He was gone all the time, but when he could, he took us hunting, camping, played catch with us in the yard and basketball in the driveway. He helped coach my little league team and later Gage's. Nathan didn't play sports and didn't like hunting or camping. They never had much in common. Maybe that's why he feels the way he does.

I set the knife down and put my hands on my mom's shoulders. "You and Steve are great parents. I'm lucky to have both of you. Nathan's just hurting. He needs someone to blame. He'll come around." Even as I say it, I wish I could make myself believe it.

Steve clears his throat from the corner of the room. I didn't see him come in. "Thanks for that, Jacob."

I turn to face him as he pulls me into a hug. "You're welcome, Sir."

***

Mom surveys the piles of leftovers. "Maybe there's some homeless shelter or soup kitchen where we can donate this." Steve and I ate as much as we could with no appetite. Mom just picked at her plate.

Steve is in his chair, passed out after drinking too much, something I haven't seen him do in years. Mom and I are cleaning up the dinner that took all day to prepare and less than ten silent minutes to eat.

"Maybe we should have had the Roberts over for Christmas."

"The Roberts?" My interest is immediately piqued.

"Juli and I talked about it—doing Christmas together this year. We thought maybe it would have been easier. Probably not with Nate around." She throws the dishrag into the sink. "How are they doing anyway?"

"Okay," I answer. *Better than us.*

"Is Tyler doing better?" She moves into the living room and sinks down on the couch.

I abandon the dishes and follow her. "I guess so. He's going back to school after Christmas break, and Mrs. Robets is going back to work."

"That's good." Mom brushes her hair out of her face. She looks so tired. I wonder if I can convince her to take a nap. "What about Jess? How is she doing?"

I study the carpet. "I don't know. I haven't seen her."

"You haven't seen her?" Mom repeats in disbelief.

I shake my head. "She won't see me."

"She won't see you? Not at all."

I shake my head again.

"What did she say when you called her?"

"I haven't."

"You haven't called her?" Mom says. I shake my head. "And you haven't tried to see her? Why not?"

I blow out an irritated breath. "She didn't answer my phone calls or emails for the last few weeks I was in Iraq. She wasn't there when I came home, and she hasn't made any effort to contact me. Seems pretty clear that she doesn't want to see me."

Mom touches my shoulder. "But you still love her."

I nod once. Then, I shake my head. "It doesn't matter, Mom. I think there's another guy."

"Lieutenant Stephens," Mom says.

I jerk my head up. Did everyone know about him but me? "You know him?"

She rubs my shoulder. "I actually invited him to the barbecue Uncle Jack threw for Gage. And he was at the memorial service."

"Were they... did it look like they were together?"

"Nothing more than friends at the barbecue, unless they were good at hiding it. She spent more time with Gage than with him."

"And the memorial service?"

Mom leans back on the couch. "It's hard to say. He held her hand, put his arm around her. We were all in need of support that day."

"And he was there to provide it.

Mom nods. "She was really sick for a few days before the service. She looked pale and fragile—nothing like herself. Juli told me Lieutenant Stephens took care of them after Matt was killed." She pauses. "He had some nice things to say about Gage."

I think about the things Gage told me about Lieutenant Stephens. *Nice* wouldn't have been the way to describe it.

Mom puts her hand on my back. "This isn't like you, Jacob, to give up so easily. If you still love her, you need to see her. Now, before it's too late."

"Now?"

"Now, tomorrow. She's probably home for Christmas. Go back early and see her. Talk about things. I know that kills you, but nothing is going to be solved if you aren't speaking to each other."

I put my arm around her. "I won't walk out on you like Nate did."

She flinches. "You aren't walking out on me like Nate. And I have Steve. She looks over at him. "Christmas is over anyway. Go, Jacob. I'll see you in a couple of months. When the baby comes."

Thirty-Nine

Possesive

H er new car is in the driveway when I pull up, a little silver hatchback. Reliable, practical—no personality at all.

No one is expecting me. I didn't want to give Jess the chance to run away. I sit in my car for a long moment, looking at the house. Why am I more afraid of approaching this familiar house than I ever was approaching a building that could have been rigged with explosives? I take a deep breath and walk to the door.

I knock. Usually, I would just walk in after that. This time I wait.

She opens the door. Recognition crosses her face, and she breathes my name. "Jacob."

She steps forward and is in my arms. I pull her close. Feel her body against mine. For that moment I wonder why I waited so long. Why didn't I go find her as soon as I got home? In that embrace, it's like no time has passed, like the space between us is gone.

I lean back and look into her eyes. Brush her hair back and lean in to kiss her.

"Sergeant Ricks."

She pulls out of my grasp. He's standing behind her.

Stephens.

Her expression clouds as she steps away and looks down at the floor.

For the first time, I see her face clearly—thinner, pale, etched with pain. The light in her eyes is dim. It makes me want to pull her close again, take away her pain. But he's already there. His hand on her back.

Possessive.

He extends his other hand. It takes all of my strength to take it. Nerve. Him standing here. His hand on my girl. Smiling at me. Shaking my hand.

"Good to have you back, Ricks. I was so sorry to hear about Gage. He was a good man, an excellent soldier."

"Thank you, Sir." Thanking him for taking my girl. Kills me to call him "Sir" even if he outranks me.

Jess won't look at me anymore. She looks like she's in physical pain. He's still touching her, his hand pressed into her back, guiding her away from me. I follow them into the house.

"We were getting ready to eat. I'm sure Juli and Paul would be happy to have you stay for dinner."

Nerve again. Acting like this is his house, and he has a say in who stays for dinner. I've known them a lot longer than he has, and I've never called Mr. Roberts anything but Mr. Roberts. His eyes hold a challenge. He thinks I'm going to bow out gracefully, make some excuse for coming by and leave. I won't give him the satisfaction.

"I'd love to stay."

"Great," he says. But his expression says otherwise.

She barely looks up at dinner. Barely eats anything. He keeps touching her—putting his hand on her back, covering her hand with his, touching her knee under the table. Reminding me they're together now.

After we eat, I let Tyler drag me out to the shop. Jess' old car is here–the '65 Mustang she called The Nag. Seeing it gives me a stab of bittersweet nostalgia. I worked on it so many times while she was in high school. It was the best excuse I had to hang out with her. Tyler wants me to help him fix it.

I wrinkle my nose as we walk in. "It smells like something died in here."

"Squirrel," Tyler says, opening the window. "I think it got into the antifreeze."

I try to focus on the car. Try to lose myself in the workings of the engine. It gets harder when Jess and Stephens come outside and their voices come through the open window.

"...why won't you come with me?" Stephens sounds impatient, annoyed. "It will be good for you to get out and do something fun."

Jess' voice is quieter. It's hard to pick out what she's saying. Something like, "I need to stay... Jasmine, shower."

"They're all expecting us to be at the party." I move closer to the window, not even trying to be casual about it, even though Tyler is standing right here. If he weren't, I'd probably be at the window, my face pressed against the glass, trying to see her face.

Now I can hear her. "I can't go."

"Because he's here."

She either doesn't answer or speaks quietly enough that I can't hear. Now I'm dying that I can't see her face.

"I know my timing is off." Stephen's voice again. He almost sounds desperate. "But there's something I haven't told you yet. I didn't want to put extra pressure on you."

Yeah right. Everything about the way he acts around her screams pressure.

"I have new orders. I'm going to Korea for a hardship tour in June. I'll be gone for a year."

"What about medical school?" There's an edge to her voice. She almost sounds like she doesn't believe him.

"There are still some things I need to do—prerequisites before I take the MCAT. I'm hoping I can finish them online. I can't get out of it. It was either that or—"

He doesn't say it, but I get his meaning–Korea or Iraq. Most of us don't get a choice.

"Come with me." Another option most of us don't have. "I could get you an apartment close to base. We could do the tourist thing on the days I'm off. You've always wanted to travel."

She's struggling with the words. "It's too soon...school...so far from my family."

"I think it would be good for you to get away from all the reminders. You can finish school when you get back. Or not. You won't have to work unless you want to. I just want to take care of you, and I don't want to be away from you that long."

Her voice is laced with indecision. "I can't. I don't..."

Tell him you don't love him.

He stops her. "You don't have to make your decision now." There's fear in his voice, like he senses she was ready to reject him outright. "No pressure about the party or anything else. I'll go back home. If you change your mind, you can come join me. Or I can stay here. Spend New Years with you."

"I don't want to take you away from your family. I know the party is a big deal for them." Her voice is stronger.

Tell him you want him to leave.

Tyler interrupts my eavesdropping, turns on the radio, loud. I get the hint and turn back to the car. My mind is spinning. I didn't know that things had gotten this far between them. He wants to take her far away from home, from her family, and, more importantly, away from me.

Forty

Blame

It's too early. I'm sitting in my car feeling like an idiot. I debated this for a long time last night. I'm pretty sure Stephens left for whatever party he was talking about. This is my chance to talk to Jess alone.

Before I decide what to do, she comes out, dressed for running. Her hair in a ponytail, with a headband covering her ears. She starts off without noticing my car. I open the door and get out in front of her. She sees me, jumps back, and screams.

I reach my hand to steady her. "Are you okay?"

She laughs. "You scared me."

"Sorry." I grin at her. Her surprise is the closest thing to a normal reaction I've seen from her yet. "What are you doing up so early?"

She raises her eyebrows like that's a stupid question considering what she's wearing. "Going for a run."

"Mind if I tag along?"

She surveys my outfit—a jacket, t-shirt, and a pair of jeans. At least I'm wearing tennis shoes. "In that?"

"Why not?" I've run in worse than this—combat boots, body armor, carrying a gun.

"I don't want you to slow me down." It almost sounds like she's teasing me. She's a lot more like herself without him around.

"I think I can keep up."

"Your choice." She adjusts her music. I'm not sure if she's turning it down so we can talk, or up so we can't.

It was worth coming, even if she's still wearing her earbuds and won't talk to me. Jess running is a beautiful thing. I stay to the side and a step behind her so I can watch her. Her running pants hit her about mid-calf. The striations in her long legs relax and tighten from her ankles to her butt. Her hair is caught up in a long ponytail that bobs up and down when she runs. It's a crisp day, but she takes her jacket off less than a mile in, so her arms are bare. The muscles in her back ripple as she runs. I'm dying to reach out and touch her, but I don't dare.

I must look like an idiot, running beside her in jeans. Somebody going by might think I'm chasing her. Actually, I am. She's pretty fast, and I can tell she's pushing herself. I'm having a hard time keeping up.

I'm not sure how far we go, how long we run in silence. She barely looks at me. We get all the way back to the house without talking. I'm not sure how to start a conversation, but I follow her to the door.

Finally, she takes her earbuds out. She looks surprised to see me. Like she didn't realize I followed her the whole way. "You can stay for breakfast. I'm going to take a shower."

I sit in a puddle of sweat on the couch, wishing I had something to change into, listening to the water run upstairs, trying not to think about Jess standing in the shower.

Tyler comes down the stairs. I'm grateful for the distraction. "What are you doing here?"

"What are you doing up this early?" I counter. I'm not sure how to explain why I'm here. "I thought you were a teenager."

He shrugs and sits down on one of the chairs. "I don't sleep so well anymore. I have nightmares a lot."

"Me too," I admit.

"Iraq?"

I nod.

He rubs his eyes, looks around him, and then he leans forward. "Tell me about it."

"About what, Iraq?"

"Yeah."

I take a deep breath. I'm not sure if I should say anything. Will I make things worse or better for him? I start talking. Basic stuff at first—the weather, the people. He keeps pushing for more. I get into this and tell him a couple of funny stories. He keeps asking for more. I'm telling him about a tense day on patrol when his expression changes. At first I think I've gone too far, that I said too much. Then, I follow his gaze.

Jess is standing behind me. I'm not sure how to read the look on her face. "Are they paying you to recruit for the Army now?" Her voice is deadly cold.

Tyler stands up. "I asked him to tell me, Jess."

"Don't listen, Tyler. It's not all the glory he makes it out to be." She turns and heads for the door.

I follow her out. "Where are you going?"

"I need to buy a present for Jasmine." She's walking fast, like she wants to get away from me.

This time I won't let her. "We need to talk."

She doesn't stop, and she doesn't answer. She's almost at her car. I grab her arm and turn her around to face me, harder than I mean to. Fear flashes in her eyes. I drop my hand, immediately ashamed. I saw Brad, her old boyfriend, grab her like that once. It made my blood boil. This time it's me.

Her voice is cold and measured. "What do you want to talk about, Jacob?"

I take a deep breath and try not to sound angry. "There are some things I need you to explain to me."

Her voice and expression don't change. "Actually, I have some things I want you to explain to me."

That catches me off guard. "Like what?"

"You were there; explain it to me."

"Explain what? Iraq?"

She nods. There's something in her eyes that makes me think that question is some kind of trap. She doesn't give me time to think. "Explain to me why my brother had to go to some God-forsaken desert and die for people who hated him. People who were happy to see him die. People who fired the grenade at him and cheered when they saw his mangled body and watched the Humvee burn. Why couldn't he just stay home? Why couldn't he be married now, happy, with Kendra? Why was he there? Why was Gage there? Why were you there?"

Her questions hang in the air—painful, angry, accusing. I don't have any answers that will satisfy her.

She pushes forward again. "I've done a lot of reading in the last few months. I've learned some things. I used to think it was all black and white. People who opposed the war were unpatriotic or selfish. Now I think maybe they're right. We shouldn't be there. We shouldn't be fighting for people who don't want us there. We shouldn't be trying to help people who don't want to be helped. We shouldn't be saving people who want us dead."

I lean against her car, wishing I knew what to say. I understand what she's feeling more than she realizes. I've felt that frustration, that anger. But as insane as the whole thing was, when I was there, it made sense. We had a job to do, and we did the best we could. Boots on the ground have a different perspective than a talking-head armchair quarterback ever could.

She's pacing back and forth. Working herself up again. I wish I could take her in my arms and give her some comfort. Physical comfort, something I know how to do. Talking is harder. What can I say that will make it better?

Nothing.

I'm the enemy. I represent everything she hates right now—the people that took her brother away.

I chose my words carefully. "When I was in Mosul, I met an Iraqi translator. I asked him whether things were better there before or after Saddam. He said, 'Better before and better after. What is the most better, is that now we can talk. Now we can complain. Now we have a voice.' That was what I was fighting for, so they would have a voice. If they decide to destroy themselves after we're gone, then there isn't much we can do about it. But at least we gave them the chance. At least we gave them a voice."

She turns to me. "I wish I could believe my brother's life was worth that."

I step forward. Put my hands on her shoulder. I want to hold her, but she pulls away. "Don't." She won't look at me.

"Is this about me, Iraq, or Lieutenant Stephens? Maybe you can explain that situation to me. You at least owe me that much."

Her brown-gold eyes snap. "I don't owe you anything. You're the one who talked Matt into joining the Army. If it wasn't for you he'd be home right now."

"You're blaming Matt's death on me? That's not fair."

"Who am I supposed to blame then? The Iraqis. The government. God?"

I'm fighting to control my temper, but I've built up too much hurt and anger to keep quiet. "Get over yourself, Jess. You aren't the only one who's hurting. You aren't the only one who lost a brother. You're so caught up in your own self-righteous grief that there's no room for anyone else. I waited weeks to hear from you, but you couldn't even take the time to tell me you'd found someone else. Maybe it was because he was there the whole time. Maybe it's because every phone call, every email I got from you was a lie."

I regret my words immediately. I might as well have hit her. I see it in her eyes. A blow to her face would have caused less damage.

She looks away. I touch her arm and try to apologize. "Jess, I'm sorry..."

When she finally faces me, the dull mask I saw yesterday replaces the pain and anger in her eyes. "I didn't lie to you, Jacob. Michael wasn't around until..." She looks at the ground. "I wish everything could have stayed the way it was before Matt died. But everything has changed. We can't go back."

Forty-One

I 'm not sure how I got here. Sitting on a couch in a stranger's apartment. Waiting for a woman I barely know to come out of the bathroom after doing whatever it is women spend so much time in the bathroom doing.

Okay, technically I do know how I got here. It's New Year's Eve. There was a bar, there was drinking, there was flirting, and then there was an invitation to her place. She's definitely hot. The guys who came with me looked at me like I'd won the prize when I walked out of the bar with her.

It was too easy. I didn't have time to think about what I was doing. So here I am, in her apartment. Sitting on Candice's (or is it Cami's?) couch.

Damn. I can't even remember her name. Candy, that's right. I used a dumb pick up line that implied she was my favorite treat.

What would Jess say if she knew where I was?

I push that thought out of my mind.

She's probably sipping champagne with Michael at his parent's mansion. I should have stayed with my mom. Our *talk* did more harm than good. If Jess didn't hate me before, now she really does.

What am I doing here?

I haven't been in this position for a long time. Actually, I haven't ever been in this position exactly. I've never gotten to this point unless a girl meant something to me. Never someone I just met.

I need this. Something to get my mind off Jess. Something to make me feel alive again. Something to make me feel real. But this isn't real. I didn't drink enough to kid myself into believing that.

She's taking forever. Giving me too much time to think.

My cell phone buzzes in my pocket. Dumb of me to even think about taking the call, but I do.

It's Jess' mom. She's trying to sound calm, but there's a note of panic in her voice. "Jess isn't with you, is she, Jacob?"

"No." I glance around the room, like I could actually find her. This is the last place Jess would want to be. "Why? Is she missing?"

"I'm sure it's nothing." She doesn't sound like she believes that. "She went out with her friends tonight. They had a baby shower for Jasmine. Taryn called me about two hours ago and said Jess had left early. That she was acting strange. She isn't answering her cell phone."

"Did you try Michael?" I try to keep the bitterness out of my voice.

"I already talked to him." Should have known she would try him first. "He's at home across the state. He hasn't seen her or heard from her. I'm sure it's nothing." I believe her even less the second time. "I'm sorry to bother you. Happy New Year, Jacob."

She hangs up, but I hold onto the phone. I can't stay here. Even if she hates me, I have to find Jess. I have to make sure she's okay.

Candy comes out of the bathroom as I'm putting my jacket back on. She's let down her hair and is wearing a lot less than she was at the bar. I turn toward the door. "I'm sorry. I have to go. A friend of mine is in trouble."

She comes up behind me and wraps her arms around my waist. "Can't it wait? I don't want to be alone tonight."

I shake her off. "I need to go. Now."

She sticks her bottom lip out in a childish pout. "You'll come back, won't you? After you help your friend. It doesn't matter how late."

"I'm sorry." I have my hand on the doorknob. "I don't think I'll make it back."

"You have my number," she yells after me. "Call me sometime, okay? We can get together."

"Sure." But I know I'll never call her.

I get in my car, not sure where to look. I rack my brain to think of somewhere that Jess might go. Where would I go? It hits me as I pull out of the parking lot—the cemetery.

I call Mrs. Roberts back and ask her where Matt is buried.

"I should have thought of that," she says. "I'll tell Paul to go there."

"No, don't." I want to be the one to find her. "I'm on my way now. I'll let you know if she's there."

It's pouring rain. The wind howls, making the trees at the edge of the cemetery bend and twist as if they're alive. "Jess!" Her name disappears into the wind. It's a big cemetery. I should have asked where Matt's grave is. I keep walking, yelling her name every few steps. I reach the far end without seeing her.

I circle around the other side, my voice gone. I'm drenched and freezing. This is stupid. She's probably on her way to see Michael. Even Jess wouldn't be crazy enough to be sitting in a cemetery in weather like this. I turn to go, but then see her car parked on the other side of a huge cedar tree.

She is here.

Forty-Two

Stone

I push through the driving rain, across the wet grass, and past the cold gray stones standing as lifeless sentinels. I move faster, call louder, but she doesn't answer. I walk up and down the rows, panicked.

Then I see a dark figure kneeling in the wet grass. I call her name.

"Jacob?" She looks up. Her hair is wet and hanging in her face. Her clothes are clinging to her body. The stone in front of her bears her brother's name, dates that are too close together, a cross, and an engraved American flag.

I kneel down beside her. "I'm here, Jess."

"Jacob? Why?" She shakes her head. "Why are you here?"

"We were worried about you. Taryn said you left them a couple of hours ago. She didn't know where you were going."

"But why are *you* here?" She looks dazed, and she's shivering. Rain streams from her hair and down her cheeks, but she's not crying.

"To get you. We need to go back to the car; you're freezing."

"After everything I did to you? After everything I said? You should hate me, Jacob. You shouldn't be here."

I put my hands on her shoulders. "If you want me to go, then I'll go. But not until I know you're safe." I pull her to her feet. She's limp, like a wet rag, like all the strength she used to have has been wrung out of her.

I wrap my arms around her, trying to keep her warm, but I'm almost as wet as she is. She trembles in my arms. I drape my jacket over her shoulders. Her car is closest so I half-carry, half-drag her to it. "Where are your keys?"

She points to the ignition. I help her in the passenger side and then start the car. The first blast of air hits us. It's freezing.

She's shaking violently. "Blanket." Her teeth are chattering. "In the trunk." I retrieve the blanket and wrap it around her shoulders.

The car is slowly warming up. I reach for my cell phone and call Mrs. Roberts to let her know I found Jess. It rings almost as soon as I hang up. A number I don't recognize comes up. The voice on the other line sounds as terrified as I was. "Did you find her?"

I'm not positive, but I'm guessing the voice belongs to Stephens. "Yeah, she's with me."

"I knew I should have made her come with me."

Definitely Stephens.

His voice becomes more formal. "Thank you for finding her. I'll start driving right now. Tell Jess I'll be there by morning."

"You don't need to do that. Jess is fine. Don't worry. I'll take care of her." I take some sadistic pleasure in saying that and in the click of my phone as I close it.

She's watching me.

I feel guilty. "I'm sorry. Did you want to talk to him?"

She shakes her head. "Why are you here? You should hate me."

I put my hand on her shoulder. "I could never hate you, Jess."

"I can't believe you came. How do you always know where I am and when I need to be rescued?"

Because you mean more to me than you'll ever know.

I can't make myself say those words. "I wasn't there when you really needed me. I wasn't there when Matt died."

She stares out the window. "There was no way you could have been. And I was the one who deserted you."

I can't argue with that.

The car is finally getting warm. Warm enough that the windows are fogging up. I think of the irony of sitting in a secluded spot on New Year's Eve in a parked car with fogged-up windows, and Jess.

She's still staring out the window. I lean over the gearshift and wrap my arm around her shoulder. "Why were you out here in the rain for so long?"

She draws circles on the window of the car with her finger. I don't expect her to answer, but she does. "They were all talking about Gage at the baby shower. Telling funny stories, things they remembered about him from the Christmas he was here and when we were little kids. They were all laughing, and then they were all crying. Jasmine got close to hysterical. She couldn't stop crying. I didn't do either."

"Either?"

She looks at me, her eyes dull. "I didn't laugh, and I didn't cry. I knew Gage longer than any of them, but I couldn't cry." She turns back to the window. "I can't cry over Matt either. It's like nothing is real anymore. I thought if I came here, if I saw the headstone, if I saw his name, then I might feel something. It didn't work. I can't even feel the cold."

I don't know what to say. I reach for her hand under the blanket. I take it between my hands, bring it to my lips, and blow warm air on her fingers.

She doesn't pull away. "I'm like one of those stones out there. Nothing gets through." She shakes her head. "Nothing but anger and hate. Like what I said to you."

I keep her hand in mine. She's looking at the floor. I want to reach over and touch her face, trace her lips with my fingers. Kiss her.

Is it wrong that I'm thinking about kissing her when she's like this? Maybe if I kiss her, I can make the block of ice around her heart melt. Only I'm not some prince in a fairy tale.

She pulls her hand from mine. Her face is closed off again, like she let too much out in her confession. "Thanks for coming after me. I think I'm warm enough to drive home now."

"Not yet." I don't move. I'm much happier where I am now than I was in my previous situation. I'm content to sit here all night, just watching her. She reaches up and tucks her hair behind her ear. I realize she's still wearing the earrings I gave her. My heart surges for a second. I squash it down. She probably forgot she had them on.

I glance at the clock on the dashboard. Twelve-fifty. The year changed without either of us noticing. "It's 2006. Happy New Year, Jess."

She voluntarily touches my hand. "I hope this one is better."

"Can I ask you a question?" She looks away, but she nods. "Are you going to go to Korea with Stephens?"

She pulls her hand away from mine. "I don't know."

"Are you in love with him?"

She shakes her head. At first I think she's saying no, but then she says, "I told you, Jacob. I don't feel anything."

Forty-Three

Addition

February 2005

I 've always hated hospitals. Mom has worked in one for years, as a surgical nurse. I've only been to that hospital a few times. I've been to this one once before, to get my head stitched after a run-in with Jess's old boyfriend and a bat. Every time I look in the mirror, the scar over my eye reminds me of her.

Everything reminds me of her. Even this.

I got the call last night. Mom, squealing, "Jasmine's water broke. The baby is coming." All night she kept calling with updates. More information than I needed to know.

Now, fifteen hours later, the little guy is here—Gage's son. Weird that he has a kid before me, a kid he'll never have the chance to meet.

Jasmine is on the phone when I come in. She looks good, for just having a baby. She's even wearing makeup.

There are a couple of pictures of Gage on the side table, one of him in his uniform, one of him and Jasmine together from her high school prom. A little rag doll, dressed in camo is sitting beside the pictures. Where the face should be is a picture of Gage. It takes a second before I realize it's one of the dolls the Army gives kids when one of their parents is deployed.

Steve is in the corner in a chair, looks like he's asleep. Jasmine's mom is in the other corner. She doesn't look happy. My mom is all smiles, bouncing around the room, holding a bundle of blankets.

She beams when she sees me. "Come meet your nephew." She hands me the bundle. He's so tiny. I'm worried about breaking him. A little red face with a crushed red nose and brown eyes stare up at me. I wonder if his nose is going to stay like that.

Mom squeezes my shoulders. "Doesn't he look just like Gage?"

To me, he looks like a baby, but I don't disagree with her. I'm thinking of how Angel had suggested a paternity test when she found out Jasmine was pregnant—*so you don't get too attached and find out it's not really his baby.*

"Steven Gage Ricks," Mom says. I catch a dark look from Jasmine's mom, across the room. "But we're calling him Stevie, Gage's idea."

I hand the baby back to my mom and cross the room to give Jasmine a hug. She's off the phone now. "Congratulations." It's all I can think of to say. I hand her a little gift bag, something Becky picked out for me.

"Thanks." Jasmine dabs at her eyes with a rumpled bit of tissue. "Sorry. It's been an emotional day."

I stand up and look around the room, wondering how long I'm required to stay. This whole thing makes me sad.

"We're going over to the Roberts' later," Mom says. "They invited us for dinner. They wanted you to come."

I shrug and don't meet her eyes. "I have plans tonight."

Mom raises her eyebrows but doesn't press for more. "Come by early Sunday. You can visit before you take us to the airport. I'm sure Juli won't mind."

"Maybe." It's easier if I don't tell her I haven't been back to the Roberts' house since I dropped Jess off early on New Year's Day. There was still a lot I wanted to say to her, but she wasn't in any state to talk then. When I went by the next morning to check on her, Michael's car was in the driveway, so I didn't stop.

Tyler catches me as I'm taking Mom's suitcase out to my car. I came late so I could get in and out without talking too much. "I found some parts for the Nag I want you to look at."

I hoist the bag into my trunk. "I'm pretty busy."

Tyler gets in my way as I try to grab the next bag. "I know you don't want to come here anymore, but I'm desperate. I'm taking an advanced auto class this semester, and we have to do a big project to pass. Dad doesn't know what he's doing. Besides, I'm tired of bumming rides off my friends."

I give in. "Sure, Ty. I'll help you. I'll come by sometime next week."

Mom kisses my cheek at the airport. She hasn't mentioned Jess once this trip. I guess Mrs. Roberts filled her in. "Do me a favor and check on Jasmine. The first few weeks after bringing a baby home are really hard, especially for a single mom. I know her mom is staying with her for a few days. I'm not sure how long."

"I will." I hand Steve the bags and hug him too. It's becoming the norm now, less uncomfortable for both of us.

"Love you, Jake." Mom waves as they walk away. "Call me if I can do anything for you."

I wish I could call after her and tell her how messed up I am because of losing Gage, then losing Jess, and just trying to get back into regular life after my deployment.

Instead, I force a smile and wave back.

Forty-Four

Comfort Zone

I immediately regret that I told mom I'd check on Jasmine. Standing outside her apartment, I hear the baby crying, shrieking actually. I knock anyway, hard so she'll hear me over the noise.

Jasmine opens the door, wearing a robe, her hair falling out of a ponytail. She looks like she's been crying too. I don't think I've ever seen Jasmine without makeup until now.

"Jake." She tries unsuccessfully to smooth her hair. "This isn't a good time."

I peer in timidly. The coward in me wants to say I can come back later. Instead, I say, "Is there something I can help you with?"

Her lip quivers as she steps aside to let me in. "He won't stop crying. He won't eat. He won't sleep. I don't know what I'm doing, and I feel horrible."

Her face is flushed. I put my hand on her forehead. She feels hot. "Did you call the doctor?"

"It wasn't that bad earlier. By the time I felt really sick, it was too late to call."

I walk through the open door. Her little apartment is a mess—strewn with baby things, blankets, diapers, bags from the hospital, and a dirty plate on the coffee table. Jasmine looks too exhausted to care. The baby is still crying. I pick him up. I had no idea such a little thing could make so much noise. "Where's your mom?" I ask over the wailing. This is way out of my league.

"She went back to work a couple of days ago. She's so tired by the time she gets home, and she isn't thrilled about...about this situation. I didn't want to bother her."

I try changing the position of the baby—bounce him, walk with him. He keeps shrieking. Nothing works.

"I can't get him to eat." Jasmine looks like she's about ready to start wailing too. "It hurts to feed him."

Her robe is open. I feel like a creep for noticing, but Jasmine's breasts have grown a lot. She wasn't small to begin with.

"The hospital sent us home with some baby formula. Maybe we can try that." Jasmine rummages through some bags on the floor. She pulls out a little bottle of premixed formula and hands it to me.

I want to hand the baby and the bottle back to her, but I'm afraid of the tears gathering in her eyes. I've never fed a baby before. I guess how hard can it be? He pushes the nipple out with his tongue and screams. I keep trying, coaxing. He finally takes it, starts sucking. The silence afterwards is deafening.

I sit on the couch and feed him while Jasmine watches. She looks exhausted and helpless. The baby must be exhausted too. He falls asleep as soon as he downs the bottle. I carefully put him back in the little crib by the coach. He sighs, but doesn't wake up.

"Thanks, Jake," Jasmine says.

I want to leave, but I know I shouldn't. "Why don't you go lie down? I can stay and watch the baby."

She doesn't argue. I know she needs to rest, but as soon as I'm alone, I panic. I have no idea what I'm doing. I need to call in the reserves. I get Mom on the phone and tell her what I've seen. I talk quietly so I won't wake up Jasmine or the baby.

"Does Jasmine have a fever?" she asks.

"She felt really hot," I answer.

"Does she have any red spots on her breasts?"

Now I'm the one who feels hot, my face on fire. "I didn't notice; I mean, I didn't look at that."

Mom laughs but tries to cover it up with a cough. "Right, sorry. Let me talk to her."

"I sent her to bed." I shift uncomfortably in my seat. "She said it hurt to feed the baby."

"I think she has a breast infection."

I'm now so far out of my comfort zone, I don't think I'll ever get back. Mom keeps going like she's talking to another woman. "Have her put warm compresses on her breasts or take a warm shower. She needs to take something for the swelling, and she needs to feed the baby. She has to empty her breasts."

"I gave him some formula." I feel guilty, like I did something wrong. "He wouldn't stop crying."

"Sleep is good for her now, but she needs to get to a doctor tomorrow. A breast pump would probably be a good idea."

Breast pump, breast infection, swelling—these are all words no guy wants to hear—except maybe swelling, but not associated with the woman who just gave birth to his brother's baby. I'll never be able to look at another woman's breasts the same.

"Tell her to call me when she wakes up. I'll try to get hold of her mom or Juli, or someone. I knew I should have stayed longer."

When Mom hangs up, I putter around the room, straightening things up. I think about turning on the T.V., but I don't want to wake anyone up. I sit in the chair and stare at my phone, not sure what to do. Mom is too far away. I'd like to call Jess. Get her opinion on things. As far as I know, she doesn't want to talk to me. I flip through the names on my phone. Jasmine needs another woman. I have numbers for a few, none I would expect to be useful in this situation. Finally, I see Bryan's number.

Becky.

Why didn't I think of her before?

By the time the baby wakes up, Becky is at the door with dinner and a black bag that's the size of a big purse. I'm afraid to ask what's inside.

Becky picks up the baby and coos over him. She sets him on the floor and changes his diaper. Jasmine appears from the bedroom. As soon as I introduce her to Jasmine, Becky crosses the room and wraps her arms around her. "You poor thing," she says. "Let me help you. Us Army moms have to stick together."

A few minutes after Becky arrives, I feel dismissed, or actually relieved of duty. I call Mom back on the way home.

"Calling Becky was a good idea," she says. "Jasmine needs all the help she can get right now. I don't want to judge, but it doesn't sound like her mom is being very supportive. When I called, she said she'd already taken off all the work she could and there wasn't anything she could do to help."

"Jasmine said her mom wasn't thrilled about the situation, I guess about her getting pregnant, or maybe her keeping the baby."

"I know they had big plans for Jasmine." Mom sounds tired. "I guess we all had plans for our kids. Things that didn't quite work out."

There's silence on the other end. I wonder if Mom is crying. Her voice is shaky. "I'm glad you went over tonight. Our family is as responsible for that baby as Jasmine's is. We need to take Gage's place. I'm sorry if it falls to you because you're there."

I get mad a few minutes after I get off the phone. Mad at Gage. For doing something so irresponsible. Getting Jasmine pregnant and then leaving.

When he gets back, I'm going to... I stop myself, remembering again he's never coming home

Forty-Five

Responsible

J asmine looks better when I check on her a few days later. She's sitting on the couch feeding the baby. She's never been shy or modest, so I see a lot more than I should be seeing.

The baby is asleep when she's done. She hands him to me while she buttons up. I stare at his little face. Now he looks like my brother—except for Jasmine's dark hair, dark eyes, and tan skin, he's all Gage. I rub my finger along his soft cheek. His mouth opens for a minute, searching. He sighs and closes his mouth. He looks content, nothing like the screaming creature I held last time.

Jasmine leans over my shoulder and smiles. "He's beautiful, isn't he? I never thought I could love anything so much." She sits back and brushes her hand through her hair. Her ponytail is smoother this time, but she's still not wearing any makeup.

"I wasn't sure I ever wanted to be a mom. It seemed like so much work. I'm an only child and spoiled." She laughs. "I guess you knew that. We would have made quite a pair of parents, Gage and I. Two spoiled kids trying to raise another one." She looks away, her eyes shining. "I like to think we could have made it work."

I watch the baby. I'm not sure what to say.

Jasmine leans against me. "This is so much harder than I ever imagined." She presses her eyes closed. A tear squeezes out and rolls down her cheek. "I don't know what I'm doing. Sometimes I think I should have given him up. Someone else would have been a better mom than I am."

"That's not true," I say.

She shakes her head. "This might be easier if Gage was coming home—if I wasn't facing the next eighteen plus years of raising him alone."

I brush the tears off her cheeks and put my arm around her shoulder. I look at her, then at the baby, and then at their little apartment. My heart aches for all of us. I consider their future and mine. I think about what my mom said about us being responsible for Gage's baby. I think about how lonely I've been since I got home.

Jasmine's damp eyelashes lie on the cheek that's resting on my shoulder. She bites her bottom lip, and I'm suddenly very aware of her mouth. I never realized how beautiful she is. Gage couldn't shut up about her, but with Jess around, I never saw it. Maybe I was missing out on something.

I lean in closer, almost close enough to kiss her.

Her eyes flutter open in and she pulls away. "Jake, what are you doing?"

I try to soften her reaction. "Maybe we should go out sometime. Get to know each other better."

She sits back and looks at me like I've lost my mind. "What?"

"I've thought about this a lot," I lie. "I like you, Jasmine. Maybe we could try—"

She laughs—laughs at me. I've never had a girl laugh at me when I expressed interest before. "Jake, you are so sweet, so old-fashioned. I believe you would actually go out with me, maybe even marry me, to fulfill some sense of honor, some sense of obligation."

I duck my head. "I didn't mean it that way..."

"Yes, you did." She's laughing again. "You know women raise kids by themselves all the time now, don't you?" Her expression softens, and she puts her hand on my shoulder. "I'm sorry. I don't mean to laugh. Being with you would be amazing; I'm sure it would be. You are so sweet, so gorgeous, and I know you'd be a great dad. But you don't belong to me. You never could." She looks me in the eye. "You belong to Jess. You always have."

I turn away. "Jess doesn't want me. She has Michael."

Jasmine hesitates, like she's not sure if she should say anything, but then she does. "I don't think she's in love with him."

My heart skips a beat. "Did she tell you that?"

She shakes her head. "It's just a feeling I have. The way she acts when they're together is just off. She's not herself anymore, and she doesn't look at him the way she looks at you." Jasmine leans back and adjusts the blanket wrapped around her son. "Jess needs time to heal. She and Matt were close. This is really hard for her."

Time again. The whole idea makes me mad without knowing who I'm mad at—at Jess, at myself, at time maybe, for moving on without making anything better.

I shake my head. "It's been really hard for me. Really hard for you. We've all had the same time to heal. Why can we get on with our lives when she can't?"

I must be louder than I think because the baby fusses. I concentrate on his face while I bounce him in my arms, but he keeps fussing. Jasmine takes him back. He settles against her chest and goes back to sleep.

"I don't know," she says. "There's no handbook for grief; it affects everyone differently. Maybe we've moved on with our lives because we had to. We have people counting on us. Jess is kind of at a different place in her life. She only has herself right now. The place I was not too long ago. I know how much Jess loved you. I think she still has feelings for you. Even if she won't let herself feel anything right now."

The constant ache in my heart throbs stronger. I wish I could believe that Jess still feels something for me, or that she feels nothing for Michael.

I stand up to leave, and Jasmine gives me a hug with the baby between us. "Thank you for everything. You really saved us. I'm sorry I laughed. It was a very sweet offer. If you had asked me three days ago, I might have taken you up on it." She squeezes my arm. "I'm happy to have you as a brother. If Stevie is anything like his dad, it will take all of us to raise him."

Forty-Six

Borrowed Trouble

March 2006

S omething about fixing a car. The way everything fits. Solving the puzzle, putting the pieces together. Comfortable—me and Tyler, in the shed, listening to the radio and the rain on the roof. I'm more content doing this than I thought I would be. Working on her car. I guess not technically hers anymore, but touching the engine almost feels like touching her. It brings back a flood of memories—Jess sitting on the fence, watching me work, talking, laughing at something I said. I always liked it when I could make her laugh. Actually, I liked everything about being with her. Now I know all I had to do was reach out, pull her into my arms, kiss her, say the word and she would have been mine—back then.

Was I really that blind?

I've thought of that a lot. What if I had paid more attention to her earlier? What if I hadn't waited so long? Would it have been easier to hold on to her now?

Tyler brings me out of my thoughts with his questions. He picked this up quickly. If he keeps working at it, someday this car may even be street-ready. Maybe even more street ready than when Jess used to drive it.

Ty leans against the side of the car and takes a long drink of his soda. "I'm still looking for a better engine, and I want a custom paint job, and glass packs like on your car. Performance-enhancing stuff, not just cosmetic."

"Slow down. I can't afford that stuff, and I have a real job." I wrap a piece of grease rag around a bolt to help me get a better grip while I loosen it.

"But your car is fast, right?"

I shrug. "It can hold its own."

"So you've raced it?"

"A couple of times, actually I..." I trail off, catching the glint in his eye. "No."

"What?" he tries to look nonchalant, but I know better.

"Hell no," I say louder.

"No, what?"

"Street racing. No street racing. It's a bad idea all around. One of my buddies ended up in a wheelchair that way."

"But you did it."

I won't answer that. "Listen, Ty, the last thing your family needs is for you to splatter your guts across the pavement."

"I'd be careful... I'm a good driver." He's looking under the hood of the car again, trying to act casual.

"If you were careful and if you were a good driver, you wouldn't try anything that stupid. Trust me, kid, sixteen doesn't mean bullet-proof."

"Okay, Jake, whatever. It was just something I was thinking of."

"Get it out of your head, and you'll live longer."

"Sure whatever. This car won't be ready for ages anyway."

I watch his face. He's still thinking about it. But he's right; this car won't be running, much less racing, for a long time. I let it go.

"Jake, I need a really big favor." Tyler is on the phone again.

"What else is new?" I make it sound like he's bothering me, but I actually like spending time with him. We're becoming like brothers. We share a loss and a love of cars, something I never had with Nate or Gage.

"I need to borrow your car."

"My car?" I laugh. "Yeah right."

"C'mon Jake, please. I have a date on Friday—a total hottie, but I need a vehicle. The Nag isn't working yet. Mom is taking her car to Portland to visit her sister, and Dad's taking his truck for a job in Bellingham."

"What am I supposed to drive on Friday?"

"You can use Matt's motorcycle. I've ridden it a couple of times. It still runs pretty good."

"I really don't think..."

"Please, Jake. I'll get it back to you on Saturday, gassed up, washed, detailed, whatever you want. This girl is is in my auto shop class. She's totally into cars and insanely hot."

I can't believe I'm softening. If this were anyone else...

He plunges into my hesitation. "I'll do anything. It took me forever to get her to go out with me. There's no way I can take her on a motorcycle."

"I don't let anyone drive my car." I'm trying to stand firm on this.

"That's a bunch of bull. You let Jess drive it for a whole year."

"Different situation." I let my breath out, loudly, so he gets the picture. "Just this once. If you're really careful. But I expect it to be washed, full tank, everything ready for me to take it on Saturday morning. A one-time deal Ty. I mean it."

He starts gushing, thanking me and promising over and over again to take care of my car. I'm pretty sure that this is a mistake, but it's getting harder for me to say no to him.

Friday night, I'm sitting in a bar on base, shooting pool when I get the call. "Jacob Ricks?" A voice of authority.

I automatically stand up straight. "Yes, sir."

"This is Deputy Clements of the Thurston County Sheriff's Department. Do you own a black and silver vehicle, license plate number..."

A cold, sick feeling floods my body. I'm praying that he tells me it's been parked illegally, that it was towed somewhere.

I know better.

"It's been involved in an accident."

Forty-Seven

Wrecked

The scene is crazy, like something out of a movie. Rain, police lights, a couple of teenage girls sitting on the curb crying. A hunk of twisted metal—my car.

I park the motorcycle and try to find Tyler. He's sitting in the back of one of the police cars. I move towards him. Then I see her.

Jess.

I didn't know she was home.

Her eyes crackle with fire—fire directed at me. I take a couple of steps toward her before she starts yelling.

"What the hell were you thinking?"

I step back. "Me?"

"Street racing, Jacob? Of all the asinine stunts. He's just a kid."

I put my hands up in front of me. "I had nothing to do with this I told him street racing was a bad idea."

"What did you think he was going to do with your stupid souped-up death machine?"

I catch one cop watching us, like he's trying to decide if he should get between us or make a bag of popcorn and watch the show.

"I don't know, go on a date? That's what he told me he was doing."

"And you believed him? I don't buy it. It's bad enough that you fill his head with your war stories; now you've got him street racing."

Tyler tries to stand up from the back of the police car. He has a bandage across his forehead and his hands are handcuffed behind his back. He's trying not to cry. "Jess, this isn't Jacob's fault. He told me not to. I know it was stupid."

Now she turns on him. "This is so beyond stupid! What were you thinking? What do you think it would do to Mom and Dad if you got yourself killed?"

"I'm sorry, Jess. I'm sorry." He sits back down, and she goes to him. Now he is crying. Crying with his hands behind his back and no way to wipe the tears or to blow his nose.

She wraps her arms around him. I step forward and put my hand on her back. At my touch, she spins around. "Don't touch me, Jacob. And stay the hell away from my family."

The cop steps forward. "You the owner of this vehicle?" He indicates the twisted hunk that used to be my car.

"Yes, sir." I walk towards him. I can feel the anger in Jess' gaze on my back as we walk away.

"This kid have permission to use it tonight?"

"Yes, sir."

"Did you know what he was planning to do with it?"

"No, sir. He told me he was going on a date."

The cop raises his eyebrows, like he doesn't believe me either. "You are aware of the modifications made to this car, correct?"

"Yes, sir. I made those modifications myself."

"For the purpose of street racing?"

"No, sir."

He raises his eyebrows again. I don't know if he's waiting for me to explain why I did what I did to my car. I'm not sure there is a way to explain it, even to myself. I'm stuck somewhere between the cocky teenager I was and the responsible adult I've become. Phrases like *contributing to the delinquency of a minor, official investigation* and even *court martial* are running through my head. I don't know what the penalty is for street racing in Washington or how liable I could be for what Tyler did with my car. The officer doesn't mention it. He finishes his questions and asks me if there is anything valuable in the car that I want to retrieve.

The money Jess left is still locked in my glove compartment. I intended to return it to her, but I haven't had the chance.

The cop escorts me to my car. I take the keys that are still hanging from the ignition and open the glove compartment. It isn't easy. The hood on the passenger side of the car is caved in. There's less than a foot of room between the smashed roof and the front dash. If Tyler had been driving with a passenger... The thought makes me sick.

I slide the envelope out of the glove compartment and then retrieve the registration and proof of insurance. Jess is talking to another cop. I'm pretty sure this is a bad time and place for me to return the money.

They haul Ty away in the police car. Jess follows. I feel like I should go with them, but she's made it clear she doesn't want me around. I stay at the accident scene and wait for the tow truck to take my car to the impound yard.

I expect to feel some sort of loss for my car, something that's been a huge part of my life since I was seventeen. I expect to be mad at Tyler.

Maybe tomorrow I will be. Right now all I can feel is sick—sick at what could have happened, sick at what's going to happen to him.

I feel responsible. Maybe, in the back of my mind, I knew what he was going to do with my car. I should have said no, and then none of this would have happened.

Forty-Eight

Storm

I fully expect Jess to slam the door in my face when she sees me. I knock anyway.

"I just need to see Tyler," I say before she has time to shut the door.

I'm surprised when she moves out of my way. She looks so stressed. I want to put my arms around her, but I can only imagine what her reaction to that would be. She closes her eyes and shakes her head. "He's up in his room. They let him come home with me. I don't think he's asleep yet."

Tyler is lying on the bed with his back to the door when I walk in. I sit on the bed and touch his shoulder. "Hey."

His side heaves with one great sigh before he rolls over to face me. His eyes are red, and he looks scared. Scared of me.

I'm sorry, Jake." he whispers. "I'm so sorry."

I don't know what to say. Part of me thinks I should yell at him—make him face this like a man. But I can't. I leave my hand on his shoulder and say, "I did plenty of stupid things when I was a kid. I made plenty of mistakes. I still do."

"You aren't mad?" The shock on his face makes him look even younger.

"Of course I'm mad. You did exactly what I told you not to do. You could have gotten yourself killed, you could have killed someone else, and you destroyed my car."

He turns away from my gaze. "I'm sorry. I'll find a way to pay you back. I promise."

"We'll figure that out later. Right now I'm just happy you're okay. You're in serious trouble, but you're alive."

He looks at me again. "Thanks, Jake."

I'm not sure why, but I wrap my arms around him and give him a hug. "You mean a lot to me, kid. Never do anything that stupid again."

Jess is sitting on the couch, staring blankly ahead, holding a mug of some steaming liquid when I come down the stairs. I approach her carefully. "Are you okay?"

"Fine," she answers.

I sit at the other end of the couch from her. She doesn't look at me, but she doesn't tell me to leave either. I can feel the barrier between us, almost as if it were something real, a glass wall I can't get through.

"I didn't know you were home. Is school out for the summer?"

She keeps her gaze straight ahead. "I'm between terms. I'm moving to Spokane in a week to start my nursing clinicals."

"Oh." When I shift my weight, I feel the envelope in my jacket pocket. I pull it out. "I forgot. I wanted to give this back to you."

She looks at me for the first time. "What is that?"

"The money you left in my car when I got home. I don't want it." I try to hand it to her, but she doesn't move.

"Keep it," she says shortly.

"I don't want it," I say again. I move closer to her on the couch, and set the envelope on the coffee table in front of her.

"You're going to need it," she answers without looking. "I'm going to guess you didn't have full coverage on that car."

"Actually, I do. I got it for the year you were driving it," I try for the joke, but her expression doesn't change.

"It's yours."

"I said I don't want it."

She sets her mug down. "Keep the money, Jacob."

I'm getting mad again. "Why do you want me to keep it? To ease your conscience?"

She finally looks at me. "What's that supposed to mean?"

"I guess it means I feel like you're trying to pay me off for leading me on for a year and then dumping me."

She shakes her head and closes her eyes. "The money is for letting me use your car. I told you I was sorry for the way things turned out."

I slide close to her, but the barrier is still there. "Why are you so stubborn? You won't let anyone get close to you. You won't let anyone help you. I know it kills you that I won't take the money. You don't want to feel like you owe me anything."

"I'm stubborn? You're the one who's still here."

"You're right. I am still here." I move closer.

"Take the money, or not. I don't care. I'm too tired to fight with you tonight." She stands up. "I made up the pull-out bed in the rec room for you. The storm is getting worse. I don't think you should ride the motorcycle home in it." She could be talking to a stranger—her voice is polite, formal, and cold.

"You want me to stay here?"

"I don't want you dead, Jacob. Besides, Dad is going to be home tomorrow morning. I'm sure he'll want to talk to you."

I grimace at the thought of facing Mr. Roberts. "Oh, so you do want me dead. Just line me up for the firing squad now."

She looks at me strangely and then laughs.

The sound catches me by surprise. "What's so funny?"

"You. The look on your face. Like you're getting ready to face the executioner. I don't know why I laughed." She sighs. "Tension breaker, I guess."

I stand and take a step towards her, daring the barrier to stop me. "It's good to hear you laugh. Even if it is at me." She looks down, but I'm already close enough to touch her. I put my hands on her shoulders. Her gaze meets mine. I touch her face, and she doesn't move. "I miss your smile, Jess." I draw my thumb across her cheek. "I miss your laugh." I trace her lips. "I miss you."

I lean in and kiss her, daring her to stop me. Her hands come up to my chest, ready to push me away, but she doesn't. She kisses me back, timid at first, but then stronger. Her arms move around my neck, pulling me closer. I drink her in, months of waiting and wanting driving me forward. I move her to the couch, lay her down while we're kissing. She's pulling me towards her. I lean against her, aching for this with every muscle in my body.

She puts her hands on my chest. "Stop!"

I pull back. There's panic in her eyes.

I get off the couch, my heart pounding. "I'm sorry. I didn't mean...I wouldn't ask you to..."

She sits up and turns away, curling up into herself into the corner of the couch. She won't look at me. She doesn't speak for a long time.

I kneel beside her. "Jess, I'm sorry. Please talk to me."

She's struggling to bring her face back to a mask of no emotion. I feel the barrier going up again. I'm desperate to stop it. "Jess, please give me the chance to—"

"I can't, Jacob, I'm sorry...I just...I can't be with you." Her voice is wavering, as if she's holding back tears.

"Am I really that hard to be with?"

"Yes."

"Why?" I swallow hard. "Because of Matthew? Because you still blame me for what happened to him?"

"I don't..." She closes her eyes, like she can't stand to look at me.

"But you do. I know you do. Jess, I'm sorry. If I could have taken his place, I would have. If I could have saved him, if I could have kept you from hurting like this, I would have. If I can do anything to help you now. I will." I take another breath. "But I need you to understand that I still—"

"Don't." She's fighting to stay in control. I reach for her hand, but she pulls it away. "I've moved on. I had to move on." Her voice is a pleading whisper. "Can't you just let me move on?"

She stands, turns her back on me and then walks away without looking back.

A knife goes through my heart.

I'm paralyzed, listening to her footsteps on the stairs. The door to her bedroom closes. It feels like my body is full of holes, like it's riddled with bullets. Worse than bullets. Bullets would at least kill me, not just leave a thousand gaping holes that will never heal.

I look at the ceiling. She's up there, one floor away. Ten stairs and a couple of steps to her bedroom door. It might as well be 7,000 miles. Worse than 7,000 miles. At least when that distance was between us, there was the promise of something on the other side.

I can still taste her lips. I can still feel her body against mine. I can still smell her hair. The soldier in me tells me I'm giving up too easily. That I should fight for her. I felt something in her kiss, something as desperate and raw as what I've been feeling. What if I went to her room and forced her to listen to me?

One thought stops me. I'm the one making her miserable. I keep pushing her. I keep coming back, even when it obviously hurts her to be with me. As long as I'm around, she can't heal.

What if Stephens can give her what I can't? What if he can make her happy again?

Rain or not, I can't stay here.

I have to get as far from Jess Roberts as possible.

The white envelope catches my eye. Something inside me turns to stone. She owes me that much. I pick up the envelope and stuff it into my pocket. I pull my jacket around me and head out into the storm.

Forty-Nine

Jess: Lies

P ain rips through me when the front door slams and the motorcycle roars to life. It's all I can do to keep from running down the stairs, from going after him and telling him I lied.

I lied. I lied. I lied.

There is no moving on. There's only being stuck in a place and time where I lost my brother, lost my friend, lost my soul, and betrayed the person I love most.

I've pushed all my emotions away, locked them up somewhere in the darkest closet of my mind, so I don't have to feel the pain or the fear or the guilt. I became a stone, a robot, a monster without any emotion.

And then he kissed me, and it all came back.

And I lied to him.

I didn't push him away because I'd moved on. I didn't push him away because I can't love him anymore. I made him leave because I felt something in his kiss.

I still love him.

That one emotion threatens to open the floodgates on everything I've kept buried. I can't risk letting them out. I can't risk feeling anything.

I'm not strong enough.

Fifty

Pillow Talk

April 2005

"Who is Jacob?"

I'm standing at the counter, reaching for the toothpaste. My roommate's question stops me.

"What?" I ask, toothbrush still in hand. How could she possibly know anything about Jacob? I've lived with Angelica for less than a month. We share a room and a couple of hospital rotations, but we haven't really talked beyond the 'where are you from, what are you studying?' conversation. I'm racking my brain, my heart racing. Who could she have talked to?

"Jacob. Who is Jacob?"

The one thing that came up in our conversation was her major, psychiatry. Every question she asks feels like she's trying to get inside my head, to analyze me. I don't need to be analyzed. I already know

I'm crazy. She's still waiting for an answer, so I continue my quest for the toothpaste and say, "An old friend. Kind of an old boyfriend."

I put toothpaste on my toothbrush and stick it in my mouth, so she doesn't expect me to answer any more questions. I'm trying to look nonchalant, but I know my face is red. My heart pounds out of my chest, even over the sound of the running water.

"Interesting." She's watching me like she's deconstructing everything, even the way I brush my teeth.

I shouldn't feed her curiosity, but I can't help it. I'm curious too. More than that, I want to know where she's getting her information. I spit toothpaste into the sink and then rinse. "What's interesting?"

"Did anyone ever tell you that you talk in your sleep?" Angelica says.

"No." I rinse again and put the cap on the toothpaste.

"If I were one of my psych professors. I'd say there are some unresolved issues associated with whoever this Jacob is."

"There aren't," I lie. "The guy I'm dating is Michael. You'll get to meet him this weekend."

I walk out of the bathroom without saying anything else. I knew I should have paid extra for a private bedroom.

"Hey babe," Michael wraps me in his arms and kisses me in front of Angelica. I try not to pull away. I'm not sure when it got so hard to kiss him back, when it all started feeling so forced. Maybe it's always been that way, and I was so numb that I didn't recognize it.

Michael is back and forth more frequently now. He leaves for his hardship tour in Korea in less than a month. I try not to think about the amount of money he's blown on plane tickets to see me. Now that I'm not in Pullman anymore, he doesn't even get to see his family when he comes.

"I have something I want to show you." He sits on the couch and pulls me onto his lap. He flips through some pictures on his phone, then stops on a picture of an apartment building. It looks far away and foreign. "What do you think?"

"What do I think about what?"

"These apartments are just outside my base. They're nice. One bedroom, a fairly good-sized living room. Close to everything. I put a deposit down."

I hand the phone back to him, annoyed. "We talked about this. I just started my clinicals. I can't leave in the middle of the semester."

"I don't mind paying a couple of months' rent until you're ready to join me."

I haven't ever said yes to Michael's idea of joining him in Korea. I haven't said no either. He keeps saying it would be good for me to get away and spend some time in a foreign country, to see something new. That it will help me forget.

"I don't want you wasting your money." I slide off his lap and onto the couch beside him.

He reaches for my hand. "I don't consider it a waste of money. More like an investment in our future."

I pull away. "Why is it so important that I go with you?" It's the closest I've come to saying no to him.

"We've talked about this." Michael's tone is measured patience with an edge of irritation, the tone he uses a lot when we he talks to me. "I don't want to spend the next year of my life without you. Korea isn't a jump across the country. I can't just fly in to see you like I have been."

"Most people wouldn't be able to fly in to see me like you have been here," I point out to him.

"I know that." He looks at me earnestly. "I just want time with you. Real time. I'm tired of the long-distance thing. We need time to build this before we make the big leap."

The big leap.

He has this all planned out. A year together in Korea, traveling when we can. Getting to know each other better, and then "the big leap."

He wants to marry me. I haven't said yes to that either.

"What if I'm not ready?"

"That's the point, Jess. To get to know each other better, to be ready when the time comes."

"What if I don't want this?"

His eyes widen and then narrow. "What's going on, Jess? Why are you getting cold feet all of a sudden?"

"All of a sudden?" My voice raises. "I haven't once said I wanted to move to Korea, to spend the year there with you, or any of it."

"Of course you have," Michael sounds like he's talking to a child. "We've been talking about it for months."

"No, you've been talking about it for months." My defiance shocks me. At the same time, I don't understand how he can't know this is how I feel. I've been silently going along with all of it, but I've never once responded with anything close to enthusiasm.

His voice lowers to a gentle note. "What's wrong, babe? This isn't like you."

But it is like me, I know it is. It's like I was before. Before I crawled inside my own head, and stopped feeling. Before I stopped standing up for myself.

"Did something happen when you went home last weekend?"

"I told you. Tyler was in a car accident." I avoid his eyes. There's more, a lot more that happened when I was home. I can't tell him whose car Tyler wrecked, or that I saw Jacob. I can't tell him I did more than that—that I kissed Jacob.

He sighs as if he's found his answer. "That must have really shaken you up—coming close to losing another brother." He pulls me into his arms. "I"m sorry. I've been insensitive. I was just excited to show you the apartment. How is Tyler?"

"He's okay. But in a lot of trouble. He wrecked the car street racing."

"Really?" Michael shakes his head in disbelief. "I guess acting out is a common grief thing for a teenager. Did he wreck your mom's car or your dad's truck?"

"Neither," I pause. Any more questions will bring us dangerously close to the truth I'm not ready to face.

Michael must sense my hesitation. "Whose car was it?"

"Jacob's."

Michael whistles. "Wow. I can't believe Ricks would do something so stupid. I mean, I know that he's reckless, but letting a six-teen-year-old kid street race?"

"It wasn't his fault." He's saying the exact thing that I said to Jacob, the same accusations, but I feel like I need to defend Jacob. "Tyler told him he was taking it on a date."

"And Jacob believed him?" Michael lets out an exasperated breath. "I'm not sure I buy that, Jess. He had to know–"

"Can we talk about something else?"

"Right, sorry." Michael studies me for a second, but instead of changing the subject, he asks, "Did you see Jacob while you were there?"

"Yes. They called him to the accident scene, and then he came by the house." I've become an expert at keeping my emotions in check, but I can't keep my voice steady.

"And?" Michael probes.

"And he talked to Tyler. He was really nice about the whole thing. He told him it was okay, that they would work things out. He's really been good for Tyler."

"Yeah, good enough to almost get him killed."

My voices raises without my permission. "I told you it wasn't Jacob's fault. Didn't you just say acting out like that was a grief thing? Tyler did something dumb. Why does it have to be anyone's fault but his own?"

Michael is nodding. "You're right. I'm sorry. Forget I said anything. How is Jacob doing?" He tries to sound casual, but I catch the suspicion in his voice.

I avoid his gaze. "I didn't talk to him very long. I..." I'm desperate for another subject. My barrier is so weak it's almost transparent. Talking about Jacob is only going to make it worse. I reach for Michael's phone. "Let me see the apartment again. How big did you say it was? I was thinking I could do some kind of study abroad, so I can still graduate on time. I could check with the university."

He smiles with relief. "That would be awesome. I'll see if my dad can pull some strings."

I catch Angelica standing in the doorway. She's shaking her head at me.

Fifty-One

Not Okay

"I thought you might be interested in this," my roommate Angelica sets a flier on my desk while I'm trying to study.

I barely glance at it. Something about free counseling at the student center. I work to keep my voice steady. "Why would you think that?"

She sits on her bed and watches me for a minute, like she's trying to think of the right words. "I think you need someone to talk to."

"Michael calls every night, and I can't get you to shut up or stay out of my business."

Angelica bites her lip but doesn't respond to my insult. "I mean a professional."

I stare at her. "I'm fine." I gesture to the on the desk in front of me. "But if I don't pass this test, I won't be, so if you don't mind." I held the flier out for her to take.

"Your friend Taryn called yesterday," Angelica says it casually, like she didn't completely trespass in my life.

"You answered my phone?"

"No. It was the apartment phone. She said you weren't answering your cell, so she got the number from your mom. She's worried about you."

"I haven't talked to Taryn in ages." Guilt slips out with that sentence. Truthfully, I haven't talked to any of them—Taryn, Mom, Dad, Tyler. I didn't even call Jasmine when her baby was born. I just sent her a 'congratulations' text.

"She told me about Matthew and about Gage." Her voice is thick with the sympathy I've been running from. She stays silent, as if she's waiting for me to tell her the whole story.

"I really need to study. I don't have time to rehash the past so you can analyze it and tell me how crazy I am."

"I wouldn't do that," Angelica's voice is quiet. She takes a long breath. "Taryn also told me about your old boyfriend, the one from high school, and the trial and everything. That's a lot of trauma to take on by yourself. It's okay to ask for help."

"Damnit," I slam the book shut. "Why can't you and everyone else just leave me alone? My grades are good. I keep a hellish schedule. I run. I'm never late for my clinicals. I have a smoking-hot boyfriend who's rich and wants to whisk me away to a foreign country to spend time together before he marries me and I'm set for life. I am fine. I just want to finish my homework and go to bed."

Angelica stands as if she's not sure whether to stay or go. It's the first time I've yelled at her. "I'm sorry. I shouldn't be pushing you into things you don't want to do, things you aren't ready to face yet. I'm just saying you've been through a lot and maybe you should—"

"Maybe you should leave me alone. Maybe you should get the hell out of my room and stay the hell out of my life."

She stares at me for a long moment. "It's my room too. But I'll give you your space." She walks to the door and leaves, shutting it behind her.

I'm fuming. Furious with all of them. How dare Taryn tell Angelica anything about me, or about Matthew or especially about Brad? How dare Angelica decide that I'm a project to be fixed? How dare any of them try to run my life?

My thoughts go deeper. How dare Jacob kiss me and open the floodgates to something I'm not ready to face? How dare Michael use my weakest moment to manipulate me into being with him? How dare Matthew join the Army and get himself killed?

I'm so worked up I throw my book across the room. I have a sudden urge to break something. I pick up my phone, ready to throw it across the room too. It buzzes with a text.

I've been thinking of you.

My fury melts into terror as I sink onto the bed. I can't get away from him, from my grief and guilt, from any of it. The mental countdown I've kept in my head is getting closer and closer to the day I've been dreading. Brad will be out of jail in less than a year. Every message from him is a reminder that he hasn't forgotten me or what I did to him.

He hasn't forgotten Jacob.

That thought hits harder than anything else.

I realize what I need to do. The only way I can keep both of us safe.

My hands are shaking as I dial the familiar number.

He picks up on the first ring.

Fifty-Two

Run Away

June 2006

"Are you sure about this?" Michael asks again. He was ecstatic the first time I called. Now that we're talking details, he's more cautious.

I try to force a smile into my voice. "I already emailed the department chair at the university and my supervisor at the hospital telling them I quit."

He's quiet for what feels like a long time. "You quit? Everything? Work and school? For good?"

"Yeah. You're right. I need a clean break from all of it. If I'm five thousand miles away..." I don't know how to finish that sentence. The phrases that comes to mind *I can get away from my past, and he can't find me.*" But I know that's not what Michael wants to hear. He wants to hear that I'm coming with him because I love him, because I can't stand to be away from him that long, because this is what I really want.

I can't bring myself to lie to him, even though I know it would make him happy.

Running away was never your style.

The voice on repeat in my head sounds a lot like Gage's. My heart aches to talk to him. He was crazy and spontaneous and irresponsible, but he could always make me feel more like me. Not like the person he wouldn't recognize anymore, or the person I barely recognize when I look in the mirror. When Gage got it right, he got it right. He knew who I really was. He knew me and Jacob were supposed to be together. Maybe we could have stayed together if I hadn't self-destructed and destroyed everything we had.

"... does that give you enough time?" There's a long pause. Michael is waiting for me to answer.

"Sorry. The phone cut out for a second," I lie. "What did you say?"

"I said, I can get you on a flight here on Friday. Does that give you enough time? Or do you need to go see your family and tell them goodbye? I'm heading out Sunday evening, but you can come later."

"Friday is fine. The sooner, the better." Better to rip off the band-aid now. Better to go before I change my mind.

"Great. I'll buy the ticket now. Don't worry about packing anything besides clothes. The apartment comes furnished, and you can buy pretty much anything you need in Korea."

"Sounds great," I force myself to sound enthusiastic, excited even. I try to convince myself that I am excited. I've always wanted to travel. Korea is a good place to start.

"I'll send you the itinerary as soon as I have it. I'm so glad you're coming with me, Jess. I love you!"

"Love you." It sounds forced, even though I know there's a part of me that loves Michael. He's been good to me. No one has ever tried harder to make me happy, but no one has failed so badly at recognizing

I'm miserable. Maybe the best thing I can do with the rest of my life is live to make him happy.

I hang up the phone and go to my room. Today is Wednesday; a flight on Friday doesn't give me much time. I need to pack. I need to do something with my car. Sell it? Give it to Tyler? His license is suspended for another six months. If I'm gone for a year, I'll miss his high school graduation. Christmas. My parent's 25th anniversary. All of it. I can't think about that. I empty my drawers, sorting everything into three piles–clothes to throw away, clothes to give away, clothes to take. That's the smallest pile. Clothes absorb memories from where and when you wore them, who you were with and what happened—memories I'm ready to let go of.

Angelica comes in as I'm working through my third drawer. She watches for a long moment.

"You're really going through with this?" She finally says. "Aren't you a little old to be running away?"

I don't take the bait.

"Dr. Diego from the hospital called. He got your email, and he asked me to talk to you about your decision. You can still take it all back. He thinks you're throwing your life away because of a guy. I told him he was right. I didn't tell him it wasn't because of the guy you were running to, but the one you're running from."

She doesn't know what I'm running from.

I keep packing, alternating between folding my clothes meticulously and randomly throwing them in my suitcase. I realize I don't have my passport. I left it at my parent's house. The only way to get it would be to go home. If I do that, I'll have to face the worry and the hurt I see on my mom's face every time I go there. I'll have to explain to them why I'm leaving. I'd planned to call them after I got to Korea, when it was too late for them to say anything about it. When I didn't have to see them or say goodbye.

"I don't have time for a lecture. I have to drive home tonight." I gather an armful of my throwaway clothes and head to the dumpster.

She follows me. "Like this? This late?"

"Right now."

I can't wait. I can't give myself time to think.

Fifty-Three

Home

I t's close to four in the morning by the time I make it home. My apartment is packed. The few things I'm keeping are in a box in the back of my car or in the two suitcases I'm taking with me to Korea. Everything else I threw away or left beside a donation bin at the Goodwill.

The house is dark. I stand in the yard for what feels like a long time, just looking at the shadowed remnants of my life–the house, the barn, everything that I once loved.

Home.

It used to be my safe place, and now it's full of things I can't let myself remember and things I want to forget.

The hollow ache in my heart threatens to overwhelm me. I force myself to keep moving. I find the key hidden in the birdhouse, and sneak in the back door. If I'm quiet enough, I can get in, find my passport and be gone before they even know I've come home.

I haven't slept for almost twenty-four hours. I've been running on pure adrenaline and caffeine, but I don't feel tired. I haven't slept well for a very long time. My body is used to it.

I leave everything in the car and go inside. I'm trying to remember when my passport is. Did I put it in my desk drawer, or in the top of my closet? What if Mom put it in the file cabinet in the office?

Whatever happens, I can't wake any of them up. I can't face their questions or the looks they'll give me when I tell them I'm leaving. I can't let them try to change my mind.

The house is so quiet. For a minute I wonder if everyone is gone. The surreal part of me imagines they moved away, or that this was never my house, or that I'm walking around in some kind of dream.

The picture on the mantel and the triangle flag in the display box beside it bring me back.

I try not to look, but I'm drawn there. I stop and put my hand on the flag. More than anything, I want to talk to Matt. I want to tell him about how badly I've messed everything up and what a disaster I've become. I want to ask him what he thinks about my running away, even what he thinks about me and Michael now.

He wanted this. He wanted me to be with Michael. He told Michael to take care of me. Is that why I've stuck with Michael, even though I know none of this is right? Is that why Michael has stuck with me?

Keep moving, keep moving.

I have to get my passport and get out of here. If I hesitate now, I'll lose what little control I have left.

I climb the stairs to my bedroom, purposely avoiding the third stair from the top, the one that squeaks, the one Matt warned me about. Damn. This entire house is full of my brother. Everything I see, everywhere I go.

I open the door to my bedroom slowly. I pause, listening for any stirrings from the other rooms, before I pull the door shut behind me. The room is pitch black, but I don't want to turn on the light. Silver moonlight slips through a gap between the curtains. I cross the room and pull them open all the way, so I can see without turning on the light.

I don't even realize he's here until I turn around.

Fifty-Four

Dream

D eep, even breathing comes from my bed. Moonlight illuminates the form that's lying there. His face is mostly in shadow, but the spike of his military short hair, the cut of his jaw, the curve of his lips are all as familiar as my own face. I watch him sleeping for a long moment. My frantic forward momentum ceases. I'm mesmerized by the figure asleep on my bed. The need to curl up next to him is overwhelming. I force myself to take a step back.

The floorboard creaks. His eyes fly open. He sits up.

It's too late to run.

His expression changes from wary, too shocked, to confused, and then to a strange sort of acceptance.

"Jess," he whispers my name. "What are you doing here?"

"I came for my passport. I was going to...what are you doing here?"

"We're going fishing in the morning. Tyler's friend is sleeping in the rec room. I didn't want to take Matt's bed..." he trails off. "I have to ask. Is this a dream?"

A giggle spills out from the storehouse of emotions I've held back for so long. That he's here, and I'm here—the whole situation is unbelievable. But also not. Jacob always finds me. Somehow he always manages to be there when I need him most. "I think maybe it is."

"Then I don't want to wake up," he says.

I don't know how to answer that. "I'm sorry I woke you up. I just need to find my passport and then I'll go."

"Go? Go where? Why do you need your passport?" He slides his legs off the edge of the bed.

"Back to school." I know that's not what he's asking.

"Tonight?" The concern on his face is familiar. "Jess, did you drive all the way here this late, and now you're going to drive all the way back?"

"Yes." I set my chin. This whole interaction feels familiar. My wanting to do something I know is dumb and probably dangerous, Jacob telling me I'm being an idiot.

"I can do it. I'm not even tired." But as soon as I say it, I am tired. More than just *I packed all day and drove five hours in the middle of the night* tired. I'm *the entire world has been weighing on me for so* long, *and I just want to curl up in a ball and make it go away* tired.

"You are tired." He stands. "At least get a few hours. I'll go down to the couch or..."

"I don't want to kick you out of your bed," I say.

He laughs. "Actually, you're kicking me out of your bed."

"I guess you're right." I don't have the energy to do anything else, so I sink onto my bed.

He sits beside me. "You want to talk about what's going on, Jess?"

"What do you mean?"

"I mean, why are you driving home in the middle of the night to get your passport? Why are you sneaking in and trying to sneak out? Why didn't you tell anyone you were coming home?"

I open my mouth to tell him that's none of his business, but a strange compulsion to tell him everything takes over. "I was going to go away. Actually, I guess I was going to run away."

"Was?" Jacob says.

"Yeah. I told Michael I would go with him to Korea. He arranged an apartment and plane tickets and everything. We're leaving Sunday. I quit my job, quit school, packed up my apartment, and then I realized I didn't have my passport, so I came to get it."

"Are you sure that's what you want?" There's no judgment in Jacob's voice, only concern.

"I thought it was."

"Thought?"

I recognize the hesitation in my voice. "I have this really obnoxious roommate. She's a psych major, and she keeps getting after me to do counseling. She thinks I have issues I need to work through. Basically she thinks I'm crazy."

"And what do you think?" Jacob asks.

"I told her I'm fine. I have a good job, I get good grades, I have a guy who wants to fly me halfway across the world and pay for an apartment in another country, so we don't have to be apart."

He puts his hand over mine, but the gesture isn't romantic, not like when he kissed me before. He's not asking me for anything. I turn my hand over and thread my fingers through his. "I didn't ask you what you told your roommate. I asked you what you thought."

"Oh, that?" I force a half-crazed smile. "I know I'm crazy. The problem is, I don't know how to be un-crazy."

"But you think going to Korea with Michael will help?" There's still no judgment or jealousy in his voice. It's like he's taken on the role of big brother again, a role I hated for him, but one that feels right. At least for now.

"I thought it would." There's that hesitation again. I'm doubting every motive I had for running away, even the idea that I'm trying to protect him. I'm still afraid, but with him beside me, that fear seems like something I made up.

"And now?"

"And now I'm not sure. I'm just..." I take a breath, not sure how to express everything that's racing through my mind. "Something has to change, Jacob. I can't keep living like this. It's like I've built my walls up so high that I can't let anyone else in. I created a prison for myself, and I don't know how to escape."

He sits in silence for a long time, just holding my hand. I'm afraid of what he's going to say, but I'm dying for something; for him to give me advice, or yell at me. Maybe even kiss me again so I know if I still feel something.

He squeezes my hand. "It took a long time for you to build those walls. They're not going to come down easily, and you won't be able to do it by yourself." He stares down at our hands clasped together. "I might be biased on this one, but I don't think running to the other side of the world is the answer either. There are people here who love you, people who want to help, but maybe we're too close to help. Michael might even be too close to help."

"Where does that leave me?" I feel very alone, even with him beside me. He just confirmed that no one can help me, not even him. He must have moved on, even if I can't.

"I think your roommate is right. It's time to stop pretending everything is okay when it isn't. It's time to stop running. Maybe it's time to let the past catch up with you, so you can feel everything you've been avoiding. Let yourself hurt so you can heal."

I stare at the pool of moonlight on the floor in front of me. I look down at Jacob's hand holding mine. Finally, I look at him.

"I think you might be right."

Fifty-Five

Jacob: Moving On

November 2006

Another weekend. Another bar. I glance around and take in the scenery. Familiar. Women in tight jeans or short skirts, low-cut blouses, too much makeup, sitting in pairs or groups, drinking and looking around casually—trying to look like they aren't looking. The guys are in jeans and t-shirts, less obviously dressed to attract interest—more obviously looking, looking for their next conquest.

I guess I'm one of them now—part of the problem. The whole thing has become a game to me, a game I'm tired of.

It's almost been almost six months since Jess showed up like some kind of dream when I was sleeping in her bedroom. I thought we'd connected, that I'd helped her. I thought she'd stay home, and we'd work things out, that things would be good between us again. That I could help her get better. Even if it meant we had to start over as friends.

By the time I came back, she was gone. Her message was obvious. "I'll never get better with you around."

I decided it was time to move on.

I've done everything I can to forget her. I don't go to her house anymore or hang out with her family, not even Tyler. I spend a lot of time in places like this and with a lot of different women. I got a new car—a Dodge Charger with a custom paint job, screaming green with black stripes over the hood—almost as obnoxious and irresponsible as the car I used to drive. I avoid anything and everything that might remind me of her.

I pretend that it's working.

I scan the crowd. A redhead catches my eye—pretty face, nice body, nice smile. Her hair is short and curly. At first glance there's nothing about her that reminds me of Jess.

I buy her a drink and we talk. Her name is Angel or Angelina, something like that. She has a little turned-up nose and a sprinkling of freckles. They make her look like a teenager, but I'd guess she's at least twenty-two. She says she's a college student. That she's only here for the weekend.

I dance with a few other women, talk to some at the bar before I go back to the redhead. She's only in town for a couple of days, easier to spend tonight with her without it needing to be more.

She's friendlier, more talkative the second time I come around. She asks me a lot of questions about the Army, about my family, about Iraq. It's easy to talk to her, like she knows me already.

A slow and romantic song comes on, so I lead her to the little dance floor. I pull her close. Her lips look inviting. I make my move. Her finger on my lips stops me. "Before you do that, I think you should know who I am."

"I know who you are," I laugh, trying to sound casual. "You're Angela..." Damn, did she tell me her last name? I can't remember.

"Angelica. But I don't mean my name, Jacob. I meant who I am." She's trying to be coy or pretending to be deep. I don't know. I'll play along. "Okay. Who are you?"

"I'm Jess Roberts' roommate."

I step backward. She has to grab my elbow to keep me from tripping over the couple behind us.

"I came here with Taryn." She nods towards a table set back at the edge of the room. I barely recognize the woman sitting there. She's cut her hair, and she wears a lot more make-up, but it's definitely Taryn, one of Jess's high school friends.

I stop pretending to dance. Only one question crosses my mind: "How is she?"

"Better," Angelica answers firmly. "A lot better than she was."

"I'm glad to hear that." I am glad, but it also hurts, because it confirms what I thought before, that as long as I'm around, Jess couldn't heal.

"She's had a lot of stuff to work through, but at least she's honest about it now. She dropped a few classes, she's seeing a counselor, and she even took up yoga. She still runs a lot, eats and sleeps not very much, but she smiles more. She even laughs sometimes."

"That's good." I'm ready to end this conversation, go back to the bar and drown my feelings another way, but one more question is eating at me. "What about her boyfriend?"

"Michael? He's in Korea now, but I'm not sure you could still call him her boyfriend."

My heart gives an involuntary leap. "Why not?"

"They had a big fight before he left. When she called to tell him she wasn't moving with him. He told her she was immature and selfish, that she'd led him on and made him blow a lot of money on her. She told him he'd never taken the time to figure out who she was or what she actually wanted, that he was only interested in the person he was trying to make her into."

"You heard all of that?" I'm thinking that Jess' roommate has a big mouth for a psych major. Something I'm grateful for right now.

"Some of it I heard. They were both pretty loud. Other stuff she told me later. We've gotten close. I think her telling him off was the catalyst for her getting better. One night she was packing up everything she owned to run away with him. Two days later, she called to tell him where to get off. I don't know where she got the courage."

A grin plays around the corners of my mouth. Maybe my conversation with Jess had more of an effect than I thought.

"They kind of got over it. He apologized, and she promised to be more honest with him. But she's not. He still calls her almost every night, but a lot of times she texts him she's working late when she isn't. She doesn't act like she misses him. Not like you'd think she'd miss the guy she's engaged to."

My heart stops. "Engaged?"

"Well, engaged-to-be engaged according to him."

"But she doesn't have a ring?"

Angelica shakes her head. "No. They have a weird relationship. Michael is he's used to getting what he wants and telling other people what to do. Kind of a control freak. That doesn't work for Jess. At least, not the way it did before."

Something like hope bubbles up inside me. I work to push it aside, but despite everything, it's still there. "Has she ever said anything about me?"

"Not at first. At first, she wouldn't even tell me about Matt. She was...I don't know, shut down. Like all there was in her life was school and her work at the hospital. It took some work, but I got her to talk to me."

"But she told you about me?"

"I asked her who you were after..." she hesitates, like now she realizes she's said too much.

"After?" I prod.

"The first time I heard your name was Jess talking in her sleep."

I'm floored. "She said my name in her sleep?"

'Yeah."

We're still taking up space on the little dance floor, but I don't care about the annoyed looks we're getting from the people as they try to move around us.

"Why would she say my name?"

"I'd guess she has some unresolved issues when it comes to you." Angelica looks unsure of herself, like she said too much again. "Things she won't talk about during the day come out in her sleep. Did she always talk in her sleep?"

"I don't know." My head is swimming.

"Maybe it would help her if you two got together and talked things out. She's here now."

"Here?" I scan the room

"Sorry, not here, here. She's at home. I drove up with her from Spokane. I've never been on this side of the state. She didn't want to go out tonight, so I dragged Taryn along, but she's not much of a–"

"Jess is here," I repeat. "Do you think I should call her, or stop by?"

Angelica hesitates. "I'm not sure how she would take that. She told her little brother not to tell you she was home."

"Oh," my heart falls. She's still avoiding me.

"But in my semi-professional opinion, you should definitely see her. Whatever was between you two needs to be resolved before she can move on."

"If I can't just show up at her house, how do I see her?"

Angelica looks thoughtful. "She'll be at a wedding all day tomorrow. I could tell you where it is if you wanted to crash it."

Fifty-Six

Crashing

I sneak into the last pew in the chapel and keep my head down. I've never crashed a wedding before. I keep waiting for someone to ask me who I am and what I'm doing here, but so far no one has. Once I'm sitting down, I scan the benches ahead of me, searching for a familiar face, or at least a familiar back.

I don't see her.

She must have decided not to come, or maybe she saw me and ran. Sounds about the way my luck has gone. I get up to leave, but the music starts and I'm trapped. The tall blond groom takes his place at the front of the room with the minister. A little girl skips down the aisle, scattering flowers. A long line of bridesmaids, arm in arm with groomsmen, walk down the aisle. It looks like this is going to be a long ceremony. I wonder if I can sneak out as soon as the procession is over.

My breath catches as the last bridesmaid walks through the door. It's her. I'm immediately jealous of the guy walking her down the aisle.

At least she isn't with him. Stephens is in Korea. His turn to be in a foreign country and my turn to have her to myself.

I wish life were that fair.

I can't take my eyes off Jess. She's wearing a dress that's shiny and clingy and emphasizes her curves. The neckline reaches her throat and crosses in the back, leaving her shoulders bare. An oval cut in the back of the dress shows the delicate curve of her lower back—probably the sexiest thing I've ever seen.

The person beside me taps my shoulder, and I realize everyone is standing. The bride walks in. I don't recognize her. She's pretty enough, but completely overshadowed by the bridesmaid at the end of the long line.

I watch Jess the entire time, but she doesn't look at me once. When the ceremony is over, she keeps her eyes straight ahead as she walks out. I'm not sure if she hasn't noticed me or if she's pointedly ignoring me.

I stand around awkwardly during the cocktail hour. Jess and the rest of the wedding party are somewhere taking pictures. A few people try to make small talk with me, asking how I know the bride and groom. I answer truthfully, "I'm a friend of a friend of the bride."

"You got dragged into the plus-one thing too," a guy who looks like he's already a couple of drinks into the open bar says. "Too bad. A couple of those bridesmaids are hot. Hard to hit on someone at a wedding when you've got a date, right?"

"Right," I bristle as I think of him staring at Jess. I grab a drink for myself. I'm going to need the extra courage to get through the part where she sees me. Even if she throws me out, watching her in that dress for the whole ceremony was worth it.

Someone announces the transition to the dinner part of the evening. I follow the crowd, taking another drink with me. As soon as I see the dining room, I know I'm in trouble. There's a map by the door and little silver frames at each place setting to show who's supposed to sit there.

"Can I help you find your seat?" The woman standing at the door with a clipboard must be the table guard. She's smiling, short with fluffy white hair, but the set of her jaw reminds me of my first drill sergeant. I scan the map, seriously considering using someone else's name, whoever they put next to Jess, but I can't find her card. Everyone behind me is waiting. My tie feels too tight, and I'm sweating under my suit.

I clear my throat. "I don't—"

"He's with me," her voice comes from behind me. "My plus one."

I turn to face Jess. She shakes her head, but she looks more amused than annoyed that I'm here.

"And you are?"

"Jess Roberts." She steps next to me.

The woman consults her notes. "I don't see that your RSVP came with a plus one."

"I'm sorry. I didn't know he was going to be here until just now." She gives me a meaningful look before studying the table map. "Can he take Kendra's place? She wasn't able to come."

The table guard looks annoyed at the breach of protocol, but she nods.

"Thank you." Jess hooks her arm through mine and leads me to one of the head tables. On the way there she whispers, "Are you so desperate for a good meal that you've resorted to wedding crashing?"

"Something like that." We stop at the table, and I pull out her chair so she can sit down. We're the first ones here, so I ask, "Who's wedding is this anyway?"

"One of my first college roommates," Jess says. She nods to the couple walking in as the crowd breaks into thunderous applause. "Nikki."

"She's pretty," I say, but I'm looking at Jess. "And you look amazing."

"Thanks," she says. "Nikki was always good at picking out things for me to wear."

"I'll have to send her a thank-you note. That dress," I pause so she can see how much I like it on her. "It's probably the most beautiful bridesmaid's dress I've ever seen."

"I'll tell her you said that." Jess narrows her eyes at me, but she seems more curious than hostile. "Why are you really here? How did you even know about this wedding or that I was home?"

"I ran into Taryn and your current roommate yesterday. She told me you'd be here."

"Angelica," Jess rolls her eyes. "She can't seem to stop analyzing me, telling me what's good for me, getting into my business."

"She seemed nice and genuinely concerned about you." I'm not sure why I'm defending the little redhead, except she made it possible for me to see Jess.

"I think I'm her senior project," Jess replies.

I look at her gently, afraid to upset the delicate balance we've started here. "Maybe it's working. You look better."

"I feel better. "She got me into yoga and meditation." She looks down. "And counseling."

I put my hand over hers. "There's nothing wrong with that. I've been going to counseling since I got home from Iraq."

"So, you'll come to yoga class with me? I'm getting certified to teach."

I imagine her balancing in an impossible pose, wearing yoga pants and some kind of cropped top. "Name the time and place."

She laughs. "Good to see you have an open mind about these things." She takes a long drink of ice water and then gets serious. "How are you doing?"

"Better now." It's the truth. I'm much better now that I'm sitting next to her.

She looks at me for a few seconds. "You look good. No dress uniform?"

"I didn't want to stand out," I answer.

She doesn't respond to that. Other people join us at the table, and the buffet opens. We get food, and Jess chats with the people at our table. From what I can tell, she knows some of them from college. I talk too, but more than anything I watch her. She laughs more easily, but there's still something reserved about her. She's quieter and somehow more delicate.

We sit through the toasts and the couple's first dance. Then the dance floor opens up to everyone. My chance to get Jess alone again. My chance to hold her in my arms.

I feel like I'm in middle school again, asking a girl to dance for the first time. My heart pounds so loud that I'm sure she can hear it, but somehow I get the words out, "Would you like to dance?"

She hesitates for a minute and then nods.

I don't think we've ever danced before, but it feels natural to lead her onto the dance floor. I want to wrap my arms around her and pull her hard against my chest. Instead, I take her right hand. She puts her hand on my shoulder. There's only one place to put my other hand. I touch the curve of her back, hesitant at first, expecting her to pull away. She steps closer, leaning in. My hand rests on her soft skin. I can feel the curve of her spine, the muscles in her back, the muscles at the side of her waist. She feels smaller, slimmer than I remember. I pull her closer, wanting to protect her.

She turns her head, and light dances from her ears. I recognize the earrings I gave her for Christmas when I was in Iraq.

"These are beautiful." I tuck a piece of hair back behind her ear. She blushes and touches the earrings. "I'm sorry. You can have them back. I always meant to return them."

"Please don't. I like them where they are." I run my fingers down her arm and put that hand beside my other hand, on her bare back. She has nothing to do with the hand I was holding but set it on my other shoulder. Easier to get close. I take a chance and step in. She doesn't pull away.

I lean my cheek against her head, close my eyes and drink in the scent of her hair and the smell of her skin. I can imagine that we're back together. That I came home to a much warmer welcome. That I bought a diamond for her finger instead of for her ears. This could be our wedding. When this is over, I'll take her away to some beautiful place. She'll be mine.

"...North Carolina?" she says. For one horrible second, I think she can read my mind, or that I accidentally said something out loud.

I look down at her. "What did you say?" She's looking up at me through her eyelashes. That used to, correction, still does, make me crazy.

"Are you going home for Christmas?"

"No. My parents are going to Mexico. I'm going to hang out with Becky and Bryan." No reason to tell her that after the disaster that was last Christmas, none of us wanted to do the traditional family thing again.

"That sounds fun. I miss having little kids around for Christmas," she says.

I want to ask her what she's doing for Christmas, if she'll be home, if she'd mind if I stopped by. I'm afraid to. It would be just like Stephens to fly her to Korea to spend Christmas with him. The song is ending. I can't let her go. "One more?" *Please.*

"Okay."

Is it my imagination or is she pulling herself tighter against my chest?

"Mom told me you've been helping Tyler. How's the car coming?"

"I haven't been over for a while. Tyler won't be driving again for a long time."

"I guess not." She looks down. "I'm sorry for the things I said. For everything that happened. I was scared and upset. It wasn't your fault."

She admits that one brother wasn't my fault. What about the other one? And when she says she's sorry for *everything,* how far back does that go? Does she mean for yelling at me, kissing me, or pushing me away?

"We appreciate what you've done for Tyler. He needs someone like you now." She looks into my eyes. "I heard what you said to him after he destroyed your car. You had every right to rip him to pieces, but you didn't. You said exactly the right thing. I was jealous."

"Jealous? Of me?"

"You're so much better with him than I am. I wish I could be what he needs." She looks down. "I wish I could be what anyone needs."

I rub my thumbs across her back, wishing I had the courage to tell her she's exactly what I need.

"That tickles," she pulls away, but she's smiling.

"Sorry, I know how you hate to be tickled," I grin back. It's good to see her smile like that. "You're beautiful, you know that."

She looks like the old Jess. She's trying to look serious, but a smirk is playing around the corners of her mouth. "Well, which is it?"

"Which is what?" I'm confused.

"First you said I was amazing, now you say I'm beautiful."

"I said you look amazing, and that you are beautiful."

"So I'm not amazing, just beautiful?" She turns her mouth down into a pretty pout. I want to kiss her. I wonder what she would do if I did. Will I ever get to kiss those lips again?

"You're beautiful and amazing. In fact, you might be the most amazing woman I've ever known."

"Thank you." The playfulness is gone. Maybe she thinks she took it too far. Her voice is shaky when she speaks again. "And thank you for what you said that night when I came home so completely messed up. You didn't push or judge me. You were just there." She swallows. "You gave me the courage to do something I'd needed to do for a long time, and the courage to ask for help."

I stare down at her. "I'm glad I was there."

She looks away and shakes her head. "You're always there. Somehow you show up exactly when I need you." She closes her eyes and leans her cheek against my shoulder. "Thank you," she whispers.

She doesn't say anything else. I'm too afraid to talk and break whatever spell we're both under. With every heartbeat, I want her to be mine again. I want to kiss her, but I'm afraid it would be too much, too soon.

The music moves to something upbeat. She pulls away. I try to hold on to her, but she slips out of my grasp.

"I'm sorry, Jacob, I have to leave early. My ride's here."

For a horrible second, I expect to see Michael in the doorway, waiting to claim her again. It's Angelica, the roommate I met two nights ago.

I grab Jess' hand, afraid to let her go. "I'll take you home, Jess."

She shakes her head and smiles. "I'm not going home. I'm going back to school. I have class tomorrow." She walks away.

I'm cursing myself. I had a full dinner and two dances. I should have said more. I should have figured out a way to tell her I still love her.

She comes back. Her dress traded for a pair of jeans and a jacket; a long dress bag over her arm. She hands the bag to Angelica and crosses the room to the bride and groom. I follow her, like I was really her plus one and not just a wedding crasher.

"Everything is beautiful. Congratulations Nikki." Jess hugs the bride.

"Thanks." Nikki hugs her back and then looks around. "Kendra?"

Jess' face darkens. "She was going to come but..."

"I get it," Nikki nods sadly. "Thanks for coming. It's so good to see you. I'm sorry you have to go early."

"Me too," Jess says, "school and work. That's my life right now."

Nikki shakes her head. "You were always the responsible one."

I'm standing off to the side, trying to look like I belong with her. Nikki turns and reaches her hand to me. "It's good to finally meet you, Jacob."

I look at her in shock. "You know who I am?"

"How could I not?" She nods toward Jess. "She had a full-on shrine to you in her bedroom our first semester of college. You were literally all she talked about."

Jess is blushing and looking at Nikki like she wants her to shut up. Personally, I'd like to hear more.

"Shrine?" I ask.

"Complete with lit incense and bowls of fruit," Nikki sounds so serious, for a second I believe her. Her eyes dance mischievously. "Okay, maybe not that bad, but she was a bit obsessed. It's good to see you two have worked things out."

I wait for Jess to contradict her, but she glances at her watch and says, "I'm so sorry. I need to get going."

Nikki hugs her again and then hugs me. I shake the groom's hand and follow Jess to the door.

When she reaches the parking lot, she stops in front of my new car. "This has to be yours."

I put my hand on the hood of the Charger. "How did you guess?"

She shakes her head. "It wasn't hard. Only, I thought you might have wanted something less conspicuous."

I shrug. "You know me."

"Yeah, I do." She runs her fingers along the side of my car. "I take it Tyler doesn't get to drive this one."

I lean against the car next to her. "Not a chance."

She looks up at me through her eyelashes. "Would you let me drive it?"

My heart beats faster. "Maybe. You didn't wreck the last one."

Angelica is keeping her distance, purposely giving us our privacy. I appreciate that.

"Would you like to try it now?" I ask.

She steps back from my car, like she said too much again. "I can't. It's getting late. I need to get on the road."

I touch her shoulder. "Jess, I—" I'm not sure how to complete that sentence. I can't just blurt out *I still love you.*

She looks up at me with a stern expression. "No more crashing stranger's weddings. The next time you need a good meal. I'm sure my mom would be happy to feed you."

I take a chance and push my luck. "What about you?"

She gives me a coy smile and bites her bottom lip. "Five hours is a long drive for breakfast "

My heart thuds against my chest. Before I can think of anything to say, she wraps her arms around me and kisses me on the cheek. "It was good to see you, Jacob. Take care of yourself."

"You too." I'm desperate to stop her, to say more, but I don't know what.

She stops with her hand on her car door. "My parents rented a condo for New Years weekend. We're going skiing." I stare at her, not sure if that's a statement or an invitation. "You'd have to share a room with Tyler, but if you want to come," she looks down, unsure, "I'm sure they wouldn't mind."

I stare at her for a long moment, trying to grasp what she just said. "You're inviting me to go skiing with you?"

"With my family, but yeah. I'll be there." Then she's talking fast, like she's embarrassed. "I understand if you're busy or if you can't get the time off. I just thought you might like to—"

"I'll be there."

Fifty-Seven

Remembering

December 2006

D oes Jess always ski like this?" I watch her head down the hill as fast and reckless as she made the last two runs.

Tyler shakes his head. "You know Jess. She isn't afraid, and she's always been aggressive, but today she's skiing like she has a death wish."

I agree. Even though she invited me here, she's shutting me out again. Her headphones are on, and she's barely talking. She acts as if she's alone, and she's skiing like something's chasing her.

"I wanted to go to the terrain park, but now I don't think we should leave her. Someone has to be around to call the ski patrol when she breaks her neck," Tyler says.

"You go ahead. I'll stay with her," I say. Maybe I can get her to open up if it's just us.

He hesitates only for a second. "Okay. I'll head that way after this run."

Jess doesn't even look at me when we get on the ski lift. She leans back and closes her eyes. Mouthing the words to whatever song she's listening to. I put my arm over the back of the ski lift. I wish I could put it around her shoulders, pull her close. Ask her what the deal is. Do something to help.

She's barely paying attention when we reach the top of the mountain. Maybe that's why when she stands up she steps on my board. She starts to wobble so I grab her around the waist and pull her against me. We're skiing and boarding at the same time. We twist, lean in together, and make it just clear of the lift exit point before we fall. Jess ends up on my lap, her legs twisted around mine.

"Are you okay?" I'm trying to extricate her equipment and her body from mine.

Tyler's kneeling in the snow, laughing hard.

"What's so funny?" Jess demands.

"You two," he gasps, holding his sides. "You couldn't do that trick again if you tried."

I look down at the mess of legs and equipment and start laughing too. Jess looks at me indignantly for a second and then laughs too. Now we're laughing too hard to get untangled. Jess leans against my chest, laughing so hard she's almost crying. "Ow," she says between gasps, "this hurts."

I reach down and pop one of her skis off. She falls. Now she's lying on top of me, her head on my chest. She's still laughing too hard to move. I wrap my arms around her and pop off the other ski.

"Okay now?" I ask as she pulls away and tries to get up.

"Better," she answers.

"Anything broken, bruised or crushed?"

She tests her arms and legs, like she's not sure. "Just my pride. I don't remember the last time I fell getting off the lift."

"Me either," I say.

"You guys looked like such idiots," Tyler says.

Jess picks up a piece of snow and throws it at him. He catches it and lobs it back. I reach up and bat it away before it hits her.

"You ready to ski this?" I latch my foot into my bindings.

"Ready to kick your butts," she laughs. "Anytime." She steps into her skis and starts down the hill while Ty and I are still getting our boards on.

She's waiting for me by the lift when I reach the bottom. She's leaning against the fence looking smug. "Told you I'd kick your butt."

"You cheated. You shoved me down at the top and then took off before I had the chance to put my board on."

"It was you, knuckle-dragger, who got your board caught under my skis." I love to see her smile when she says that. She looks like the old Jess.

"Yeah, whatever," I say.

"So what happened to Ty?"

"He headed to the terrain park." I wonder how she's going to feel about skiing with just me.

"You can go with him. I don't mind skiing alone."

"I'll stick with you for a while if you don't mind. I'm a little old for the terrain park." I follow as she slides into the back of the line.

"You're not that old. You're just worried that I'm going to kill myself or someone else."

"The thought occurred to me. You're a maniac on skis."

She shakes her head, but doesn't answer. When we get on the lift, I sit near the middle, close to her. I'm waiting for her to turn her music back on, but she doesn't. She leans back and looks away from me.

A shadow moves across her face. I stretch my arm over the back of the chair and touch her shoulder. "You want to talk about it?"

She shakes her head and closes her eyes. "It's hard to be here. We spent a lot of time on this hill when we were kids. There are just a lot of reminders." I slide closer and put my arm around her shoulders. She doesn't say anything else, but she doesn't move away either.

When we get to the top, she says. "There's somewhere I need to go. I'll see you at the bottom."

"I'm going with you."

She shakes her head and takes off her skis. I plant my board and follow her as she hikes up the mountain. She doesn't stop me.

I don't ask her where she's going, even when she ducks under the out-of-bounds tape and goes into the woods. I catch up with her just as she reaches a little clearing. There are trees on one side and a breathtaking view of the mountains on the other. I don't know what significance this place has for her. She's struggling not to show how much she's hurting.

She takes her helmet and her goggles off. "I almost expected it to be the same."

I don't answer. I don't think she's talking to me.

She walks over to a tree and kneels down and drags her hand through the snow. She doesn't move or speak for a long time.

I take a chance and get closer. I put a hand on her shoulder. "What is this place?"

She looks up like she just realized I followed her. "This is where Matt proposed to Kendra. For some reason, I thought it would be the same." She closes her eyes and leans against the tree. "I keep looking for Matt. I keep thinking he's got to be here somewhere."

I kneel next to her in the snow. "Tell me about that day."

She's quiet for a minute and then nods. "They made a table and chairs. And there were candles, and lights in the trees and champagne, and—" she stops, stands up, and crosses the clearing. A wreath decorated with white roses hangs in the lower branches of a tall pine.

She touches the wreath reverently.

I put my hand on her shoulder. "Did you bring this here?"

She shakes her head. "I don't know where it came from."

"Maybe your mom brought it up, or Tyler?"

"They don't know about this place. It was just Kendra and Matt and me and... Michael," she turns away from me when she says his name. "They were so happy. Matt had so much ahead of him. How could it all just be over? How can he just be gone?" She stands up. "I shouldn't have come here."

I take my glove off and put my hand against her cheek. "It's okay to remember, Jess, even if it hurts."

She takes a shaky breath. "That's what my counselor keeps telling me, but I kept everything buried for so long, I'm not sure I know how to feel," she pauses and looks directly in my eyes, "about anything."

Fifty-Eight

Below Zero

I can't sleep. I haven't snowboarded in a long time, so I'm tired and sore, but my mind won't turn off. I keep replaying moments from today—times when Jess let her guard down and let me inside the barrier. Like when I put my arm over the back of the lift and she didn't move away or when I touched her face in the little grove. It doesn't help that I'm acutely aware of her presence in the room next to mine. I saw when her door was open that our beds are on opposite sides of the same wall. There are only a few inches separating us. I touch the wall and think about her lying next to me. No wall between us.

I'm going crazy.

I sit up and slide out of the bed, trying not to wake Tyler up, but I do. He rolls over. "What are you doing, Jake?"

"I can't sleep. I'm going for a walk."

"You're nuts. It's freezing out there." He wraps his blanket around himself to prove his point.

I don't have a response for that, so I just fumble around in the dark for my boots and a shirt, and then open the door to the hallway. A little blue night-light gives enough light to get my bearings. I pause at Jess' door, listening. I can't even hear her breathing.

I sneak my jacket out of the closet and open the door as quietly as possible. A blast of frigid air hits me, almost making me change my mind. Instead, I zip my coat up to my chin and go out. The moon reflecting off the snow makes it almost as bright as daylight.

I'm walking fast to stay warm and thinking faster, thinking about Jess. Wondering where we are now. Friends? Can we be more? If I try to push it, what's going to happen? Would she welcome me, or would she push me away like before? And what's the story with Stephens? Is she done with him, or on some kind of break?

A voice from somewhere above me interrupts my thoughts. "You lost, soldier?"

I look up. Jess is leaning on the balcony of our condo. I was so absorbed in my thoughts that I didn't realize I had circled back behind it.

"What are you doing up?" I call back.

"What am I doing up? What are you doing walking around in the middle of the night? Sneaking back from some girls' condo?" She's too far away to read her expression. I don't know if she's teasing me or if she really thinks that's where I've been.

I hold up my hand. "No, nothing like that. I couldn't sleep."

"So you decided to go for a below zero stroll?"

"Yeah. What about you?"

"I couldn't sleep either." Her hair falls loosely over the balcony, and her face glows in the moonlight like some haunting ghost of girlfriends past.

"You want to come out for a walk?" I ask.

She pulls a blanket around her shoulders. "No way. It's freezing out there."

"Can I come up?"

She shrugs. "Sure."

I want to race up the stairs, but I remember in time that everyone else is sleeping. I open the sliding door quietly and walk out. She's sitting on a chair with a blanket wrapped around her, looking at the mountains across the road. "It's beautiful, isn't it?"

"Yeah." I answer, but I'm not looking at the mountains. I sit on the chair next to her, lean over and blow on my hands to warm them up. I forgot to grab gloves.

She turns. "You look cold."

"I am actually." I look at her blanket. "Will you share?"

She nods. I pull my chair over, but the blanket isn't long enough to cover both chairs. She slides to the very edge of her chair. The seat is wide, but still not big enough for two. I can only sit next to her on the chair if we both sit sideways with our butts hanging off the side—not very comfortable. Finally, I pick her up and set her on my lap. I brace for her reaction. She tucks the blanket around both of us. "Better?"

I wrap my arms around her waist. "Much."

She leans back, looking at the mountains again. "It's so peaceful here. I'm glad I came. Things are so crazy with school and work at the hospital. I guess I needed the time off."

"What are you doing in your nursing courses?" I want to keep her talking—keep her with me as long as possible.

"Different rotations. Right now we're doing peds—the pediatric wing. I love it. The kids are great. I think that might be what I want to do when I graduate—work in a pediatric hospital."

"You'd be good at it."

"Kids are easier than adults sometimes. But also harder. It breaks my heart to see them sick or hurt."

"Kids are great." I'm looking for a way to score points on the kid thing. "I've been hanging out with Little Stevie once a week so Jasmine can take a couple of classes."

Jess shakes her head, and her hair brushes against my cheek. "How are Jasmine and Stevie? He's almost one, right?"

"Ten months, and a terror, like his dad. Jasmine is talking about going to stay with Mom and Steve so she can get back to college full time."

"It must be nice to have Little Steve around. Like Gage isn't so far away."

"Yeah. Jasmine is part of our family now, too, kind of the sister we never had. They could never take Gage's place, but it helps fill the hole." I don't mention the other gaping hole, the one that Nathan left.

She leans against me and closes her eyes. I'm wondering if she's fallen asleep when she lifts her head up and looks at the stars. "Do you think that they're still out there? Matt and Gage, do you think they still exist somewhere?"

I take a second to think. It's a deep question, one I've thought about myself. "I can't imagine Gage just fading away. There was too much life in him. Matt too." I think for a minute, trying to choose my words carefully. "I've seen some terrible things—people who lost their families, their homes, everything. But in Iraq, more than at any other time in my life, I knew, there has to be something more than this. Look at the mountains, and the snow, and everything around you. That all didn't just happen. Someone is out there making sure it's all taken care of. I think He's taking care of our brothers too. I don't believe they're gone forever."

"I used to believe that," Jess says softly. "Now I'm not sure."

I pull her against me. "Jess, I..."

She pulls away and stands up. "It's really late. We should go to bed."
She sets the blanket on my lap and turns to go inside.

I sit for a minute more after I watch her go. I wonder what I said
that scared her away this time.

Fifty-Nine

Breakfast

I wake up to Tyler shaking my shoulder. "Get up!"

"No way, kid," I pull the covers around me. I rarely call Tyler 'kid' anymore, only when he irritates me.

"Oh c'mon old man." Tyler is pulling the blankets off. I pull back. When did that kid get so strong?

"Sorry, I'm sleeping in today. I'm going for the half-day only. I was up late last night."

"Yeah, no kidding, what time did you finally get to bed?

"It was something like two o'clock."

"What were you and Jess doing so late, anyway?"

How did he know I was with Jess?

Tyler is sitting on the edge of his bed. "Never mind, I don't want to know. She is my sister."

"Talking, we were just talking."

"Sure, whatever." He doesn't sound convinced. "Come on, you're awake now, you might as well get going."

"Nope, call me in a couple of hours."

"Hey Tyler," Mr. Roberts calls from the hall. "Everyone else wants to sleep in. Why don't you and I go get a few runs in, just the two of us?"

I can't see his face, but I can imagine Tyler rolling his eyes when he calls back, "Sure, Dad." To me, his whispers, "Thanks a lot."

"No problem," I reach down and grab the covers and wrap them around me. Mr. Roberts confirmed what I already suspected. Jess is still asleep in the next room.

After Tyler leaves, I run my fingers over the wall that separates us; six inches of two by fours, plaster and drywall. Six inches I would gladly remove with my bare hands if I thought the reception on the other side would be a good one. Last night was a good night. Even if all we did was talk. Friends again, at least. I'm almost ready to hope we can be something more. If I could just figure out how not to spook her.

I close my eyes and think of Jess; how good it felt to hold her last night. The smell of her hair. The softness of her body. The sound of her voice.

A knock on the door brings me out of a deep sleep. My dreams and reality merge as her voice comes from the other side of the door.

"Jacob, are you decent? Can I come in?"

"Just a minute," I call back.

I look around the room. It looks and smells like two guys have been sleeping here. I have a sudden urge to clean things up. Make it look okay for her. I pull on a shirt and stumble around, moving Tyler's smelly socks and my coat out of the way. I stub my toe on the edge of Tyler's bed and catch myself mid-curse.

She's laughing. "What are you doing in there? C'mon. Let me in. I brought breakfast. It's going to get cold."

I can smell bacon, eggs, and something sweet. I imagine her outside the door, in her pajamas, waiting. Breakfast in bed, won in a card game ages ago. I didn't think I'd ever be able to collect on that bet.

I open the door. She's already dressed. Her hair is pulled back in a ponytail and she's holding a tray. "It's about time." She walks past me. "This is heavy."

She looks around for a place to set the tray. It's a small room and cluttered with Tyler's stuff. There isn't anywhere to put it. "Back in bed," she orders.

I obediently climb into the bed. She tries to set the tray over my legs, but the sides aren't long enough. She takes the tray away, kicks aside a pair of Tyler's pants and sets it on the floor. She puts a napkin on my lap and then puts the plate on top of it.

"Can you reach this?" She points to the the tray on the floor.

"I'll manage." That was the wrong thing to say. She heads for the door.

"You want to share?" I pat the side of the bed. "There's plenty here. Three stuffed crepes, bacon, scrambled eggs, milk and juice. I could down it by myself, but I don't want her to leave.

She hesitates. "I already ate."

"C'mon Jess. You're in for an athletic day. You need a hearty breakfast."

"Okay." She sits beside me on the bed.

I cut a piece of the crepe and offer it to her. She shakes her head. Halfway to my mouth, a strawberry slice falls out and slides down my chest and into my lap.

She laughs. "You need help with that." She tucks another napkin into my T-shirt and then takes my fork away. She cuts a piece of the crepe and feeds it to me. "Is that better?"

"I'm pretty sure I can feed myself," I say, but I don't take the fork back. There's something incredibly sexy about her sitting on the edge of my bed, feeding me breakfast.

"Shhh, just eat." She shovels another bite into my mouth.

"You have a bite too." I reach for the fork to feed her. She holds it out of my reach and then cuts another piece. She leans over the plate and slides it into her mouth. A bit of whipped cream gets on the edge of her lips. She licks it off.

She feeds me another bite. "I'm getting good at this."

"At feeding me?"

"Feeding people in general. There's a little boy at the hospital. He's six. He broke both arms in a car accident. He always wants me to feed him." She forks a piece of egg and puts it in her own mouth. "He has deep brown eyes like yours and freckles like..." She stops. I know who she's thinking about. If I remember right, Michael Stephens has a face full of them.

"I was worried about leaving him," she continues. "He doesn't eat very well unless I'm around to feed him."

"Where are his parents?" I ask.

Her face goes dark. "His dad comes as much as he can. His mom didn't survive the accident."

"Oh, I'm sorry."

She puts the fork down. "I've been thinking about what you said last night. It reminded me of that little boy. He asked me if I knew where his mommy was now, but I couldn't answer him. He told me later he'd figured it out. He said that his mom was still around, but he couldn't see her, because she was an angel. He said she had to be there because moms don't leave their kids alone when they're only six."

"I think he's right," I say. "And I think if we ever really need them, Gage and Matt will be around too."

She nods and twists the corner of my blanket. "I've learned a lot from those kids. They do more for me than I do for them. Helping them keeps me from getting so caught up in my own problems."

I nod at her. "It was like that in..." Do I dare say it? "In Iraq. Not all the time. But we got the chance to do some humanitarian stuff. That helped a lot. Made me feel like we were doing some good. I mean, I know we were, but it helped to be one on one. Helping people up close."

"I'm glad you got the chance to do that." She smiles, but she doesn't pick up the fork.

I continue eating, feeding myself and watching her. She looks far away. I wish I knew what she was thinking.

She shakes her head as if to clear it. She leans down and retrieves a glass of apple juice and offers it to me. I take a drink and hand it back. I'm trying to think of something to say to her. I want to put my arm around her, pull her close and offer her some comfort. I'd probably scare her away again.

Mrs. Roberts appears in the doorway. "I'm glad you two are up—well, sort of. I just heard from the guys on the radio. Tyler ran into some of his friends, so he's having lunch and then boarding with them. I'm going to ski with Dad as soon as he gets back. I guess the two of you are stuck with each other for the day."

Jess sticks her finger in the whipped cream and dabs it on my nose. "I think we can handle that."

Sixty

Letting Go

I can't remember a better day of snowboarding. The weather totally sucks—cold and windy, near whiteout conditions at the top.
The snow is icy with just a little powder. I barely notice any of it.

I have Jess.

It's like we erased the last year and we're back, not together exactly,
but back to being comfortable, back to being friends. I love watching
her laugh. I love pulling her close on the lift and keeping her warm.

The weather clears with just a few runs left. We run into Tyler and
a bunch of his friends at the terrain park. They're practicing jumps,
sliding the rails and doing all sorts of crazy stunts. I try, but no way I
can keep up. I'm too out of practice.

Jess tries a few jumps too, but eventually she just sits in the snow
and watches. I sit down beside her and watch too.

Tyler slides over beside us. "Did you see that?" he asks. We make the
appropriate appreciative comments. "I'm pretty good, but you should

have seen Michael. He was incredible." My stomach twists when Tyler says his name. "He did this backflip and these jumps. He plops down in the snow. "Right Jess?"

"Yeah, he was great," Jess says. She stands up. "I want to get a couple more runs in. You can stay here if you want, Jacob."

"No, I'll come," I stand up beside her.

"I'm coming too," Tyler says. "I want to get a couple more runs in too." He yells to his friends and follows us down the mountain.

Jess is skiing too fast. She launches off the lip of a cat track, catches an edge when she lands, and crashes hard. Her skis fly in different directions. She rolls and then slides for a couple of hundred yards before she stops. Tyler goes for one of her skis. I grab the other on the way down to her.

"Are you okay?" I kneel beside her in the snow.

"Fine," she answers. Her hair and face are covered in snow.

"Are you sure?" I brush the snow out of her hair.

"Man, Jess, that was really stupid." Tyler hands her the other ski.

"Thanks," she says.

I reach for her hand. "Can I help you up?"

"I got it." She stands slowly.

We clean the snow out of her bindings. She leans on me and stomps into her ski, but it doesn't stay. She tries a couple more times. I kneel down and look at the binding.

"I think it's messed up," I say.

She shakes her head. "Old skis."

Tyler kneels beside me. "You should have let Michael buy you those expensive skis for Christmas like he wanted."

She kneels down and examines the binding. "There are a lot of things that Michael wanted to give me, that I didn't want."

I'm surprised at the bitterness in her voice, but I can't help but be happy about it. "I'll carry your skis down."

"You don't have to do that. It's only a little way from here to the bottom. I can make it that far on one ski. I don't want to mess up the rest of your day. I'll see you at the condo."

"I'll follow you down," I say.

"I'm fine." I want to argue with her, but the tone in her voice and the look on her face make me think she wants to be left alone.

I watch her start down the hill and then follow Tyler.

I bomb the next two runs; I want to get back to Jess and make sure she's really okay. On the way back to the condo, Tyler tells me about a party that his friends are having tonight. I nearly forgot it was New Years Eve.

"You're invited, but I don't want Jess to come. Too much like having Mom there," he says.

I start to answer, but the voice coming through the door of the condo stops me. Tyler opens the door and we step inside.

"...with some other guy," Jess is saying.

"She has the right to get on with her life," Mrs. Roberts' answers. "It's been over a year."

"Not here, Mom, she can't bring him here," Jess bites back. "And a year isn't that long. I thought she loved Matt."

"Hon, the amount of time you spend grieving doesn't have anything to do with how much you loved someone."

"Don't try to defend her."

Mrs. Roberts sighs. "Matt wouldn't want Kendra to stop living."

"Don't tell me what Matt would want. Matt wanted to marry Kendra. He wanted to live, but he can't want anything anymore. He's dead."

"Jess," Mrs. Roberts says.

There's no answer but footsteps on the stairs and a door slamming shut.

I wait in the doorway, but Tyler walks inside to his mom. He folds her in his arms. "Kendra?" he asks.

Mrs. Roberts nods. "Jess ran into Kendra and her new boyfriend. I knew they were here. I saw them yesterday, but I didn't tell Jess. I didn't think she would take it well." She pulls away from Tyler and sinks into a chair. "What are we going to do with her?"

Sixty-One

Whatever it Takes

C hopping wood should be a good way to get rid of my frustrations. I chop enough for the next four people who rent this condo. It doesn't help. I can't decide whether I'm mad at Kendra or Jess, or just fed up. I want to shake Jess, and tell her to snap out of this, but I know that won't work.

Things were going so well.

I carry a load of wood inside to start a fire. Earlier, I was thinking about doing the whole bit—dinner, candles, cozy fire, our own little celebration. Now I'm not sure how she'd take it.

We're alone. Her parents went to have dinner and play games with friends in another condo. Tyler headed off to the party he told me about. I told him I wasn't interested.

The wood is damp, so I'm having a hard time getting the fire going. I swear and throw down my gloves in frustration.

"Dad uses this when the wood's too wet." I turn around, startled. Jess kneels on the floor beside me and hands me a bottle of lighter fluid.

"Thanks."

She isn't exactly smiling, but she doesn't look as mad as she did before. "If you get the fire going, I'll bring us something to eat."

I take a chance and tease her. "You're going to cook?"

She smiles back faintly. "I think I'll just reheat. There are a lot of leftovers."

"Sounds good." Maybe tonight won't be a total bust after all.

The fire is taking off when she comes back carrying two plates. It's a sampling of the food we've been eating for the past couple of days. I'm starving, so I eat fast. She picks at her plate, takes a couple of bites, and sets it aside. She leans back and closes her eyes.

I watch her for a second. "Not hungry?" She shakes her head. "Tired." She shakes it again.

I set my plate down and reach for her hand. She doesn't open her eyes, but she doesn't pull away either.

"When am I going to be normal?" she asks. "Like today. I was doing fine. I let myself think about things without the hurt, remembered some good things. Seeing Kendra...with someone else... here. I can't handle that. I know it's not fair. She has the right to get on with her life. We all have the right to get on with our lives. Only I can't. I'm stuck, like it happened yesterday."

She's talking. This is what I wanted, I guess. It scares me. I don't know what to say; how to ease her pain, or how to help her anger. I try to remember some of my post-combat counseling, take a breath and try my best. "Things will never be normal again. Not the way it was before. You're living with a gaping hole. We all are. Normal doesn't exist. Sometimes it's just survival, but we can't stop living."

"How are you surviving? Your hole is at least as big as mine. You were in combat and saw horrible things. You lost other friends. You lost your brother too. But you keep going. How?"

I lean back against the couch and think. "I guess the thing about being at war, or being in any intense situation like that, is that life takes on a different meaning. You understand how fragile it is, how short. It leaves you with a better idea of what you stand to lose if you wait too long to live your life."

She stares into the fire. The light picks up the gold flecks in her eyes. "And what if you're so afraid of what you might lose that you can't start living, or keep living, or do anything at all?"

I move closer to her on the couch. "What are you so afraid of losing, Jess?"

Her eyes meet mine. "You."

The air is sucked from my lungs. "Me?"

"I know it doesn't make any sense. But I've thought about it a lot. I was so afraid of losing you after Matt died that I did everything I could to push you away, to make you hate me. If I lost you that way, at least then it was on my terms, at least I felt like I was in control." She pulls her hand away. "Do you know what I felt when my dad told me that Matt was gone?"

"I can imagine."

"No. You can't, because what I felt was relief." She bows her head. "Because it wasn't you. What kind of sister is grateful that her brother is dead because it wasn't her boyfriend? And when I saw how much Kendra had lost, and then Jasmine, I was glad it wasn't me, but I knew how easily it could have been. You told me you would have taken Matt's place, and I know you would have. That just made it worse. I wouldn't have let you take his place. Seeing Kendra today brought it all back. She's happy, she's moving on, and so much of my guilt is because of her." She's curled in on herself on the other side of the couch. Her arms are wrapped around her shoulders and she's rubbing them, even though the fire is blazing and the room is hot.

My mind searches for something, anything that I can tell her that might make this better. "I think you're feeling a kind of survivor's guilt. We talked about that in post-combat counseling. *Why did I live when someone else died?* You can't change what you feel. In Mosul, some guy dies who has a wife and four kids, and I'm happy it wasn't me. I'm happy I get to come home. I get to be with you. And I feel guilty as hell."

She looks up at me. "But it wasn't your fault. You're not the one who chooses who lives and who dies."

"But you do?"

She looks down again. "It's not the same. Matt was my brother."

"And you didn't choose for him to die. And there's no way of knowing what choice you would have made if it were up to you. We don't know why Matt and Gage didn't come home, and I did. You loved Matt. I loved Gage. It doesn't mean I should stop living out of guilt that my brother is dead, that he has a kid who will never know him. Pain happens, loss happens, but so do a lot of good things." I put my hand under her chin and lift her face to mine. "Maybe being happy it wasn't me was your brain's way of coping with it—finding something positive in a horrible situation. It doesn't mean you didn't love Matt. It doesn't mean you don't miss him."

She doesn't look away. "All this time I've been horrible to you. Everything I said. All the stupid reasons I came up with to hate you, so I could justify pushing you away. And what happened with Michael." Her eyes close in shame. "I'm sorry, Jacob. I know it's not fair for me to ask you to forgive or forget, or... but I'm so sorry for everything I did to you."

I put my hands on her shoulders. "We all do stupid things when we're hurting and afraid. We can get past this."

"What if I'm still afraid?"

I look into her eyes. "Then you can be afraid with me." I'm reminding her of a pact we made when she was a little kid and she confessed to being afraid of the ski lift—a pact that she reversed when I told her I was afraid to go to Iraq.

For the first time, I see something like hope in her eyes. "You'll forgive me?"

I move closer. "Yes. I can't guarantee things will go back to the way they were, or that you won't get hurt again. Life is unpredictable and hard, but I know it's better when we're together. I'll do whatever it takes to hold on to you, if you'll let me." I wrap my arms around her and say the words I've been holding in for too long. "I still love you."

She buries her head in my chest. "I'm sorry, Jacob. I'm so sorry." She's sobbing now. Her tears are making my T-shirt wet. I pull her onto my lap and cradle her in my arms. "It's okay, it's okay, it's okay," I say over and over again, feeling that somehow, now it is.

I'm crying too. Hiding it better than she is. She looks up at me with her eyes still wet. "I need you to understand. I never stopped loving you. I won't ever stop loving you."

The barrier between us melts. I'm not sure who moves first. I only know her lips are on mine.

We're still kissing when the clock chimes midnight.

She pulls away. "Happy New Year, Jacob."

"Happy New Year, Jess."

She smiles, tracing her finger over my lips. "It will be. I'm sure of it."

"I am too."

It feels like the beginning of what could be the best year of our lives. Whatever it takes, I'm not letting her go ever again.

Sixty-Two

Complicated

I t takes me less than five minutes to change, throw a couple of pairs of pants and a few T-shirts, my razor and a toothbrush into a bag. Eager would be an understatement. Today couldn't possibly have gone any slower. Now that I'm off, I'm free to get on the road. Free to go see Jess.

It's been three weeks since I saw her, three weeks since we got back together, three weeks of talking on the phone for hours, getting to know each other again. Three weeks of wanting to hold her, wanting to kiss her again. Three long weeks, and now I can be with her.

I throw my bag onto the back seat of the Charger and climb in. I don't even have the key in the ignition when my cell phone buzzes. A text from Jess.

Have u left yet?

I text back: **Just starting
the car. Can't wait to see
you.**

Her reply: **Don't leave.
Not a good weekend for
u to come.**

That answer stops me.

**What? You don't want
me to come?**

It takes her a second to repeat:

**Not a good weekend for
u to come.**

Y?

Complicated.

I stare at that for a long time. What's complicated? Why didn't she just call me with a straight answer? Why is she texting this? My mind fills with a thousand unwelcome thoughts. What are the odds

Stephens bought a plane ticket and surprised her? That sounds like him.

Complicated? I want to see u.

She doesn't answer. I sit in the car debating. If he is there, I should go. I can't let him get close to Jess again. Maybe it's something else. Maybe it's someone else. The excitement and anticipation that made me crazy all week deflate. The unanswered questions are killing me. One more comes through:

I'll explain l8tr.

Later? Maybe I should call her now, demand an explanation. I can't. She's texting for a reason. Maybe he's there with her now. I'm being paranoid. It's probably something else—a big test or extra shifts at the hospital. I grip the phone in my hand. I'll wait. I have to trust her.

I shove the car door open and stand up, wondering what I'm going to do this weekend if I'm not with Jess. How am I going to keep myself sane?

My phone buzzes again. Another text. Maybe this will answer some of my questions.

Turn around.

"What?" I say out loud. "I didn't even get the chance to leave."

A voice says, "Turn around."

She's standing behind me, leaning on her car. She might have been there the whole time. I was in such a hurry to get on the road that I didn't notice her.

I cross the parking lot in three quick steps and wrap my arms around her. I kiss her hard then pick her up, set her on the hood of her car, and kiss her again. She wraps her legs around me and pulls me close.

When I finally pull myself away, I cup her face in my hands. "You scared me."

She grins. "I scared you?"

"All this *complicated,* and you didn't want me to come. I thought you'd changed your mind."

"Sorry." She traces my lips. "I wanted to surprise you."

"You definitely did that."

"Is it a good surprise?"

I look into those incredibly sexy brown-gold eyes. "Any surprise that ends with me kissing you is a good surprise." I kiss her again to prove my point.

"I did some rearranging and got the weekend off. I left right after my 12:00 class, so you wouldn't have to drive all the way to Spokane."

"I'd rather I drove it than you. But I love that I don't have to wait five hours to see you."

"I'm pretty happy about that myself." She leans in and kisses me again. "So what do you want to do this weekend?"

"I kind of like what we're doing now."

"Me too." She stops me as I'm leaning in for more. "But I told Mom we'd be home for supper."

"Supper with your parents?" I say in mock horror. "Isn't it a little early in our relationship for me to meet your parents?"

She hits me. "You've been there lots of times."

"Not in this capacity."

She puts her lips next to my ear. "You mean as my boyfriend?"

I love to hear her say that. I love having her breath against my ear. I love having my arms around her. "Do you think your dad will be cleaning his gun when we get there?"

"Probably. He's always cleaning or restoring some gun."

"Let me guess, he took it up when you became a teenager. Once you're happily married, maybe he'll find a less violent hobby, like golf."

"I can't imagine my dad golfing."

I shake my head. "Me neither."

She leans into my ear again. "So you're scared of my dad?"

"Not scared exactly, let's just say I have a healthy respect for a guy who owns his own arsenal and has a beautiful daughter."

"I promise to protect you." She kisses my neck and then slides off the hood of her car. "Shall we go?"

I take her hand. "There are some people I want you to meet first. Do you mind?"

She shakes her head and follows me into the barracks. A couple of guys lounging around stand up when they see Jess. I know they're impressed.

"Guys," I say, "I'd like you to meet my girlfriend, Jess. Jess, these are the guys."

Harrison steps forward and offers his hand. I immediately don't like the way he's looking at her. "PFC Phil Harrison," he says. "If you ever decide to dump this loser and get with a real man, give me a call."

Winters shakes her hand next. "That goes for me too, ma'am."

Jess wraps her arm around my waist. "Thanks, but I'm pretty happy where I am now."

Watching the way they look at her and remembering the stories they like to tell makes me regret bringing her here. I move so I'm between them and her. "We need to get going."

"Don't forget what I said." Harrison touches Jess' shoulder.

I resist the urge to hit him for touching her and pull her closer. I didn't realize how rough these guys are until now. I won't be bringing her back.

Sixty-Three

Rain

I t's too early again. Jess' house is quiet. Seven o'clock Saturday morning, and it looks like no one is up. It was close to 2:00 am when I left last night. I didn't ask, but I get the idea that the days of being a welcome overnight guest at the Roberts' house are over. At least for now.

I'm used to being up early. I couldn't sleep, anyway. All I could think about was Jess and being with her again. I'm sitting in my car, feeling like an idiot, when Mr. Roberts comes out of the house. He sees me, so I get out.

"Morning, Jake." He picks up the newspaper from the front steps "Jess and Ty are both still asleep, but you can come in and have coffee with me." It's more like an order than an invitation. The idea of being alone with Mr. Roberts makes me nervous. I'm a grown man. I've been in combat. I deal with grown men all the time, but being around Jess' dad makes me feel like a teenager again. I follow him into the kitchen, and he pours me a cup of coffee.

"Kids take after their mom," he says. "They like to sleep in. I've always been an early riser. I had to get used to that when we got married." He leaves the paper on the table. "You want some breakfast?"

"No, thanks." I sip my coffee.

He looks at me across the table. I feel like I'm being appraised. "You and Jessica are dating now?"

"Yes, sir." I feel myself sitting up straighter.

He clears his throat and smooths the paper. "Dads have this reputation for chasing guys away, for trying to protect their daughters. I guess I'm as guilty of that as anyone. Probably more so." He takes a drink of his coffee. "Most of the guys who came here after Jessica deserved to be chased off. I guess you know that." He shakes his head. "Don't worry, I won't be chasing you off. At least not yet. This is the happiest I've seen her in a long time."

He stares down into his cup. "Losing Matt was hard on all of us, but maybe hardest on her. For a while I thought we were going to lose her too. All that's changed now. I think you have something to do with that." He looks up at me and nods. "Thank you."

"You're welcome, sir."

He picks up the paper and shakes it to unfold it. "It doesn't mean I won't have my guns out from time to time. Just as a reminder."

I look at him to see if he's serious.

His eyes are twinkling. "You're a good man, Jacob. You hurt her though—"

"Dad!" Jess is standing in the doorway to the kitchen. Her face is red.

"Hey, hon," Mr. Roberts says. "You're up early."

"Apparently not early enough." She walks across the kitchen and sits on my lap, defiant, like she's daring her dad to say anything about it.

He grins and turns back to his paper.

"You want to go for a run?" she asks.

"Love to," I answer. She slips off my lap, and I stand up. "Thanks for the coffee."

Mr. Roberts nods.

This time I came prepared with running shoes and a change of clothes. I let Jess drive my car. I get the idea that she's enjoying the drive, taking the long way around. We end up at a trail that runs through the middle of the woods.

The day is cold and damp with a little fog. Jess is wearing running shorts—short running shorts—and a WSU sweatshirt. She's not wearing makeup, and her hair is pulled back in a ponytail. She looks amazing. No headphones this time. She stays beside me, and we talk while we run—nothing important, just talk.

We get down the trail a good couple of miles when the weather changes. "Maybe we should head back." I'm watching an ominous black cloud heading our way.

"Afraid of getting wet?" she teases. "I thought you'd lived here long enough to get your webbed feet."

"Up to you," I say.

She looks at the cloud. "Yeah, maybe we'd better turn around."

Five minutes later, the cloud erupts into a downpour. We're getting completely drenched, and Jess is laughing. I grab her hand and pull her with me under a giant cedar. She whirls around to face me, still laughing. I brush my hand across her cheek to catch a drop of rain running down her face.

"Isn't this great?" Her face beams.

"The rain?"

"The rain. Running. Being with you, just being alive. It's incredible." She walks out into the rain again, throws her head back, and catches raindrops in her mouth.

I walk over, pick her up, and kiss her. We stand there kissing in the rain, like a scene from some cheesy romance—completely drenched but incredibly happy.

Sixty-Four

Parts

"Shot," Tyler says, "shot, shot, shot, and almost shot." He's pointing out the parts of the Nag's engine that need to be replaced. "I need to get an entirely new engine."

Jess is leaning against the workbench like she's bored. "Why don't you get an entirely new car?"

Tyler looks at her like she's an idiot. "And give up a body like this?" He touches the side of the Nag reverently. This car is vintage, Jess. You aren't going to find anything better."

"I already found something more reliable," she says.

Tyler gives me a look that says, *She doesn't get it.*

Jess wanders away to the other end of the shed. She's looking out the window through the rain. "Is that your old car, Jake?"

I walk up behind her and put my chin on her head and look at the canvas-enshrouded lump that used to be my car. "Yeah," I say.

"Dad lets you keep that hunk of junk on our property?"

"Ouch," I say. "Have some respect for the deceased."

"Sorry." She turns around and wraps her arms around me. "It's just not like Dad. He's usually so into keeping everything neat and junk-free around here."

"He likes me. He said I was a good man." I kiss her nose.

"He also told you not to hurt me." She touches my lips. "You'd better listen or that car will go straight to the dump."

I look into her eyes. "I would never hurt you, Jess." I lean down and kiss her.

"Arhhhh," Tyler throws down the wrench he was holding. "I liked it better when you two hated each other. How am I ever supposed to get this thing running if you two are kissing all the time? Jess, you're banned from the shed. Go read or find something else to do." He gestures towards the door.

Jess walks over and hugs her brother. He ducks and pulls away. "Please, can I stay?" she pleads. "I'll stay out of the way, I promise. I won't distract Jacob."

He pulls back and shakes his head. "Doesn't matter. I don't know where I'm going to find a new engine for this, even if I had the money for it."

"Does that thing out there have an engine?" She gestures towards the corpse of my car.

"Yeah," I answer. "But it was probably messed up in the crash."

"It wasn't damaged," Tyler says. "I checked. The roof is all caved in, but the engine is intact."

"So put that engine in the Nag," Jess says, like it's a simple thing.

I shake my head. "Changing out an engine is a big deal. There are all sorts of conversions involved. Besides, it's a different make. I don't think there's any way that engine would be compatible."

Tyler walks over to the window and looks out at my car. "I don't know. I might have to do some research on that."

Sixty-Five

Spring Break

March 2007

D oesn't this fall under the official definition of redneck?"

My head snaps around at the sound of Jess' voice. She didn't tell me she was coming home. She's pointing at the tree with an engine hanging out of it, extracted from the Nag.

I cross the yard and have her in my arms before she can make any more comments. I kiss her long and hard, not even caring that Tyler is watching. "You're home." It's all I can say when we stop kissing.

"For a whole week," she answers. "Spring break baby."

"Why didn't you tell me?" I haven't released my hold of her. "Let me guess. You wanted to surprise me?"

"That and I wasn't sure I'd be able to get the time off. I had to do some major switching around of shifts at the hospital. I called in a bunch of favors. I think I may have promised one lady my kidney or my firstborn or something."

"I'll try to make it worth it." I kiss her again.

"Great, just great," Tyler's voice behind us. "Now we'll never get this thing done."

Jess backs away from my arms and walks over to her brother. She puts her hand on his shoulder. "I'll stay out of the way, I promise. You guys can still work on rebuilding your car. I'll just watch. But," she grins at me, "Jacob is mine from 9:00 at night until Dad kicks him out."

Tyler says something under his breath, but I'm too happy to care.

I glance at my watch again. I have another hour of this. We're at a community fair—PR stuff. Showing kids the Humvees and tanks. Time's dragging, and it's making me crazy. I want to be done with this already. I want to get back to Jess. She said she was sleeping in and then going shopping with Jasmine. I won't see her until this evening.

This kid is getting on my nerves. Asks me a million questions, pokes every button he can find. Asks me if I've ever shot anyone. His mom is a few hundred yards away, yapping on her cell phone. The other guys are gathered by the tank, evaluating and making comments about the women walking around the fair. I glance up to see if the kid or his mom heard what they're saying. The mom shuts her phone and calls the kid over.

"Maybe you should check to see who those ladies are before you say something like that." Bryan looks disgusted.

I missed who said what, but I know who they're talking about. Jess and Jasmine are coming toward us. Jess is holding a soda, and Jasmine has Little Steve in a stroller.

Since we're in public, I let the guy's comments go. I don't let being in public stop me from showing them that Jess belongs to me.

"No kissing on duty, Jake," Bryan says.

I pull away, but leave my arm around Jess' waist. "I've seen you kiss Becky when you're on duty, lots of times."

"She's my wife, and I outrank you," he says. He smiles at Jess. "It's good to see you."

"Good to see you too, Bryan." She hooks her fingers in my belt loop. "How are your boys?"

"Crazy as usual. You should come over while you're here. Becky would love to see you." He looks at me. "Do you two want to come over for dinner?"

"We can't. Jess' brother would kill me if we deserted him tonight. We're getting close to finishing the car. We'll probably know tonight if all the work we've done is for nothing."

Jasmine pulls Stevie out of the stroller. As soon as he's free, he heads for the Humvee. I catch him on the way, pick him up, and hold him above my head with one hand. "Say Uncle Jake."

He squeals and kicks his legs.

"Say it."

"You'd better put him down," Jasmine says. "He just ate. He might throw up on you."

I bring him down to face level. "Un-cle Jay-ake."

He mumbles something that sounds more like "bumba bake." I tell him, "good job" and put him down. Then, I follow him to the Humvee and help him in.

Stevie pushes the buttons and says, "Tuk, tuk." Jess looks inside the Humvee, but I don't think she's watching him. I put my arm around her waist.

"Do you know where they were sitting?" She asks suddenly. "Where Matt and Gage were when the grenade hit them?"

I avoid her eyes. I've looked into the report, so I know exactly what happened, but I don't think it's a good idea to fill her in on the specifics.

She puts her hand on my face and turns my chin toward her. "I want to know."

I take a breath. "Matt was the gunner, so he was sitting here. Gage was on the left, behind the driver."

She touches the seat where Matt would have been. "Where did the grenade hit them?"

"Left and back. They've ramped up the armor since then. An explosion like that now probably wouldn't..." I stop when I see the look on her face.

"Did you see them? After they were killed, did you see them?"

"I was flown over by helicopter for the unit memorial service. I was there when they loaded the coffins onto the plane."

"So you didn't see what they looked like after?"

I shake my head.

She steps back. "I started my ER rotation last week. The first night they brought in a sixteen-year-old who'd been in a car accident—totally torn apart. I couldn't help but think about..." She shakes her head. "I don't think I would have wanted to see them, but sometimes I wonder if it would have been easier to say goodbye if I'd seen Matt's face."

I pull her against my chest and kiss her forehead. She leans there for a long time.

Jasmine is talking with the other guys. Post-baby, Jaz looks good. She has on a low-cut blouse and tight jeans, normal for her. I watch the guys close, feeling protective of Jaz, like she really was my sister. Jess looks up and follows my gaze.

"Maybe I should warn her about those guys. They're a bunch of dogs."

"Maybe we should have warned her more about Gage. Not that I didn't try." She takes a breath. "Don't worry about Jasmine. Being a mom has changed a lot of things about her. She's too smart to get mixed up with guys like that."

Jasmine walks over like she knows we're talking about her. She pulls a camera out of her diaper bag. I set Stevie on the hood of the Humvee, and we all stand in front of it while Bryan takes our picture. "For your parents," she says. She picks up Steve and wrestles him into his stroller. "We need to get going, Jess. He needs a nap."

I kiss Jess lightly on the lips. "Tell Ty I'll be over as soon as I'm done here."

"Love ya," she says. I watch her walk away.

"Your girlfriend is hot—those long legs—must be pretty good." Harrison walks by with a load of gear. I'm cleaning up the Humvee. Moving as fast as I can so I can get on the road to Jess' house.

I don't look up, but my grip on the hose tightens. Listening to those guys on the way back to base was about all I could stand. I keep wondering if I ever sounded like that. They weren't stupid enough to talk about Jess and Jaz that way in front of me. One guy asked me for Jaz's phone number. I'm not giving it to him.

"So is she?" Harrison stops in front of me so I can't ignore him.

I don't answer.

"Must be pretty good for you to drive 300 miles just to be with her."

I set the hose down and turn it off—slowly.

"C'mon, Ricks," he starts again. "You never give details. You have to give us something. Help out guys like Vincent over there who are going through a dry spell."

Bryan glances up from the forms he's filling out. "Shut up, Harrison. You've got work to do so we can all get out of here."

"Yeah, right, I got it." He walks a couple of steps and turns around to face me. "You ever get tired of her, send her my way."

I don't even realize I've moved until I feel his nose explode against my fist. When I pull back, my hand is wet with his blood. I'm ready to throw another one, but two guys have me from behind. Harrison lands one punch on my jaw. Another couple of guys pull him back.

"Cool down, Ricks," Bryan is holding onto me. "Stop struggling. We aren't going to let you hit him again. I don't think you want to spend tonight answering to the MPs."

He releases his hold on me. "Harrison, go get yourself checked out and cleaned up. You might want to start with your mouth."

"This isn't over," Harrison mutters when they let him go, blood dripping between his fingers as he holds his hand against his nose.

"Yes, it is," Bryan says. "For both of you. I don't want to get anyone else involved in this, but I will if I have to." He moves away from the group. "Sergeant Ricks, you're with me." Bryan only uses my rank in official circumstances. He must be pretty mad. "The rest of you finish up here."

As soon as we're out of earshot, he says, "Listen, Jake, I'm not saying that he didn't deserve that, or that I wouldn't have done the same thing, but you have to keep things clean right now. You're going before the promotion board in a couple of weeks, and from what I've seen, you're going to need that pay advancement."

I stop walking and turn to face him. "What's that supposed to mean?"

"Looks to me like you're in love." He cracks a smile. "If I were you, I wouldn't wait much longer."

"Much longer for what?"

"Do the math. We've been here almost four years. We're not going to be at Fort Lewis forever. My guess is you don't want to leave here without her."

Sixty-Six

Frankie

S he's been a good sport about this. Bought pizza for us and brought it out to the shed. Stuck around even though I know this is boring for her. It's nearly midnight. Way past her nine o'clock "Jake is mine" curfew, and she's going back to school tomorrow.

She brought a blanket and a beanbag chair from the house. She's been curled up on the floor, reading. Now it looks like she's fallen asleep. I watch her breathing; it makes me want to curl up beside her, wrap my body around hers, kiss her awake.

Tyler's voice shatters my thoughts. "I need you to hold this while I bolt it in place."

I lean over to help him.

"We've almost got it. I can feel it. Frankenstein is about to rise."

"Frankenstein?"

"Or Frankie. The Nag doesn't seem to fit anymore. We built this thing from dead car parts, so I think that works. I'm thinking about painting it green. Not lime green like yours, but a dark metallic green."

"You're getting way ahead of yourself." I shake my head. "It has to run first."

"It'll run." He finishes tightening the bolt. "In fact..." He steps back and slams the hood shut.

"Are you sure about this?"

"Only one way to find out. I'm trying it."

He crawls into the driver's seat, takes a deep breath, and turns the key. It clicks. Tyler swears, loud. Jess flinches in her sleep.

Tyler walks over to the engine, discouraged. "I don't get it."

We both peer into the engine. Tyler tugs on a couple of wires. Moves some things around.

"Did you put gas in it?" Jess asks, coming up behind me.

"Of course I—" Tyler smacks his forehead. "Right."

He walks over and gets a gas tank from the corner. "How could I have been so stupid?"

He pours in the gas, then climbs back in the car. He stares at the ceiling, maybe saying a prayer. He turns the key.

Jess jumps as the engine roars to life. I stand in dumbfounded amazement. Tyler is yelling as loud as he can, "It's alive! It's alive!" He revs the engine. "Open the garage doors, Jake. Let's see if it will actually go forward." The gears grind. The car moves out of the garage. He takes it out and down the driveway, turns around and circles back.

"I can't believe you guys actually did it!" Jess screams. I wrap her in my arms and kiss her in celebration.

Jess steps back, and Tyler almost knocks me to the ground with his bear hug. "Frankie lives!"

"Frankie?" Jess asks.

"Tyler's new name for your car," I explain, "Like Frankenstein."

"You changed her gender?" Jess puts her hand on her hip.

Tyler wraps his arm around Jess' waist. "We might as well have, with all that we did to it, but Frankie could be a girl's name."

"Are you two going to take her out?" Jess says.

"We can all go," Tyler says generously.

"No, that's okay," she answers. "You and Jake go."

I can see Tyler struggling with this. "You two go. They were your cars. I'm not supposed to be driving yet, anyway. My license is still suspended."

Jess starts to argue with him, but I grab her hand. "We won't go very far."

"You can't. I didn't put much gas in the tank. If you let it run out of gas, I will come looking for you."

I take it slow, not willing to ruin all of our hard work by being impatient. We drive to the end of a county road. I flip the car around and put it in park.

"Why are you stopping?" Jess asks.

"Shh," I say, "I'm listening to the engine."

She unbuckles her seat belt and slides next to me. I wrap my arm around her shoulders and look into her eyes. The moon shines through the car window onto her face. Her hair is all over the place, messed up from her nap on the floor. There's a smudge of makeup under one eye. She's gorgeous. She kisses my neck, and I forget about listening to the engine.

"Are we really going to let Tyler have this car?" She murmurs in my ear. "I mean, it kind of feels like our baby."

I raise my eyebrows.

"You know—your muscle and my body."

"Wow," I brush my hand through her hair. "It sounds incredibly sexy when you say it like that." I pull her into my arms and kiss her. She reaches her hands up under my shirt and slides them down my back. She leans back on the seat, pulling me with her.

I kiss her lips. She lifts her chin, so I move to her neck, changing my position so I can get closer to her. The steering wheel and gearshift keep getting in my way. I wish the seat were longer. "Not a lot of room in here. Have you ever made out in a Mustang before?" I kiss her again and breathe into her neck. "Never mind, I don't want to know the answer to that question."

"And I know I don't want to know what you've done in a Mustang." She slides her hand across my chest. I couldn't hear the engine now even if I wanted to. My heart is pounding too hard.

Her phone buzzes. She moves to check it. Fear flashes in her eyes, and she pulls away abruptly.

"What is it?"

"Nothing." She shoves the phone in her pocket.

But I saw the message.

Thinking of you.

"We should probably get back. I don't want Tyler to come looking for us." Jess avoids my eyes.

I want to ask her who the text is from, but I can guess. Stephens gets back in a few months. She told me she broke things off with him, and I trust her, but I get the idea he's the kind of guy who doesn't take no for an answer.

Sixty-Seven

Jess: Paper Trail

I don't look at the text again until I'm back at my apartment, far away from Jacob and the questions he might ask if he saw it. I close my door. Angelica is in the living room with a guy we work with at the hospital, one she won't shut up about. I doubt she'll come into our room for hours.

I stare at my phone. It's late Sunday night, but he said to call anytime.

I hesitate. It feels safer to ignore the text. Acknowledging who sent it makes the whole situation too real, but the messages have been coming more and more frequently, and I only have a couple of months left. Jacob would be furious if he knew what I'm keeping from him, but we just got back together. Things are good between us, and I don't want to mess that up.

It takes four rings before he picks up.

"Jess." It sounds like he was asleep. "Are you okay?"

"Yeah, I just." I reach up and pull the curtains shut. How many times have I told Angelica to keep them closed? "I got another one. A text this time." I hold my breath, bracing for the doubt I know will be in his voice when he answers.

"You're sure it's from him? He shouldn't have access to a phone."

"I'm not sure about any of it. I just know it's the same message I've been getting for the last two years."

He breathes into the phone. "Right. Forward it to me. I'll add it to the paper trail."

"I will." I lean against the window and close my eyes, frustrated and tired. According to Mr. Harris, the lawyer my parents hired after I shot Brad, a *paper trail* is the best (only) course of action I can take right now. There's no proof any of the messages are from Brad, but they might be enough for a restraining order when he gets out. Or not. I started saving the messages a month ago. I called Mr. Harris for the first time three weeks ago after the police said there wasn't anything they could do about it. The messages have been coming more frequently and in different ways—letters, emails, and now a text—always the same four words:

I'm thinking of you.

I don't know what Brad has planned after he gets out of jail, but I know he hasn't forgotten that I'm the one who put him there.

Sixty-Eight

Jacob: Don't Wait

I walk around the mall three times before I can make myself go into the jewelry store. I try to be casual, but I'm sweating. I know nothing about rings or any other jewelry. Yeah, I may have hit it out of the park with a cheap silver locket ten years ago, but I've had no experience since then. Mom bought Jess' earrings. This is a special kind of torture. Bring on the water-boarding. I think I'd prefer that to looking for an engagement ring.

Maybe I'm getting ahead of myself. It's only been a couple of months since we've been together. Well, a couple of months, the year in Iraq, the three years I've been at Fort Lewis and all the time we spent together when we were kids. Is that long enough?

The lady standing behind the glass case is blonde and pretty. She has a huge smile, a row of sparkling white teeth. Nothing threatening about her, but I shy away from her friendly "May I help you?" and shake my head.

I keep my head down, looking, but not really looking. What am I doing here? Do I really want this? The whole thing: a lifelong commitment, a wife, a family. Am I ready for this?

I need another lap around the mall to sort things out. I'm about to walk out of the store when a ring in the corner of one of the display cases stops me. I step forward to look. It's a simple ring, a twist of silver and a single diamond, but something about it says Jess. Something about the curves on the side reminds me of the little locket I gave her a long time ago.

The clerk takes it out of the case. I hold it between my fingers and watch the light reflect off the diamond. I can imagine it on Jess' finger. I wish I could imagine what her reaction will be.

I check the price tag and grimace. Between my new car payment and all the dumb stuff I did before I got Jess back, my savings is shot. I might be able to swing the ring if I get the promotion I'm in line for, or if I sell my car.

I shake my head. Is this what I really want? Sell my car, get a wife. Make that commitment. Jess' face comes into my mind. What would it be like if she were really mine? What would it be like to have her waiting for me every night when I came home?

This is the rest of my life—the rest of our lives. I know I've never loved anyone this much before. A future with her is easy to imagine. I can picture her glowing with the roundness of pregnancy, carrying our baby. I can see her pushing our daughter or son in the swing, being a mom to our kids. I can see us getting old together, being one of those cute old couples celebrating a 50th wedding anniversary.

I look at the ring again.

The only thing I know for sure. I can't leave Fort Lewis without Jess.

I buy the ring. Lucky for me, my credit is good. I qualify for convenient monthly payments. I'll put the car up for sale when the details are all worked out. I guess that means if she says yes.

The sparkly-toothed clerk puts the ring in a little velvet box and smiles at me. "She'll love it, but if it isn't quite what she wants, you can bring it back and exchange it for something else."

She didn't tell me what to do if it's me she doesn't want.

I manage to get to my room without anyone seeing me. I'm not sure what I would say if anyone tried to talk to me right now. I pull the box out of my pocket and set it on my desk. I open it and look at the ring from a distance. My heart is pounding as if I ran ten miles. Now what? I step forward and pick up the ring between my fingers.

My phone rings. I pull it out and check it. For the first time ever, I'm hoping it isn't Jess. I'm not sure I can talk to her now.

It's my mom. Almost as bad. Mom has a sixth sense about things like this. She always knows when to call. Like when I was assigned to Fort Lewis, she called almost immediately after I got my orders.

I consider not answering the phone, but I know I have to tell someone. Mom is probably the best choice.

"Hey hon," she says. "How are things?"

"Pretty good," I answer.

"How are things on base?"

"Good." I study the diamond in the light of my room, and run my finger over the patterns on the sides.

"What have you been doing lately?" she asks.

"Lately? Like when lately?" My reaction sounds like I'm hiding something.

"I don't know. How about today? What did you do today?"

I take a breath. "The usual."

She sounds suspicious. "How are things with Jess?"

"Good, great actually," I try to keep it casual, but I know she's not buying it. I roll the ring between my fingers, wondering how to tell Mom. The ring flips out of my grasp, flies across the room, and bounces along the floor. I swear.

"What was that?"

"Just a minute, Mom." I set the phone down on the floor and retrieve the ring. I put the ring back in the box, shut the lid and then go back to the phone.

"Okay, what's going on? And don't say nothing. I know you too well. You sound nervous, or stressed, or something. Did you hear from the promotion board?"

"No, it's not that."

"What then?"

I touch the box. "Mom, what do you think about me and Jess...what would you say if I told you..." I take a deep breath and just blurt it out. "What do you think about me marrying Jess?"

She laughs, "You want to know what I think about you marrying Jess? The beautiful, sweet daughter of one of my best friends, the girl who has been in love with you since she was a little girl, the girl who would make a great mom and a great wife? What do I say to that? How about this, Jake? What took you so long?"

I touch the velvet box. "I'm glad to hear you say that because I bought something today."

"A ring?"

"Yeah."

"Oh, Jake, congratulations!" She practically squeals. "When do you think you'll get married?"

"I haven't asked her yet. If she says yes, it will have to be soon. I'm expecting new orders." I'm waiting for Mom to give me some encouragement. I want her to say, *Of course she'll say yes.*

She talks slowly. "She loves you a lot. I'm pretty sure that this is what she wants, but..."

I don't want to hear buts at this point.

"But she's still very young. And there's her education to think about." The practical side of Mom takes over. "Maybe she could join you wherever you end up after she graduates. And then there's the whole Army thing."

"The Army thing?" The phone slips and I have to rub my hands on my pants. My palms are sweating.

"Being an Army wife isn't easy." She sighs. "I know that better than anyone. And Jess has already seen the worst of it. It takes a strong woman to be a warrior's wife. My gut feeling is that Jess is the kind of woman who can handle it, but it's up to her."

It feels like Mom is giving me the *don't be disappointed* talk. The one she gave me when I was twelve and tried out for the all-star baseball team.

"It's the right thing to do," she finishes. "You have our blessing, you know that. You couldn't have made a better choice."

Sixty-Nine

Jess: Germany

M y phone rings, jerking me out of a nightmare. My hands shake as I reach for the phone.

"Jess, did I wake you up?" Becky's voice slows my heartbeat.

"Yeah," I admit, "but I need to be up, anyway." I glance at my clock. I missed my early-morning yoga class, but I can still make it to my lab if I hurry. I haven't been sleeping well again, and when I do sleep, I have nightmares I can't quite remember.

"Sorry, I won't keep you. I just got some insider information that I think you should know."

I sit up. "Insider information?"

"Yeah. Bryan got his orders. We're going to Germany."

"Wow. I'm excited for you, but I'll miss you guys. Germany's pretty far away."

"It is, but you don't need to miss us. You could come."

I shake my head, confused. "To Germany? With you? Do you need a nanny?"

She laughs. "That would be awesome, but I'm sure I can't afford you. My insider information says that most of their unit is going to Germany too, meaning Jacob is likely being transferred as well."

"Oh." My heart falls. "Germany is so far away."

"You could come with us," she repeats. "Wives get to go on this one."

"I'm not exactly—"

"Yet," Becky says. "Like you said. Germany is far away. Think about whether you really want to be that far from Jacob again."

After she hangs up I start thinking about it—all of it. How much I'd hate to be that far away from Jacob, how much I love him, but also how I'm not finished with school. As far as marrying Jacob, for me, it's become less of an *if* and more of a *when*. I think, or at least hope, he feels the same.

I get dressed, too distracted by everything Becky told me to worry about making my lab on time. Angelica walks in, a cup of coffee in her hand. She sits on my bed. "Did you have a good spring break with Jacob?"

"The best," I answer.

"I'm glad. I want details tonight. I have to get to class. I just wanted to tell you Michael called."

"Michael?" I ask. He's so far from my mind now that it takes me a second to register who she's talking about. "Why would he call?"

"I don't know, I mean, I assume it was Michael. The connection was terrible, so I couldn't tell who it was, but he sounded far away."

"What did he say?"

"Just, *tell Jess I'm thinking of her.* If you ask me, that's borderline creepy, especially since you broke up with him, but maybe he meant it in a friendly way." She stands. "I just thought you should know so you're prepared if he calls again."

"Thanks," I answer, hoping she doesn't notice the tremble in my voice.

Seventy

Jacob: Orders

May 2007

"How's it going, Jake?" Vincent's voice behind me makes me jump. He laughs. "Man, you've been on edge lately."

Bryan puts his hand on my shoulder. "He's right, Jake, is there something going on that you'd like to share?"

He keeps prodding, trying to get me to spill something. So far I haven't told anyone but Mom about the ring. She's sworn to secrecy, and Mom is pretty good at keeping secrets. I'm avoiding the Roberts' house, Becky, and Jasmine—too much estrogen, too many prying moms.

My original idea was to do something romantic, like what Matt did I had ideas about the barn loft or the beach near Jess' house. But Jess is up to her neck in work and school. She won't be coming home until her term ends at the end of next month. I haven't gotten my orders yet, but the rumor is that it will all happen pretty soon. I don't want to run out of time.

I'm going to see her this weekend. I'm not sure what I'm going to do, how I'm going to ask her. I only know I have to do it soon, before I go crazy.

"I have something here that will either eliminate your stress or add to it." Bryan hands me an envelope. "A summons from the Command Sergeant. He wants to see you in his office. It must have something to do with your promotion."

I dress carefully for my meeting—every button, every badge in place, my shoes polished to a shine. He makes me wait outside his office long enough for me to be sweating by the time he calls me in.

He's sitting behind a big desk. He stands and we exchange salutes.

"Sit." He says.

I sit while he makes a show of shuffling through some paperwork. "Sergeant Ricks," he starts slowly, "I've gone over your service record and the notes from your commanding officers. Impressive. The word from the review board is in." He slides a big paper envelope across the desk. "Congratulations, Staff Sergeant Ricks."

"Thank you, sir," I take the envelope and watch him, waiting to be dismissed.

"The advancement comes with a transfer," he continues. "You'll be joining a unit at Fort Bragg. You have a months to get things squared away here. Then they need you. They're deploying to Iraq at the end of August. They're glad to be getting someone who has your experience. I expect to hear good reports about you, Ricks."

He stands and dismisses me with a smile and a clap on the shoulder, like he just did me a big favor.

I salute and walk out of the office in a daze. My head is spinning. All the plans I made, everything I'd counted on has changed.

Jess.

I get a sick feeling in my stomach when I think about what this means for her, what it will mean for us.

I pack for this trip to see Jess more slowly than I usually do. Through our phone conversations, she knows something's bothering me, but I haven't told her what it is yet. The ring feels heavy when I slide the little box into my glove compartment. This whole thing carries more weight since I talked to the Command Sergeant. Since I got my new orders. Since I found out I am going back to Iraq.

I thought about leaving the ring back at the barracks. I'm not sure if I should give it to her now. I don't know if I should tie her to me now—the way that Matt tied Kendra to him before he left, or even the way that Gage tied Jasmine to him.

I feel the weight in my chest too. I know that this is going to crush her. I hate that I have to tell her this.

The drive to see her gives me too much time to think. A million times I think that I'll take the ring back. That I won't tell Jess anything about it. That I should leave without asking for a commitment. A million more times I think that I can't leave without tying her to me. That I can't leave without knowing she'll be there when I come back.

Seventy-One

Jess: Bound

I keep listening for his car, checking the window.

Two steel-gray envelopes hide in my top drawer, taunting me. I haven't turned them over to the lawyer yet.

"Michael" has called a couple more times, always with the same message: *Tell Jess I'm thinking of her.*

But it can't be Michael. I haven't talked to him in months, and he's still in Korea.

I've been trying to figure out how to tell Jacob about the messages I've gotten from Brad. It's probably something we should figure out together, but Jacob is already stressed about something else. I hear it in his voice whenever we talk. He told me he got the promotion, so not that. I'm guessing it's because he knows he's being transferred and he's not sure how to tell me. I'm hoping it's because he has something planned, that there's something he wants to ask me.

If not, I'm prepared to ask him. Tradition be damned. I'm going to ask Jacob to marry me. If he says yes, we can get married as soon as possible. If I have to finish my last semester at another college, or wait until we're back. it's okay. I'm ready to stop doing the distance thing and just be with him. The sooner, the better. I've never cared about a big wedding like Kendra. Something simple, maybe in the barn or my backyard—sweet and romantic, just our family and close friends. We can be far away by the time Brad gets out of jail. More importantly, we can stay together.

I don't know what I'll do if he says no.

His car pulls up out front. I stand at the window, waiting. He stays in the car for what seems like forever. He leans over, as if he's putting something in the glove compartment, and finally gets out.

I don't give him a chance to knock. I open the door, jump into his arms, and wrap my legs around his waist. I'm kissing him before he can even say my name.

He carries me to the couch. Then pulls away, looking at my empty apartment. "Where is everyone?"

"Out. They won't be back for hours." I lean in to continue what I started.

He pulls away. 'That's good. We have a lot to talk about."

"Talk?" I tease him. "My apartment is completely empty; we're finally alone, and you want to talk?"

"Yeah." His face twists like he's in pain.

I slide off his lap. "Are you okay?"

He reaches for my hand. "There's something I need to tell you."

I hate to see him so worried, so I jump in. "I know about your transfer."

"You know?" Relief floods his face. "And you're okay with it?"

"On one condition." I lean into his ear. "Take me with you."

He looks confused. "Jess, you can't go with me."

"I could if we were—" I stop, and look down, embarrassed. Obviously, he hasn't been thinking about the same thing I have. I feel foolish, like a little girl again, begging for his attention and jumping to a place he's not ready to go.

"If we were...married," he finishes after the long, painful pause it takes for him to figure out what I mean.

I nod.

He laughs, but there's something guarded about it. "I'm not sure if I should take that as a proposal or an acceptance, since I didn't get the chance to ask."

I can't tell if he's serious or so caught off guard he doesn't know how to respond. I work to keep my voice light. "We could call it both, or..."

He nods, and now I'm wondering if that's his answer. None of this is going the way I thought it would. He's holding something back. "Who told you I was leaving?"

"Becky. She said your entire unit is going to Germany."

A shadow passes over his face. "She was wrong. Not everyone is going."

"So you're staying?" The thought gives me hope and terrifies me at the same time. I won't have to say goodbye. We won't have to rush into anything, but I'll have to tell him about the messages Brad has been sending me. I probably should have told him a long time ago.

"No." He rubs his thumb across the back of my hand. "I'm not going to Germany, and I'm not staying. My promotion came with a transfer. I'm joining a unit at Fort Bragg."

"Fort Bragg, isn't that in North Carolina, near your parents? Your mom will be happy." I force enthusiasm into my voice because I still don't know what he's thinking. "I could see if I can finish my last term there and then we—"

"I won't be at Fort Bragg very long."

He sounds so serious that I'm afraid to ask, but I do. "Why not?"

"The unit I'm joining is deploying to Iraq six weeks after I get there. I'm going too."

I pull my hand from his and cover my mouth. "No." I shake my head. "No." I stand and stumble a couple of steps away from him. I can't process what he just said. I can't let him go. I can't lose him. I lean my head against the wall and close my eyes. He comes behind me. I turn and wrap my arms around him. He kisses my forehead, and I lean against his chest, my tears soaking into his T-shirt.

"I'm sorry. I should have warned you this was a possibility. I know guys who are already on their third tour in Iraq." He leans back so I'm looking in his eyes. There's a fire there that I haven't seen for a long time. He cups my chin. "Marry me, Jess. Before I go or after I get back, it doesn't matter. I just want to be with you. I just want you to be mine."

I step out of his arms. "No." There's more strength behind the word than I thought I had left.

He looks thunderstruck. "No? You don't want to marry me?"

"No. I don't want you to go to Iraq. I just got you back. I don't want to spend the next year waiting and worrying."

He puts his hands on my shoulders. "It will be okay. It's only a year, and things have settled down some. Iraq isn't as dangerous as it once was."

My heart clenches in fear, anger rises in my chest and comes out in my voice. "Do people still die there? Can you guarantee that you'll be coming back?"

"No. But you can't guarantee that you won't get hit by a bus tomorrow."

I step away from him, wanting to protect myself, wanting to push him away. "You're right. There are no guarantees. So we shouldn't make promises we can't keep."

He closes his eyes. "Jess, don't do this. You're upset. We both are. We should—"

"No." It comes out with more force than the first time. "They can't make you go again. Tell them you won't go."

His voice is calm, but with an undercurrent of irritation. "I don't have a choice, you know that."

"You do have a choice. You're not a slave to the Army. Michael didn't have to go to Iraq."

His name makes Jacob's lips tighten. "I'm not Lieutenant Stephens."

I know I'm pushing it, but I can't stop myself. "Your brother was killed in Iraq. Isn't there some *Saving Private Ryan* clause you can invoke? We could go to the media, ask them to—"

"No." His no is even more forceful than mine was. I step back. His voice is full of a conviction I've never seen before. "I took an oath. I gave my word. I'm not going back on that."

I ask the question I know isn't fair. "Not even for me?"

He shakes his head. "No. And that you're even asking me...that you ever thought I would... shows me you don't know me at all."

Too late, I realize I pushed him too far.

"You knew who I was when we got together. You knew how important this is to me. You knew, Jess. Don't act like any of this is a surprise. If you want me, really want me, then you have to take everything I am and that means accepting that I'm a soldier first."

I shake my head. I can't accept that. I can't let him go for another year, knowing he might not be coming back. "It was just a dream, wasn't it? I loved you, and you loved me. We were together, and we thought we could live happily ever after, but that's not how the world works, is it?"

His righteous indignation dissipates. It's replaced with a kind of anguished resolution. "You're right. This won't work. I can't go back on my word, not for you, not for anyone. I love you with everything I have, but that's never going to be enough for you. I can't give you what you want. I've already given too much of myself to the Army."

My chest hurts. "What are you saying?"

"I'm saying maybe it's time to admit defeat. I can't make you happy. I can't be the man you want me to be. I should step aside and let someone else try."

I stare at him for a long time, afraid to move, afraid to say anything. The muscles in his jaw work, but the rest of his face could be made of stone. I pushed him too far. This is really over. I take the earrings out of my ears and press them into his hand.

"I'm sorry, Jacob." A sob rises in my throat without my permission. I turn away so he doesn't have to see my tears.

Part of me wants to take back everything I said and beg him for forgiveness, but I know he's right. I'm not strong enough to be the woman he needs. I'm not strong enough to be a warrior's wife.

"I'm sorry too," he says. He slides the earrings into the bag he came with and walks out the door.

Seventy-Two

Jess: Self-Preservation

July 2007

The police officer looks over the little stack of cards. She's some kind of domestic violence specialist. We've already gone through the texts and emails from Brad. Her expression is sympathetic, but not encouraging. It took all the strength I had left to come here. For the first couple of weeks after Jacob walked out, I folded in on myself again. Worse than before. This time, I didn't even pretend to function. I barely got through my classes, my stellar grades for the rest of the term were the only thing that saved me.

Ironically, the sudden deluge of messages brought me back to myself. Some sense of self-preservation caused me to push past my guilt and pain, bypass my unhelpful lawyer and try the police again.

"I'm sorry, but there isn't much I can do for you. He's still in jail and, as far as I can gather, he's been a model prisoner. There's no proof that he sent any of these messages."

"Someone could have been helping him. The messages seem harmless unless you know the context. Brad knows how to work the system. He's very good-looking, and he can be charming when he wants to be."

She nods. "They usually are. That's what makes them so dangerous. No one knows what kind of person a guy like Brad really is until—" She sighs. "The law isn't always on your side in this. Domestic stuff...is tricky. Frankly, you were lucky that he served any time at all. You'll be notified when he gets out. Other than that, he's pretty much free to do whatever he wants."

"So I'm supposed to just wait around for him to come for me?" I ask.

Her mouth is set in a firm line. "No. I wouldn't recommend that. I've seen too many domestic violence victims get hurt or worse after their attackers have served their meager debt to society. Are you by yourself? Do you have a husband or a boyfriend or even a dog?" She looks down at her notes. "What about the man who helped you before?"

I swallow the lump of pain that comes every time someone mentions Jacob. "He's gone."

"Right. Then, I recommend you do everything you can to protect yourself. Change your number, get a big dog, move out-of-state if at all possible, don't make it easy for him to find you."

I nod as the weight of what she's saying sinks in. I can do all of that except leave the state. I'm going to finish my degree; that much I've promised myself. After that, I'll go somewhere far away.

She stands up and closes the door to her office. "Do you have a gun?"

"No. But I know how to shoot."

"Whether you know how to shoot a gun or not is a moot point if you aren't willing to use it. Could you shoot to kill if you had to?"

I think about the conversation I had with Michael about being afraid to kill someone. Then I think about what happened last time. Jacob isn't around to come to my rescue this time. If Brad comes again. It's all up to me.

"I could do it."

She nods somberly. "Legally cover your bases as much as possible. Get a restraining order. Document every attempt at contact. Get a concealed carry permit and watch your back."

"I will." I promise.

Seventy-Three

Jacob: Goodbye

I t's not the goodbye I'd hoped for or one I ever wanted, but it's one I know I need to give. The little box is heavy in my pocket. No one knows I kept it, that it was too hard to return, that even now, it feels like it belongs to Jess. Even if she doesn't belong to me.

I wonder if I was too harsh on her. She's young. She's been through a lot. We could still–

No. I stop my thoughts from going down that path. I'm pretty sure that in the course of our tumultuous relationship we used up all the chances we had.

Tyler is waiting for me on the front porch. I won't go inside. Neither of us is equipped for this to be a long goodbye. This conversation might go better if we were bent over the engine of a car, but we don't have anything we can work on right now, and I don't have any time left.

"Hey," he says as I mount the front steps of the Roberts' house for what is probably the last time.

"Hey," I answer back.

"You decided to give me your car after all," he nods to the Charger. We've joked about it a couple of times, me leaving my car for him, the way I did for her—but I'm not coming back this time.

"Still no," I reply. "How's Frankie doing?" I indicate the monstrosity we created, sitting in the corner, still unpainted, still reminding me of her.

"She's hanging in there. Not as fast as yours, but she runs okay." He looks at his car with the kind of pride that only comes when you get something the hard way. It strikes me how much Tyler has grown up since I've known him. He's almost taller than I am and more filled out than most kids his age, but it's the self-assurance and hard-fought maturity in everything he does that makes him look older. It's easy to forget he still has one more year of high school. I don't know where he's going from there, but whatever life throws at him, he can take it.

"I have something else I want you to take care of for me." I slide the velvet box out of my pocket. The lid comes open, and the ring bounces across the sidewalk. I kneel down to pick it up.

"Wow, this is all so sudden. I don't know what to say."

I put the ring back in the box. "I love you, dude, but not that way." I stand up and get serious. "Put it in your dad's gun safe. I'll come get it when I get back." I hesitate for a long moment. I don't want to bring this up with him. I saw how hard things were for Tyler after Matt died, but he's mostly a man now. "If anything happens to me, I want you to give it to Jess."

His anger surprises me. "She changed her phone number. Moved into a new apartment. She hasn't been home for a long time. She's gone again, the way she was before. Jess isn't coming back to you, maybe not even to us. I don't think you owe her anything."

I look at the ground. He's right, I'm a sucker or a glutton for punishment—when it comes to Jess, I'm never sure. Maybe he understands this better than I do. "I know. I don't expect anything from her. Just keep it safe for me, okay?"

He takes the ring. "I'm sorry. I'm sorry my sister's so messed up. I'm sorry for all the shit she's put you through. You don't deserve it."

"Thanks," I say.

His voice gets husky. "No matter what, you'll always be my brother. Take care of yourself."

I pull him into a tight hug. "I will. Love you, bro."

Seventy-Four

Jess: Old Friends

August 2007

My feet hurt and I'm exhausted. Not the good exhausted I used to get after a long run or a productive day. The kind that comes after a bone-wearying day in the ER. The kind that won't let you sleep, even though your body is screaming for rest.

The tiny one-bedroom basement apartment I moved into is dark and unwelcoming. It's cold even in late summer, but it's cheap, and no one but the old lady who lives above me knows I'm here. I got a job at a small hospital as an aide, in an out-of-the-way little town not too far from home, but far enough that I don't think he'll find me.

Originally, I was going to go home for the summer, so I could be closer to Jacob. Back then I had all kinds of plans for the warmer weather, lots of time with him, maybe even a wedding. Now I have very little to look forward to beyond surviving another semester of school and then graduation.

I rummage through the fridge for something to eat even though I'm not hungry. A buzz from my bedroom sends electric prickles down my spine. It's coming from my old phone.

I have a new phone and a new number—one I've only given to my parents—but I haven't gotten rid of my old phone yet. I keep trying to convince myself it's because I might need it for evidence if Brad calls or texts me again, not because it's the last remaining tenuous connection I have to Jacob.

I let it go to voicemail, then go into the bedroom to check. I don't recognize the caller ID. Whoever it was didn't leave a message. I move to shove it back into my drawer. It rings again. This time the caller ID is familiar. My heart skips a beat. I know I shouldn't answer it, but I do.

"Jess, it's so good to hear your voice." His voice is familiar and comforting. "Where have you been? I've been trying to get hold of you for weeks."

"Hi Michael. It's good to hear your voice too." And it is, maybe because I've been so lonely, maybe because Michael has always represented a kind of security to me.

"I'm back in the states and I'd love to see you."

I hesitate. "I don't know if that's a good idea. I..."

"Just as friends," he says quickly. "You can bring Jacob. I could get someone to double with."

"Jacob and I aren't..." I close my eyes. I'm not sure that telling him this is a good idea.

"Aren't what?" His voice is soft and sympathetic.

I have a sudden urge to just talk. There's so much weighing on my mind, so much I've kept to myself. I need someone to talk to. "We're not together anymore. He's deploying to Iraq, I couldn't deal with it, so we broke up."

"I'm sorry to hear that." He doesn't sound sorry. "That must be so hard for you. I'm kind of in the middle of a breakup of my own."

A twinge of unwelcome jealousy hits me. "I'm sorry. I didn't realize you'd been dating anyone."

He laughs. "Not a person. The Army. I'm done with the Army."

I don't know whether to offer sympathy for that or not. He sounds more relieved than anything. "What happened?" I say instead.

"Completely out of my control, actually. Turns out I have a heart condition, nothing too serious, just enough to earn a medical discharge."

"Now what?" I ask.

"I think it's called getting on with my life. I've finally been accepted to the University of Washington Medical School, so I'll be in Seattle."

"That's great; congratulations." I lean back on my bed, the constant knot in my stomach loosening. It's good to talk to Michael as a friend, with no guilt.

"It means a lot more years of school and paying tuition on my own, but I can handle that. At least I won't owe the Army anything when I'm done. What about you? You have to be close to being done with school."

"One more semester."

"And then what?"

"I don't know. I'll look for a job. I'm thinking somewhere out of state, maybe farther."

"Why so far away? I thought you liked it here. Your family is close." He hesitates. "In a couple of months I'll be closer."

"It's a long story."

"Sounds like something we should discuss over dinner. I'll be in Seattle in a couple of days, taking care of some details at UW. If you're free, I'd love to see you. You could come up, or I could drive down."

"I'm not home. I'm–" I stop myself. I've been careful not to tell anyone where I am, but Brad doesn't even know Michael exists.

"Still in Pullman? I could make a quick trip to see my family. I'm sure they'd love to see you."

"I'm not there either."

"What's going on, Jess?" His voice is rich with concern. "You sound stressed. Are you working too much, or is it the whole thing with Jacob? He's a complete moron for letting you go; I hope you realize that."

I don't want to talk to him about Jacob. It feels disloyal, even if we aren't together. "It's a lot of things."

"It sounds like you need some time away from everything, a good meal, and a friend to talk to. Name any place in the state of Washington—no, any place in the world and I'll take you there, even if it's just for dinner and friendly conversation. I miss you, Jess."

His offer is incredibly tempting. It strikes me that Michael could be the solution to all my problems. He has the money to take me away from here. He's out of the Army. I could try things with him again, see what it would be like if there was nothing holding me back.

I take a breath. "You're incredibly sweet as always. You've been such a great friend, but I can't."

As good as he's been to me, as good as he obviously still wants to be to me, I can't accept Michael's help. I can't pretend I'm in love with him, even if I know it will make him happy. Even if it might save me.

There's a long silence on the other end. Finally he says, "Because you're still in love with him." There's a hard edge to his voice that I've never heard before.

I don't have the words to explain, or deny, or confirm what he already knows. He's right. Not that it makes a difference now.

"I'm sorry, Michael. I hope you have an incredible life. You deserve it. But please, for your sake as much as mine, don't call me again."

I don't wait for his reply. I hang up, then turn off the phone and put it back in the drawer. I promise myself I'll have it disconnected tomorrow.

Seventy-Five

Jacob: Thinking of Her

I sit at the clunky computer in the corner of the room that used to be Nate's. He traded it in for an expensive laptop when he went to college. What he did with the laptop after he dropped out, I don't know.

I know this one doesn't get used much. Or it didn't. I imagine Mom will use it to send emails to me during my deployment like she did last time.

Email.

The excuse I made to myself and to the sparse crowd gathered downstairs to say goodbye is that I needed to check my email to make sure nothing has changed. I implied the *change* I was checking on was the where's and when's of my deployment three days from now.

I can pass that lie off to Steve, maybe even to myself, but I know Mom saw through it. When I asked about the computer, she gave me the same worried look she's been giving me since I got here.

It's not like I'm expecting another last-minute Hail Mary intervention to save my relationship with Jess. Last time I was only a few hours away, and there was a lot less hurt and fewer harsh words between us. Even as I curse her, blame her, even try to hate her, I get that it's not fair of me to ask her to go through the months of fear and the excruciating memories this deployment will dredge up. I get that we'll never be good for each other. I get that it's time to cut ties and admit defeat.

I still miss her.

"Some people are just not cut out for this life," Mom said. She knew it was thin comfort, even if it's the truth.

"Better that you know now," Steve said, no comfort implied. Just his usual gruff practicality. Again, he's right, but that doesn't make it any easier.

If I were more like him—practical to a point that borders on stone cold—I'd be downstairs drinking with the few neighbors and shoestring relatives who've gathered for this little send-off. I might even try to make small-talk with our next-door neighbor's pretty niece. She's about my age and at least superficially interested. I wouldn't be waiting for this brick of a computer to come to life so my last hope can get dashed.

When it comes to Jess, I'm more of a masochist than I care to admit.

Even Jasmine is telling me I need to let Jess go. She and Little Stevie moved into Gage's room so she can finish college with free room, board, and babysitting. Mom is thrilled to have her grandson close, and both my parents love Jasmine. I'm glad they'll be here. The two of them make our house feel more alive and less empty.

I scroll through a list of unread advertisements, resisting the urge to go back to the emails I saved from before. Rereading and remembering what we had can lead to nothing good.

I'm about to shut it all down, close up the computer and go back downstairs to drinks and goodbyes and maybe even some superficial flirting with a pretty girl to see where that leads. An email at the bottom stops me. I don't recognize the sender, or really anything about the email, except the subject line.

Thinking of her.

My blood runs cold. I immediately know who it's from. Brad. Jess' old boyfriend who's spent almost three years in prison for assaulting both of us. He's not supposed to contact either of us, but if he can get my email, he can get hers.

Thirty-six months minus time served, I do the math in my head. His sentence ended two weeks ago. Somehow, in the middle of everything going on. I missed that. Once when I brought up that he would be out soon, Jess said she wasn't worried about it. She was lying; I could see it in her face, but I didn't want to push it then. I assumed I'd be there to protect her when he got out, or that she'd be with me, somewhere far away from him.

I open the email and my blood boils. It's filled with pictures of her: running, leaving her counselor's office, her eyes closed as she balances on one foot in the yoga studio she started going to, through her apartment window, getting out of her car to go to work at the hospital.

Besides the pictures, there's one line of text, a date. 2006–08—20 three days from now, the day I deploy.

His message is clear. He can get to her any time he wants, and he will, as soon as I'm out of the way.

I reach for my phone and dial her number, praying she'll answer. I get a message that her phone was disconnected, and I remember Tyler told me she'd changed her number.

I try Tyler's number, then both of her parents. No one answers.

She told me she was moving home for the summer, so I try her house phone. No one answers. I find the phone number for the Thurston County Sheriff's office and call them. I'm shuffled around for what seems like hours. Finally, I get on with someone who knows something.

The officer on the other end has a voice that's lazy and unconcerned. "Forward the pictures to my email and I'll take a look, but if he's served his sentence, so there's no direct supervision or check-ins he needs to do. Basically, he's free to live his life."

I'm getting desperate. "He's obviously stalking her. Can you send someone to check on her, or at least warn her?"

He sighs. "You could contact her yourself."

"I don't have her phone number, her new address or—"

"I see." The officer says, and I hear it in his voice. *Are you sure you aren't the one stalking her?* After a long silence, he says. "Probably the best thing you can do is come down and file a restraining order. You said you were a victim too, and he isn't supposed to have any contact with you. That would at least give us an excuse to talk to him when it was served. It might take a few days to process though."

I work to keep my voice even. "I'm across the country in North Carolina. I'm deploying to Iraq in three days. I can't just come down, and I can't wait days for you to talk to him."

There's silence for long enough that I think he's hung up on me. Finally he says. "I see. If you can get me the address of where Miss Roberts is currently living, I can send a patrol car down to do a welfare check on her. Best I can do."

I tell him her home address, the only place I think she might be. "Would you like a call back once we get there? How soon depends on the availability of our deputies."

"Yes, please." Automatic politeness kicks in, even though I want to throttle him through the phone.

I call Tyler again. No answer. Mr. and Mrs. Roberts. No answer.

I run downstairs. The murmur of voices stops as soon as they see me. "Do you have Jess' new number?" I yell at my mom.

She stares back at me. "Jacob, I—"

"It's important," I snap.

She exchanges a glance with Steve. "No. I didn't realize she had a new number."

"She does, and I don't have it. I tried her parents and her brother. None of them answered." I sound desperate, even to me.

Mom steps toward me. "Her parents are in Alaska on a cruise for their anniversary. They won't be back until next week. I don't know where Tyler is."

"Jaz, do you have her new number?"

Jasmine stands. "No. Sorry."

The three of them look at me like I've lost it. Actually, the entire party is looking at me like I've lost it.

Mom puts her hand on my arm. "Jacob, what's going on? Why do you need to—"

"He's coming after her. Brad. Brad is out of jail, and he's going to find Jess. He sent me an email—pictures of her taken without her knowing it. He's been stalking her."

"You need to call the police," Steve says.

"I did that. They won't do anything beyond a check of her house. I gave them her address, but I don't even know if she's there." I push past Steve. "I have to go. I have to find her. "

He puts himself between me and the door. "Hold on, son. You're over 2,000 miles away. You deploy in three days. There's nothing you can do from here. Send the pictures to the police. Let them do their job. Your mom and Jasmine can keep trying to get hold of her parents."

"I can't just—"

He puts his hand on my shoulder. "There's nothing you can do for her."

Steve is using his *the discussion is over* tone. I've never pushed back on it before, not even as an adult. "What if I'm the only one who can find her? What if I'm the only one who can help her?"

In the back of my mind, I hear Jess' voice from a long time ago. *How do you always know how to find me? How do you always know when I need to be rescued?*

"I'm sure there are lots of people who are closer. People she's actually speaking to," Steve's dig hurts just enough for me to get his point. I get it, but I don't care. I need to know she's okay.

"Michael," Jasmine says suddenly. "He's back, isn't he? He might know where she is."

"Good idea." I'm almost desperate enough not to be jealous that Michael might have her new number if I don't.

"I have his number," Mom admits. "From the barbecue way back when. Unless he changed it."

"Let's try it," Jasmine says.

Steve ushers the guests out. Mom looks for Michael's number in her phone. I go back to the computer, thinking I'll take a closer look at the pictures and maybe see when the next plane leaves for Washington.

I zoom in on each of the pictures. The backgrounds are familiar, but too blurred to be sure where they were taken. I don't know much about computers, or photography, or any of it. I think there's a way to figure out when or where a digital picture was taken. Something about the file, but I don't know how to find it.

There's only one person I can think of who might know.

I haven't spoken to my brother for almost two years. I've been too mad to call him first, and I'm guessing he feels the same way. He may have gotten a new number like Jess. He probably won't answer.

The phone rings seven times. I'm trying to figure out what kind of message I might give to to his voicemail when a suspicious voice answers. "Jake?"

"Nate!" I want to cry at the sound of his voice. There are so many things I want to tell him, so many questions I want to ask, but I don't have time. "What kind of information can you get from a digita. picture?"

The other end is quiet for a long time. I think he hung up on me. Finally, he says, "You haven't talked to me in almost two years, and this is what you call for? I only answered because I thought someone ha died." Now I'm sure he's going to hang up.

"Wait, Nate, please. It's important. I need your help. Jess is in trouble."

"Jess?" he asks.

He still cares about her. He might even still be in love with her. I can tell by the way he says her name. I talk fast, explaining the situation, hoping I can leverage that to get him to help me.

Once I get it all out, he's silent again for a long time. "I'll text you my email. Send me the pictures. I'll see what I can figure out."

Seventy-Six

Jess: Overthinking

Weekends are the worst. There's nothing to do but hang out at my empty apartment and think. I can't go for a run. I don't have any homework because I'm not taking classes now. I can't focus enough to read or watch TV. I keep thinking about what Jacob is doing right now. He could already be in Iraq.

I think about what the next year will be like, knowing he's there, but not knowing what's going on. If something happened to him, I'm sure Trina would let us know. Beyond that...then I think about beyond that. What's it going to be like when he's home? When I find out he's dating someone, getting married, moving on with his life?

That spiral of thoughts will lead me to the bottom of a pit I'm afraid I won't be able to climb out of. I struggle to pull myself out of my funk. There are still a couple of things the police officer suggested I haven't done yet. My lease doesn't allow pets, so a dog is out for now. The part of her advice that I've been avoiding comes back to me.

I need a gun.

My dad has an entire arsenal in his gun safe. She warned me it would need to be one that is registered in my name to cover my bases legally, in case... Then I remember. I do own a gun. It's a rifle my dad bought me for my eighteenth birthday. He tried to get me to go hunting with him. I couldn't stomach it, so I've only used it for target practice. It's not something I could carry as a concealed weapon, but it is registered to me. I haven't shot a gun since I shot Brad in the leg. After everything that happened before, the thought of shooting it, even in self-defense, makes me sick.

But I don't want to be dead either. I have some idea of what my death would do to my parents, and Tyler, even Jacob.

No one's home. My parents are celebrating their anniversary with a cruise, and Tyler is backpacking with his friends—a last hurrah before they start their senior year. I could get my gun, get in and out without having to answer questions. I don't want to make them worry about me any more than I already have.

I make myself get up and grab my keys.

Seventy-Seven

Jacob: Give Away

"Sargeant Ricks. Good to hear from you," Lieutenant Stephens says when Mom hands me her phone. "Jess told me you're deploying to Iraq again. I hope everything goes well."

"You've seen her lately?" I'm relieved enough not to be jealous. Almost.

"I talked to Jess a couple of days ago, why?" He still has that tone when he talks about her—possessive. Maybe they're already back together.

"Do you know where she is now?"

"I'm not sure I should–"

"Please, it's important," I say. "I think she's in danger. I got a bunch of pictures from her old boyfriend. The one who was in jail. He's been stalking her, and I think he's getting ready to come after her."

"Yeah. He's been sending her messages too," Stephens says.

I'm shocked. "What messages? When?"

"For a long time, actually. She got a card from him right after Matt was killed, and one on her birthday."

"What?"

"She didn't tell you?"

"No."

"At first it was cards, then emails, lately it's been texts, even a few phone calls."

"That's why she got a new phone number," I say. It's no comfort that she didn't just get a new phone number to avoid me. For whatever reason, Jess didn't feel like she could tell me that Brad has been contacting her for a long time, even from prison. But she told Michael.

"That makes sense," he says thoughtfully. "Probably why she wasn't up for dinner in public when I asked her."

My head and my heart are battling for dominance. My heart wants to keep Michael as far away from Jess as possible. My head tells me he might be the only one who can keep her safe. Steve is right. It's stupid to think I'm the one who has to come to her rescue right now. She didn't even trust me enough to tell me about the messages from Brad.

"Where are you now? Are you close to her? Could you find her and make sure she's okay?"

"Pullman, and of course. I'll go find her right now."

I take a long breath, feeling like I'm giving her away. Stupid, because she's not mine anymore. "Promise me you'll keep her safe. Promise me you won't let him get to her."

"Don't worry, Ricks. I promise. I'll take care of her."

Seventy-Eight

Jess: Safe

The drive was excruciating. A hundred times I thought about turning around. If Brad is looking for me anywhere, it would be at my house.

I don't plan to stay very long.

I stop at the top of the hill and look down on my yard to make sure there are no extra cars in there. It's empty. I park my car in the garage so no one can tell that I'm here. I go in through the garage door, past the kitchen that somehow still smells like my mom's baking and dad's barbecue, past Matt's picture on the mantle, and the family picture above it—now almost four years old. I ache at the loss of the family I had. I know it will never be the same. There's always going to be an empty place, a hole where Matthew should be. And then there's what I've done to them. I wonder if I'll ever be able to repair all the damage I've caused.

I go upstairs and bypass my bedroom, heading straight for the office and Dad's gun safe in the closet there. I have the combination memorized—Mom and Dad's anniversary date—today, actually. They've been together for twenty-five years.

I think of my parents miles away in Alaska, or on a ship somewhere. Their marriage isn't perfect, but I've always known they love each other. I wonder if I'll ever have that, or if every relationship I have will end in pain and destruction.

A ping on my phone makes my heart race. My parents are the only ones who have this number, and Mom told me she wouldn't be able to contact me while they're gone.

I breathe again only when I see that it's Mom.

Jess, where are you? Jasmine has been texting me, asking where you are. She's really worried about you.

I text back.

Home.

I open the safe and reach to the back to pull out my rifle. A little velvet box falls out. I bend down to pick it up, confused. At first I think it's Kendra's ring, but as soon as I open it, I know. It was supposed to be mine. The half-proposal Jacob gave me at my apartment was the real thing. He'd planned it, even bought me a ring. And I'd messed it all up by asking him for the one thing he wasn't willing to give me.

Why would he leave it here?

The thought hits me. He left it for me because he thinks he's not coming back. I sink to my knees in front of the closet, holding the ring as the tears push through.

My phone buzzes again, as if Mom senses how much I'm hurting.

Is everything okay?

I want to tell her everything. I want her to come home and make me feel safe the way I once did. But I don't want them to worry about me. I want my parents to have fun and celebrate and forget all the horrible things they've been through in the last few years.

I'm good. Just picking up some things here. Let Jaz know I'm okay. I'll message her when I get back to my apartment.

Stay home tonight, please. I don't want you driving back to your apartment alone.

I think about that for a long moment. Maybe she's right. The idea of walking down the stairs into a dark basement by myself is terrifying.

K. I'll stay here.

Are you sure you're okay?

No.

Fine. Good. I hope you're having fun. Happy Anniversary! Love you!

I can't ruin their anniversary.

Thanks! I'm turning my phone off now. The texting rates from the ship are astronomical. Talk to you soon. Love you.

I hold onto the phone for a long time, wishing I could say more to her. Maybe when they get back. Maybe I can ask for help then.

I take the rifle and a box of ammunition out of the closet. Just before I close the safe, I catch sight of one of my dad's handguns, one I've shot before. It's small and easy to handle. It would be better to keep with me, at least until I work up the courage to buy my own gun. I put my rifle back and take the smaller gun instead.

Seventy-Nine

Jacob: Risk

"T he pictures are all at least four months old." Nate says.

His call pulled me out of a fitful sleep, filled with dreams of Jess and Iraq. I don't remember anything concrete, only that she was in trouble and I couldn't get to her.

"That old?"

"Yeah. They're all extremely creepy. This is the guy from before, Brad?"

"It has to be. I don't know who else would be stalking her." Brad should have been in jail then, but maybe he got out without my knowing. Maybe that's why Jess started hiding right after we broke up.

"What did she say about it?"

I hesitate for a minute. "We aren't exactly on speaking terms."

"Idiot," Nate says.

"What?" I say.

"You're an idiot when it comes to Jess. You always have been."

I'm waiting for him to tell me to get over her, to stop acting like a whooped dog, like everyone else has. I'm ready to defend myself and say, "I broke up with her."

Instead he says, "You're an idiot for letting her go. You have no idea what you have with her. You have no idea what I would have given to have her look at me the way she looks at you, even one time. Hell, I'd be happy if any girl looked at me that way."

"Angel?"

"Long gone."

"I'm sorry."

"Don't be." He lets out a long sigh. "What happened with Jess?"

I keep it brief. I'm positive Nate will agree with her, that I should have done what I could to get out of the deployment. He stays quiet as I finish up. "It's an impossible situation. I can't not go to Iraq. Jess can't accept that."

"Did you give her time to process the whole thing, or did you just lose it when she asked you to stay with her?"

"I lost it," I admit.

"Everything is so black and white with you, Jake. You forget that people have different opinions and different views of the world. You fly off the handle when someone questions your loyalty, especially when it comes to the Army. I know you'd never go against your oath. I'm sure Jess knows that too. But she probably would have appreciated it if you had listened. She might have even come around to your opinion."

I sit for a long moment, realizing he's right. "What do you think I should do?" I ask.

He laughs. "You're asking me for advice about a girl? That's a first." He's quiet for a minute. "First thing, save her life. You're pretty good at that. After that, try not to be so hardheaded."

"I'm a couple thousand miles away and deploying in less than thirty-six hours. There's nothing I can do to fix either situation beyond what I've already done. I sent the police and a guy who's closer to check on her."

"You're going to let someone else rescue her? You must trust this guy a lot if you let him take your place."

I consider what he's saying. "I don't actually, not when it comes to her, but–"

My call-waiting beeps. It's an unknown number. "I've got to go. This could be her," I say.

"Let me know how it all turns out," Nate says.

"Thanks I–" but he's already gone.

I hurry to answer the phone. Immediately, I know it's a cop on the other end. "Sergeant Ricks? I have good news for you."

"You found her?" I ask eagerly.

"No, the house was dark and unoccupied. But I was able to get some information about the inmate you asked about."

"Brad? Did you find him?" I ask.

"In a manner of speaking. He's still in jail. Before he was released, additional charges were brought against him, charges that had been dropped due to a lack of evidence and are now pending."

"What does that mean?" I ask.

"It means your friend is safe, at least from him. There's no word on when he might be released, but you and Ms. Roberts will be informed when he is."

I think I manage a thank you, but I'm not sure. The surge of relief is short-lived. If Brad isn't out of jail, he couldn't have taken the pictures. He isn't the one who is stalking Jess. Could this whole thing be someone's idea of a sick joke?

Jasmine comes into my room, her hair piled on her head. She's wearing the shorts and tank top she sleeps in, but it doesn't look like she's been sleeping.

She sits on my bed. "I got Jess' mom to answer a text. She said Jess is at their house. She's staying there tonight. I already let Michael know. He's still in Pullman, so it will be awhile, but he said he'd get there as soon as he can." She gives me a hug. "It will be okay, Jacob. Jess is tough, and I know you don't want to hear this, but Michael is almost as obsessed with her as you were. He'll keep her safe."

"Right," I say, but something is nagging at the back of my mind. Something I'm missing. Someone is stalking Jess. If it's not Brad, it could be anyone—a patient from the hospital, some guy from one of her classes, someone else who is obses— I stand up. "What did you say?"

Jasmine is at the door of my bedroom. She turns. "I said, try not to worry. Jess is–"

"Not that. What did you say about Michael?"

"I said he'll keep her safe."

"No. You said, 'He's obsessed with her.'"

Obsessed. Possessive. Controlling. All things I've heard people say when they described Michael's relationship with Jess. I've seen it too, how Jess wasn't herself when he was around, how he seemed to always be telling her what to do. How he wanted to take her away—not just from me, but from everyone she loves.

"What are you saying?" Jasmine asks.

But Michael was supposed to be in Korea until June. If the pictures are four months old, it couldn't be him. Unless he wasn't there, or he came home early, or... I grab my phone again, this time dialing Bryan's number. It's early in Germany, but he picks up on the first ring.

"What can you tell me about Lieutenant Stephens?" I ask, almost before he's said hello.

"Stephens?" His voice is husky with sleep. "Why do you need to know?"

"I'll explain later, but it's important. You were in the same unit before Fort Lewis, right?"

Bryan hesitates. I'm not sure if he's thinking or if he's not sure how to answer my question. "Yeah. He was a good guy, but...I got the idea he was always hanging on by a thread. Physically he was as good as anyone, but mentally...I don't know. There were some rumors about a hunting accident when he was a kid, something that messed him up and maybe should have disqualified him from service. Someone told me he had friends in high places who kept covering for him, but there were a lot of guys who were jealous because he had money. It could have just been that." He's quiet again. "Funny that you should ask about him. I heard he just got out."

"Out?" I ask.

"Out of the Army. A few months ago. His deployment to Korea was cut short, and he came home, some medical thing."

My heart freezes. "How many months ago?"

"Four or five maybe, I'm not—"

"Do you know what kind of medical thing?"

"No idea. Jake, what's all this ab–"

"Thanks for the info. I'll explain later." I hang up, and start rummaging through my drawer for some clothes and my wallet. I grab them and turn to Jasmine. "Call Michael back, tell him you were wrong, that Jess isn't at her house, that she's back in Pullman, or Spokane, wherever will take him far away from her."

"Where are you going?" She's looking at me like she thinks I've lost my mind. Maybe I have.

"To the airport. I'm going to Washington. It was Michael. It is Michael. At least I think it is. And I sent him there. I asked him to take care of her."

"Jake, you're not making sense," Jasmine says. "You can't just—"

"What are you doing, Jacob?" Steve is standing in the hall, blocking my way.

"I have to go. I have to make sure Jess is—"

"You have no proof she's in any real danger. Nothing to go on but blind fear. She could have sent those pictures to you herself to get you to come running back."

"She wouldn't do that," I say, trying to move past him.

He doesn't move. "She's not your responsibility. What are you going to do when you get there and find her with him? When you risk everything you've built your whole life on only to find out she's been playing you this whole time?"

I keep my voice steady because I know he might be right about all of this. I've always had blinders on when it came to Jess, but I don't think I'm going into this situation blind. "If I'm wrong about all of this, if she's with him and safe, then I can let her go. But she's not. I don't know how to explain it, but I know, I know she's in trouble. I know if I don't go, something is going to happen to her. I could never live with myself if—"

"Think about it, Jacob. Think about what happens if you don't show up for your deployment. Think about what you're risking. At best you lose your promotion, at worst—"

"I know. I know what I'm risking. But I also know what I stand to lose if I don't find her."

Eighty

Jess: All or Nothing

I wake up with my heart racing, confused about where I am. It takes me a minute to remember that I'm home, in my own bed. I lean back on my covers and try to relax. Then I hear something outside. It sounds like a car circling the house, then pulling into our driveway. I stand and go to the window, opening the curtains just enough to see outside. The yard is empty.

I'm paranoid.

I should just go back to bed, wrap up in my blanket and try to go back to sleep, but I know I won't. A little blue box of memories sits on my dresser. I have this sudden urge to see the pictures of Jacob I have there, to pull out the locket, and rub it between my fingers.

I bring the box back with me to my bed. I turn on the little lamp on my nightstand and open it. The first thing on top of the pile is a picture of me and Jacob on the couch together. I stare at the girl in the photo and think of how young and naïve I was. How much I was in love with Jacob then. How hard I tried to get his attention. How I thought we were destined to live happily ever after.

The girl in the picture knew so little about grief and loss and real life.

The locket is next. I run the smooth surface over my lips, remembering the first kiss, and the second, and so many that came after. I close my eyes against the tears. Someday, I hope I can look back on my time with Jacob with sweet memories instead of heartbreak.

I leave the picture and the locket on my nightstand and put the box back on my dresser. As I go to put the lid back, another picture stares back at me. Michael and I in parachute gear, our faces flushed with excitement. I pick it up and look closer.

I don't regret telling him never to call me. Michael, with his grand gestures, and money and plans for my life, never understood what I wanted or who I was. It took being away from him to realize how much of me he had tried to control when we were together. I flip the picture over and re-read the message he wrote when he sent it to me.

Looking forward to our next adventure. I'll be thinking of you. Love, Michael.

My heart freezes. I re-read the message. Then I examine the handwriting, realizing for the first time how similar it is to the notes I've been getting. I'm confused. Were the notes from Michael all along? Maybe he thought they were a sweet gesture, something romantic. Maybe I misread them the whole time.

But why do it anonymously?

I remember the night in my bedroom. The night I asked Michael to kiss me. He asked about the card I'd gotten. He noticed it upset me

If he realized how much it bothered me, why didn't he just tell me it was from him? Why would he keep sending them, and the texts and the emails, and the phone calls? Angelica said they were from Michael, but I assumed she'd misheard him. She said the calls all appeared to have a bad connection. What if that was on purpose?

I'm not sure what to do, where to go from here. Have I been hiding for nothing? Pushing everyone away for nothing?

A car door slams outside. I jump and move to the window. A tall figure walks toward the front door, a figure I would recognize anywhere. He stops at the little birdhouse on the front porch and grabs the key.

The front door opens.

Eighty-One

Better this Way

Jacob

It's dark and rainy when I land at SeaTac Airport. I mostly maxed out my credit care, but I caught a red-eye at the last minute, thanks to a helpful counter attendant, who has a son in the Army.

Her name is Jessica.

I have a return ticket that will get me back in time for my deployment and a message to my commanding officer explaining why I left.

I'm driving as fast as I can on rain-slicked and mostly empty roads. I rented the fastest car they had, but it's still too slow. It's been over seven hours since Michael said he was on his way to Jess—plenty of time for him to get to her. I hope he bought the diversion Jasmine gave him and didn't go straight to her house. If not...I press the gas down harder.

I'm not sure what I'm going to do when I get there. It's not like I could bring a weapon on the airplane. Jess's dad has a full gun safe, but I don't know the combination. I hope I don't need a gun. I hope I find Jess alone, and that I can convince her to come back with me. She can stay with my parents until things get sorted out with Stephens or whoever sent the messages and the emails.

I crest the hill that leads to her house, and my hopes for a clean get away are shattered. There's another car in her driveway, a Lexus. I grab my phone and dial 9-1-1. I learned my lesson last time. This isn't a situation I want to go into without support.

Jess

I stay still in my bedroom, wishing I hadn't turned my lamp on. I think about my options, places I could hide until he leaves. He doesn't know I'm here.

The door between the kitchen and the garage opens and closes. He's seen my car.

"Jess," he calls. He starts up the stairs.

I pull on the jeans I was wearing when I came, reach under the bed and get the pistol I took out of Dad's gun safe. I tuck it into the back of my waistband and pull a sweater out of my closet to cover it. The whole time I'm thinking I'm being paranoid. This is a knee-jerk reaction to the trauma I'm still holding onto from Brad. Michael is my friend. He would never hurt me. The cards were just a way for him to show he still cares. Maybe he isn't even the one who sent them. He just came to check on me.

I steady my breathing and try to keep my voice calm. "Michael?"

He moves into my doorway and flips on the lights. "Jess, are you okay?"

"Yeah, I...what are you doing here?"

"Jacob called me. He's worried about you. He said someone emailed a bunch of pictures of you to him. He thinks they're from your old boyfriend. The one who's in jail."

"Brad?"

He moves closer. "Yeah, that's the one. He said they were pictures that were taken without you knowing it—when you were running, at the yoga studio—that kind of thing."

My mind races. If he's telling the truth, if Jacob really sent him, if he really got pictures like that of me...I haven't been to a yoga studio since before I broke up with Jacob. If there were pictures of me there, it couldn't have been Brad. At most he's been out of jail for a couple of weeks. I can't tell if Michael is making it all up, if I'm paranoid or–

He steps forward and puts his hands on my shoulders. "He asked me to take care of you, just like Matthew did. I gave my word as a soldier, and that's something I take very seriously. You need to let me take care of you."

"Thank you for coming." I work to keep my voice steady and then realize maybe I shouldn't. Michael is here to play hero. If I let him have that role, if I play along, maybe I'll be okay.

He cups my face in his hands. "It's been so long since I've seen you. You look so beautiful. I've missed you so much."

"I've missed you too." I force myself not to pull away, not to stiffen as he presses his lips against mine. I wrap my arms around his neck and focus on kissing him back, hoping he doesn't move his hand down far enough to feel the gun. He does.

He pulls it out. "What is this?"

"Sorry. I was alone and," I look down. "I've been getting weird messages too, for a long time. Cards in gray envelopes. Texts. Phone calls from someone saying they're thinking of me." I wait for him to tell me it was him, that he was worried about me. That he just wanted me to know he was thinking of me.

He doesn't.

"The gun is a good idea, but I should hold on to it, and we should get out of here. The first place he's going to look for you is your house. I'll get a hotel in Seattle. Two rooms if you want. But it would probably be better if we stayed together."

I reach for my phone. "Shouldn't we go to the police? If Brad is really—"

He puts his hand on top of mine. "I already called them. They said there's nothing they can do for you. But don't worry about that, I'm here I won't let—"

We hear it at the same time. The low growl of a sports car. I know without knowing how that Jacob is in that car, that he's coming for me, even if he's supposed to be on the other side of the country. Even if he's supposed to be on the other side of the world.

I can't let Michael get to him.

I wrap my arms around him. "You're right. We should stay together."

I lift my face to his and kiss him.

Jacob

I pull into the driveway, for the first time wishing I hadn't rented such a loud and conspicuous car. There's no chance for stealth, so I pull up right in front of the house. I look up at the window of Jess' room. Her bedroom light is on. Two shadows hold each other behind the curtains. They're kissing.

It's just the way Steve said it would be. For a second I feel like an idiot, like I've fallen into their trap and their upstairs laughing at me. Then the taller shadow, Michael, lifts his arm. There's something in his hand—a shape I recognize immediately.

He has a gun.

My first instinct is to storm through the front door, race up the stairs, and overpower him. I realize that's a good way to get shot, maybe to get Jess shot too. Something Gage told me comes back now. A *helpful hint in case you ever need it. The tree in the back leads directly to Jess' bedroom window.* I didn't ask him how he knew that, but I trust he knew what he was talking about.

Jess

I'm doing everything I can to keep Michael from looking out the window, but when we hear the car door slam, he moves me behind him. "Stay back." He peers out the curtains and swears. He lowers his voice. "He's here."

He can't know I know who's out there. "Brad?"

"Yeah. Stay here; I'll go make sure he doesn't get in."

I pull him into another kiss, stalling for time. "Be careful."

"I will." He nods solemnly.

As soon as he's out of my room, I reach for my phone and dial the number I've had memorized since I was seventeen.

"Jess." He answers immediately. "Are you–"

"I'm okay. Michael is out there. He has a gun, please, go back to your car, lock the doors and–"

"Open your window. I'm coming up."

Branches scrape against the house. I run to my back window and pull it open. Jacob climbs in. I wrap my arms around him. We only get a second.

"Step away from her." Michael's voice is behind me.

I turn to face him. "Michael don't–"

Jacob moves in front of me.

"I said, step away from her." He points the gun at Jacob's head.

"Do what he says, please," I say to Jacob. "He won't hurt me."

Michael gestures for me to come to him. I agonize for a second, but then move to stand beside him. He wraps his arm around my waist. He keeps the gun on Jacob, talking fast. "It was him all the time, Jess, don't you see? He was the one sending you the messages. He was the one who took the pictures. He wanted you to be afraid so he could be your hero. He's been trying to get between us from the very beginning. He asked me to come here tonight, so he could get rid of me. He knew you'd never stay with him as long as I was around. You believe me, don't you?"

I turn around to face him, look into those beautiful green eyes and understand he's giving me a kind of twisted confession.

"Yes," I answer.

"I did all of it for you, so we could be together. I love you, Jess."

I try not to choke on the words, "I love you too, Michael."

"That's what I was waiting for." He pulls the trigger.

Jacob

The gunshot reverberates through my head. I stumble, step toward her, and fall forward. Something warm drips from the side of my face.

She's screaming my name, but her voice is far away, under water.

His voice. "Turns out I had the courage after all."

Another gunshot.

"Me too."

She's on the floor beside me. I reach for her hand.

"It's better this way."

Eighty-Two

Jess : The Ties that Bind

I'm shaking, my teeth rattling inside my head. I pull the scratchy blanket someone finally gave me around my shoulders, but it doesn't help. The orange jumpsuit is too thin. They took my clothes. They were covered in his blood. I did everything I could to stop it. I used all the training I had from the ER, but it just kept coming.

The police arrived just a few minutes after I shot Michael. If I had waited a little longer, if I had somehow kept him talking...if I hadn't taken the gun out of the safe...but I can't think about that now.

I don't even know if Jacob is alive or dead. I only know this is my fault.

My lawyer said as much in our brief meeting. "If you're lucky, this will go down as manslaughter, but it doesn't look good, especially considering your prior experience."

I could only nod to him and to the judge when he set my bail.

Whatever happens to me, I deserve it. Maybe not for killing Michael, but for all the mistakes along the way. The worst one was letting him get to Jacob.

A jail matron comes to the door. "Your bail has been posted," she says.

I follow her out. Mom and Dad must have come from their cruise and paid a lot of money they couldn't afford to get me out. I destroyed their anniversary too.

The woman in the foyer of the jail looks vaguely familiar. Her face is drawn and pale, her eyes are a deep emerald green. I look up in surprise as Karen, Michael's oldest sister, hands me a bundle of clothes. "Get changed. I'll give you a ride to the hospital."

I can only nod. I don't know what she plans to do with me, but if whatever inspired her to post my bail gives me the chance to see Jacob, I'll take whatever punishment she has in mind.

She doesn't speak again until we're in her car. "How are you doing?" She asks.

I shake my head.

"Right, dumb question." She pulls out of the police station.

"Why did you...?" But I don't have the strength to finish that sentence.

"You might say I'm the self-appointed family representative. Not that any of the rest of them know I'm here, but I thought you were at least owed an explanation."

I'm not sure what she means. The side of her jaw is working, like she's trying to keep from crying. After a few moments of silence, she asks, "What did Michael tell you about our sister Kaylee?"

I search my addled memory for the name before it comes to me. "He told me she was killed in a car accident when she was fourteen and he was sixteen, that they were very close."

Karen nods. "That's not quite true. Kaylee died in an accident when she was fourteen, but it wasn't a car accident. It was a hunting accident. Michael was the one who pulled the trigger." She's quiet for a long moment. "Kaylee wasn't like the rest of us girls. She was more like Michael. She loved skiing and hunting, and sports. They did all of those things together. It was an accident, a terrible, tragic accident—more her fault than his, really, but it broke something inside of him. His grades tanked; he stopped doing all the things he loved; he stopped living.

"My dad's solution was to put him in ROTC. It was a family tradition, he'd been an officer before he retired from the Army. Somehow he thought the discipline would help Michael. On the surface, maybe it did. His grades improved, he went back to skiing, he started being more of himself, almost but not quite. Michael has always been a people-pleaser. He wanted my dad to be proud of him. He didn't want my mom to worry about him. He tried not to let anyone see how much being in the Army crushed him. I'd moved out of the house by then, but I saw what a horrible choice it was. My dad refused to.

Tears squeeze out from under my eyes. I hurt for Michael, for Jacob, for all of us.

"From what I've heard, he wasn't always great at hiding it in the Army either. He got shuffled around a lot, because the officers over him weren't sure what to do with him. Dad still had some friends in the Army, higher-ups who were willing to pave the way and keep things quiet—his drinking, his temper. Still, I think he was heading for another crash. Then he met you."

Karen turns to look at me, and I'm not sure how to take her expression.

"Michael was most normal when he was with you. Most like the person he was before. I think we were all hoping you could fix him,' she looks away. "That's why we tried to push you together, why Mom and Dad were willing to pay for an apartment for you in Korea, when they realized he wasn't going to get out of that assignment. That wasn't fair of us. There was no simple fix that would have worked for him, but hard fixes and facing the truth aren't top priorities in my family. Success, pressure, keeping up appearances—that's what's important. Getting kicked out of the Army and not getting into medical school pushed him over the edge."

I'm struggling to process everything she said to me, I'm stuck on one minute detail. "He told me he'd gotten into UW medicine, that he was starting in a couple of months."

She shakes her head and puts the car in park. We're in front of the hospital. "I don't know what's going to happen with you legal-wise, that's not my area of expertise. But even if no one else in my family will do it, I'll tell the truth about what was going on with my brother."

I sit for a long moment, not sure what to say. "Thank you," I finally say. "For bailing me out, for bringing me here, and for telling me the truth."

I reach to open the door. Karen puts her hand on my arm. "I came here first. I had a consult with the surgeon. I've seen the prognosis, and it isn't good. Even if Jacob comes out of this, there's no guarantee he'll be–"

"Don't," I say to her with more strength than I thought I had left.

She sighs. "You're young, you're beautiful, you've already been through more than anyone your age should have to go through. If he loved you as much as I think he did, he wouldn't want you to stop living because he's not…"

I pull away, hating that she's using the past tense when she talks about Jacob. I won't accept that—no matter what the outcome of all of this—as long as he still wants me. I won't leave him ever again.

Eighty-Three

Jacob: Breathe

The darkness is full of noise, cries of anger, pain, and fear. Explosions, smoke and mud. The acrid smell of gunshot mixes with blood.

I fight and fade. The images become clear, then fade away. I can't open my eyes.

The noise changes.

The whoosh of machines. Pain. Fog I can't escape. Something solid and smooth and warm. A hand in mine.

Voices.

"The surgeon did everything she could, but there's still a lot of damage. The prognosis isn't—"

"Don't." Her voice.

Steve's voice. "We need to consider what will happen if he can't breathe on his own. He wouldn't want to live this way. You need to prepare yourself. I'm not trying to be cruel, but we can't live on false hopes."

"Hope." She laughs, but it's the kind of laugh that hurts. "If false hope is all I have, I'll take it."

"You've always been incredibly stubborn. Especially when it comes to him. We're grateful for that." Mom's voice breaks.

The hand releases mine. My fingers won't move. I don't have the strength to hold on.

It all comes back. Pictures of her. Calling with no answer. The flight to Seattle. Driving. Finally, finding her. The kiss. His taunting face. The shot. Her scream. Another shot.

Silence.

Her arms, holding me together, while she fell apart. "Don't leave me, don't leave me. Don't leave me."

I still can't open my eyes, but know he's standing next to me–his crooked grin and dancing eyes. He puts his hand on my shoulder. "Don't worry, bro. I've got you."

He fades away.

We're alone now. I have no perception of time. It could have been minutes, or weeks, or years. Her footsteps pace the room. The machine noise and her hand have become the only constants in an existence filled with confusion and pain—for both of us. It might be better if I let go.

"Whatever happens," her voice is close, whispers of breath on my face, "I'm here as long as you want me."

Me too.

I want to lift my head, meet her lips, tell her I'll never leave her again. I can't make my body move. She stands and paces again. I breathe, a little blip on the machine.

She comes back, "Jacob?"

There's something in my mouth that keeps me from talking. I try to move my lips, to say her name. Another breath, another blip. She leans closer, grips my hand. One finger moves, then another. I squeeze with everything I have left, knowing it's not enough.

She leans over, her lips on my forehead. "I love you. Forever."

This time when the darkness overtakes me, it's warm and welcoming, because I know what waits on the other side.

Eighty-Four

Jess: Protection

August 2008

"There's still the question of who killed Lieutenant Stephens. The shots were too close together to determine who shot whom and when." The lawyers in front of me are arguing. Behind me, Michael's family stares daggers into the back of my head. I don't have the courage to turn around and face them.

I'm not testifying this time. My lawyer didn't think it was a good idea, and I agreed with him.

"I'm just saying, it's unlikely that Staff Sergeant Ricks, wounded as he was, could have made the fatal shot."

I swallow a sob that threatens to break me. I've gone through that night a thousand times, wondering what I could have changed—not gone home, left the gun in the safe, called the police as soon as Michael walked in. None of that compares to the choice I made when I saw

Michael's hesitation, when his grip loosened on the gun, and I twisted it around and pulled the trigger.

"Staff Sergeant Ricks was an experienced combat soldier; in an intense situation like that, his training would have kicked in."

"Fingerprints from all three were on the one weapon in the room, and since Ms. Roberts is the one person who wasn't injured and because she's pleading the fifth, I think it's just as likely..."

It's better this way.

I didn't understand why Jacob had taken the gun from me when I knelt beside him, but I know now. He was dying, bleeding to death on my bedroom floor, but he was still protecting me.

"You cannot use Ms. Roberts' refusal to make a statement as evidence against her," the judge reminds them. She's a tall woman, an ex-soldier, with a serious face and a reputation for doing everything by the book. "Ms. Roberts obviously felt threatened. Lieutenant Stephens shot Sergeant Ricks with the intent to kill. Everything else is irrelevant. It's a simple case of self-defense. I'm dismissing all charges."

I'm stunned. I was prepared for the worst—to go to jail. In no realm of possibility had I considered that the judge would throw the case out.

Behind me, Sylvia is sobbing, Michael's sisters are too. I want to turn and tell them I'm sorry, but my lawyer told me not to talk to any of them, especially not to express any kind of guilt. As everyone stands, I find the courage to look behind me. Kelsey gives me a dark look before she puts her arm around her mother and walks out. I turn away.

"How is Jacob?" I look up. Karen is waiting for me.

"Getting stronger every day." It's my canned answer, one I hope is true. It's been a long and painful recovery. "He wanted to be here, but he doesn't remember anything from that night, and he's still not talking very well. It all felt like too much to put him through that."

She nods. "I'm glad he's doing better. I hear congratulations are in order. When is the big day?"

I twist the ring on my left hand. "He said he doesn't want to do it until he can stand with me at the altar. I'm pushing for sooner."

Karen looks around, but the rest of her family is gone. "I'm glad for the way things turned out today, and I'm sorry again—for everything you've been through."

"I'm sorry too." The words feel hollow. Nothing I could say can express how sorry I am—for everything.

She nods as if she feels the same way and walks out.

Eighty-Five

Jess: The Last Kiss

I shift my weight, but the chair I've been sitting on too long still digs into my hip. A trickle of sweat slides down my neck. I reach to scratch my nose as a piece of bangs falls into my eyes.

It must be a hundred degrees in the barn, and I've been waiting so long.

"Hold still and don't touch your face. You'll ruin your makeup," Jasmine pins the errant curl back in place.

"Jessica, are you up here?"

My heart pounds at the sound of his voice. I hold my breath.

"Jess?"

"Absolutely not," Kendra says. "It's bad luck for him to see you before the wedding, and the two of you have had all the bad luck you can take."

His steps are slow and heavy with the added thump of his cane, but he's walking, climbing stairs even, something he wasn't ever supposed to do again.

I shake my head and bite my lip to keep the tears from sliding out. They come anyway.

I stand up against their protests. I'm not in my dress yet, so it's not like it matters whether he sees me half-done. My dress hangs on a hook in the corner. It's a simple satin gown, long and form-fitting. Kendra couldn't talk me into something more elaborate, but I gave in when Jasmine suggested the low-cut back. I knew Jacob would like it.

Mom transformed the barn with lights and flowers. Dad built a little dressing room at the top of the stairs. Tyler painted everything. We're having a small wedding, like I wanted—family and close friends. Jasmine, Taryn, and Kendra are my bridesmaids. Tyler, Bryan and Nate are the groomsmen.

His face at the top of the stairs surprises me. I step back, and he laughs. He looks amazing in his dress uniform, even if it hangs loose now. Seeing him in it makes the tears flow freely, because I understand the depth of what he gave up for me.

He reaches up and wipes a tear away. "Don't cry, Jess. I never could stand to see you cry."

"You're going to ruin—" Jasmine starts and then shakes her head in defeat. "You have five minutes."

"Sorry to go against protocol, but I have something I want to give you. I meant to do it before now, but it wasn't ready. Nate just picked it up for me. I thought you might want to wear it for the ceremony."

He hands me a little silver locket, the same locket he gave me all those years ago. It's been repaired—the scuffs buffed out, and it has a new chain. I open it to a picture of the two of us together, years ago.

I'm eleven; he's fifteen. His arm is around my shoulders, my hair is crazy, thick glasses shroud my eyes, but I'm smiling.

"Mom found that picture. I thought you'd like it, to remember what we were before. Let me help you put it on." Jacob says, and I realize I've been staring at the locket without moving.

"Okay." I pull my hair up out of the way and turn around.

His fingers tremble, and he struggles with the clasp, but just as I decide to help him, he pats it in triumph. I rub the little heart between my fingers, still not convinced that any of this is real.

He puts his hands on my shoulders, turning me around to face him. "Promise you'll never take it off."

I finally meet his eyes. "I promise."

"Just to be sure, I'd better give you something else." He has a look on his face, unsure, like he's trying to decide something. My heart beats so loud I'm sure he can hear it. He leans close to my face.

And kisses me.

On the lips.

Long and so sweet that I never want it to end.

He pulls away. I can barely breathe.

He looks up and pushes a curl off my forehead. "I did that now because I'll never get the chance to kiss you again...as a single woman."

"Save it for the altar, you two," Jasmine breaks in. "You'll have lots of time to kiss later; right now we need to make you beautiful."

"Jess is already beautiful," Jacob says.

"And he's mine, so I can kiss him whenever I want."

I put my hands on either side of his face, pull his lips to mine, and kiss him one last time before we begin the rest of our lives together.

The End

For R and B and so many others who've sacrificed everything for our country.

Author's Note

This book was originally written about 15 years ago. I've lived in Lacey, Washington, where this book is set, for almost 27 years. (Although I never used the name "Lacey" to describe where Jess lives.) We're about fifteen minutes from Fort Lewis (now JBLM) and have had many friends in the military in the years we've lived here. (Including the family of three boys that inspired this story.) In 2004, my friend's husband was killed in the attack on Mosul mentioned in Chapter Ten. It was a devastating and eye-opening experience. He was an incredible man, with an incredible wife, four kids close to the same age as mine and many happy years in front of him. It brought home just how much our men and women in the military and their families sacrifice for all of us.

I've never been in the military, and none of my immediate family members are in the military. I've relied on the experience and help of others to write this book. I know I've made mistakes and taken dramatic license in some areas. Please forgive me for that. I have the deepest respect for military personnel and families. Thank you for all you do. If I got things wrong, I'm so sorry. This was hard for me to write because I was constantly worried about trivializing or over-dramatizing someone else's experience. I believe in the power of stories, even love stories (especially love stories) to build bridges of understanding, so I'll keep writing and hoping it touches someone.

I hope you enjoyed Jess and Jacob's story. They've lived in my head for a long time now. Maybe after this is finally published, they'll let me move on. Part of me hopes not. They're the first characters that I ever put into a complete story. It's evolved a lot over the years as I've evolved as a writer. I'm still not sure I got it right, but this feels like the best version of their story.

Thanks for letting me tell it.

Also by Jennifer Shaw Wolf

The Second Kiss

Jess never told anyone about her first kiss, her crush on the too-old-for-her boy next door, or what his departing gift meant to her.

Jacob has been gone for six years, and a lot has changed. The shy, awkward little girl he left behind has grown up. Jess is a high school senior with plans, popularity, and a football star boyfriend. Just as everything she's worked for falls apart, Jacob is back—assigned to the Army base near her home. Is this her second chance at love, or will Jacob only see the little girl he left behind?

The Extra

Desperate for cash, a starving student takes a job as an extra on a B-list horror movie and finds herself in a fight for survival.

To get your free copy of "The Extra," subscribe to my mailing list, and get access to free content, visit my website at:
jennifershawwolf.com

The Body in the Bookshop

Inheriting a bookshop and the island that comes with it could be the solution to all of Emmy's problems, or it could be the last thing she ever does.

Emerson Fox's ADHD has left her with a do-nothing degree, a jilted ex-fiancé, mounds of student debt, and a knack for forgetting important things while focusing on obscure details. When a disastrous blind date leaves her stranded in a quaint bookshop on a tiny island in Washington's Puget Sound, the last thing she expects is to find the bookshop's owner has been murdered. Even more shocking, he's left a will that names her as his long-lost niece and sole heir to his bookshop and the entire island. Emmy can't claim her inheritance until she unearths a long-buried family secret, convinces the only police officer in town (and the other half of her disastrous date) that she's innocent, and finds the focus she needs to solve her uncle's murder.

Dead Girls Don't Lie

Jaycee and Rachel were best friends. But that was before. . .before that terrible night at the old house. Before Rachel shut Jaycee out. Before Jaycee chose Skyler over Rachel. Then Rachel is found dead. The police blame a growing gang problem in their small town, but Jaycee is sure it has to do with that night at the old house. Rachel's text is the first clue-starting Jaycee on a search that leads to a shocking secret. Rachel's death was no random crime, and Jaycee must figure out who to trust before she can expose the truth.

Breaking Beautiful

Allie lost everything the night her boyfriend, Trip, died in a horrible car accident - including her memory of the event. As their small town mourns his death, Allie is afraid to remember because doing so means delving into what she's kept hidden for so long: the horrible reality of their abusive relationship.

When the police reopen the investigation, it casts suspicion on Allie and her best friend, Blake, especially as their budding romance raises eyebrows around town. Allie knows she must tell the truth. Can she reach deep enough to remember that night so she can finally break free?

Meant to Die

Ever since her twin sister died at birth, Miranda has walked with the dead. But what she knows about death has kept her from living life. Then she meets Remy, a little girl with a different view of life and death. Remy sees people on the brink of a violent end, people who were never meant to die. When Remy shares her visions with her, Miranda has to decide whether to team up with this fearless girl and a restless spirit to solve a string of decades-old murders. But can someone who's spent her life in fear find the courage to catch a killer, even if it means she might be the next to die?

Acknowledgements

Fifteen years ago, I sat down to write my first book. I didn't have a clue what I was doing, but I promised myself I'd push through until the end. At the time, I didn't know how hard writing a book really was. When I reached the point where I thought I needed feedback to see if I was wasting my time, I sent a few chapters to my niece, Ashley. I asked her to tell me what she thought. Instead of giving me a critique, she simply asked, "Is there any more?" I sent her more and got the same response. I'd like to thank Ashley, my first reader, because that simple question kept me going until I finished the book. That first attempts became the first book in this series, *The Second Kiss*. Finishing that one gave me the motivation to finish *Kiss Me Goodbye*.

I also want to thank my sister-in-law Angela, "real author," MFA extraordinaire, for reading my horrible first draft and telling me she loved it, and then "change everything." More than anything else, that prepared me for working with an editor. Thanks to my earliest readers, Kristy and Christie—sisters by birth and sisters by choice and David, my biggest supporter. Thanks to Kimmie for being the second voice that kept me moving forward. Thank you to Sam for helping me sort out some of the military family stuff and for telling me this story "devastated" her (I hope in a good way). Thanks to Shylah for not being afraid to tell it like it is. Thanks to the brothers from our little cul-de-sac for inspiring great characters. Thanks always to my romantic inspiration—my husband David. Thank you to all the men and women who serve at Fort Lewis and in the armed forces across the nation and around the world and the people who love and support and pray for them. I see your sacrifices, I see your courage, I see your devotion to a cause greater than yourself.

Thank you to my Father in Heaven, the Great Creator, for the right words at the right time and for a life filled with discovering who I am and who I can become.

Jennifer Shaw Wolf was the kid you see hiding behind a stack of books from the public library. She read her way through life, routinely falling in love with fictional characters and daydreaming about her perfect love story. She looked up from her books long enough to create a love story of her own, get married, and have four amazing kids. She lives with her Prince Charming and an incredibly spoiled (but also very charming) dog in the mysterious green forests of the Pacific Northwest. Her favorite things are reading, writing, and spending time with her family, which now includes three wonderful in-law kids, two beautiful grandkids and another on the way!

If you enjoyed reading *Kiss me Goodbye* please consider posting a review on Amazon or Goodreads. Reviews help indy authors like me get their books out of the noise of Amazon and into the hands of readers.

Thank you for your support!

www.ingramcontent.com/pod-product-compliance
Lightning Source LLC
Chambersburg PA
CBHW070902260626
47162CB00007B/2534